PRAISE FOR THE NOVELS
of
SANDRA KRING

"Touching... surprisingly poignant... builds to an emotional crescendo... The book becomes so engrossing that it's tough to see it end." —*Washington Post*

"Heartfelt... Strong characters, a clear community portrait and a memorable protagonist whose poignant fumblings cloak an innocent wisdom demonstrate Kring's promise." —*Publishers Weekly*

"Sandra Kring weaves an intricate and heartwarming tale of family, love and forgiveness in her sensational debut novel.... Kring's passionate voice is reminiscent of Faulkner, Hemingway and Steinbeck.... She will make you laugh, have you in tears and take you back to the days of good friends, good times, millponds and bonfires. This is a piece destined to become a classic and is a must read for devotees of the historical fiction or the literary fiction genre." —*Midwest Book Review*

"Sandra Kring writes with such passion and immediacy, spinning us back in time, making us feel the characters' hope, desire, laughter, sorrow, and redemption. I read this novel straight through and never wanted it to end." —Luanne Rice, *New York Times* bestselling author of *Last Kiss*

"Earwig Gunderman will capture your heart and challenge your conscience.... *Carry Me Home* is a plainspoken, nostalgic account set in the 1940s, but the story of a brother's love, and the healing powers of family and community in the aftermath of tragedy, is timeless." —Tawni O'Dell, *New York Times* bestselling author of *Sister Mine*

THANK YOU
for
ALL THINGS

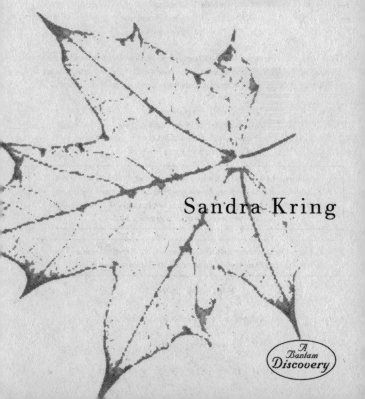

Sandra Kring

A
Bantam
Discovery

THANK YOU FOR ALL THINGS
A Bantam Discovery Book / October 2008

Published by Bantam Dell
A Division of Random House, Inc.
New York, New York

This is a work of fiction. Names, characters, places, and incidents either are the product of the author's imagination or are used fictitiously. Any resemblance to actual persons, living or dead, events, or locales is entirely coincidental.

Bantam Books and the rooster colophon are registered trademarks and Bantam Discovery is a trademark of Random House, Inc.

ISBN 978-0-553-59233-7

Printed in the United States of America

www.bantamdell.com

OPM   10   9   8   7   6   5   4   3   2   1

HUMBLE BEGINNINGS

We cannot deny

that often

a truth and a lie

have the same

humble beginnings,

intended to keep

someone from harm,

but in the scheme of things

both have the same intensity

to reduce someone to tears.

—*dodinsky*—

Thank you for
all things

THAT SKINNY eleven-year-old boy sitting across the table from me with the wispy dishwater-blond hair and glasses, that's my twin brother, Milo, short for Myles. He's got his long nose pointed down where his physics books and sheets scribbled with mathematical equations are neatly lined up at 180-degree angles on his end of the table. This is where Milo is likely to stay until bedtime (even though Mom says we have to study only until four o'clock), mumbling to himself and moving his face closer and closer to his work and getting more and more fidgety, until he's reaching for his inhaler. Then Mom makes him stop for the day and go to bed.

Milo is "profoundly gifted." One of those scary-smart geniuses who could have started college while still in diapers. Milo is going to be a physicist one day. His dream is to get a paper on string theory published in the globally renowned journals *Nature* and *Physical Review* and to prove some startling theory in quantum mechanics so he can earn himself a place among the leading geeks in the physics field.

Mom had me tested when she sent Milo, but I know it was for no other reason than that she didn't want me to feel left out. Same as she had the eye doctor give me a Sponge-Bob SquarePants sticker when Milo got his last eye exam, even though my eyes are as sharp as a hawk's, and even though I didn't know who the little character was. We were six when we took that test. Mom hid the results when they came, but it wasn't hard to figure out where she'd hidden them, since she puts all of her important papers in one place: her file cabinet, in a folder marked *Important Papers*.

"Don't be disappointed," Mom told me when she found me sitting on my knees alongside the file cabinet, staring down at our scores: *Lucy Marie McGowan—144. Myles Clay McGowan—180.* "You have a photographic memory and you're an exceptionally creative child. These IQ tests don't adequately measure either trait. If they did, you'd have scored every bit as high as your brother." Later that day, she handed me a quote by Albert Einstein that she had jotted on an index card: *Everything that can be counted does not necessarily count; everything that counts cannot necessarily be counted.*

Milo and I are homeschooled. Mom says it's because *we* have special needs and would only fall through the cracks in a public school system. But in reality, it's because we'd have to go to an inner city school here in Chicago because there's no money for a private school for the gifted, and she's afraid that Milo would get knifed or shot on the playground for being a freak and a geek. She's also afraid that if people knew just how smart he is, he'd be hounded by the press and doctors and develop mental problems, which would be an easy thing to do, since the experts believe that profoundly gifted kids are more fragile than others (they sure got that one right!). And, of course, I have to be homeschooled if Milo has to be.

Mom agrees that I should become a psychologist when I grow up, and either get into people's heads and cure what ails them or test and study gifted kids. Not because she has a particular fondness for shrinks—she doesn't!—but because she believes that kids should be steered in the direction of their gifts, and I happen to be people-smart.

After I convinced Mom that my interest lies in human behavior, she started checking out psychology textbooks from the college library for me: social and personality psychology, cognitive and experimental psychology, abnormal psychology, clinical psychology, you name it. I enjoy the parts of them I can understand, but like Carl Jung said, "Anyone who wants to know the human psyche will learn next to nothing from experimental psychology. He would be better advised to abandon exact science, put away his scholar's gown, bid farewell to his study, and wander with human heart through the world." I know *I* learn more by studying live people. Not that I have many people to study, mind you, because for the most part we live like recluses. So I watch my mother and my grandmother, the people who sit on the stoop downstairs on the rare days we leave the apartment, and sometimes Milo. Undoubtedly, though, studying Milo would be more beneficial if I were going to be a botanist.

When I told Mom that I'd like to become a psychologist (although I'd rather be a figure skater, even if I do have weak ankles and my balance isn't up to par. And even if I don't know how to skate, period, much less do a double axel or a triple lutz), she brought me home a little present that I know was meant to show me that she supports my decision. "I know how much you've always liked puppets," she said when I opened the cloth Sigmund Freud finger puppet that came with a little chaise longue. "They have magnets on the back, so you can stick them to your computer tower."

Milo got upset when I put Sigmund on my index finger and bobbed him in front of his face, asking him if he thought that having an overprotective, overanxious mother was what made him such a sissy. He punched me in the arm for teasing him, but it didn't hurt, because Milo is even smaller than I am and his fist is only about the size of a walnut.

In all honesty, if I can't be a figure skater, and if I have to cure people of what ails them, I'd rather be a shaman. My grandmother, Lillian, snuck me a book about a shaman in Africa. I thought it was cool the way he traveled to the underworlds in search of the missing pieces of people's souls to heal them.

Mom got upset when she found the book tucked under the dirty clothes in my hamper. "Take that book back when you leave, Mother," she snapped. "And stop filling Lucy's mind with that crazy crap." My grandmother scoffed at her, saying, "What a shaman does is every bit as real as the shadow at our feet, our breath in winter." Unfortunately, there's no school that gives a degree in Shamanism. And, anyway, where would I set up my practice? I'd probably have to go to a remote village in some Third World country and risk dying from cholera or dysentery and get paid in dead chickens, not money. That would suck, because being poor sucks.

Besides worrying about our education and Milo's mental and physical well-being and me getting a complex because I'm not as smart as my brother, Mom worries about us running out of money. Every time I bring up the mail from downstairs, she looks at me like I'm carrying in a poisonous snake, wrinkles her nose, and says, "Just set it on the kitchen table," where it'll sit for days until she musters up the courage to open the bills.

It's because of our money situation that Mom sold out and started writing Christian romance novels, even though her love is literary fiction *and* even though she's an atheist who happens to be bitter about love. What was she supposed to do, though, after she sold her first novel, *The Absent Savior*, three years ago, to a prestigious press on the East Coast and it sold only four hundred eleven copies? It didn't earn enough to allow us to buy a frikkin' case of boxed macaroni and cheese, Mom said, so she scrapped her second work-in-progress and started writing Christian romance, which is where the big bucks are. She's ashamed of writing them, so she isn't using her real name, Tess McGowan, but instead uses the pen name Jennifer Dollman. Her advance-reader copies are still sitting in a box in her closet, unopened.

Last month we stopped by Wal-Mart to buy sunscreen on our way to the public pool—a rare treat, brought on only because of my grandmother's sudden, not completely irrational fear that Milo was suffering from a vitamin D deficiency because he won't drink milk and doesn't play outside in the sun. Never mind that Milo doesn't play, period, and that there's no place to play outside our apartment but the street, even if he did. We were almost to the checkout line when Milo happened to spot Mom's Christian romance on a cardboard display at the end of the aisle. He pointed to it and said, "Look, Mom, your book!" He grabbed a copy and ran his fingertips over Mom's pen name and said, "Jennifer Dollman, that's you!" Some lady behind us in a T-shirt that had a picture of Jesus on the cross and the words *Follow the Leader* stretched across her chest heard him and got all excited.

"You're Jennifer Dollman? Oh, my *gawd*! My book club is not going to believe this! We picked your book for next month's selection, and I'm reading it right now." And Milo—who may have an IQ of 180 but has absolutely no common sense—said, "Yes, she's Jennifer D——"

Mom clamped her hand over his pale lips and backed away, but the woman rushed forward. It was as if she'd entered the rapture early, and she couldn't stop gushing. She was on chapter seventeen, she said, and she "absolutely adored" the trials and tribulations of Mom's protagonist, Missy Jenkins, and bless Mom for upholding the sanctity of marriage and not allowing Missy to be sweet-talked into sin by that good-looking philanderer Chase Milford. Mom quickly told the woman that it was a misunderstanding, her son only meant that it was the same book that is sitting on her nightstand. The woman started to protest, her finger wagging over Milo's head. "But he said——"

"No. No. The author and I share the first name. That's all he meant. My son . . . he's . . . he's learning disabled."

Mom almost yanked Milo's poor little arm out of its socket as she dragged us out of the store, Milo shouting, *"Learning disabled? You called me learning disabled?"* the whole way, the sunscreen left on the candy shelf for some weary-footed employee to march back to the pharmaceutical department. When we got home, Mom sat us both down and lectured us about not airing our dirty laundry in public.

"Can we tell people that you edit academic books?" I asked, and Mom said we could.

"What about your articles? Can we tell them that you're a travel writer?" Milo was referring to the many articles Mom writes each year, advising gonna-be travelers on where they should go and what they should see in exotic places like Shanghai, Bali, and even Roatán, that magical island off the coast of Honduras where many go on vacation, then decide to never leave. The truth is, Mom has never been to any of these places. She gets photographs e-mailed to her by a woman she knew in college who dropped out of school to become a flight attendant. She likes to brag about all the places she's been by sending Mom photos. Then Mom researches the places online and writes the article. I rolled my eyes at Milo's question. Milo should have had the sense to figure out that since Mom's travel articles are every bit as deceptive as her Christian romances, they, too, would be off-limits.

Mom has a lot of issues, frankly. And, unfortunately, at least some of them began with the woman who just burst through the door. Her mother, Lillian. And although I don't know if my grandmother is right and I am truly a bit psychic, I do know the minute she swoops into our apartment on this morning in mid-September that this visit is going to generate more than the usual amount of sparks.

MY GRANDMOTHER stands as still as a soldier in rank, her royal-blue tunic floating around her as though it's still responding to her morning tai chi movements. Lillian is sixty-two years old. She is tall and has chin-length hair, dyed to match the roasted-almond color it was when she was young, and it is every bit as light and airy as the clothes she wears. She also has big boobs and legs almost as good as Tina Turner's. "Good morning, Oma," I say, calling her the German name for Grandmother that she prefers because she likes the sound of it, even though she's not German.

Oma leans down to press her cheek to mine, and her chunky fertility goddess earring clips me on the nose. Her

breath and hair smell like cigarettes. Oma is tense this
morning—unusual for her—and she doesn't look down at
me when I try to tell her that Deepak Chopra has a new
book out, even though she worships the ground he walks on.
Instead, she looks toward the desk at the other end of the
living room.

As always happens when Oma searches for anything in
our living room, a cloud of distress darkens her hazel eyes.
Oma thinks living rooms should be spacious and cozy, with
soft woven rugs strategically placed, plants to breathe oxygen into the air by day and carbon dioxide by night, colors
to support positive moods, and the furniture feng shui–
arranged to let the chi flow through the room freely. Our
oblong living room has none of these things. Its smudged
walls are the color of a faded army blanket and filled with
calendars, charts, and graphs, and the floors are scuffed
wood, with only one rug, a rubber welcome mat, placed at
the door to leave your soggy shoes on. The room is cramped
with Mom's cluttered desk, stiff-backed chairs, computers,
stacks of books that never made their way to the leaning,
pressed-board bookcase, tea- and coffee-stained mugs, and a
vintage chrome kitchen table that Milo and I use for our
work space.

"There you are," Oma says when Mom straightens up in
her chair after plucking the Bible—King James version—
off the stack of books at her feet.

"Ma, is this important? Because if it's not, I really wish
you'd at least plan your stops for after four o'clock."

Oma, never one to give long-winded verbal drumrolls
before she states her business, is suddenly stammering.
"Yes, it's important. Very. I, well ..."

Mom looks up, tucks an unyielding strand of paler-than-
Oma's brown hair behind her ears, and blinks impatiently.

There are purple pouches under Mom's eyes because she's not been sleeping well. Three times in the last week, I've heard her pacing late at night, then going out, the dead bolt clicking behind her, and coming back an hour or so later. The last time I waited until she returned, then got out of bed under the guise of having to pee, and we met face-to-face as she was coming out of the bedroom. Even in the dim light, I could see that her eyelids were puffy, her red capillaries a road map of misery. I called her on it too, because that's just the way I am, and she got all nervous and claimed that she had an eyelash stuck under her contact.

Oma clears her throat and straightens herself up to her full five-foot-nine height. She takes a deep cleansing breath, then says, "Tess, I need to ask you a favor. A big one." That's when Mom's cell (the only phone we own) rings.

Mom answers it and listens for a time, her mouth falling open in disbelief. She stands up and paces as Oma and I watch her and wait. "Run that by me again?" Mom listens and then tosses her head and flattens her bangs back with her palm until her eyebrows lift. "A notice would have been nice, for crissakes!"

Mom hurries into the kitchen, Oma and I following her, Oma uttering, "What is it, dear? What's wrong?"

Mom dips her head to the side to hold her cell against her shoulder, then riffles through the stack of unopened mail. She picks up an envelope and rips it open. She skims the papers inside, then lifts her head and asks the caller, "How long will this take?" She mutters a couple of choice cuss words and tosses her phone on the table. Oma and I follow her back into the living room.

"What's wrong, Mom?" I ask. She's skimming four stapled pages, her face bunched with worry.

"Apparently the department of health caught wind that

this place is full of asbestos, lead paint, and about every other hazardous material known to man. They're condemning the building until it's cleaned up."

Oma gasps. "Oh, my God! So that's what those inspectors were doing here last month, when you thought it was only a routine check." Her gaze sweeps over the apartment and she pulls me to her, her hand subconsciously drifting to my neck, as if she's trying to keep the lurking toxins from slithering down my throat. She glances over at Milo, who has his head up, staring. I stare back at him. "Oh, my. No wonder that boy's had so much trouble breathing," she says. She keeps me tucked under her arm and hobbles me across the room so she can place her arm protectively around Milo too.

"We have to have our stuff out of here by the end of the month. They're promising us relocation benefits for displaced tenants, but what in the hell is that going to amount to? And how long will it take to get it? Shit." Mom's face has gone the color of asphalt—the color of the "yard" she no doubt imagines for us when we are forced to move into a cardboard box. "I paid off my past-due bills and my credit cards with my advance, then had to run them up again, and it'll be a couple more months before I see any royalties. Who knows how long these repairs will take. Shit!"

"Honey, your language," Oma says.

Mom collapses on her office chair and lets the letter drop onto her lap. Her arms fall over the armrests and dangle limply. "It looks like we're going to have to barge in on you for a while, Ma, though how we'll all fit into your tiny utility apartment is beyond me."

"You can't," Oma says, but there doesn't seem to be an ounce of regret in her voice. "They're changing the carpets and renovating the bathrooms in our complex. They did the first floor last week, and they'll start in on mine next week. I've already told them that I won't be there. I can't bear to be around all those horrid glue fumes. I could even smell them wafting up from the first floor, and they made my sinuses and throat burn like they were on fire. Lord knows what they would do to Milo's asthma if he were there."

"Oh, this is just great," Mom says.

"It *is* great, honey! Now things will work out perfectly."

"What things?"

"You and the children coming to Timber Falls with me."

Mom stops blinking. She stares up at Oma like she's gone mad.

"Honey . . . your father is dying. Your aunt Jeana called last night. She's been taking care of him since his first stroke, but now she's convinced that her Chihuahua has a brain tumor and she wants to hurry him back to his vet in Pennsylvania. Besides, she says she's fulfilled her sisterly obligations to Sam and that if I don't relieve her immediately, she'll put him in a nursing home. He developed congestive heart failure after his second stroke too, so she says it won't be long."

"And this is *our* problem *how*?" Mom says, once she can close her mouth enough to say anything.

"Tess, I promised your father years ago that I'd never let him go to a nursing home if it ever came to this. That man never kept one of his promises to me, but still it's important to me to honor mine."

My ears are perked up like a German shepherd's at the mention of my grandfather, because if there's any topic Mom views as more taboo than her Christian romance writing, it would be the topic of fathers. Hers *or* mine.

"You've got to be kidding, Ma. You divorced that man

twelve years ago, and neither of us has spoken a word to him since. And *I* certainly never promised him anything."

"No, you didn't. But you owe it to yourself to go."

"To *myself*?"

"That's right." Oma stands taller. "You've got unfinished business with him, Tess. And that unfinished business has ruined every relationship you've ever had."

Oma is referring to Mom's most recent boyfriend, no doubt. Peter. The man I hoped would become my dad. Peter is tall, built like a logger, and has sandy-colored hair just a shade darker than mine, so strangers would probably think he's my birth daddy. He keeps it tethered in a ponytail that hangs halfway down the back of his leisure jackets. He teaches poetry and poetics—the analysis of the art of poetry, if your IQ score happens to be even lower than mine—at the university. He fishes, hikes, grows violets, and writes poetry, of course.

Every time Peter came over, he'd stop at Mom's desk, give a kiss to the top of her head, or her lips, depending on which she presented to him, then walk over to our work-table. He'd come to me first, pick up whatever book I was reading, flip back a chapter or two, read me a sentence at random, then ask, "Where?" I'd close my eyes, turning pages in my mind until I found the passage he'd quoted, and answer something like, "Page one fifty-six. Fourth paragraph!" Peter would laugh every time, shaking his head in admiration for my photographic mind, and shout, "Yes! Yes! She does it again!"

Then, in the exaggerated swagger of a pompous professor, he'd move to Milo's side of the table, take a haughty, comical stance, lift his finger into the air as he thought, then ask questions such as, "Mr. McGowan, 17.5 raised to the power of 653?" or, "Mr. McGowan, what day of the week will it be on January twenty-fourth, 2046?" Milo would give him a swift, accurate answer, and Peter's laughter would fill the whole room like warm sunshine. When the little game was over, Peter would set one Hershey's Kiss with an almond inside on each of our palms, then grin with the pride of a real dad before heading to the kitchen for tea.

Peter was going to take us to Vermont next spring and we were going to help tap maple trees and make syrup, a yearly tradition for Peter and his family. We were going to meet his dad, a widower who, at the age of sixty-four, can walk on his hands clear across his yard (so he would probably appreciate a woman with Tina Turner legs), and his niece, who is twelve and has read *Little Women* fifteen times. A week ago, though, he showed up and handed Mom a poem he'd written on a coffee filter. A poem, he said, that would explain why he needed to break things off with her. He didn't pick up my book or ask Milo a question that day, but after he handed Mom the poem, he hugged me good-bye, squeezed Milo's shoulder, and left our Hershey's Kisses on the table next to our computers. I still have that Kiss.

Mom's hands trembled as she read the poem while still standing by the door where he'd left her, and when she was finished, she tossed it into the paper shredder. Then she rested her hands on her scarred desk to steady herself and sat down to resume her work. I ran to the window and looked down to watch Peter waggle through the old people and little kids clogging the stoop. "Don't let him go!" I screamed. "Mom, please! Call him back! Call him back!" But she didn't. Instead, she asked me if I'd finished my report on archetypes and warned that, if not, I should get busy.

Later, when Mom disappeared into the kitchen to nuke

our frozen dinners, I dug through the paper shredder and tried to find the strips of coffee filter. It would have been impossible to put them back together, so it probably didn't matter that Mom caught me and scarfed up the scraps and shoved them into the trash. "That's okay," I shouted, crossing my arms across my chest. "I know why he broke up with you, anyway. You have an attachment disorder, that's why. I don't need his poem to tell me that."

"It's like my intuitive, Sky Dreamer, says," Oma announces, her voice grabbing my attention and yanking me back to the here and now. "Sometimes we need to go home to find the parts of ourselves we left behind before we can truly become whole."

"Your intuitive? What in the hell are you talking about?"

"Sky Dreamer, my intuitive. I told you about her, Tess. I met her at that psychic convention I went to in California last November. Remember?" Oma pauses to cough. "She told me that each of us—you, me, Lucy, Milo—we all left parts of ourselves back in that town, in that very house, and in our relationship with Sam. She said that this trip will help us reclaim those parts and cleanse our family."

"The twins were newborns when they left Timber Falls. What could they have possibly left behind but spit-up? Besides, the only things that sound like they need cleansing to me are your lungs. Did this Sky Walker tell you to quit smoking too?"

"Sky Dreamer. Her name is Sky Dreamer."

"A rose by any other name is still a charlatan," Mom says.

Oma looks down at the chair opposite Mom's desk, and I hurry to remove the stack of books, folders, and notebooks from its seat. Oma pats my back as she sits down and props her other hand on the baggy white purse now resting on her legs. "Tess, you've always had an aversion to the concept of 'going home.' When you were three years old, you'd plug your ears every time you heard Bing Crosby's 'I'll Be Home for Christmas' play on the radio. And do you remember what you did to that Home Sweet Home pillow Marie made me for my birthday?"

Mom picks up the Bible and her pencil and runs the tip of it down one of the parchment pages. "I don't think we need to go into this, Mother," she says. Mom calls Oma "Mother" only when she's upset. The rest of the time it's simply, "Ma."

Oma turns to me. "My best friend in Timber Falls, Marie Birch, made me a needlepoint pillow for my birthday one year. It was beautiful. Burgundy and peacock blue, some gold. Your mother hated that thing from the moment she saw it. She swiped the seam ripper out of my sewing box and hid it under the sofa cushion. Then, whenever I left the house in the evening, she'd take it out of hiding and pluck at those tightly woven threads, letter by letter, word by word, until the whole adage was gone.

"I couldn't for the life of me understand how the threads could have come loose, period, much less over the words only. That is, until I found the seam ripper under the cushion."

"That's enough, Mother!" Mom snaps. "Crissakes, like I don't have enough on my mind now, and you have to bring up old crap that doesn't have a damn thing to do with the problem I'm dealing with today."

Oma turns her attention back to Mom. "Oh, but it has everything to do with your problems today. Don't you see that?"

Oma sets her purse on the floor, then parks her arms

on Mom's desk and leans in. "Scoff if you want, Tess, but I believe that you've always had these aversions because, deep down, you've always known that one day you'd have to go back home and deal with the pain you never dealt with. Did you think you could rid yourself of it simply by leaving Timber Falls? Honey, it just doesn't work that way. Think of the toxic waste they dumped in the ocean back in the sixties. Was it gone because we couldn't see it? No. It washed up on other banks, just as toxic as ever. Tess, you know what I'm talking about. On a soul level, you know."

I look at Mom. I don't know what Oma is talking about, but Mom certainly does, because her navy-blue eyes pool with water. My throat tightens then, because when I see her pain, the emotion swelling under my breastbone makes me want to cry. I glance over at Milo to see if he's empathizing with Mom too, but he's not even looking at her. I know Mom would have to start wailing before he'd notice that she was in distress. And considering that Mom's lids are already blinking like windshield wipers, I know Milo isn't going to notice.

Oma leans over and presses her hand—the one sporting a sapphire half-moon ring surrounded by diamond chips— over Mom's hand that's holding the Bible. "Honey," she says, her voice soft and pleading, "I need you to drive me to Timber Falls. Would you do that for me?"

Mom leans back in her chair and slams the Bible down. "Take the bus. I'm not doing it."

Oma sits erect and gasps, "Oh, Tess. I can't do that! You've seen the people who take the buses. God bless their pitiful souls, but I'm afraid of them."

"Then drive yourself. You have a car." Mom is referring to the 1965 wine-red Mustang coupe that Oma's last boy-friend, Roger, gave her. The one he had a new CD player and Bose speakers installed in, so that after his heart bypass surgery he could take Oma to see New York, Frank Sinatra crooning the whole way. He had a heart attack the day before his surgery and died, leaving Oma his car. It's sitting in a parking garage somewhere in the city, the storage paid for two more years.

"You know I can't drive a standard, Tess."

"Then sell the damn thing and buy an automatic!"

Oma takes a deep breath, then drops her hands to her legs and positions them in shuni mudra—the tips of her middle fingers touching the tips of her thumbs—to give her patience. She takes a cleansing breath as Mom mutters, "Oh, Jesus," and rolls her eyes before she looks back down at the Bible.

When Oma is done breathing, she looks at Mom with tofu-soft eyes, but she doesn't say anything. She just stares until Mom looks up.

Mom studies Oma carefully under a hem of bangs. "Okay...now that you're all 'centered,' maybe you'd like to come clean and tell me the *real* reason you're so determined to get me back there. Or to go yourself, for that matter."

"I don't know what you're talking about," Oma says in a voice higher pitched than normal.

"Of course you do. Cut the crap, Mother."

Oma takes another cleansing breath. "Okay," she says. "Maybe there is another reason, but that doesn't mean I'm not sincere about honoring my promise, because I am."

"And what would that other reason be?"

"Your father's leaving you the house, Tess."

"What?" For a moment, the only sound in the living room is the sound of Milo's pencil scratching paper.

"Well," Oma finally admits, "it wasn't exactly his decision. It was your aunt Jeana's. Sam made her executor of his will a couple of years back, and Jeana's decided that you should get the house."

"What's the catch?"

"You get the house only if you spend this time with him. Now, before he dies."

Mom bolts out of her chair, pacing behind it, one hand on her hip, the other rubbing her forehead. "You've got to be fucking kidding me!" Mom says, smashing Oma's calm to bits with that f-word. Before Oma can respond, Mom puts her hand up. "Okay. I'm sorry. It just slipped out, but, Ma, you've ... I ... God, I don't even know how to respond to something this absurd."

"Oh, I know what you're thinking. That this is typical Jeana behavior, manipulative and controlling. But I believe that her intentions are good."

Oma gets up, circles the desk, and puts her hand on Mom's arm. "Honey, please. You have to stop and think this over. What are you going to do until you get your royalty check? Run your credit cards up even higher? I know you're almost broke, and I'm not in a position to help you. And now with you having to move out of here for a while ... Well, it can't just be a coincidence that Jeana called when she did. It just can't be."

Oma lets go of Mom—probably because Mom has just deflated and is suddenly too emotionally drained to stomp away—and Mom leans her back against the wall, rumpling her chapter-by-chapter outline on oversize paper tacked behind her. She grabs the sides of her face, stretching her eyes and mouth into a replica of Edvard Munch's *The Scream*.

"Tess, you know I wouldn't ask you to go back there with the children if ... well ... if he was the same man he used to be. But he's not. He's old and frail, and he's dying. You need this for your spirit, and you need this for your bank account. I talked with Marie last night, and she said that property prices are going up astronomically now that so many folks from here and Milwaukee are buying land up there so they can vacation and retire in the pristine north woods. Your father's house sits on forty acres of hardwood. As soon as he passes on, you can sell the place and rest assured that if these romance books you're writing don't do more than this one run—which they probably won't, only because your intentions aren't genuine, I might add—you'll be able to support these kids for a good long time."

Mom sits back down on her chair. Hard. She sighs and runs her fingertips in tiny circles over her temples.

Oma turns to look at me and then at Milo, who is wheezing over his books. "It would do the children good to get some fresh country air and sit a little closer to the earth. They'd have acres of trees to climb and grass to run on."

I get a lump in my throat when Oma says this, because besides dreaming of being a figure skater and a shaman, I dream of running barefoot on grass. There's grass and a few trees in the park we pass on the way to the university where we borrow our books. Whenever we pass that park, I press my face against the grubby bus window and ask Mom if we can *please* stop. And every time, she says that we will when we aren't in such a hurry. But I know that a lack of time is not the real reason. The real reason we can't stop is that the park is filled with homeless people stretched out on park benches, their small bundles wadded into pillows, and with crack whores who do obscene things with men for money so they can buy more crack. And then there are the bangers from the People Nation, or the Folk Nation, who congregate there at night sometimes to exchange money for drugs, or shoot each other, or whatever else it is those scary gangsters— the same boys who will stab or shoot Milo if he goes to school—do. After the bus passes the park and I sink back against the seat, Mom always promises that one day soon, when we have more time, we'll take a different route and stop at a nicer, safer park, but we never do.

Oma gets up, clasps her hands together softly, and asks who would like tea. I'm the only one who says yes, so Oma invites me to help her make it.

We go into the kitchen and I get out the basket we keep our tea bags in while Oma fills the teakettle. There's tea to pick you up, calm you down, put you to sleep, wake you up, clear your mind, help you focus; any mood you could possibly want is in those little pouches of tea. Unfortunately, I don't think the tea itself can alter moods enough, because after Mom's literary novel bombed, she drank gallons of tea laced with Saint-John's-wort, but in the end she still needed to go to a doctor to get an antidepressant so she could get out of bed. The Paxil didn't make her happy, but she did get out of bed and start writing her Christian romance book.

"I don't remember my grandpa Sam," I say, as I rummage through the bags.

"Of course you don't, Lucy. Not consciously, anyway. You and Milo were newborns when you saw him last."

"Well, at least we saw him once, even if we were too small to remember. We never saw our dad, though, did we? Not even when we were newborns."

"No, dear," she says, giving my flimsy blond hair a stroke. She looks as sad as I feel, so I choose guarana chai tea for the two of us, to boost our spirits, and calming chamomile tea for Mom, if she decides she wants some after all. "Your mother, I'm afraid, chooses the kind of men I once chose. Men like her father. Selfish men who only respond to their own wants and needs."

"Not Peter," I say. "Peter paid our rent the month before

Mom's advance check came, when our charge cards were maxed. And when Mom and Milo had the flu last winter, he brought them Tylenol and juice, even though he was sick with the flu himself."

"True, dear. But then your mother didn't choose to stay with him, now, did she?"

As Oma digs through the cupboard for the honey, I put her tea bag and mine into the two cups that are sitting side by side. I take the tea-bag strings and twist them slightly at the ends so they are entwined. Just as Oma and I are intertwined in some way I can't quite put my finger on but that she explains by saying our souls knew each other before we came into this world.

Oma's got a point. Mom didn't choose to stay with Peter. Just like she—obviously—didn't choose to stay with my father.

Mom didn't tell me his name until I was nine years old. And I'm sure she did it then only to rid me of the notion that figure skater Scotty Hamilton was my father. "He's got to be our dad!" I told Milo, after seeing him skate on some PBS special at Oma's (we don't have a TV, but I can watch a little at Oma's as long as it's a PBS program). "He has the same fine blond hair that we do, and he's short and slight of build like you. And doesn't my nose look like his, the way it turns up at the tip? Milo, look!"

After I saw Scotty, I scoured the Internet for articles and photographs and printed them out. His bio convinced me even further that he was our father; an unidentified childhood illness had made him stop growing. This, I was convinced, presented a genetic explanation for Milo's small stature, even though the doctors never said there was anything wrong with Milo, except for his asthma and poor muscle tone from lack of physical activity.

I glued the articles into the scrapbook Oma had given me for my eighth birthday and taped his pictures above my bed, giving each one a caption. I'd look at them while I turned down my covers. Once I was tucked in, I'd make up stories about how things would be once my father and I were reunited. Then, until I fell asleep, I'd see flash after flash of those moments. Our first tearful, joyful hug. Dad proudly introducing me as "My daughter, Lucy," to Katarina Witt, Brian Boitano, and all of those old-timers he used to skate with. Dad holding my hands and pulling me across the ice, coaxing me along with tips on how to keep my ankles from folding over like the peak on a soft-serve ice cream cone on a summer day. And, finally, Dad and I sailing across the ice once I'd quickly mastered the sport, my short skirt bobbing, the breeze from our speed brushing my smiling cheeks as he tossed me into the air and gently caught me.

Mom wasn't upset the night she came into my room to tuck me in and saw Scotty's photos tacked on my wall, but she got upset later in the week—that quiet, stiff kind of upset—when she noticed the caption: *Dad, 1997, the year I was born. Taken right after he was diagnosed with a cancer that could have killed him, but, thankfully, didn't.*

She opened her mouth to say something, then stopped, bent down to kiss me good night, and walked out of the room. The following week, though, when she caught me "skating" across the kitchen linoleum on two sheets of waxed paper, yelling, "Daddy, Daddy, look at me!" as I tapped my feet across the floor with steps I was sure were every bit as intricate as his, she told me to stop it, "Now!" And a couple days after that, when she strolled over to check on how my assignment on French literature was coming along, and she saw me typing *Dear Daddy*, in the contact box of Scotty's MySpace fan page, she lost it. "Scott

Hamilton is *not* your father! Stop this nonsense right now!" And when I yelled back that he was—that he *had* to be— she shouted, "That's crazy! Your father's name was Howard. You got that? Howard Smith. Not Scott Hamilton!"

I was daydreaming that my dad, Scotty, was at the peak of an extension on a triple lutz when Mom caught me writing to him and said this. And that heavy, gut-carving feeling I get in my middle when I think of not having a dad suddenly, painfully exploded, until I was certain it had cracked my breastbone. Just as the ice cracked under Scotty when he landed his jump and, to my horror, he slipped under the ice to be gone forevermore.

It took a few weeks to forgive my real dad for drowning my fantasy that Scotty was my father, but before I knew it, the name Howard Smith began ringing through my head like church bells. I became obsessed with saying his name and would mutter it under my breath while I worked, until Milo—who, like a lot of profoundly gifted kids, is a tad on the hypersensitive side when it comes to sounds, smells, and tastes—stopped working long enough to toss a pencil at me and to tell me to shut up.

I begged Mom to tell me more about Howard Smith. Things like what he looked like, if he figure skated, and what kind of hands he had (because I happen to think that hands reveal a lot about a person), but Mom's darkening eyes warned me that the topic of my father was every bit as shameful and off-limits as the topic of her romance novels. I tried squeezing information out of Oma then but knew instantly that Mom had gotten to her first, and for whatever reason, this time Oma was going to honor Mom's wishes and tell me nothing. "When you're older," was all Oma said, to which I reminded her that I was nine years old and probably going to start my "moon time" in a couple of years and was therefore old enough to know the truth.

After that, I scoured Web sites that help you find missing people for tips, then searched the Web for e-mail addresses for any Howard Smiths I could find—even one in France! I told each one that he'd probably find it useful having Milo and me in his life. I listed all the talents we have, just to support my claim. Under Milo's name, I put reasons such as: *He could balance your checkbook and do your income taxes for you, compute more accurate odds for the lottery or racetracks if you're a gambler, and be your walking calendar so you could pay your bills on time.* For my talents, I listed things such as: *I could make you tea to help you adjust your moods and tell you if a potential business partner is honest or not, based on his eye movements and body language. I could tell you what page you left off on in your book, if you happen to be one of those readers who doesn't use bookmarkers because you think you can remember but you never do.* Out of the couple hundred I spammed, only one Howard Smith wrote back, and he asked me for a photograph— one in a swim suit or, better still, in the nude, so he could look for any physical resemblances between me and his nieces.

"I'm letting your mother chew on this for a bit," Oma says, then lifts her teacup to her glossy peach lips. "You know how she is. She's not a rash person and always needs time to warm up to an idea."

"In that case, I think you'll be waiting about a century, because that's how long it will probably take for her to warm up to this one."

"Necessity will sway her, Lucy, which in this case is a blessing. She needs this. Financially and spiritually."

"Oma?" I ask after a time. "Did my grandfather know how to ice skate?"

Oma tosses her head back and laughs. "The only ice that man ever skated on was the ice over his own heart."

Oma gets quiet, thoughtful, then says, "I shouldn't think and talk like that. It'll bring bad karma. I take it back. And, anyway, I'm exaggerating. Sam cared a lot about a great many things. His children and his wife just didn't happen to be among them."

Oma is referring to Mom, of course, and Mom's twin brother, my uncle Clay. Uncle Clay lives in Mill Valley, California, where he has—in Mom's words—nipped and tucked his way to fortune as a highly sought-after cosmetic surgeon. I've never met him, which figures. Every year, though, his wife sends one of those photo Christmas cards. Uncle Clay has a girl, a year younger than me, and two younger sons. I don't know much of anything about the girl, Britney, except that she does well in school and likes to sing and that she looks like a very nice person. Three Christmases ago I wrote her a letter that started, *Dear Cousin Brit,* and in it I told her about myself and asked about her. I never got around to mailing it, though, which is just as well since I told fibs in the letter anyway. Things like how I have six best friends and how once we all visited the underworld together. And also that I figure skate and was being groomed for the 2006 Winter Olympics in Italy, which of course she'd have found out was a lie by now.

"Oma?" I ask—but I don't have time for my next question about Grandpa, because Mom comes into the kitchen. She pats her hand on the teakettle to see if it's still hot, then, as she's getting down a cup, she says flatly, "Okay, I'll drive you there. Tomorrow morning. But I'm not staying longer than to stretch my legs. And don't even ask me to, because obviously I need to get back here to start packing and figure out where in the hell we're going to set up our cardboard box."

Oma stands, her face glowing with hope—either because of the guarana tea, Mom's compliance, or both—and she gives Mom a hug. "I'm so happy that you've decided to go where the powers that be are leading you, Tess."

"Nonsense. I'm only giving you a lift because I'll never get a moment's peace for the rest of my life if I don't."

Mom, whose arms are limp at her sides as Oma hugs her, is crushed up against Oma's big breasts. And muffled or not, I hear her words when she says, "Just so you know, I could deal with you a hell of a lot better before you turned into this New Age freak."

And Oma says, "I love you too, honey."

T HE NEXT morning, Oma stays with us as Mom takes a bus to the parking garage to pick up the Mustang. Oma looks down at our single piece of luggage waiting on the floor. "This isn't all of it, I hope."

"Yes. Mom said we're not staying, so a few books and one change of clothes and one pair of pajamas—in case we stay in a motel tonight—is all we need."

Oma shakes her head and hurries off to our room, me tagging after her. She opens Milo's drawer and begins digging through it, pulling out extra pairs of jeans, T-shirts, sweatshirts, socks, and underwear. "Get yourself more things too, Lucy," she says.

"But Mom said—"

"Oh, you'll be staying a good long while. Now, get your things."

"How do you know we'll be staying a good long while? Mom said—"

"I called Sky Dreamer last night. That's how I know," Oma says in a singsong voice. "Milo? You have an extra inhaler or two to bring along?" she calls into the living room. "And don't forget your jacket, Lucy. A hooded sweatshirt, and something warmer too. It'll be cooler up north."

"Milo, you have extra inhalers?" Oma asks again when we go back into the living room. Milo says yes, then fidgets. "What's the wind speed today, and what direction is it coming from? Do you know, Oma?" Oma blinks at him, because she has no clue about today's wind, much less why he's asking.

"He wants to calculate how long it will take us to get to Timber Falls," I say, falling into my old habit of speaking for Milo. It's one I developed way back when I was two and Milo's verbal skills were lagging behind mine—a "boy thing," and a twin thing too. "He's calculating the exact time we'll pass through each town along the way—down to nanoseconds, no doubt—and he can't be precise unless he knows the force of the wind."

"Oh," Oma says, as she sets down our newly packed bags and moves to our worktable. "I'm sorry, dear, but I don't know. We'll catch the weather on the radio while driving." She picks up a piece of paper scribbled with equations, turning to me for explanation.

"He's accounting for the amount of traffic he believes there will be at precisely eight-sixteen, which is what time he guesses it will be when Mom gets back and we get in the car. Of course, now he'll have to readjust his calculations because we have three extra bags."

"Be sure to calculate some extra time in there for our wayside stops, Milo. We girls need to stop often to pee." She pats his head, which is now bent over the paper he plucked out of Oma's hand so he could recalculate. That's when Mom's key rattles the lock.

We look like we're moving a library as we head down the three flights of stairs. Milo and I grunt under the weight of our books, as we wait behind Mom and Oma, who are moving slowly with bags slung over their shoulders and arms, our luggage bumping down the stairs behind them. "Shit," Mom says, when she bangs her laptop bag against the grimy wall. Her phone rings while we're trudging down, but she can't reach it in her purse with her arms so full, and she says "shit" again.

On the ground floor, we meet the superintendent. He's got his arm propped on an industrial broom. He looks tired. "Tell them to fix the goddamn elevator while they're at it," Mom snipes.

"That be the least of our worries here, Miss McGowan," he says.

As soon as we get outside, Oma calls hello to two old black women, and one young one with dyed, rust-colored hair, who are watching two little kids chase green leaves that they've plucked from the branches of one of the three potted trees on our block. The trees were planted by an environmental group after the emerald ash borers killed the old ones that reached clear to our floor and they had to be sawed down to stumps. One girl has both of her fists packed, and she tosses them in the air, her cheeks the color of apple butter and going chubby as she laughs. She looks so elated that I can't even be angry at her for desecrating the poor tree.

I stomp my shoe on a rolling leaf and ask the little girl

to pick it up and hand it to me. She tucks it between the two
fingers I lift slightly so I don't drop my psychology books.
She waits for me to throw it, but I'm not going to. I'm going
to save it.

"Come on, Lucy!" Mom snaps from where she stands
next to Oma at the opened trunk, checking voice mail on
her cell phone.

Oma has her things loaded in the trunk already. Her
toiletries and New Age paraphernalia are packed in two
pretty tote bags that are wedged alongside three matching
moss-green pieces of luggage. She lifts a Curves bag that
has the toe of a tennis shoe peeking out from between lime-
green fabric and holds it in the air so Milo can tuck his stack
of books beside her things. As I watch her arrange our bags,
I wonder if one needs to arrange things in a feng shui sort
of way even in a trunk.

Milo gets motion sickness easily and can't read in the
car no matter how much Dramamine he takes, so he keeps
out only one notebook and a library CD for inside the car:
Richard P. Feynman's *Lectures on Physics, Vol. 19.* I keep out
my book on somatic disorders and use the soft leaf for a
bookmark, even though I know exactly where I've left off:
page 293, second paragraph down.

The car smells like leather. Mom slips behind the steering wheel, and Oma gets in on the passenger side. I sit behind Mom, and Milo behind Oma. "Poor Roger," Oma coos
softly, as she digs in her purse and pulls out a pewter clip
that she fastens to the visor above Mom's head. It has an angel on it and says, *Angels, protect me on my journey.* She taps
it once she has it in place, then mutters a short prayer. I see
Mom's eyeballs scoot up toward her forehead, as if they are
looking there for some explanation that would explain her
mother's "wackiness."

I'm excited as we weave through the busy lanes. It's been ages since I've ridden in a car. I wait for cars to coast parallel to us, and watch the people inside. In many of them there are whole families: a mother, a father, kids, and sometimes a dog. I watch a green Toyota pull up beside us. The mother is dozing, her auburn head pressed against the glass. In the backseat, a boy and girl, younger than Milo and me, are slapping at each other's hands in some sort of game and laughing when their hands miss each other. I glance over at Milo, who is staring out the window, seeing nothing but his thoughts, and I wish he wasn't the stereotypical genius: serious, frail. An old man in a boy's body.

"Oh!" Oma says to Mom, once we are out of Chicago and traffic lets up some. "I've got to tell you what Marie said when I talked to her last night. Oh, how that woman makes me laugh!" Oma pauses to giggle. "I don't know how, but somehow we got on the topic of finding a bra that supports but is comfortable. And Marie told me that when her daughter, Sue, was visiting over Labor Day weekend, she took her to Victoria's Secret to buy her a good bra for her birthday." Oma laughs again, and, surprisingly, so does Mom.

"She took her to *Victoria's Secret*?"

"Yes! Can you imagine that? Marie said the bras these days look like body casts for boobs. She said...oh, land's sake, I can't even spit it out..." Oma's laughter is so hearty that her whole body shakes. She swallows her giggles enough to say, "She said that at our ages, filling these new-fandangled bras is like filling a Jell-O mold. You just pour them in and wait for them to set." Oma's hoot fills the whole car.

"You should call Mitzy when we get to Timber Falls," Oma says once she settles down and gets done dabbing her eyes.

"Who's Mitzy?" I ask.

Oma glances over her left shoulder to look at me. "Your mother's best friend throughout childhood." Oma looks over at Mom. "You even kept in touch through most of college, didn't you?"

"I haven't spoken to her in years, Ma," Mom says, her voice reserved again.

"Well, you should. Old friends are such a blessing. Marie started to tell me something about her, but the battery on her phone was dying, so I told her I'd call her when I get settled in and we'll catch up."

"Ma, I won't be there long enough to see anybody. I plan to just drop you off and turn around."

"Oh, Tess, don't be silly now. A round trip in one day is too much."

"We're going and coming back in one day?" Milo asks, his skin tone already looking a little green from his queasiness.

"If I get too tired, I'll stop and get us a room on the way back."

"You don't have money to throw away on a motel room, and besides, even if you did, do you know how many dead skin cells and traces of bodily fluids are soaked into those mattresses? It's unsanitary!"

Mom sighs but says nothing.

Oma has a Dasani water bottle that she filled with water run through a Brita pitcher, and Mom has a travel mug filled with coffee. They both take a sip of their drinks, and for a time there's no sound but for the hum of the tires on the road and the scratching of Milo's pencil.

I've never been able to talk openly about the grandfather I never knew, but I feel it must be okay now since we're on our way to see him. "Is Grandpa Sam paralyzed on the left side? Is he going to speak with his words all jumbled?" I'd done research online to learn about strokes so I'd know what to expect.

"Actually, no," Oma says. "Neither of his strokes were the usual kind. They were in his frontal lobe, Aunt Jeana said."

"I know about strokes in the frontal lobe!" I say, too loudly, judging by the way Milo flinches. "That part of the brain serves as the doorway to our emotions. Our social conscience is located there, and that portion of the brain also tells us when to stop doing an activity." And maybe just to be a little mean—or because I'm still annoyed that Milo won't play in the car with me like a normal sibling—I add, "Gee, Milo. Maybe you had a stroke. Mom should mention your symptoms to the doc on your next visit."

"Lucy," Mom warns, and Oma (who obviously absorbed only the first part of what I said or she'd have snapped my name too) says, "Well, isn't that interesting. It shouldn't surprise me, though."

"What do you mean?" I ask.

"Well, your grandfather spent his entire life trying to shut the door on his emotions. I guess he finally succeeded. So sad." Oma turns her head to look at Mom. "And isn't it ironic, Tess, that he should lose his social conscience too, when once that's all he had? You remember how he fretted about what others thought of him?" Mom gives a little grunt, then sips her coffee.

"Do I look like him?" I ask.

Mom's body presses against her seat hard enough to jiggle it. "Let's change the subject, shall we?"

"Oma started it!" I say.

Milo glances over at me. "No she didn't. You're the one who brought up Grandpa first." I keep my hand low so

Mom can't see it in her rearview mirror, and I reach across the seat and give Milo's scrawny leg a hard pinch. "Ouch!" he says, and Mom tells me to keep my hands to myself.

Oma is oblivious to all of this. "Yes, I do believe you resemble him some. Through the eyes."

"Mine are the same shape as Mom's, but lighter blue."

"Yes, and she got the shape of her eyes from her father. Sam's are lighter than hers, and more gray than blue. He has flecks of yellow in them, though, like your mother has." I ask Oma to borrow her compact so I can check for yellow flecks in mine. I hope I don't find any, though, because once I read a book on Chinese face reading, and it said that yellow shards in the iris point to a vengeful temper.

While I'm looking, Mom and Milo get into a debate about the genetic likelihood of children getting one parent's eye color as opposed to the other's. I find no flecks of yellow and hand Oma back her mirror. I don't listen to Milo and Mom but only stare out the window, waiting for another family to pull up alongside us.

After a time, the high-rises give way to suburban clusters and, finally, to open fields. Milo gets excited when he sees three high-tech windmills spinning against the sky, and he starts rattling away about renewable resources versus fossil fuels. He sounds like a PBS program. A dull one, at that. I like facts. I love them, actually. But only if they're about something interesting. Mom joins in on the debate, but she's left to discuss it alone once Milo decides he needs to calculate something or other, no doubt it having to do with a windmill's rotations.

"What's our new house look like?" I ask.

"What did you say?" Mom asks, her eyes in the rearview mirror scrunching into cat's eyes. "Why did you call it *our* new house? Who said it's ours?"

"Oma," I say defensively.

Mom's head snaps toward Oma, even though she's in the middle of changing lanes to pass a semi. "I did not say I was taking that house!"

"And I didn't tell Lucy that you were," Oma says calmly.

"Grandpa Sam gave us his house?" Milo asks.

"No, he did not! He wouldn't give me a damn drink if I was dehydrating on the Sahara and he came by on a camel weighted one inch off the ground with bottled water!"

Oma doesn't comment. She reaches into the tote bag stuffed with treats for the road and pulls out a box of organic granola bars and asks who would like one. After she hands Milo and me one each, she reaches back in her tote bag and takes out a CD and pops it in, and the whole car fills up with the mournful but soothing calls of humpback whales.

As we cross the border into Wisconsin, Milo checks his calculations and utters a "Yes! Within 3.5 seconds! Right on schedule," and Mom says, "Oh, goody," under her breath in a tone that can only be called sarcastic.

"Did you know that every pod of whales has their own song?" I say to no one in particular. "And that even if one gets separated from the pod, they never forget that song, no matter how long they've been away from the others or how many miles apart they are?" Nobody says anything until Milo asks if he can listen to his Feynman lectures now. Mom tells him he can.

chapter

FOUR

AS MUCH as I've always longed to be among trees, I begin to feel smothered the farther up into Wisconsin we get. The trees, already beginning to color, edge closer to the highway, then crowd together so tightly that only slivers of flickering sunlight can squeeze between them.

Mom is unsettled too, but I suspect it has nothing to do with the encroaching forest. The top of her head, visible over the seat, is pressed tightly against it again, as if she's bracing herself.

Oma does not look unsettled but contemplative. Her head slowly cocks from side to side as we pass houses with lawns as big as parks. Places she probably remembers passing during her days as Grandpa Sam's wife.

Oma married my grandpa in 1970. She was twenty-four. He was forty and recently divorced. It's the kind of "love story," I overheard Mom say once to Oma, that gets men locked up nowadays and earns them a spot on Wisconsin's list of sexual predators. Grandpa Sam and Oma met when Oma went to stay at a friend's cabin in Timber Falls for one week. It was love at first sight, Oma said, and they were married three months later. Right after the wedding, they moved to Chicago so Grandpa could make better money and realize his dream of building the biggest and best sawmill in the Midwest. Oma worked in a factory, and every penny she earned she put into their savings for that sawmill. They stayed in Chicago for four years, then Grandpa decided that city life wasn't for him. So they headed back and bought the house that Grandpa lives in now. Our house. And a year later, my mom and Uncle Clay were born.

Oma rests her head closer to the side window and peers up. Her whole body perks when she sees something. She taps the window glass. "Oh, look, children! An eagle!"

I have to almost lay my head on Milo's lap to see him, but there he is, soaring above the treetops on Oma's side of the road, heading in the same direction we are. There is a slight upward curve to the tip of his wings, which are spread wide as though he's claiming the whole sky. He's beautiful, with his regal head capped in white feathers. "Wow! He's gigantic! His wingspan must be a good six feet!" I say.

Milo glances out. "I'd say closer to seven," he says, then quickly turns his attention back to his notepad.

Not to be outdone by Milo, I add, "The eagle's scientific

name is *Haliaeetus leucocephalus*." Milo doesn't even glance at me when he corrects my pronunciation.

"He's beautiful, isn't he?" Oma says, her voice all dreamy with wonder. "Did you know, Lucy, that the Ojibwa people believe that if you offer an eagle tobacco, he will carry your prayers to heaven?" Her head is still leaned back, her face bent toward the sky.

"Really?" I ask, scooting forward as far as my seat belt will allow me to.

"Tess, stop the car! Now!"

Mom is mid-sentence, trying to snag Milo into a new discussion. She stops talking and looks over at Oma, who is digging in her purse.

"Just stop the car! Hurry!" Oma says as she pulls a Virginia Slims from its pack.

"Jesus, you can't wait fifteen minutes to have a smoke? We're almost there!" Mom steers the car to the gravel alongside the pavement, and Milo groans and grabs his belly when it jostles.

"Come on, Lucy!" Oma says, springing open her door while the car is still rocking from the stop.

"Open your door, Mom!"

"Hurry, Lucy," Oma says, as she waits outside with one hand on the door.

I don't wait for Mom to decide to open her door so I can get out. I scoot myself into the front seat and dive out Oma's door.

Oma and I hurry to stand in the tall grass along the ditch. Oma points to the bird, who has lit at the very tip of what I recall from our early studies of tree species is a northern pine, set off the road some thirty yards behind us. The eagle glances down at us, then turns his curved beak elsewhere.

Oma breaks the cigarette into her palm, then gives me

a pinch of tobacco. She whispers so as not to scare him away—or because this is supposed to be a sacred moment. "Now say a prayer, then toss the tobacco into the air as your offering," she says.

Oma holds her tobacco up high, closes her eyes, and starts muttering her prayer. I'm not sure if she's praying to God, though, because she's calling Him "Creator Spirit," and about seven other names. I close my eyes too and say my prayer in my mind. *Please, God, if You exist, please help me find my real dad. And if You can't do that, please bring Peter back to be my dad. And if You can't do either of those things, then would You at least crack the door to Grandpa's emotions open a little, so that when he gets to know me he can feel fondness for me? Also, can you make my ankles stronger so I can be a figure skater, even if I don't have Scott Hamilton's genes to give me a boost?*

When I'm done, I open my eyes and see that Oma is still softly muttering her prayer, both hands lifted toward the eagle. She barely finishes her "We thank you for all things. Amen," when Mom honks the horn, causing Oma, me, and the bird to startle. The eagle opens his wings and springs from the branch, lifting above the treetops. Quickly, I open my fingers, and the breeze takes the tobacco flakes and scatters them to the ground.

As we hurry back to the car, Mom opens her door and cranks her head around. "Damn it, Mother. What did I tell you about filling Lucy's head with that crazy hocus pocus, New Age crap?" She opens the door wider and leans her chest against the steering wheel and tells me to get in.

"There's nothing New Age about it, Miss Smarty Pants," Oma says, and I giggle. "Native Americans have been sending their prayers up with Eagle for centuries."

As soon as I get settled in my seat, I look for the eagle. When I spot him, he's only a speck swirling in the sky.

"Put on your seat belt and find something to read," Mom tells me.

But I can't read, of course. I'm too excited. So is Milo, but only because when we come up alongside a wooden sign saying, *Welcome to Timber Falls*, the stopwatch that Peter gave him says he's only off on his estimated time of arrival by four seconds and who knows how many fractions of a second, even though we made one uncalculated stop to pee, one so Oma could smoke, one so Oma and I could pray, and yet another so Milo could vomit.

I stare out the window, my face so close to the glass that I can feel my breath against my lips. The stores lining the streets are small, the tallest of them only two stories high. Behind the storefronts' masks of fresh paint and pretty stenciled lettering, the sides of the buildings are shabby, their rear ends sagging.

There are fewer people milling around Main Street than what I'd see out in front of our apartment building on sweltering summer days. As I gawk, Oma does too. She says things like, "Oh, look. The Rexall drugstore is still here," and, "Oh, my, now, does any town this size need both a Hardee's and a McDonald's?" And Mom says, "What an oppressive dump."

When we get almost to the north end of the main street, the road veers off to the east, and at the bend there's a landscaped yard and a big, beautiful, Victorian-style house. "Look at that!" I say. "I wish that was the house we were going to inherit from Grandpa Sam."

"We're not going to inherit anything from your grandfather!" Mom snaps.

Milo winces because, once again, the volume in our voices is cranked up enough to put his ears on overload.

"Oh, look, Tess," Oma says as she points to the house I've just singled out. "They've turned the Millard mansion into a historical landmark. Harlan must have passed on, then." Oma turns to me. "Joseph Millard built that home, along with most of the town. He was a timber baron and the founder of Timber Falls. Your grandfather went to school with his great-grandson, Harlan."

"Harlan and Samuel," Mom huffs. "Wisconsin's own Hatfields and McCoys. Legends in their own mind."

"Who are the Hatfields and the McCoys?" I ask, but Oma ignores that question and addresses Mom's grumble.

"Your father and Harlan sure did carry that ruckus into their generation, now, didn't they?" Then she looks over her shoulder into the backseat. "Harlan and your grandfather didn't get along. Something about Harlan's family and ours and land that our family believed was taken out from under our noses by the Millards during a bout of bad luck."

"Dad wanted that stupid mill just so he could become a somebody and keep Harlan from gloating about our family's downfall. And that's what made him turn into such an asshole, when——" Mom stops. "Oh, let's change the subject," she says as we swing around the bend. I turn around in my seat to catch a last glimpse of the remarkable house.

Oma's still cranked around to watch the house pass. "Harlan must have given the house to the city. He never married and didn't have any children, so I suppose..."

"He was probably gay," Mom says, but Oma shakes her head. "Oh, Tess, you know that's not true. He was in love with Maude Tuttle."

Oma points ahead to a house we're approaching. It's large, three stories, painted pale yellow with white trim, and though not as grand as the Millard manor house, it's easily the second most extravagant house I've seen in this town so far. "That's Maude Tuttle's house right there," she tells me. "It used to be ... well ... a house of ill repute."

"What's that?" I ask, and Mom scowls at Oma.

Oma giggles. "Good heavens, when I first moved here, they were still doing raids on that place when a complaint came in, though halfheartedly, since on any given night you could bet that one of Timber Falls's most elite would be found there.

"Well, anyway," Oma says, stifling her laughter. "The only woman Harlan ever loved lived there. Maude Tuttle. I wonder if she's still alive. Hmmm. Anyway, what a beautiful woman. She'd cut you like broken glass if you looked at her twice, but she was absolutely gorgeous. Had she been in her prime today, she'd be the hottest plus-size model this country's ever seen. Harlan loved her dearly."

"Why didn't they get married, then?" I ask.

Oma starts giggling again. "Oh, he couldn't marry a girl like Maude Tuttle; he had his family name to protect."

"Crissakes, as if they were the royal family," Mom says.

"She loved him, though—or at least what he did for her. Enough that after he became her only ... well ... *boyfriend* she dyed her pretty blond hair red, because Harlan liked redheads." Oma leans across the console and whispers (but loud enough for me to hear, because what I wasn't given in ankle strength, the acuteness of my hearing makes up for), "Women said that the hair on her head wasn't the only hair she dyed red for him either," and Mom says, "Too much information."

Oma tips back upright in her seat. "She stayed loyal to him, though, and I'd like to believe that it was because of love rather than that he bought her out of the business and set her up pretty for the rest of her life. Harlan was one good-looking man in his day. Marie said once that Harlan was good-looking enough to make even Mother Teresa tingle in her naughty places."

"Mother! I hardly think this story should be part of the kids' educational tour of Timber Falls. For God's sakes, keep your voice down when you talk like that."

Oma taps Mom on the arm. "Oh, Tess. Loosen up. Sex is a natural part of life, and the children are already pubescent. Why, soon Lucy will begin her moon time, and—"

"Her *menstrual cycle*, Mother. Her MENSTRUAL CYCLE!"

Milo glances up. "Do you people have to talk about such things in front of me?"

"Oh, so you mean Maude Tuttle was a prostitute and that she turned tricks like a crack whore!" I say, finally getting it.

"Lucy Marie McGowan! Where on earth did you hear such a term?" Mom shouts.

I don't dare tell her it was online—not with Mom confident that she has all the bad sites blocked—so I say, "From the stoop downstairs."

Mom growls under her breath, and Oma shrugs. "You can't protect them forever, honey. Even though I agree that children are growing up too fast. Good Lord, I was in the store last week, and they had thong panties in a children's size four. What are they thinking? When did kids stop being kids, anyway?"

"When people like you started talking about things they shouldn't in front of them, that's when!" Mom snaps.

O UR NEW home—if only Mom will have it—sits just a short distance beyond the cluster of new constructions about two miles west of town. The small house, two stories high, is dingy white, like city snow. It has shabby, barn-red shutters alongside the front windows, one pulled loose and cocked, and a small entranceway that juts out from the front of the house like a dog's snout. The lawn is spacious, the tall trees fringed with long blades of grass a mower couldn't reach. The same shaggy fringe clings to the half-dilapidated fence that boxes in the house.

"Oh, look how the house has fallen to ruins," Oma groans.

"It looks exactly the same as it's always looked. Like a dump."

Mom pulls the car down the drive and brings it to a stop. She opens her door but just sits there, staring at the house. I don't wait for her or Oma to get out before I shove against Mom's seat and squeeze by, then rip off my shoes and socks, even though it's chilly and windy, and step onto the cool grass. And then, for reasons it would probably take Sigmund Freud himself to figure out, I flop down on my belly, press my cheek against the ground, and skim my arms and hands over the silky grass.

One car door slams. "What are you doing?" Milo asks. I feel him standing beside me, but I don't open my teary eyes, and I don't answer, because I have no answer. Instead, I feel the earth solid under me and the grass pricking against my clothes. I hear the scattering of a few dried leaves making soft tinkling sounds as they skip past me, and I want Milo to shut up so all I hear is their sound.

A screen door squeaks, followed by the yips of a small dog. I turn my other cheek to the grass, open my damp eyes, and see a tiny dog charging toward me, followed by a little woman every bit as skinny as the dog, with gray hair almost as short. "Chico! Chico!" the woman calls. Her voice, too, is every bit as high-pitched and yippy as the dog's.

The dog reaches me, still yipping, his diminutive body popping off the grass with each one. He's a homely thing, with bulgy eyes and a red rhinestone collar around his neck that looks big enough for him to jump through.

The other car doors slam as Aunt Jeana reaches down to scoop up the dog hopping at her feet.

"Jeana," Oma says. I close my eyes again but know they hug politely.

"These are Sam's grandchildren. This is Milo, and that's Lucy."

Milo shows his good manners by saying hello, but me, I just keep my eyes closed and wish them all to go away, because lying here feels more prayerful than giving tobacco to an eagle, and more personal than using the bathroom.

"You're looking well, Lillian," the yippy voice says, and then it lowers. "Tess," she says, her mouth making the s's in Mom's name sound like the hiss of a snake. "I'm glad you decided to come."

"Aunt Jeana," Mom volleys, in a voice cooler than the air.

"Did she fall?" Aunt Jeana asks, talking about me.

"No," Mom answers.

"Then what's wrong with her?"

Oma's voice is blissful as she says, "She's just savoring her first real meeting with Mother Earth."

Aunt Jeana says, "Hmmm," and Mom snaps, "Lucy, get up. Now!"

There is the chatter of Aunt Jeana's and Oma's voices and the *whomp* of our trunk slamming. The voices and yipping fade, then disappear behind the clack of the closing screen door, and still I lie on the grass, stroking, sniffing, and loving the ground I lie upon.

When I was six years old, Marcus, a man Mom was dating, took us on a train trip to the East Coast to see the Atlantic Ocean. Marcus was thin, fair skinned, and rubbery to the touch, like a piece of string cheese. We traveled there on a vintage passenger train with red velvet seats and hanging chandeliers in the dining car that rocked above our heads as we ate our omelets. I don't recall much about the trip itself, except that Milo vomited most of the way and that when you flushed the toilet, a trapdoor opened and the water and waste splattered onto the rocks and railroad ties bumping by beneath us. I excused myself often, flushing and watching, and wondering how it was that the health department could allow such a thing. But what I remember most of all about that trip, our only vacation ever, is the ocean. I didn't know how to swim, so Marcus carried me out 'til the water was washing his colorless chest hairs, then he stretched me across his arms and just held me there. I closed my eyes as the waves lapped over me, and I went as mute as I am now and wished for the moment to last forever. It didn't, of course, nor did Marcus, though I'd wanted him to be my dad too.

Only when my belly cools to the point where I start to shiver do I roll over and sit up. I draw my legs up and wrap my arms around them. I tuck my chin on my knees and look past the yard, past the patch of trees, at the rolling hills dotted with houses that, from this distance, look as tiny as the houses on a Monopoly board.

It is quiet here. Peaceful. I smile as the breeze brushes my cheeks and dries my eyes as if I'm ice skating. I look to the north of the house, where the red maples in low-lying spots are blotched with deep red, and to a patch of sugar maples that are just beginning to tinge with a brighter, orangier red, and I wonder how tall those trees were when Mom was a kid and if she climbed them or raked their leaves into piles and jumped in them, as I've always heard country kids do. I look at the line of upstairs windows and I wonder which of them belongs to her childhood bedroom and if Oma ever read her *Goodnight Moon* before tucking her in.

I head to the house. Inside, it smells like frying hamburger, oatmeal cookies, and poop. I stand inside the entranceway and see shoes—including Milo's tennies, Mom's loafers, and Oma's beaded slippers—lined up on a rug alongside a narrow, short pair of oxfords. I take off my tennies and pair them up with Milo's, and hang my jacket on the coatrack beside the door. There is a man's hat propped on the tip, wool and charcoal gray. I lean over and study it. The silk band rimming the inside is stained darker in the front, as though it has sopped up a million drops of worry.

I can hear the women's voices, and when I step into the living room, I can see into the kitchen. Oma is standing at the sink, running her hand up the tiny shelves that sit beside the window. Mom's shoulder and hip are peeking out from behind the door frame.

Milo comes into the living room and looks at the TV, from which an excited man standing before a rotisserie oven is shouting, "That's right, just set it and forget it!"

"It's an infomercial," I explain, knowing he doesn't get it by the way he's blinking at the screen. "I studied them for my paper on pop culture." Then, "Where's Grandpa?"

Milo shrugs and sits down on the couch, refusing to allow his back to rest against the orange and yellow afghan that looks older than us. He opens the top book on his stack, but his eyes keep darting around the room. He looks like a fish on pavement.

My eyes wander above him, where a plaque hangs next to a gob of artificial flowers. The plaque bears my grandfather's name, Samuel McGowan. "Milo, look at this."

"What?"

I try to keep my voice quieter than the ones coming from the kitchen, and that's no easy feat. "Grandpa's last name! It's the same as ours!"

"Yeah? So?"

I'm almost shaking. Around the same time I learned

that Scott Hamilton was not my real dad, I asked Mom and Oma what my grandpa's name was. I asked because a girl my age, Sonya, had moved into apartment #426, and for a short time I entertained being her best friend, like she asked me to. That notion didn't last long—mainly because her idea of fun was making her Barbie doll hop up and down the front steps, and a girl named Lativa found that game more to her liking than I did, and also because after just five short weeks she announced that she and her mom were going to go live with her grandpa in Minnesota. The mention of her grandfather was the first time that it really dawned on me that just as I had to have a father someplace, so did Mom. So I asked if I had a grandpa and what his name was. Mom didn't answer me, but Oma did. And all she said was, "Yes," and, "His name is Sam." I never thought to ask his last name. I just assumed that it was the same as Oma's—Larson.

Milo shrugs. I scoot alongside him and hiss into his ear, "You idiot! If Grandpa is a McGowan too, it can only mean one of two things. Either our father was Mom's first cousin or we're bastards. I'd bet on the second—even though in-breeding often produces a genius or two among the idiots."

Milo shrugs again, then fiddles to perfectly align the books stacked on his lap.

"We're bastards. I can't believe it."

"So? Lots of couples cohabitate and have children and never marry."

"Yeah, well, Oliver Twist was a bastard, and look where that got him."

I can see I'm not going to get anywhere with Milo—not surprising—so I let the topic rest and I look above him, where an 8×10 photograph hangs in one of those cheap,

black metal document frames. In the photo is a man holding a sheet cake that says, *Happy Retirement,* and there are
men and women surrounding him, holding up beer glasses.

I kneel on the arm of the sofa so I'm higher and stare at
the picture that has to be him, my grandfather. He has
broad shoulders and dark hair that sits like chocolate frost-
ing, thick and swirled over the top of his head, exposing a
wide forehead like Mom's. He's wearing a dark suit. His
eyes are indeed shaped like mine, but they look more so like
Mom's. His broad smile looks like no one's. Well, except
maybe for the man on the infomercial.

I leave Milo and go into the kitchen, where Aunt Jeana
is busy taking brown bottles down from the cupboard. Chico
is trembling at her feet. One by one, she sets the bottles on
the counter, reciting their names and times per day Grandpa
needs to take them. "And don't forget his aspirin every day."
There is a plate of oatmeal raisin cookies on the counter
and chopped hamburger sizzling in a small fry pan on the
stove. As Aunt Jeana lists the medications, she pauses now
and then to glance into the pan.

Chico has been yipping at me since I entered the kitchen,
and Aunt Jeana scoops him up and kisses the top of his bony
head, then whispers, "Hush now," into his paper-thin ear.
He stops barking, his bottom snaggletooth catching on his
upper lip.

"Sam's napping. That's pretty much all he does anymore. I moved him into that room," she says, pointing
toward the door that's slightly ajar, just around the wide,
arched doorway connecting the kitchen and living room.
"He couldn't go up and down the stairs if he tried at this
point. He doesn't talk much, but he will answer you if you
ask him questions. It sure has been lonely around here,

though. I'm just glad I had my Chico and my programs." She nods toward the small TV propped on the counter, where some woman with heavy makeup and dark roots is addressing herself at normal volume, while a mannequin-perfect man stands inches behind her, his head tilted as he ponders her thoughts, even though he should be able to hear every word she's saying. On the floor under the TV are two ratty, hard suitcases and a fluffy dog bed that looks like a hat an old Russian man would wear in a blizzard.

"I've tacked his medication instructions and his schedule here," Aunt Jeana says, tapping the paper Scotch-taped to the inside of the cupboard door. "He likes his coffee black and some cinnamon in his oatmeal. And, oh, no celery in his food. He hates celery. Even chopped fine, he can taste it." Oma has a slight smile on her face, and I know that she's wondering how it is that Aunt Jeana could have forgotten that she lived with the man for years, so no doubt knows these things already. "Oh, and watch it, because he likes to turn on the stove and walk off."

Jeana keeps rattling off instructions as Oma circles the room. Oma stops and touches a clock in the shape of a rooster. Mom doesn't move. She stands still, her arms wrapped around her middle, bunching her shirt so that a peek of skin shows. As I watch her, I wonder how it can be that Mom, five foot six and thirty-three years old, can look dwarfed and as young as me in this house.

"Oh, and watch the back door. I don't know what the fascination is with that shed back there, but twice now he's gotten loose and I've found him standing at the door, looking confused. He still thinks he can drive too, though where he thinks he's going is beyond me. I hid his keys on the back of the top shelf, right here," she adds in a whisper.

Aunt Jeana plucks a chunk of steaming meat out of the pan and pops it into her mouth, chewing it as she rattles off more instructions and excuses why she needs to leave today. Besides Chico's brain that needs scanning, she lists reasons such as: "My plants have probably all died by now," and, "I haven't mailed back my Book of the Month Club card, and I don't always care for the featured selections." She pauses, plucks the chewed meat from her tongue, and puts it into Chico's mouth. He gums it happily. "He's missing so many teeth that it's hard for him to chew," she explains when she looks up and sees that we're all staring at her. Well, Oma and I are, that is. Mom is turned away, gagging.

"Which reminds me: Sam is having problems swallowing, so you need to—"

"Please don't tell us that we need to prechew his food," Mom interrupts.

"—feed him soft foods," Aunt Jeana finishes her sentence, and her eyes squint tight. "No, that wasn't what I was going to say. But I'd hope that if your father needed it done, you'd do it for him, simply because he's your father, if nothing else. That man raised you and paid your way through college. And he's leaving all of this to you." Aunt Jeana waves her bony hand, encompassing the room, so dramatically that one would think she was motioning to a whole kingdom.

"What time does he go to bed at night?" Oma asks, to distract her, I'm sure.

"Actually," Mom says, facing Aunt Jeana, "he didn't."

"Mom said Grandpa Sam wouldn't stop to give her water if—" I say, and Oma glides over and reaches around my shoulder, past my cheek, and pats my mouth shut before I can finish the sentence.

"What time does he turn in for the night?" Oma asks again.

But Aunt Jeana won't be distracted. Her beady eyes are boring into Mom's face like stingers as she tucks another clump of hamburger into her mouth. "Didn't what?" she asks Mom.

"Support me through college. He didn't give me a damn red cent for school. And *he* isn't leaving this to me, you are. I'm curious as to why."

Aunt Jeana grabs the meat from her mouth and holds it out to Chico. There are little gray specks left on her tongue, like scattered mouse turds, when she talks. "You are his daughter," Aunt Jeana says. "In spite of everything. And considering that you or your children wouldn't—"

"And Clay is his son," Mom interrupts. "Don't such fine riches typically go to the firstborn son?

"But we know why you've chosen me instead of him, Aunt Jeana. This place holds no sentimental value for Clay—not that it does for me. No monetary value either. This dump wouldn't be fit to be an outhouse on one of his properties. Clay would have absolutely no use for it, but I'm sure you already know that, because no doubt you've already offered it to him. And you certainly wouldn't want it for yourself, it being so far from *Choke-o*'s doctor. As for selling it for the cash, you'd have to rid it of all this worthless junk, list it with a broker . . . It would be work. And you don't need the money, since Uncle Willie left you richer than God, so why would you bother?"

Aunt Jeana gasps, and Oma hurries to her. She gently pinches Chico's skeletal paw between her fingers and bobs it. "Ohhhh, poor little darling. His eyes do look a bit dazed, don't they?"

Aunt Jeana's attention turns from Mom to her dog. She

cups her hand under Chico's chin and lifts his head to peer into his protruding eyes. He makes choking noises, so she lowers it.

"We should let you go now, Jeana. Didn't you say you fly out tonight?"

"Yes. I'll have to wait around for a few hours, but I want to get this rental car back or they'll charge me for another day."

"Well, I'm sure you're eager to get this poor little thing back home to his doctor. Thank you so much for the instructions and for the cookies. They smell delicious. Did you leave your phone number so I can call you when . . . well, you know."

"On the inside of the cupboard door where his medications are kept," Aunt Jeana says. "Oh, and I washed a load of his bedding, but I didn't have the chance to throw it in the dryer yet."

"I'll take care of it, Jeana. Thank you for everything. Lucy, help me take Aunt Jeana's things to her car, please." Oma hands me Chico's bed.

"We should get going too," Mom announces after Aunt Jeana leaves. Mom is blinking her eyes, and she rubs at them with her fingertips. Oma watches her, and I watch Oma, silently pleading with her to do something, and hoping that Sky Dreamer is right, because I don't want to leave just yet.

"Are you coming down with a migraine?" Oma asks.

"Just a little haloing," Mom says.

"Good heavens, Tess. You can't drive with a migraine. You're tired too. Stay the night, at least."

Mom tips her head toward the living room. "He's getting anxious," she says, motioning to where Milo is fidgeting on the couch.

"It's because he has no work space," I tell them.

"Then let's give him a place to spread his things out," Oma says. She hurries into the living room, where Milo is still sitting stiffly, fidgeting as he reads. "Come in the kitchen, Milo," Oma says. "You can spread your things out on the table, just like at home."

Oma ignores Mom's protests as she helps Milo get situated, then she asks me if I'd like a tour of the house. I nod.

Oma opens the basement door. "We'll start at the bottom so I can get that bedding in the dryer and work our way up," she says.

I follow Oma downstairs. The basement is poorly lit, with a bare bulb hanging near the washer and dryer. Webs of dust dangle from the back of the wooden steps.

Two of the walls have wooden shelves attached to the concrete blocks, mostly empty but for a few jars of foods floating in cloudy juice. Another wall is bare, and the fourth is tacked with corkboard and a few hanging tools. While Oma pulls ropes of sheets out of the washing machine, I spot a sled in a darkened corner, propped against the wall.

"A sled!" I shout, and hurry to it. Oma's voice follows me. "That belonged to your uncle Clay and your mother," she says.

I bend over to admire the sled. Before Uncle Clay's wife started sending photo Christmas cards, they sent us regular store-bought cards. One year they sent us one with a picture of children dressed in Christmas reds and greens on the front, sledding down a hill. I kept that card tacked on my wall until it fell down and disappeared behind my bed. Thinking of it now, I wonder if my longing to be a figure skater and my longing to sled like the children in that picture doesn't stem from some deeper-rooted longing for winter snows and ice, and if so, why? It's not as though I've never seen snow before. All winter long it's tossed past our apartment windows, and when we come and go, I see it fall and turn to brown slush under tires.

I stroke the dusty wood of the sled. There's not a nick anywhere on it, and the red lettering on the seat is still glossy under the dust. "It looks brand-new. Did they even sled with it?"

Oma shrugs. "I imagine they did. Eventually." It is an odd comment, but one I don't have time to probe her about, because Oma is heading up the stairs. "Come on," she says. "I'll show you the rest of the house."

We leave the dryer whirring and go up the stairs. I've seen the kitchen and living room, and even though I still haven't seen what's behind the three other doors off them, where I want to go next is upstairs. "Can I see Mom's old room first?" I ask.

"Yes. As soon as I check on your grandpa."

Oma opens Grandpa's door only slightly when she peeks inside to check on him. I tuck my head under her arm and take a peek into the room, which is darkened by heavy shades. Grandpa is only a long, snoring mound on the bed. Oma shuts the door before I can get a good look, saying that we'll not disturb him. "Come on, I'll show you the upstairs, and your mother's room, now."

Mom and Milo are settled at the table when we pass through the kitchen. Milo has his books and notebooks open and now looks as comfortable as he does at home. Mom looks anything but comfortable, though she's got her laptop open and is typing. As Oma and I head up the stairs, Mom calls after me, "Don't get too cozy here, Lucy. We're only staying long enough for me to stretch and get some ideas down for my next chapter before I forget them." Oma looks at me and grins as though we share a secret.

Back home Milo and I share a tiny bedroom, even though, in my opinion, we're too old to. We each have a single bed with one nightstand jammed between them. To get over the books that are stacked on the floor at the foot of each of our beds, we have to walk to the end and long jump. Mom's childhood room has books too. Classics mostly, lining shelves along the wall. The shelves, like the woodwork throughout the house, are painted thick with white glossy paint.

I instantly fall in love with Mom's spacious old room, with its pale pink and cranberry flowered wallpaper and long windows dressed in filmy curtains that obviously were once wedding-white. There's a small nightstand with gouges in the wood next to the full-size bed and a vanity clotted with dried nail polish. And, best of all, there's an old rolltop writing desk, the veneer on the writing area bubbled and cracked in places.

Oma stands in the center of the room, her hands on her hips as she swirls in a slow circle. "Your mother had this room filled with posters of rock stars by the time she was twelve. She pulled them all down when she left," she says, moving to the wall and running her fingers over the tiny patches where triangles of glossy paper sit trapped under yellowed strips of tape.

Oma shakes her head. "I can't believe your grandpa's third wife didn't clear out this room." Her peachy lips form a circle then. "Oh, I wonder..." she says, as she heads to the closet.

"Oh, my gosh, they're still here!" Oma reaches past the cardboard boxes closed with duct tape and runs her hands over the stack of notebooks beside them, their edges frayed and waved like potato chips. There are at least five dozen notebooks in the stack, bound with a thick rope made of braided yarn.

"What are those?" I ask.

"Your mother was born a writer," she says. "I think she kept notebooks of her thoughts and happenings from the time she was old enough to write her ABCs.

"I put most of the things she left in the attic, along with her toys, but I left these more personal items here, thinking she'd be back for them soon. I'll have to tell your mother they're here." I reach to take a notebook from the stack, but Oma taps the back of my hand and closes the closet door. "Come, I'll show you the rest of the upstairs."

We just step into the room where Oma slept when she lived here—the room that makes a haze slip over her eyes—when Mom calls from the bottom of the stairs, "Ma! Can you come down here?"

I follow Oma down stairs that creak as we walk. Mom is blinking rapidly. She points toward the living room, where Grandpa Sam is slowly shuffling across the room with a walker, his back to us. The thick dark hair he wore in the photo is thin now, and sidewalk-gray. Long wisps almost four inches long swirl straight up from the top of his head like the hair of a troll doll. He is wearing long underwear bottoms that show the crack of his butt, a sleeveless undershirt, and one slipper. His arms, underneath sagging skin, aren't much bigger than Milo's.

"Sam?" Oma says, and he lets go of his walker and turns ever so slowly with shuffling baby steps. He stops when he sees us all staring at him and stares right back at us.

Oma brushes past Mom and goes to him. She gives him a warm hug, the kind of hug missionary workers probably give starving kids in Third World countries. She pulls back and places her hands on the sides of his head. "It's Lillian, Sam. Your second wife. Do you remember me?"

"Lillian," he says flatly.

Oma gives him a kiss on his slackened cheek. "And, Sam, these are your grandchildren. The twins." Oma steers me to stand in front of her. "This is Lucy. And the boy on the couch is your grandson Milo."

I can't stop looking at Grandpa Sam's eyes. Not only because they are shaped like mine (but for his lids, which droop over the outer edges of his eyes like sheets on a poorly made bed) but because the dullness in them is somewhere between the glass eyes of the antique doll that Oma keeps propped on her bed back in Chicago and the deadened eyes of the superintendent's nephew, who has an IQ of 70, tops.

While Milo and I are saying hello to our grandpa, Oma laces her arm through the crook of Mom's and leads her to her father. "Sam? Do you know who this is?"

He does not blink.

"Come on, Sam," Oma says through a smile. "You know who this is."

Mom grumbles, "Mother!" under her breath, and pulls out of her grasp.

"Course I know who that is," Grandpa says slowly, his voice as dull and lifeless as his eyes, but without a slur anywhere in his sentence. Oma waits for him to say Mom's name out loud, but he doesn't. He grabs his walker and starts to move.

Oma steers Grandpa toward a salmon-colored chair that has a remote control on the arm so it can rise up to meet his butt, then take him back down again. Once he's sitting, Oma squats down next to him. She takes the hand that is sitting listlessly on his bony leg. "Sam? You remember years ago when I promised you that I'd come take care of you in the end if you needed me to. So you'd never have to go into a nursing home? Well, that's why I'm here."

"Where's Jeana?" he asks.

"She's gone home, Sam. She went back to Pennsylvania."

He pivots his head in water-sprinkler slow motion and asks, "Where's Millie?"

"Who's Millie, Sam? Your third wife? An old girlfriend?" She glances at Mom. "Hmm, he had a dog named Millie. Do you think he's talking about the dog he used to have, or an old girlfriend?"

"Same difference," Mom says.

Oma glares at Mom, and Grandpa stares at the TV, which is now running a regular commercial. Oma takes the remote from the end table and pushes buttons 'til she finds the History Channel, then sets the remote down on the arm of his chair. Only when Oma looks up and says, "Tess, could you..." do we realize that Mom has left the room.

I follow Oma into the kitchen, past where Milo sits, already deep in his studies. "Where's your mother?" Oma asks him. He points to the back door, which is slightly ajar, a rusty screen door showing. Oma squeaks it open and slips out, only partially closing the heavy door behind her. I follow Oma to the door and stand still, peeking through the gap to watch them through the mesh screen.

Mom is sitting on the back porch—or deck, or whatever it's called when it has no walls, when it's only a large surface of grayed boards with six pillars holding it off the ground—her legs dangling over the side. Oma sits down beside her.

The backyard beyond them is spacious, with two clothesline poles made of rough wood in the shape of crosses. There is a dog tied to the pole, which Oma must notice at the same time I do. "Oh, poor thing." The dog is black and looks like a Labrador but for a white splotch between his eyes and a patch of long hair that runs down his back like a Mohawk. He is sitting on his haunches, wriggling, as though he wants to bark.

"You okay, honey?" Oma asks, ignoring the dog for a moment.

"I'm fine," she says. I've never heard tears in my mother's voice before, but I hear them now.

Oma sighs. "It's a shock seeing him like this, I know. It was for me too. He was always such a proud man."

"Arrogant is more like it," Mom says.

Mom's head rotates like an oscillating fan set on *slow*, as she looks over the yard. Her legs are bouncing. "You remember how upset he'd get if anyone pulled in the yard? He never wanted anyone he was trying to impress to see this place. And oh, God forbid if someone did dare to stop in when there was a speck of dust on the furniture or a newspaper laying out. You busted your ass to keep this place clean. And it looked decent, considering he wouldn't let you have a dime for upkeep, but it was never good enough. *We* were never good enough."

"Oh, you know your father. First saving every penny for that sawmill, then for his retirement." Oma sighs. "Isn't that the way it goes, though? We get caught up in getting ahead, planning ahead, and for what? Whatever money he could have left at this point is useless to him. What does any of it matter in the end but who we loved and how we loved them."

Mom leans back, propping herself on hands that are splayed behind her. "He was such an ass about money," she says. "And about most everything else." She is quiet for a time, and the dog watches her, squirming as though he's waiting for her to say more, just as I am.

"You know what's the first thing I saw when I came through the door? Grandma's old mirror, hanging in that same odd place—not centered on the wall but hanging where you hung it that night, butted too close to the archway. And all I could think of when I saw it was how insane it is that you stayed with him all those years."

"There was purpose in even that, Tess."

Mom huffs, "What was that? So you could experience hell here on earth?"

"Oh, Tess..."

I want to hear more, of course, but Milo interrupts by nudging me out of the way. "Oma," he calls. "Grandpa keeps switching the TV channels and won't stop. I can't concentrate when he does that."

"I'll be right there, honey," she says. Rising, Oma pats Mom on the shoulder, and says, "Tess? Could you please stay for a while? Even a couple of days? I know you don't understand why I had to come back and do this, and I don't suppose there's any way I can really make you understand it, but my choosing to be here doesn't mean it's easy for me. I have my memories too."

"I have to get back to the city and pack. Figure out where in the hell we're going to live while they gut our building."

"I know. But just a couple of days?"

Mom doesn't answer, but she gets up and I back out of the doorway to let them inside. "I'll take care of your grandpa, children, but will you please go untie his dog from the clothesline and bring him in? His dishes too."

Milo stares after Oma as though she's asked him to give up his studies to trim her hair or stitch a seam in her workout sweats. I grab his arm and tug him out the door.

"I like it here, don't you?" I ask Milo as we walk across the lawn.

Milo has his pencil tucked behind his ear like a geek. "I don't know," he says.

The dog hops on his back paws as we near, his tongue flapping. I pick up the dented metal dish that is tipped upside down, and Milo picks up the one that is crusty inside with bits of dried food. "Poor thing," I say. "Aunt Jeana prechews her dog's food but lets Grandpa's dog's dishes go empty."

I reach out to pet the dog and he leaps up, his toenails digging into my stomach. "Down!" I snap, and he instantly crouches to lie flat-bellied against the ground. His tongue and tail continue to wag. "Ouch, that hurt!" I tell him, rubbing my still-stinging stomach.

Milo's never petted a dog before. He reaches out, his hand flat, patting rhythmically on the top of the dog's head, bouncing it as if it's a basketball (not that he'd know how to handle one of those either). The dog tilts his head and slobbers Milo's wrist with his tongue, getting a rare laugh in return.

Milo reaches down to unfasten the chain at the dog's collar, and as he does, a tin medallion in the shape of a bone dangling from his collar flutters against his hand. "Hey! It says *Feynman* and the address of this house."

"Must be his name," I say, stating the obvious.

Milo's mouth is gaping, like he's gone dumb.

The second the dog's loose, he starts running in circles around the yard, going so fast that you can hear his feet thumping the ground. "Come here, Feynman!" Milo shouts, and the dog stops, looks at us, then grabs a small branch from the grass and runs it back to us, dropping it at Milo's feet.

"He wants you to throw it," I say.

"Why?"

"So he can fetch it, idiot. It's what dogs do."

The minute Milo cocks his arm back, Feynman takes off at a good clip. He's halfway across the yard before he realizes that the stick isn't going that far. Feynman watches the branch go up in a tight arc and drop a mere fourteen or fifteen yards from Milo, then he comes back to fetch it. He drops it at Milo's feet again, and Milo laughs. "I think he likes you," I say, and I try hard to keep the jealousy I'm feeling out of my voice—not that Milo would have noticed even if I hadn't.

I've always wanted a dog. Not a dog like Aunt Jeana's— the kind that yip nonstop and feel like dried-out buffalo wings to the touch—but a dog like Feynman, big and cuddly. And not so I could toss sticks to him but so that I could talk to him like a friend. A man down the street back home has a dog, a beagle. He lets me pet it when he comes past the stoop, and he is always whispering to it, and the dog's eyes work like sponges, soaking up everything as though he understands. A dog would be the best listener, since they can't repeat one single word said to them. It just figures then that, as much as I'd like a dog like Feynman to tell my secrets to, the dog likes Milo best.

Milo runs toward the house, and Feynman tears after him—no doubt because he thinks Milo's legs are two skinny sticks worth chasing—and beats him up the steps easily, then wags his butt until Milo opens the door. I pick up the empty dishes and take them inside.

We stand watching Feynman as he first laps his water, then buries his muzzle in the food dish, saliva dripping as he crunches furiously. Oma enters the kitchen and drapes her arm around me as she watches Milo crouch down alongside Feynman, patting his head some more, so that the poor dog's snout keeps whacking the sides of his metal bowl. "He would probably like it if you scratched him behind the ears," Oma says.

Milo looks up and grins, then starts scratching. "Guess what, Oma? The tag on his collar says his name is Feynman. Like Richard P. Feynman, spelled the same! Could he have been named after *the* Feynman?"

"I've no doubt but that he's named after your Feynman. Your grandfather was quite the science buff. You'll see what I mean if you go into the study off the living room, across from where he sleeps now. It was his private sanctuary. A room full of treasures for a boy like you."

Milo hurries off to find them, and Feynman follows. "Weird," I say. "Milo was just listening to that guy's stupid CD in the car, and now he finds out that the dog here is named after him. That's quite a coincidence."

"Oh, honey, there's no such thing as a coincidence. It's synchronicity." Oma smiles blissfully.

"As in the synchronicity Jung studied?" I say. "When two or more seemingly pure chance events coincide, forming a connection that has extraordinary and particular meaning for the one who observes it? Those meaningful connections between the subjective and the objective?" (A definition I read—more or less—on page 367, first paragraph down, in a study on Carl Jung himself.)

Oma laughs softly and pulls me to her. "My little Lucy," she says. "As bright as the stars." She gives me a kiss on the top of my head. "There are no accidents. Just remember that."

"Wanna bet?" Mom says as she comes into the kitchen to refill her coffee cup. "I think the old man just crapped his pants."

THAT NIGHT I sleep downstairs with Oma (who snores!) so she can hear Grandpa Sam if he needs her, and Mom sleeps up in her old room. Milo beds down on a roll-away in Grandpa Sam's study, even though there are two empty bedrooms upstairs. Mom doesn't like dogs, so she wouldn't have told her secrets to one of Grandpa Sam's but to those notebooks instead. Secrets that will tell me why she looked at Grandpa with an odd mixture of fear and revulsion as Oma steered him into the bathroom for his shower. A reaction, I think, that stems from something deeper than the fact that he smelled worse than a neglected baby.

When I wake in the morning, Oma's side of the bed is

empty. I go into the kitchen and see Oma out the window, doing her tai chi in the backyard. Grandpa Sam is still asleep, and Mom is at the table, her hair damp from a shower, her "breakfast" before her: a cup of black coffee, a Paxil, and three ibuprofens (they mean her neck is stiff and sore again, which Oma says represents her stubbornness and inflexibility, her resistance to "seeing what's back there," and which Mom insists stems from nothing more than her poor posture at the computer). Mom gets up to get a glass of water so she can down her Paxil. She gives me a morning hug as she waits for the water to cool. "Know when I love you best?" she asks.

"When I'm sleepy and squishy," I answer while rolling my eyes because I've had to answer that question every morning for as long as I can remember. I go to the cupboard and root around inside, looking for cold cereal.

Mom fills her glass and shuts off the faucet. She gazes out the window, her Paxil momentarily forgotten. "You ever notice how after your Oma finishes one of her wacky rituals, she wears the same glazed expression as a fundamentalist after a revival?"

"I've never seen a fundamentalist after a revival," I say, as if I'm every bit as left-brained as Milo. I open the next cupboard.

"Well, they look just like...well, never mind. Now she looks more like a—" and she stops. I shut that cupboard, because the only cereal I can find is a tub of oatmeal and a yellowed box of Cream of Wheat. I slip over to the window to stand alongside Mom. Oma is wearing a silk kimono-style negligee, scarlet red, and she's got one hand on her hip while the other one floats a cigarette from her hip to her mouth and back again, strings of smoke wafting.

"Like Maude Tuttle?" I say, and Mom whacks me lightly on the back of the head.

Oma comes in, humming, while Mom is digging in her gray leather purse. "Oh, you must be about ready to leave," Oma says.

"Where we going?" I ask, my body and voice instantly tightening at the thought that Mom is taking us home already—giving credibility to Oma's belief that the mind and body are one, and that all thoughts give way to emotions, and all emotions cause an instantaneous body reaction.

"She's going to town to get some things," Oma says. She floats to the stove and pulls two soft-boiled eggs from a small pan and brings them to the old scuffed blender on the counter. She cracks them, scoops out the runny insides, then dumps them, along with a small carton of plain yogurt, over the top of a peeled, spotted banana. "There's nothing much here but frozen food, probably old and loaded with chemicals and sodium. That's not food."

"It looks like food to me," Mom says.

"Well, I won't eat it," Oma says. "And I certainly can't in good conscience feed it to these children." Mom mumbles under her breath that she won't need to worry about feeding Milo and me because we'll be heading out, but Oma ignores her. "Which reminds me," Oma says. "Don't bring back any genetically altered, hormone-laced food either, you hear?"

Milo comes from the study, Feynman at his heels, and Oma pauses long enough to tell him good morning and to ruffle his already ruffled hair. Then she starts in again, saying she won't spend money on any "Frankenfood."

"What in the hell is Frankenfood?" Mom asks.

Milo yawns. "Food that's been genetically altered by inserting genes into it. You know, like Frankenstein. Genes to make crops disease-resistant, add nutrients, delay ripening of fruit...that sort of thing." He rubs the crust out of the corners of his eyes. "Eventually they'll splice in vaccines and antibodies." Feynman prances at Milo's feet, looking up with admiration.

"Well, I won't eat it," Oma says. "Not if I can help it."

"Oh, for crying out loud," Mom says as she grabs a small brush from her purse and runs it through her hair. "You eat it all the time, whether you realize it or not. Why do you think a head of lettuce lasts a month instead of two days before turning brown? And they say there's not a kernel of corn left that hasn't been genetically altered."

"Who are *they*?" I ask, being a smart-ass and nothing more, only because Mom is so big on us citing our sources in our papers. She ignores me.

"In developing countries, a million children die each year, and millions more go blind from vitamin A deficiencies," Milo says. Aside from the fact that he's in pajamas with little space rockets and moons spattered over the flannel, Milo looks and sounds like he's giving an oral report: chin up, shoulders back, but with his hands flat at his sides because he still hasn't caught on to the necessity of using hand gestures to make a point.

"By inserting genes from a daffodil and a bacterium, which the body converts to vitamin A, researchers can combat this deficiency. And by adding another gene derived from the French bean, the iron content of rice can be doubled."

I make my face serious. "So, do they have a gene they can inject into profoundly smart boys to make them more human?" Mom barks my name, adding the "Marie" for good measure.

I utter an apology I only partially feel, then blink in surprise as Mom herself gets nasty when Oma tells us that

Greenpeace calls this altered food "biological pollution," and says she agrees. Mom retorts with a sarcastic, "Don't gripe, Ma. Who knows, maybe they'll start injecting anti-toxins and other preventive substances into your tobacco to keep you from dying of lung cancer."

"Mom!" I say, and Mom's apology sounds even less sincere than mine.

"Say what you want, Tess, but it will be a disaster. Mark my words. We humans are far too egocentric. What makes scientists believe they possibly know enough about the balance of the natural world—God's design—to tamper with it? And when they realize their mistake, when there's not even one pure grain of rice left in the world, what then? Not that it matters, since at this rate we'll obliterate ourselves, anyway." Oma turns to me. "Do you know what I heard on the news? They injected brain cells from a pig into the brain of a stroke victim! Can you believe it? And not only is she having seizures now, but she's—"

"Oinking?" Milo interjects, and I start giggling.

"Wow, Milo made a funny!"

"Milo," Oma says. "Was that nice? And, Lucy, it's no laughing matter. Now that woman is susceptible to the horrendous diseases swine get. With the DNA of humans and pigs mixed, this means that these diseases could spread like wildfire through the human population. It's insane."

"Oh, for crying out loud," Mom says. "Can we just end this discussion?"

Mom takes her jacket down from the hook beside the back door. "Where's the list?" Oma scoots around her, squeezing up against the door frame. With her eyes closed, she lifts her arms as she takes a full breath, bringing her hands together. Then she turns her palms facing out and, as she exhales, swooshes her hands to her thighs in one sweeping movement.

"What in the hell are you doing now?" Mom asks, one arm shoved into her jacket sleeve.

Oma doesn't answer until she does it two more times, and when she opens her eyes, her smile has returned, her calm intact. "Cleaning my space of negativity," she says. "You should do it. A lot."

Mom rolls her eyes.

"My list is over by the toaster," Oma says. "And you'll need to drop off the cable payment. I see it's past due. I just forged Sam's name on the check."

Oma goes back to the blender, and Mom's words are chopped away by the loud whirring grind it makes. When Oma shuts it off, Mom is screaming, "—in the hell am I going to find *that*? And what is it, anyway?"

"What's what, dear?"

"Xuan fu ha . . . or however it's pronounced."

"It's a Chinese remedy. I thought it would be good for your father. He sounds congested." Oma pours the black speckled mixture that looks like snot from the blender into a bowl, and I cringe, because my stomach's every bit as weak as my ankles.

"And I can find that in Timber Falls where? At the Rexall drugstore, maybe? Right between the Depends and the One A Days?"

Oma giggles. "There's a health-food store over on Seventh Street. I found it in the yellow pages this morning. Nature's Garden. It's right next to Larson's Building and Home Supplies," she says. "And pick up some organic bananas while you're there, okay?" Mom rolls her eyes again. "Oh, and that reminds me—stop in at Larson's too, will you? In their flier, they're advertising a sale on bird feeders. Get one, and some sunflower seeds. It will give your father something to look at when he sits in his chair. There's plenty of cash stuffed in my checkbook. Take what you think you'll need."

Mom's face flushes when she pulls Oma's wallet from her purse.

I think of Mom going to town, and suddenly I want to go too.

"Hey, can I go with you, Mom?"

"May I," she says. Then, "No."

"Why not? I want to see the town!"

"You've got work to do, Lucy. It's a school day, remember? Have you even given one thought to your oral report? It's to be fifteen minutes long. That's a lot of research and a lot of work."

The oral report is something Mom makes Milo and me do every year. Last year, she had us present them to the residents of Golden Lawns Retirement Home—they'll take anything for entertainment, I guess. I did mine on aging and based most of it on James Hillman's book *The Force of Character: And the Lasting Life*. I talked about the mental and spiritual transformation of old people as they near death. I thought the topic was fitting and would give them some comfort, but it didn't. Most of them were slumped in wheelchairs, and frankly, I don't think they even knew they were in a nursing home, much less close to death. And the ones who still had their wits intact grimaced like I was spitting lemon juice into their eyes. Milo gave his report on string theory. I don't think that even the ones who were with it understood a single thing he said, but they loved his speech anyway—even though he doesn't use hand gestures.

They smiled and fussed over him like he just stepped out of Charles Dickens's *A Christmas Carol* and a mean boy had stolen his crutch.

"Our oral reports aren't due until late November. And you haven't even found a place for us to give them yet. I'm not going back to that nursing home."

"Nonetheless," Mom says as she closes Oma's purse.

I cross my arms across my chest. A sign of defensiveness, I know, and although I think looking vulnerable would serve me better, I can't help myself. "I don't see why I can't go! You and I never get to do anything by ourselves."

"Ohhhh," Oma says, obviously reacting to my pouty words rather than my clamped arms. "It would do her good to get out, Tess. Lucy is very extroverted. She needs the stimulation of people. Besides, it would be a nice mother-daughter outing for the two of you."

Mom sighs. "Okay, hurry and get dressed then. You've got two minutes."

As I'm heading up the stairs to dig in my bags, I hear Oma say to Mom, quietly, but not quietly enough, "Don't worry, honey. People have moved on to new gossip after this many years."

WE STOP at the cable office first, to pay Grandpa's bill. "Oh, you must be Sam McGowan's daughter. I'd know those eyes anywhere," the woman behind the counter says after she looks at the check and invoice Mom set on the counter. "I heard you and your children and mother were back in Timber Falls—you can't keep anything a secret in this town." She laughs, a wad of pink gum bobbing on her tongue as she taps the back of Mom's hand playfully. "Anyway," she continues, "I think it's so wonderful that you and your mother came home to care for Sam. But of course you would. He's a wonderful man."

I'm watching the woman carefully, intrigued by how her tongue comes out beyond her teeth when she says *th* words yet, strangely enough, doesn't cause her to lisp. She holds out her hand to Mom. "I'm Connie Olinger," she says.

Mom takes her hand and shakes it quickly. "I'm in a bit of a hurry, so if I could have my receipt..."

"Oh, yes, of course," Mrs. Olinger says. She fumbles for the glasses that dangle against her chest from a white cord, then props them on her powdered nose. She punches a few keys on the keyboard before her, then sighs. "This darn computer is froze up again. I'll write you a paper receipt." She plucks her glasses off her nose and lets them fall like a bungee jumper, then roots around behind the counter.

"When my son, Barry, finished high school, he got a job at the paper mill where your dad worked. And right off the bat he had a problem with one of the young men there, Tad Wilmington. That roughneck picked on my Barry something fierce, did anything to make him out to be a lazy fool. He'd find ways to make it look like Barry was slowing down the production line, and he'd say such horrible, mean things. Making fun of Barry's size, because my Barry's husky, so that the other guys would laugh." Connie Olinger cups her hand around one side of her mouth—the backside facing me, as though I won't be able to hear what she's about to say—"Calling him 'gay' even."

She plunks a thick book on the counter and begins paging through it to find the next empty receipt. "Poor Barry could hardly stand to get up for work after a few weeks of that. He gained twenty-two pounds, just from the stress.

"I told him to see the foreman, but a lady who worked

on Barry's line told him not to waste time with him but to take the problem right to Sam. Barry did, and your father said he'd take care of it the next day. He did too. He stopped by on his way home from work and told me himself, 'Today will be the last day of *that*, I can assure you.' Like your dad said, nobody should have to be bullied and humiliated at work like that."

"Hmmm," Mom says. "And did he happen to mention if he thought it was okay for people to be bullied and humiliated *outside* of the workplace?"

Mrs. Olinger tilts her head and her smile quivers with confusion, but only for a second. She rescues her glasses and returns them to her nose as she licks her first two fingers, then leafs through the filmy pages of the receipt book again. "Barry didn't stay working there long, though. Even though things got better, he just had too many bad memories. Plus, he wanted to make something of himself. He had some schooling, and now he breeds cows."

"You must be very proud," Mom says, and there's no mistaking her sarcasm, though I think Mrs. Olinger just did.

"Barry still talks about what your dad did for him, though." Mrs. Olinger fans a few more pages of the receipt book, then tosses her pudgy hands in the air. "Why, this book must be all used up. I'm sure I've got a fresh one here, though."

"That's all right. The canceled check will suffice," Mom says.

"Oh, dear, I wouldn't want you leaving without proof of payment. I'm supposed to give everyone a receipt. I'll just write you one on our stationery. How will that be?"

Mom looks agitated enough to spit. She shifts from foot to foot while Mrs. Olinger tears a piece of white paper from a tablet and looks for the pen that's sitting five inches from her hand. "Dear, you just be sure and tell your father that Connie Olinger from the cable office says hi. You know, we're just all so glad that his stroke was not so bad that it ruined his speech and left him half paralyzed. Mel—he's the loan officer over at First National—he ran into your dad after his first stroke, and he said that he was still the same good ol' Sam. Your dad's so fortunate it wasn't so bad."

"He's not so fortunate, Mrs. Olinger," Mom says flatly. "His second stroke left him brain-dead for the most part, and today I'm picking him up diapers."

Mrs. Olinger's pink lips pull away from her teeth as she grimaces.

"Lucy, you bring out the receipt. I'll be in the car." Mom scurries out the door without saying thank you or good-bye.

"Oh, dear, your mother is upset. But of course she'd be, coming home to find her poor father in that condition." She writes out the receipt, and as she hands it to me, she says, "What's your name, honey?"

"Lucy."

"So nice to meet you, Lucy. Please tell your grandpa that Connie and Barry Olinger say hi."

"I will," I say with a smile, taking our receipt.

I slip into the car, where Mom is checking over Oma's list. I study her with quick glances. Mom has never been the type to yammer with strangers. Not like Oma, anyway. But she's typically not rude to them either.

"Okay, let's see," she says, her tone efficient. "We'll stop at Larson's for the bird feeder first. The health-food store is next door. Then we'll walk over to Fuller Street to the Rexall. The IGA isn't far from there."

As we drive slowly down the streets, Mom gets more

and more irritated, until she's looking like she could benefit from another hit of Paxil. "Can't these people use the crosswalks? Look at that, he didn't even look to see if anything was coming! And what's up with the mullets? Gee, maybe Milo found the secret to time travel and zapped us back to the 1980s. Backward hick town."

We get the bird feeder and seed, then go to the health-food store, where a pasty-looking, thin-as-a-bookmark woman with blotchy skin helps Mom find the herbal remedies on Oma's list, all except for the xuan fu ha, which she says they don't have but could order, to which Mom says, "Forget it."

"Oh, Mom," I say as the clerk starts ringing up our purchases. "Oma wants us to pick up some lemongrass tea too. She forgot to put it on her list. And we're supposed to ask for a tea that will help Grandpa's mind function better. Help his memory."

"Oh!" the pasty woman says with more vigor than you'd think possible for someone so pallid. "There are several herbs that help fight memory loss. Gingko biloba, DHEA, gotu—"

"Just what's on the list," Mom says. "And the lemon-whatever."

The woman plucks another box off the shelf behind her and sets it down by the organic bananas and a few other boxes. "Lemongrass tea increases your psychic powers," she says as she's ringing up our purchases. Mom looks stressed already, so I don't mention that Oma wants it for exactly that purpose: When she gets back to Chicago, she is going to interview for a job with a psychic hotline. The plan is to boost her abilities with herbal remedies and practice 'til then.

We put our purchases in the car, then walk down the

street toward the Rexall. We aren't even past the Dollar
Tree when a voice calls out Mom's name.

A woman jaywalking across the street is waving her
arms at us as she runs on her tiptoes, her dark, chin-length
curls bobbing. She is young, petite, and cheerleader-cute.

"Oh, my God! It *is* you!" the woman shouts, and Mom
cries out, "Mitzy!"

They hug, Mitzy bouncing in Mom's arms.

"What are you doing back in Timber Falls?"

Mom cringes. "Just drove Ma here. She's determined to
take care of Dad until he croaks."

Mitzy takes Mom's hands and pulls back, and they
swing their arms like they are dance partners. "Oh, you
look terrific! Trim as ever."

"You look the same too," Mom says, to which Mitzy
says, "Cut the crap. I'm fifteen pounds heavier, and all of
it in my hips. But what the hell, that's life, huh?" Mitzy
laughs with her whole body, like a baby.

"Oh, my God, is this your daughter?" Mitzy says. She is
only about two inches taller than I am, so she doesn't need
to look down as she examines me.

"Yes. This is Lucy."

Mitzy rescues my hair from the breeze and pats it to my
shoulder. She taps my cheek. "Aw," she says, "you're beautiful." In reality, I'm just slightly above average in appear-
ance, but because Mitzy doesn't strike me as the type to give
false praise, I decide that she thinks all children are beautiful.

"Milo, my son, is back at the house."

"We're twins," I add.

"You are? Oh, wow." I'm relieved that Mitzy doesn't ask
if we are identical twins, as many people do, even though

any village idiot should be able to see the absurdity in such a question.

"Oh, Tess, I've thought of you so many times. How on earth did we let ourselves lose touch for this long? What's it been, twelve years, thirteen years?"

Mom and Mitzy are talking over each other as we shuffle from side to side to make room for people passing by on the narrow sidewalk, until Mitzy asks if we have time for coffee so they can catch up.

We go to a little place called Coffee Beans, Incorporated, which I quickly learn used to be Sparks, a restaurant where Mitzy and Mom would stop for Diet Pepsi and cheese pizza. The place is cramped with heavy, pale wooden chairs and tables, and one wall is lined with booths sporting thick teal-blue cushions. The walls are decorated with prints and country-style crafts tagged with price stickers. Fake ivy and clear Christmas lights are strung from the ceiling, and tables with more craft items are tucked here and there. "Wow, this place sure looks different," Mom says.

Mitzy leads the way to the counter, and we examine a menu written in pink on a chalkboard. We decide we're ready for lunch, so we order three tuna croissants and a nonfat decaf for Mitzy, a vanilla latte with whipped cream for Mom, and a hot chocolate for me, then we slip into a booth.

"God, I can't believe you're here!" Mitzy says. "I missed you so much. We have so much to cover. How's your mom? Where are you living now? Oh, tell me everything!"

"Well, Ma's gone New Age nuts," Mom says, nodding her head slowly. "Reiki, tai chi, feng shui, Pilates, you name it, she does it."

"*Your* mom?" Mitzy's laughter is like the tinkling of wind chimes.

"Yes. She even has an 'intuitive,' for crissakes."

"An intuitive?"

"Yeah. You know, a psychic."

They both roar with laughter—causing me to glare at Mom—and when they finish, Mitzy says, "Well, I suppose she needed something, and whatever works for her, the more power to her. And your dad? How's he? I heard about his strokes."

"He's deteriorating," Mom says. "Fast, I guess."

Mitzy bites the inside of her cheek as she studies Mom. "Is it hard, seeing him again?"

"Yeah," Mom admits. She glances over at me and squirms against the cushion. "Lucy, go wash your hands, please."

I hold my hands out and flip them over. "They're clean!" I know why she wants me to get lost, of course, but I just like funning her now and then.

"Go," she says.

WHEN I come out, Mom suggests I look around at all the "pretty" things. I roll my eyes, but I do what I'm told. I examine reprints on the wall and the chunky wooden angels and animals on the tables. I wait for Mom and Mitzy to lean across the table, their mouths both going, until I figure that they've forgotten about me, then I wander close enough to hear them. I kneel down behind Mitzy's side of the booth, as if I'm examining figurines on the bottom shelves of a display case.

"...this robust, stomping, strong-bodied man who was larger than life," Mom is saying. "And I look at him now: skin sagging from his bones, jowls limp, deadpan eyes. In diapers, after today, and it's...I don't know. Confusing, I guess."

Mitzy groans. "I always felt so bad about the way he treated you guys. God, you remember graduation day? What a nightmare that turned out to be. Clay taking off for who-knew-where, not bothering to stay in town for the ceremony for your sake, at least. I knew how much you wanted the two of you to march together. And then your dad had to go and make the day even worse.

"I remember we were all standing together in the hall, right after the ceremony: you and me, your mom and dad, my folks, and Walker came up to you—a dick, always, that guy, but playing the proper principal at the moment—and Mr. Louis came, and couple of other teachers joined us too, though I can't remember who…"

"Reynolds, and Lukes," Mom fills in.

"Yeah. Anyway, I remember how Mr. Louis congratulated you on your scholarship. He was polite enough not to mention that Clay didn't show up to receive his. He shook your hand, then he turned to your folks and said, 'You must be very proud of this young lady. Salutatorian, president of the National Honor Society, four-year gold medalist at the state forensics competition…' He went on and on, listing all of your accomplishments. Your mom was looking at the medallions hanging around your neck as he praised you, and she looked so proud. She put her arm around your shoulder and tipped her head down to press it against yours. It was so sweet! And then your dad destroyed the whole moment with one line: 'Second place. Shit. You might as well come in last if that's the best you can do. My boy knew that. That's why he didn't bother coming today. He didn't want to humiliate himself.'

"I could have slapped him, Tess, and I think Mr. Louis wanted to, too."

"Yeah, well…"

"Louis adored you, of course. He jumped to your defense, saying that you were the brightest, most talented student he'd seen in his thirty years of teaching. That you could write description and sympathetic characters far better than most published authors twice your age, and he said that you'd make your mark on the publishing world one day."

I can feel Mom's unease right through the wood between us, and I know that she's thinking of her Christian romance novel and hoping Mr. Louis never learns that she's Jennifer Dollman.

"It should have been such a wonderful day for you, but he ruined the whole thing with that damn comment. He even ruined things for your ma. She had been shoving aside any bit of extra money she could squeeze out of your dad for how many months to buy you that word processor. She was so excited to give it to you after the ceremony, but considering how he turned the day into crap, even that excitement was spoiled for her—or maybe not. You know your mom."

"Word processors. Unreal how archaic they seem already, isn't it?" Mom says. Then, "Enough about me. We haven't even talked about you yet. How's Brian? Any children? I feel so guilty not knowing any of these things, so tell me anything, and everything, please."

"Brian and I aren't together anymore, Tess. We divorced almost five years ago."

"Oh, Mitzy!" Mom says, and she sounds genuinely surprised and sorry. I stand up and move to stand next to a shelf filled with porcelain rabbits where I can not only hear them but also see them.

"And I was pregnant twice, but I don't have any children. I had my first miscarriage when I was two and a half months along, and then a year later I gave birth to Dylan, fourteen weeks early. The hospital didn't even have a breathing tube small enough to get down his throat. He cried when he was born, his cry as tiny as the mew of a newborn kitten. They called for the medicopter to take him to the preemie unit in Marshfield but canceled the call because he was failing so fast. They knew he couldn't hold his own until the helicopter got there."

I don't have to try to be still when I overhear this. My whole body stops, even my breath.

"Ohhhh, Mitzy." Mom's voice sounds muffled, as if she's speaking while underwater. I glance up and see that she has her fingers pressed over her mouth. I've noticed that this is a gesture people make when they hear something tragic. A gesture, I figure, that is probably innate and goes back to the caveman days, when the instinct to hush oneself when danger was lurking was necessary in order to avoid being preyed upon. Back when I came up with it, I told Milo my theory and he verbally discounted it, but I could tell he was impressed.

"It's hard to lose a premature baby," Mitzy says. "To everyone—even my mom—it was a *pregnancy* I lost. A dream of what might have been, like my early miscarriage. But I lost a baby that time. One I could see, and hear, and hold. One who died in my arms. I didn't just lose a dream of a baby, I lost a child. I'm not even sure that Brian realized the difference, since, of course, I cried plenty the first time too.

"He was off playing a softball game when I went into labor, and I had no way to reach him. He stayed out drinking with the guys, and by the time he got home and saw Mom's note, Dylan had been dead for five hours. They asked him if he wanted to see him, but he said no. I held that baby for two hours after he died—until they gave me an injection and pried him from my arms—but he didn't even want to glance at our son? God, I hated him for that."

Mitzy twirls her mug to the right and then to the left, back and forth, back and forth. "It's no wonder our marriage fell apart after that. I was so grief-stricken that I even cried in my sleep the first two weeks."

"Of course you did. Of course," Mom says softly.

"I know now that men handle grief differently—and Brian was really still a boy then. But at the time, I looked at him, running off to play ball, or to fish, or to sit and shoot the bull with his buddies down at Hap's Tap while I was at home breaking into a million pieces, and I saw it as him not caring."

"Of course," Mom says.

"We knew it was going to be a boy, so I'd painted the nursery blue and put up a border of little footballs, basketballs, baseballs. When I got home from the hospital, the room was stripped. Brian's mother had done it. Packed all of the shower gifts away, took the border down. I know she thought she was doing me a favor—getting rid of anything that might remind me of my baby, as if that would help me forget—but it was the wrong thing to do. I held such a grudge that I told Brian I didn't want her in my house anymore. He reminded me that she'd lost her first grandchild too, and he wasn't going to even ask her where Dylan's things were.

"The wooden rocking chair was still in the room, cluttered by the old spare bedroom set Brian's mother had moved back up from the basement, and I'd sit in that chair rocking for hours, holding myself and crying. Brian couldn't take it. One night when he came home drunk and found me rocking, he lost it, telling me to get over it already."

Mom puts her hand over her mouth again, then removes it and takes Mitzy's hand. "Oh, how that must have hurt," Mom says, sounding more like Oma than Mom. "I can't believe Brian would say such a thing. Well, I'm not doubting you, I'm just saying that Brian...he was always so..." She reaches out with her other hand and takes both of Mitzy's.

"He was drunk. Really drunk. As he was most of the time by then."

"But still, that's no excuse. God, that pisses me off. That baby was his son too. Oh, Mitzy. I'm so sorry I wasn't there for you. I didn't know. Had I, I would have come, no matter where I was or what was going on with me."

Mitzy dabs at her eyes. "I thought of calling you. You were my best friend, Tess, but how could I have called when I wasn't there for you when *you* needed *me* the most?" They mumble apologies, then Mitzy says with a sad, slow laugh, "Remember when the only thing we feared about pregnancy was getting fat and getting stretch marks?"

"Yeah," Mom says. "Ironic, isn't it?"

Mom looks up, scanning the room to find me, and I quickly grab a wooden ornament off the shelf and pretend I'm admiring it. I start humming to show her just how wrapped up in my own little world I am.

"About two weeks after that incident, Brian had three of his buddies over, helping him build a deck. He'd wanted a deck for some time, and his folks bought us a kit for our anniversary. I couldn't have cared less. Anyway, I was in the kitchen making subs for their lunch when Brian came in and headed for the nursery. When he came back through the kitchen, I could see he had something tucked under his arm. It wasn't hard to guess what it was.

"Brian had won a football—signed by Brett Favre—in

a raffle right after we learned that I was carrying a boy. He decided to put it away and give it to Dylan on his tenth birthday. When I went outside to see what he was up to, there he was, tossing that football into the air as he dove off the unfinished deck, reenacting some play or other, I guess. His dumb friends were laughing. He got to his feet and was about to toss it to one of them, and I just went nuts.

"I charged him. Clawing and kicking at him. And when I got the ball from him, I dropped to my knees and bawled until spit was stringing out of my mouth. The guys left in a hurry, of course, and Brian just stood there staring at me, his fists clenched.

"I knew I was acting crazy, but I couldn't stop myself. I wanted him to stop me. To hold me and tell me that he understood. That I'd feel better in time. That he loved me. Anything. Instead, he told me, 'I'm outta here,' and he left."

Mom lets go of Mitzy's hands so Mitzy can rummage in her purse for a Kleenex. After she blows her nose, she looks up at Mom and continues.

"I never heard from him after the divorce, but every year on Dylan's birthday there's a basket of fresh flowers on his grave that I like to believe come from him."

The waitress comes then, carrying our sandwich plates on a round tray. She talks all chirpy, oblivious to the tears in Mom's and Mitzy's eyes. She's wearing a nose ring in each nostril and dreadlocks filled with beads in assorted colors. The bottom of each drab brown lock has been dipped in white wax and dotted with pink at the very tips. "Those look good, don't they? I'm starving myself. Is there anything else I can get you girls?"

Mom shakes her head.

"Any refills on your drinks? Extra onions for your sandwiches?" Ms. Dreadlocks takes the pencil that's stuck in her ratty mess, and she scrapes at her scalp as she talks. "I like lots of onions on my tuna. It doesn't do much for the breath, but, hey, it tastes good. And I like to crumble a few of those kettle corn chips inside the bread too. The extra crunch is good. I was just telling—"

Mom scoots my plate closer to hers, as she looks up at the woman in disbelief. "Crissakes. What's the matter with you? Can't you see you've interrupted a private, emotional conversation here? And if you've got to scratch your head, for crying out loud, don't do it over our plates! What could possibly make you think we'd want you interrupting our conversation, much less powdering our croissants with your dead skin cells?"

Mitzy's dark eyes get even larger than they already are, and a cloudburst of laughter breaks out of her.

"Well, really . . ." Mom says, as the waitress leaves in a huff, and Mitzy laughs all the harder.

Still laughing, Mitzy waves for me to join them.

Mom scoots over so I can slip into the booth. Their coffees are half gone, and the ice in my soda is melted. "I'd ask for a pitcher of water, but she'd probably spit in it now," Mom says.

Mitzy laughs, as though she does not have tears clinging to her lashes. Mom doesn't laugh, though. She is looking down at her plate, her shoulders as limp as the Bibb lettuce peeking out from her sandwich, then she reaches over and rests her hand on my leg (a gesture driven, I'm sure, by thoughts of how sad it would have been had she lost me when I was born). Mitzy looks at Mom, tilts her head, and smiles sadly. "I've made you sad, but you don't have to be. I'm okay now, hon.

"I'm living in delicious sin with Ray Dayton. He's ten years older than us, so you probably don't remember him, but he is the sweetest, most considerate man in the world. The first time he made me laugh, I started crying. I didn't say why. I didn't need to. He took me in his arms and said, 'Dylan would want his mommy to be happy again.' That was it for me. I fell head over heels in love with him that second."

"How long have you been with him?" Mom asks.

"Lemme see. Going on three years now."

"Any wedding plans?"

Mitzy picks up her fork and knife and begins cutting her tuna-stuffed sandwich in half. "Nah. He'd like to. He's in his forties. He's ready for kids."

"And?" Mom asks.

"I can't go through that again, Tess. Just can't. But I can't ask him to give up his dream of having children either, so I don't know."

I look at Mom, who's looking at Mitzy with one of those let's-talk-more-about-this-later looks.

"What about you?" Mitzy asks suddenly. "Anyone special in your life?"

"There *was*," I say, and Mom tells me to shut up and eat, forgetting already how lucky she is that I didn't die at birth. Mitzy takes her cue and shuts up about it too.

They catch up on gossip about their graduating class, and then, while I'm munching my last potato chip, Mitzy says, "Oooh! Oooh! That reminds me! I read your book, *The Absent Savior*!"

"Well, I knew about the retired schoolteacher from Vermont who read it and wrote me ... I was wondering who the other person was," Mom says, laughing at her own joke, even though I know she doesn't think it's funny. "How'd you find out about it?"

"From Pamela Kort. I ran into her one day, right here in Coffee Beans. I hadn't seen her since graduation. She got her thighs lipoed, and she looked great. Anyway, she's out on the East Coast now, teaching at the same university that published your book. She told me all about it, and I ordered it online as soon as I got home. Oh, Tess. All I could think of when I read it was how Louis was right. I meant to write you through your publisher and tell you that, but... well. I'm sorry.

"Anyway, it was a beautiful book. And it wasn't hard to see that the 'absent savior' in the book was really Rachel's father, not Asher. It was her relationship—or lack of it—that—"

Mom interrupts Mitzy by glancing at her watch with such exaggeration that a 1940s starlet would have felt threatened. "Shit! Sorry to interrupt you, Mitz, but, wow, where did the time go? I've got to get this stuff back to Ma. I can't believe she hasn't called me yet." I scoop my pickle and grapes up as Mom scoots me out of the booth with her butt.

"Oh, okay." Mitzy looks a little dazed. "How long are you staying in town?"

Mom sighs. "A day or two at the most. Ma asked me to stay a few, but no way can I do that."

"Let's get together, though. Please? How about my place. Breakfast, tomorrow morning?"

Mom nods and Mitzy quickly jots her address on a sticky note, and then they play tug-of-war with the check.

They hug on the street, then Mitzy hugs me. "I'm afraid your mother and I hogged up all the time, and I didn't even get to find out one thing about you."

"That's okay," I tell her. "There isn't all that much to tell, since I'm still only a child."

Mitzy laughs and hugs me again. "Precocious, just like her mother, I see."

As Mom and I walk to the car, an older woman pauses to give us a second glance, and Mom grabs my sleeve. I have to trot to keep up with her.

By the time we get to Oma's car, Mom is her old self again: quiet, emotionless, lost in her own thoughts. I know about personas, of course, those masks we wear to make impressions on others. And seeing Mom as she is now, and remembering how animated and soft she was with Mitzy, I wonder which—if either—is Mom's true self. "We'll grab the groceries and get back," she says. She's distracted as we shop, and she doesn't say a word as we drive home. That is, not until we're pulling up the drive. Then she stares up at the dirty-snow-colored house and mutters, "Someone shoot me. Just frikkin' shoot me."

I T'S EVENING, and Mom and Milo are at the kitchen table, engrossed in their work, while I help Oma dry the dishes. Mom and Oma aren't speaking, because a bit ago they had an argument about Mom suddenly wanting to head back to Chicago that very instant. Oma guilted her for even thinking of having two children on the road in the middle of the night, and now the only sounds in the kitchen are the tinkling of plates as we put them away and an occasional huffy sigh from Mom.

Oma sets her cup of lemongrass tea on the counter and asks Milo—who has his nose almost scraping his book on the table, his inhaler in hand—if he'll help her get Grandpa

Sam to the bathroom so she can give him a bath. Right now he is in the living room, flicking channels again, the volume suddenly blasting. "Oh, dear," Oma mutters. "There he goes again! He's been doing that with the clicker all day. Come, Milo."

Oma goes into the living room and asks Grandpa Sam nicely for the remote. The channels keep flipping, and then Oma doesn't sound so patient. "Oh, my God! Sam, give me that. Give me the remote!"

I hear the stations flick quickly, so I think it's Grandpa still doing the flicking, but then Oma shouts out, "Oh, my God. What channel was that? They said after the commercial...here! Tess, come here. Quick!"

I race into the living room, where Grandpa Sam sits in his lift chair, his arm outstretched, his hand still clutching the remote, even though Oma is manning it. Mom is right behind me. "Jesus, that thing loud enough?" she says, half drowning the voice of the reporter, who's saying, "And in Chicago, fire rips through a recently condemned apartment complex on the lower south side."

Oma waves her hand at the TV as the pretty black reporter says, "Sylvia Decker is on the scene with this live report..."

"I saw it while he was flicking!" Oma says, then she shushes us, even though she's the only one talking.

The camera shifts to a burning building, and my throat tightens when I realize it's our building, red lights splashing against the brick, flames shooting like protruding tongues mocking the screams of sirens and people. Mom gasps.

I recognize a face from the stoop, and I search the crowd huddled on the street, looking for the rest of the tenants I know. I don't know many of their names, but I know their faces. I look for the little girl who handed me the leaf, and her dark-skinned mother with the rust-colored hair. I search between shoulders for the faded, little old Japanese man I call "Mr. U" because he is so bent over that he looks like the letter *U* tipped on its side. I look for the strange man two doors down who leaves his door open when the summer heat is oppressive—even if he is in his underwear—and you can hear his parrot talking in human words with more clarity than the old man uses when answering him. I don't know any of them well, really, yet I'm suddenly worrying about them all as if they are family when I don't find them in the quick camera shots. "Many of them probably moved out already, Lucy," Oma says to comfort me.

The camera slides up the side of the building, revealing fire shooting out of every window on the second floor and smoke billowing out of the rest. I feel like crying. Our building was butt-ugly, as Mom often said, but it was home. And everything but what we have here with us is melting and burning up, including our computers.

The cameras move to the front stoop, where masked firemen are carrying out bodies on stretchers, two with white sheets sheathing their faces. Some people are being helped out of a window into a metal cage, their faces darkened with soot and smoke and fear as they are lowered to the ground, where paramedics wait to clamp oxygen masks over their faces. Seeing them, I forget about our things and the building itself and worry about the people again.

"That son of a bitchin' slumlord!" Mom says. "He couldn't wait until the building was evacuated before he torched it, now, could he?"

"Oh, dear, I had a sinking feeling just last night that

something bad was going to happen. That's what made me stop you from leaving," Oma says, as though her lemongrass tea had already done its job.

Sylvia Decker yammers on, shouting, saying nothing, because there's nothing she knows beyond what she can see, which is exactly the same as what we can see.

"Oh, God," Mom groans. "All of our things. Our books. Our clothes. Furniture. Everything."

"Did you have renter's insurance?" Oma asks.

"How in the hell could I have renter's insurance? I could hardly make my rent."

"Our computers. My notes..." Milo says, and he looks ready to cry. Oma sits down beside him and pats his back as though she's burping him. "They're only things, Milo. Things can be replaced."

"Not if you don't have a dime to replace them with," Mom says.

Their exchange leads me to do a running tally of what things of mine are now being consumed by the flames shooting out of the very window where I stood watching Peter leave, and I decide that I've lost practically nothing of value in that building, except my computer, and maybe my pictures of Scott Hamilton, a pair of summer shorts I especially like (that probably wouldn't have fit me by next summer anyway), a couple of scrapbooks, and my Sigmund Freud puppet. And then I think of how grateful I am that my important things—the words I read, my memories— are safely stored up in my head.

"Shit," Mom says.

We're still watching the screen when Grandpa Sam grabs the remote from the arm of the couch and starts ramming buttons again. By the time Oma swipes it back, the news has moved on to a segment about some Hollywood couple that's split up.

Mom doesn't say anything. She just goes out the front door.

Oma, Milo, and I sit for a moment, no one making a peep but for Feynman, who is suddenly at Milo's knee, his butt wagging, small whines vibrating the flappy skin hanging from his neck.

"Go on and take him out to do his business," Oma says.

Milo looks up at her. "Does this mean we have to stay here now?"

"For a while, yes. I'd imagine so."

Milo looks forlorn as he pats his scrawny thigh, cueing Feynman to follow him. Oma grabs her cigarette case and follows them out, and I follow her.

"Oma?" I say, as we stroll slowly through the backyard, Oma smoking and watching Feynman running in circles around Milo. "I was sad and scared for the people and our things when I saw the report, but I felt glad too. Glad because Mom and Milo and I weren't in it. And because it means I'll probably get to stay here longer. Did I just create some bad karma?"

Oma wants to hug me, I can tell, but she won't touch me while she's exhaling hundreds of toxins.

"Oh, honey. No," Oma says. "It's only human to think like that. Why would God punish someone for being the very thing *She* created them to be?"

Oma flicks the ash from her cigarette stub on the grass, then grinds it out with the heel of her slipper. With the butt still in her hand, she puts her arm around my shoulder and we stand quietly together for a time.

"Oma," I say. "It's synchronicity at work again, isn't it?

You want us to stay longer, and I want to too. Mom wanted to leave so we could get back and pack and now there's nothing to pack, and we have nowhere to live but here."

Oma is looking toward the front yard, where Mom is pacing, her cell phone to her ear. Mom pulls it away and bangs on the keys, then puts it back to her ear. "My little Lucy. As bright as the stars," Oma says softly, sadly, and I smile even though I'm sad, because I love the sound of her voice when she says those words.

T HE NIGHT of the fire, I sleep with Oma again, even though I could have avoided her snores by sleeping in one of the spare rooms upstairs. I didn't want to be alone. The next morning I wake in an empty bed, take a shower, and find Milo and Oma in the kitchen, Grandpa Sam sitting at the table with them. "There's oatmeal on the stove, and your muffin and juice are here on the table."

Oma catches a clump of oatmeal that is slipping down Grandpa's chin, and she scoops it back in. She plucks a raisin off of his dish-towel bib and pops that back into his mouth too. "Your mom went off to have breakfast with her friend Mitzy. She told me to see that you two get straight to your studies after breakfast."

"Why are you telling *me*?" Milo asks. He's not offended, just sincerely confused.

"So she doesn't have to single me out, stupid," I say. "I think we all know that you don't need any prompting to study. To breathe, maybe, but not to study."

"Lucy," Oma says with a sigh. "I really wish you wouldn't speak to your brother like that."

"Yeah, sorry," I say.

While we eat, I keep my eyes on my oatmeal, on Milo, or on Feynman (who happens to be contentedly licking his testicles while lying at Milo's feet), rather than on the oatmeal spurting out of Grandpa's mouth. Now that he's awake, I want to watch him, to study him, but not while he's slobbering his food.

"We have a paper to write too, Lucy," Milo says. "Don't forget about that."

"I was going to write mine on the relationship between Freud and Jung, but how am I supposed to do that now, with no Internet or books to use for my research?"

"You always write about them, so why would you need to do more research? It's not fair either," Milo huffs, "that Mom lets you pick them for your subjects all the time."

"Your mom is going to stop at the library this morning," Oma explains, "and she's also going back to the cable office to order the Net. Did you check Grandpa's library? Maybe he's got some books in there you could use, if you choose another subject."

"There are no biographies in there, and Lucy always does hers on people," Milo says.

"Are you sure there aren't?" Oma asks.

"There's not if he says there aren't," I tell Oma. "He'd

know because he's reorganizing all of Grandpa's books according to the Dewey decimal system." Oma blinks at Milo like she's not sure what to make of him, but of course she doesn't say anything.

"Does it have to be someone famous?" Oma asks.

"I don't know. Mom's never said. But I'd imagine so. If they're not famous, what could there possibly be to write about?"

Oma laughs. "Oh, dear child, everyone has a story. Take your grandpa here, for instance. He lived in a boxcar. How many people—famous or otherwise—can lay claim to that?"

"A boxcar?"

"Yes, you know. One of those cars on a railroad train that are always filled with that pretty graffiti."

"I know what a boxcar is, Oma. I'm just asking why."

She pats Grandpa Sam's face with the corner of a towel. "Well, your grandfather was born in 1930, just months after the stock market crashed. His dad was already struggling to make ends meet, and when the country slid into the Great Depression, they lost everything they owned. Sam's father had worked for the Soo Line before the Depression and they lived next to the tracks, so I guess it was a feasible option when they lost their house and their land."

Oma glances at Grandpa and smiles sadly. "Once, he'd have thrown a fit for my mentioning that, because it shamed him. He was always such a proud man."

Oma tries to give Grandpa Sam another spoonful, but he slowly lifts his hand and swats the spoon away. "That's shit," he says.

"Your mother got her potty mouth from him," Oma says as she gives Grandpa's face a final swipe, then carries the bowl to the sink. While she's swirling his bowl under a stream of water, she says, "Sam was ten years old when his dad kicked him out. They didn't have money to feed all those mouths, and the older ones had to leave to find work. He worked on a farm for a time, then rode the rails, going from town to town, city to city, taking whatever odd jobs he could find. A year after Sam left, we entered World War Two and the economy turned around. That's when your great-grandpa decided there was money to be made, and he summoned Sam home so he could help him make it."

"Flora brought me biscuits," Grandpa Sam says, and Oma asks him who Flora was. He doesn't answer, though.

While Oma is filling the sink with dishwater, Grandpa stands on shaky legs and reaches for his walker. "Where are you going, Sam?" She shuts off the faucet and cranks her head around and watches him shuffle into the living room. "He must be going to watch TV."

Oma is drying dishes and humming something that sounds like a Gregorian chant and I'm at the table pretending to do my geometry when Milo comes out of the study and says, "Is Grandpa supposed to be outside? I just saw him outside my window, looking in."

Oma drops her dishcloth and hurries out the door. I dart after her.

"Sam! Sam!" Oma yells, as he shuffles his feet across the grass—one slipper missing, a dented lunch box in his hand. "Lucy, catch him before he reaches the road. Hurry!"

I reach him in time and take his arm. He's breathing hard. He looks down at me, seeing me as if for the first time.

Now that I have him, I'm not quite sure what to do with him, so I just hang on to his wrist and wait for Oma to reach us. I use those few seconds to stare into his face. His eyes show confusion, but the rest of his features look drawn and sad. I think of him working hard since he was a boy, and how now he's wearing diapers, wandering around with an empty lunch box, and I know why his face is frozen in sadness.

"I can't find my truck keys," he says. "Where are my keys?"

"Come on, Grandpa," I say.

He lets me turn him and steer him toward Oma, who is shaking something out of her slipper. He asks her where his truck keys are too. She takes his lunch box. "Come on, Sam. Let's go back inside."

He slips his hand out of hers. "I want my goddamn keys. Where'd you put them?"

"Come on, we'll go inside and find them."

I know Oma means well, but according to what I read, to go along with a stroke victim's fantasies only serves to confuse them more.

"Grandpa Sam?" He stops and wags his head to the side so he can look down at me again. "You can't have your keys. You've had strokes, and your mind and body don't work well enough to drive. Or to go to work anymore. But maybe if you want to go someplace besides work, Mom can drive you."

"I start at seven. It's after seven."

It isn't.

"Lucy," Oma whispers. "Don't."

"No, Grandpa. You don't work anymore. Sorry. But maybe you can tell me about the jobs you've had when we get inside, okay?"

Grandpa lifts his finger and points to his forehead. "My brain's broke," he says, and I can't tell if it's a question or a statement, but I say, "Yes."

I take his hand and help lead him back to the house and into his lift chair. His chest is heaving by the time we get him settled, and his face is contorted into a sob, even though his eyes are dry and no sound comes from him.

Twenty minutes later, Oma has Grandpa Sam reclining in his chair, and she's standing over him, her opened hands hovering a couple of inches above him while some twangy Japanese music plays from a beat-up boom box. I go to the table and spread out the textbooks I brought from home, but none of them grabs my interest at the moment. "Sam, don't bat at my hands like that. I'm opening your chakras," Oma scolds.

With Oma busy clearing Grandpa Sam's chakras, Milo lost in his books in the study, and my own reading dull as plain toast, I glance at the stairway off the kitchen and bite my lip. Then, without giving myself time to ponder what kind of karma will boomerang back to me for this one, I rip off my shoes and head up the stairs in stocking feet, walking gently because the boards are prone to creaking.

I open the closet door slowly so it won't creak either, and without moving the stack, I untie the pink cord of yarn that Oma tied around them. I pull out one of the spiral notebooks, closing the door quietly behind me, and take it to Mom's old bed.

The notebook I grab is blue, and the cover is worn bare in spots where an eraser rubbed the color off. The date—December 21 to January 5, 1985—is written over one erased bar and, above it, Mom's name. I quickly calculate Mom's age to be ten, when she was in the fifth grade.

I feel like a window peeker when I open it, yet I don't stop myself. Not when I see the childish penmanship inside: fat, round letters, with circles for the dots over *i*'s. Pencil-drawn wreaths and Christmas trees decorate the top of the page.

I run my fingers over the paper, feeling the small creases her pencil chiseled years ago. I feel as though I've gone back in time to meet a potential new friend. One who, it just so happens, will be my mother when she's grown.

I got the only A today on our chapter test in Mr. Thorton's class. Mitzy got a C+, but she didn't glare at me like that Trudy Millard did. I hate Trudy. I hope she cuts herself when she trips over those big feet and stabs her buck teeth so far into her bottom lip that doctors can't dislodge them. Then she'd have to shut her ugly face and stop telling me I'm a cheater when I do better than her and stop calling Mitzy the "Pygmy Pixie."

Ma told Dad my grade while we were at the table. Dad was shoveling forkfuls of potatoes and gravy dotted with corn kernels into his mouth (it's so gross the way he mixes his food!), The Timber Times folded in half and held to his side so he could read without dipping the paper in his plate. Ma pointed to my ace paper hanging on the fridge. Dad didn't look up when he told me to keep it up, get a good education so nobody can keep me down.

I looked over at his work boot butted up against the leg of the table. Dad used to let Clay stand on them when he was little, then he'd take Clay's hands and walk him around the room. I don't know why I thought of that when Ma told Dad about my paper, but I did.

I skim the other entries, but there's nothing in them, it seems, other than more of her good grades, the snotty remarks Trudy made, and that she and Mitzy made s'mores at Mitzy's house. So I get up and grab another notebook from the stack and leaf through it:

December 19, 1989:

Mom is fourteen.

I hate Trudy Millard! She knows I like Brandon Wills, and that's exactly why she saw to it that she got his name for our gift exchange. Mrs. Billows said we could exchange names ourselves but that it had to be with someone besides our best friend.

It's my own fault. Brandon asked me if I wanted to, right after lunch. I wasn't expecting him to ask me, and while I stood there acting like an idiot because I was in shock, Trudy butted right in and said, "I'll exchange names with you, Brandon!"

Trudy was wearing a new burgundy shaker sweater. I hated my sweater today—the grass-green one, unstylishly short, with hard, nubby lint balls on it that I picked for the whole bus ride. No matter how much plucking I do, there they are, sticking to my sweater like the boogers Clay rolls and tosses at me.

Mitzy said Brandon only said yes because he knows that Trudy's rich, so he thought he'd get a better gift, because he certainly didn't say yes because of Trudy's good looks, since she's uglier than a pit bull's ass—so screw him, in his Gap clothes. That's how mad Mitzy was at Trudy. Mad enough to swear, even though I've only heard her swear a few other times in the whole seven years since we've been best friends.

I want a new sweater for Christmas. A shaker sweater, like everybody else is wearing. I was going to tell Ma the minute I got home and even show her what one looks like in my Seventeen *magazine. Not that I'd look that great in it. It doesn't look like I'll get Mom's nice boobs. More like Aunt Jeana's corn-kernel-sized ones—the Niblet variety.*

Mom was in the kitchen when we got off the bus, a kettle of ground beef smoking on the stove, cans of kidney beans and whole tomatoes left unopened next to the burner. The kitchen stunk of scorched meat and burnt onions. Ma's head was down, her forehead pressed against one arm.

I slammed down my schoolbooks, but the thump didn't wake her. I hurried to the stove to stir the meat and dump in the remainder of the ingredients. Clay went to the cupboard for the peanut butter jar, saw we were out of crackers and bread, and picked up a Pringles can, giving it a shake to see if it was worth the bother of opening the lid.

Ma woke when Clay cracked the cupboard door shut. She sniffed, then jumped to her feet. She thanked me when she saw the chili simmering, her words slurred from sleep as she explained that she only meant to shut her eyes for a minute to try and get rid of her headache.

I glanced into the living room, but of course there was no tree in the stand. Only the box of ornaments I brought downstairs last night. When I asked Clay to go cut that balsam at the edge of the yard, the one the robin's nest fell from last spring, he asked why. Duh!

Clay held the Pringles tube upside down and poured the last of the crumbs into his mouth, not caring that orange crumbs were sprinkling all over his sweatshirt and the floor. I reminded him that it's only six days until Christmas, and that's when he got snotty. He made some rude remark like, "Yeah. We'll just put up our tree and then we'll have a regular Hallmark Christmas, won't we, Ma?" I hate the way Clay talks to Ma!

Ma ignored Clay's barb, just like she ignores most of Dad's—except when they are directed at Clay or me. Then she reminded me that Dad said he'd cut a tree tonight. She said this as if Dad's word is anything close to a promise.

"Like he said he'd build the biggest and best sawmill in the Midwest and make us rich?" Clay said then, reminding me of how I hate him just as much as he hates Dad.

When Dad got home and Ma asked him to get the tree, he balked, and she said nothing. At least not until he took off his work clothes, leaving them in a heap on the bathroom floor, and she went to pick them up. Balsam needles fell out of the cuffs.

"Looks like you cut a tree for somebody," she said. "But obviously not for your kids." She reminded him that I've been asking for a tree for two weeks now.

I told Ma it was okay, making sure I said it loud enough for Dad to hear. Then I leaned in close enough that her hair tickled my nose and pleaded with her not to start a fight over a stupid Christmas tree.

Ma didn't say anything else. At least not with her voice. But she slammed pans and clinked plates as she emptied the dish drainer and put dishes away. I knew without looking that she had tears in her eyes when a stack of pans and lids came clattering out of the cupboard. I was in the bathroom when I heard the avalanche, and I stopped my pee midstream so I could hurry to her and plead with her to let it drop.

"Here, you want noise? I'll give you noise, you stupid bitch!" That's what Dad shouted from the living room.

I didn't see Dad pick up the ornament box and throw it, but I heard the thud against the living-room wall and the tinkling of shattering bulbs.

I bolted to the living-room door, just as Ma did. It's weird how we always do that. Rush to him when he's upset, even though we should be running in the other direction.

The ornaments were scattered across the floor, and a hole was jabbed through the box where Dad's boot had gone. The

*Styrofoam bulb I'd made into the face of Millie, Dad's dog—
even though my kindergarten teacher said we were supposed
to make Rudolph, just because I knew Daddy would like a
Millie ornament better—was smashed, his brown pom-pom
nose gone, leaving only a small, fuzz-covered splotch of dried
Elmer's. I swatted the real Millie out of the way before she
scarfed it up in her mouth and picked up the broken ornament.
Dad looked down at the crushed Millie in my hand, but he
didn't say anything. I doubt he even noticed that it was Millie
in the first place.*

*The fight ended with Mom cleaning up the Christmas
mess as she wiped her eyes.*

*Tonight I don't care that Trudy Millard is going to get a
Christmas gift from Brandon. I hate him anyway, so I'm not
going to cry about it. He's a male, so therefore stupid and not
worth my bother. Trudy Millard told Jennifer Logan that
she's going to marry Brandon one day. She can have him! I'm
never going to get married. Not even if I decide I want kids
someday. I'm just going to go to a sperm bank to get those.*

I stop reading for a second and stare at the wallpaper facing
me. The house here in Timber Falls is quiet—at least when
Grandpa is sleeping and the TV is off—and it's hard to
imagine it filled with the sounds of slamming pans and
shouts. It makes me feel sad for Oma and Mom. I keep reading, though, hoping that she at least got the sweater she
wanted.

December 24, 1989:

*We're having turkey for Christmas dinner. Last year we
had one measly, skimpy chicken. The same as we have on
ordinary Sundays, baked until the skin is tree-bark dry.*

Granted, Ma tried to make it look like a turkey by stuffing its tiny ass with dressing and garnishing it with parsley sprigs, but it only made it look more pathetic.

We have a real turkey this year because the paper mill gave all the employees a certificate for a free one. When Ma told Marie about the coupon, she came right over to drive Ma to the IGA to get it, saying that if she waited, they'd all be picked over.

Clay thinks the turkey is an indication that this Christmas will be better than last in all ways and that he'll get the .22 he asked for so he can shoot clay pigeons with his dorky friends. As for me, I'm not convinced we'll get good gifts this year, and I'm not even sure it matters, because what I want now, more than anything else, is boobs, a boyfriend, no fighting on Jesus's birthday, and one of Dad's toboggans.

Dad has been making and selling toboggans for two years now. Ma says he's made one for us this year, though. Not one for each of us—yet—but one to share, because he's had too many orders and because he's had to put in too many over-time hours at the mill. I hope he got the toboggan finished, but I'm not sure if he has, because on Saturday he was putting on his boots to go out to the shed to work when the phone rang. He looked funny when he said, "Okay, okay, I'll be right there." When he hung up, he told Ma he had to go in and not to expect him home until close to morning. That's how it is when there's a major breakdown at the mill. Sometimes Dad has to work two days straight, because time is money. Clay was pissed when he first heard that Dad had only one toboggan for us, saying he had all year to make us each one. I don't mind, though. Clay and I can take turns using it.

Dad's in his workshop tonight. I can see the lit bare bulb through the shed window and his dark head bent over his workbench. I suppose he's rubbing the bottom with beeswax, which is the last thing he does. Liz Gardiner got one of Dad's toboggans for her birthday last month, and she said he told her that if you keep it coated on the bottom with beeswax, it will glide down the hill all the faster.

Just about a mile down the road, there's a hill behind Henry and Nordine Bickett's house. A tall hill, perfectly sloped, that begins at a clump of red pine we can shimmy between, then nothing but hill that empties into a field beneath it. Clay says we'll be able to sail like the wind down that thing, and I told Mitzy that we should have a sledding party there and invite everyone we like—which doesn't mean Trudy Millard! Clay will crash it, of course, along with his creepy friends, and they'll be smashing into everybody and talking dirty, because they're all dumb enough to think that that kind of behavior impresses girls.

As soon as we open gifts on Christmas Eve and that toboggan is in my hands, I'm going to call Mitzy and tell her I got it. Mitzy doesn't open gifts until Christmas morning, and she asked for a sled, so then all we'll have to do is wait for morning to know if our party's on.

Clay must have decided that one toboggan is better than none, because he stopped being pissy about it and decided that we're going sledding as soon as the sun comes up on Christmas morning—just me and him (weird, because the only thing we ever do together anymore is fight). Clay has his boots propped by the door, an extra pair of socks he swiped from Dad's drawer stuffed inside and waiting. I'm going to wear the boots Clay outgrew last year, which are still too big for me, but with extra socks they'll do. Clay says we'll sled until dinner is ready—which should take considerably longer, since it's turkey this year, not a 3.5-pound chicken—come home to eat, then sled until dark.

I have to go. I'm going to help Mom clean.

I turn the page and glance at the date of the next entry: *Christmas Eve night.* I want to read about them sledding, but before I can turn the page, Oma calls to me. I quickly tuck the notebook under the bed with the next entry I want to read facing up (because the pages aren't numbered, so even with my sharp photographic memory, I might have a bit of trouble finding it quickly), then I hurry to the top of the stairs and call back, "I'm up here!"

Oma is at the bottom of the stairs, wiping her hands on a towel—hands that are red from hot water and scrubbing, because she had to cleanse them well to remove the "disease" that came from Grandpa's Sam's blocked chakras. "Oma? Since Mom said she wants to sleep in the guest room now, can I sleep in Mom's old room? I like that room, and you snore."

"Who says I snore?"

"I do."

"We'll see," she says. "But you'd best come down here and get to work, young lady. Your mother will be upset with us both if you don't do your schoolwork while she's out."

At the bottom of the stairs, the bathroom door is shut. Feynman is sitting on his haunches watching it, so I know Milo is in there. "I'm going to use the bathroom up here first," I say, "since Milo is using that one." Milo, the idiot that he is, yells, "I'll be out in a second," from behind the door, and knowing Milo, he probably means literally one second.

"I can't wait," I yell, and hurry off. I lean out of the bathroom doorway and listen. I don't hear anything, so I creep to the end of the hall to see if Oma's still at the bottom of the stairs. She's not. Then I hurry back to Mom's room and pull the notebook out from under *my* bed.

Christmas Eve night:

Christmas Eve dinner was a joke. One big, fat, stupid joke! I thought it would be different this year—or I hoped it would be—but it wasn't.

Ma was at least semi-happy when I got downstairs this morning. She was smiling as she measured flour into a bowl so we could make gingerbread cookies, like we always do on Christmas Eve.

Ma got teary-eyed when she told me how she wanted to get Clay and me nice gifts this year. She knows how disappointed Clay is going to be when he doesn't get the gun he asked for. I suggested that maybe Dad could give Clay one of his, but all Ma said was, "Well, you know how your father is." And, yes, I know how he is. How Ma has to beg for every dime he hands her, and every time she does, he asks her where the last ten or twenty bucks he gave her went. It upsets me when he does that, but I know he's scared that we'll run out of money or that he'll never have his dream. It's only fear that makes him say those things.

Dad was a boy during the Depression, and he always tells us that we don't know how it is when you have to go to bed hungry because there's no money for food. I think that's why he hoards his money like he does. And besides that, Dad wants to save every dime he makes because he's got his heart set on building a lumber mill. In a year or two, if First National will give him the loan (which he thinks they will, considering he's got forty acres for collateral, and he'll have a hefty down payment saved), he's going to build the biggest and best sawmill in the Midwest. Dad always says that then we'll have so much much money we'll be swimming in it, and the Millards will be kissing the asses they kicked. I smile every time Dad says something like that, because he looks happy then. And we'll all be happy when Dad gets happy.

I wanted to tell Mom that a lot of gifts don't matter, so she wouldn't be upset with Dad. I wanted to tell her that after Christmas vacation, when Mrs. Paulson asked us all to stand up and recite what gifts we got for Christmas, I'd make up my gifts, like I do every year, so that none of us has to be embarrassed. But I didn't say that to her, because I knew it would only make her sadder. What I did tell her, though, was that if I got my toboggan, and if Dad carved her something special out of wood, those gifts would be more than enough.

We had fun making the cookies, contorting the cutout shapes to look like people we know. Mom giggled 'til she almost fell off her chair when I made Aunt Jeana, stretching the cookie's body 'til it was as narrow as a pencil and then taking a paring knife and gouging out two deep-set eyes so close together that she looked like a Cyclops. Mom told me it looked just like her. She giggled when she told me I was terrible.

And then the phone rang.

Mom was still laughing when she answered it. She asked who was calling, then said, "Nordine? Is that you?" She stopped laughing.

There is only one Nordine in town (or maybe anywhere in the whole world), so I knew who she was talking to. Nordine clerks at the Holiday gas station by day and waitresses at a supper club on the outskirts of town by night. Everybody always raves about how pretty Nordine is, and I guess she is, even if she's got to be as old as Dad. She's blond, trim, and has the kind of face that should be on a ceramic Christmas angel. Nordine is the mother of little Ralphy, the puny kid who played Rudolph in this year's Christmas program. He stunk at acting, but he broke all of our hearts just by entering the stage, skinny-necked and pale as a snowflake, the plastic clown's nose clamped over his, so big that it was making his eyes water.

Nordine is the wife of Henry Bickett, a hot-tempered little drunk who hasn't worked a day in his life and won't take care of Ralphy while Nordine works, so she has to drag him to work with her, even if that means keeping him up until after eleven o'clock on school nights.

Ma called Dad, her hand clamped over the receiver. She told him it was Nordine Bickett and that she sounded like she was crying. Ma sounded confused, though I'm not sure if the confusion was about why Nordine was crying or why she'd call our house and ask for Dad.

Dad yanked the phone from Mom and started toward the bathroom, but Clay was in there. He stretched the cord as far as it would go in the other direction—'til he was standing under the archway between the kitchen and living room. Dad's voice was as high-pitched as Mickey Mouse's and sounded totally fake when he said, "Nordine? Hello there!"

Ma came back to the table where I was sitting, plucking excess dough from around the cookie shapes. She pretended she was looking at my Marie cookie as she bent over me, but her attention was on what Dad was saying on the phone.

Dad didn't talk long, and he listened more than spoke. Finally he said, "It's okay, Nordine. You can trust me when I say that won't happen."

Dad hung up the phone and hurried to grab his boots from the mat by the door.

Ma asked Dad what Nordine wanted, and Dad told her, "Never mind." He grabbed his keys and went out the door.

Ma and I both stood at the kitchen window, watching as Dad stomped a trail through the fresh snow, straight to his workshop. He left the door partly open as he slipped inside.

"Oh, God, don't tell me…" Ma said when the curled tip of a toboggan peeked through the doorway.

My heart sank as Dad carried a toboggan the color of honey around the side of the house.

I ran to the spare bedroom that overlooks the driveway and pulled back the shade. Cold wind from the leaky window frame chilled me—or maybe it was the sight of Dad tossing our toboggan into the back of his pickup, then driving away.

"Tell me you didn't do it, Sam," Ma said when Dad got home an hour later. "Tell me you didn't give away your kids' toboggan to that woman."

Dad shimmied his feet out of his boots, and snow clumps rolled from the cuffs of his work pants onto the newly waxed floor. "I didn't give anything to 'that woman.' I gave it to her kid," he said.

"Oh, but, Sam…"

Dad turned to her. "Shut the fuck up." And Ma did. At least to him.

The minute Dad turned on the TV, Ma asked me to watch the last batch of cookies in the oven, then she dialed Marie's number. She stretched the phone so that the cord was hardly spiraled so she could talk from the bathroom, where Dad couldn't hear her. Minutes later, Marie's truck pulled into the yard and Mom opened the drawer where she kept her grocery money, then hurried out. When she came back, she made Clay and me go stand in Dad's study, which is on the opposite side of the house from the driveway, so we wouldn't see what she was bringing in and hauling into the basement—as if Christmas wasn't already ruined.

I pause and let the notebook rest on my legs. My stomach is clenched so tight it hurts, and my eyes feel hot, like tears are boiling behind them.

When I had my computer, sometimes I'd sneak in a

game of Spider Solitaire when I got bored with my school-work. It's a glorified version of solitaire, played with ten columns of cards instead of seven. I like playing it better than regular solitaire because, if you don't win, you can just click *Restart this game again.*

When I first started playing it, I wondered if maybe the cards were delivered in such a way that it was impossible to win a particular game no matter what move you made. But after a few failures and then an ultimate win on the same board, I saw that the difference between winning or losing often depended on one simple move. Maybe there'd be two cards facing down—two blind choices—and you'd choose one and lose the game the first time, then you'd play it again and choose the other card when the same choice presented itself, and you'd win. I remember wondering then if life didn't play by the same principles as a game of Spider Solitaire and whether making one simple move over another might make the difference between winning or losing in the end. I think of this game as I run my fingers over the notebook on my lap, and I wonder if maybe Grandpa Sam would have won Mom and Uncle Clay's love forever if he'd just made the other choice and not given their toboggan away.

I dab at my damp eyes—I'll have no explanation for crying once I get back downstairs—and I continue reading, hoping that Mom and Uncle Clay ended up with at least one reason to be happy on Christmas Day.

Christmas morning:

This morning I unwrapped a blue sweater made out of the same material and knit in the same style as my grass-green lint-ball sweater, and Clay got a model of a Camaro. In place of the toboggan that should have been was a sled with metal runners. Dad's name was written on the tag—in Ma's handwriting, of course—a Holiday gas station price tag dangling from one blade (Ma never thinks to remove price stickers from gifts).

Clay took one look at that sled and said Dad might as well use it for firewood in his shop because hell was going to freeze over before he used it.

"What the hell's wrong with you?" Dad asked. "Ralphy's six years old. You want a six-year-old kid to think that he wasn't good enough for Santa to bring him anything?" Then Dad told him how Nordine's husband—"that horse's ass," he called him—spent what money Nordine had saved for Christmas to buy a useless junk car for parts and how he couldn't let a little kid like that go without a Christmas. He told Clay to grow up, then reminded him that with the grades he got this semester, he was lucky to get anything.

When Clay stomped off, bawling, Dad told him to shut his "baby-ass mouth." And when Clay's feet pounded up the stairs, Dad shouted after him, asking him what in the hell was the matter with him that he couldn't see that a store-bought sled was better than a stupid homemade one. Then Dad yelled at Ma for telling us he was making the toboggan for us in the first place, since it was supposed to be a secret, and had it been kept that way, Clay wouldn't be carrying on like a "sissy."

But it wasn't Ma's fault that we found out. I had weasled it out of her over a week ago, after she sent me out to the shed to tell Dad that dinner was done. And there he was, sitting in a pool of curly wood chips, his flannel shirtsleeves rolled to his elbows because the wood stove was burning hot. He had a stick with a bunched rag at the top and was dipping it into a pot of water boiling on a hot plate, then brushing it over the end of the planks.

He didn't look up when I slipped inside the door and told him dinner was ready. He set the stick down and slid what he once told me was the brace over the wet tip of the planks, then he pinned his knee below the brace so he could bend the wood. I didn't get to see him do it, though, because he told me to go so he could concentrate on what he was doing. The second I got back inside the house, I asked Ma if the toboggan was ours. She wouldn't admit that it was, but I could tell that it was by the sparkle in her eyes, and I ran to tell Clay. Now I wish— for Ma's sake, and Clay's, and mine—that I'd never asked.

"Lucy?" Oma calls up the stairs.

I scramble to tuck the notebook back in the closet. "Yes?" I call back, delivering it in a short clip so, hopefully, she can't tell that I'm hanging out of the doorway of Mom's room rather than in the bathroom.

"Your schoolwork, honey," Oma says.

I crouch down and scoot across the hall and into the bathroom, where I flush the toilet. "Comingggggggggg," I yell.

I go downstairs and take my place at the table and open a book. "You okay?" Oma asks. "You don't look so well, and you were in the bathroom an awfully long time. Maybe you should have some ginger root tea."

"I'm fine, Oma," I say. I make a note to practice my expressions in the bathroom mirror so I can stop showing my guilt when I'm being snoopy.

I watch Oma as she sits on a stool next to the phone, a New Age supply catalog spread on her lap, and listen as she orders a portable Reiki table, some essential oils, a Pilates exercise ball because her stomach's getting flabby, a book on boosting your psychic powers, and *The Tibetan Book of the Dead*. I hear Grandpa's snores in between Oma's recitation of item numbers, and I just feel sad.

I know Mom didn't have any reason to lie in her own journal, but I want what she wrote to be a lie because I don't want to think of soft, kind Oma being sworn at. And I don't want to think of Grandpa Sam not being a good husband to her or a good dad to Mom and Uncle Clay.

When Oma is done on the phone, she looks at me again and her pretty eyes squint until they rim with feathery lines. "You *sure* you're okay, Lucy?"

It's the lemongrass tea. I'm sure of it. And I know there's no distracting her. I look down at the novel Mom brought me home from the library. Some new young adult book with a picture of a sad-eyed girl on the cover. "Oh, it's just this book I'm reading," I say, even though I haven't even finished reading the first page yet and have no idea what it's about.

Oma picks up the book, scans the copy on the back, and fans the pages a bit. "It doesn't sound like a sad story to me," she says. "But maybe it's the emotions that were present in the author as she wrote them. I'll bet if you took ten writers and gave them each ten words from the endless pool of words to choose from, even if they ended up arranging them in exactly the same order, you'd still feel something different from each one, depending on who wrote them. A story, a painting, a piece of music—anything created—gets infused with the emotions and the essence of who created them.

"I'm a sensate, a highly sensitive person, just like you are. Here..."

Oma plucks a carved cardinal from the windowsill, explaining that Grandpa Sam carved it before his fingers got crippled with arthritis, and puts it in my hand. "Close your eyes as you hold it. See what you feel." I take it reluctantly, hoping it's not like when she handed me a chunk of amethyst and asked me if I felt the energy. I didn't.

I do as Oma says, holding it and concentrating, just as she does when she holds her rocks and gems. For a time I'm aware of nothing but the fact that she's watching me, waiting, hoping that I feel something.

At first I don't feel anything, but then I start to see something, though I'm not sure if I'm only making pictures up in my mind. I see Grandpa Sam sitting on a stool, bent over, a curved metal-tipped tool scraping the wood and sending blond curls to the floor. And I know that he feels fragile as he carves it, even though he's big and strong as he was in the picture hanging in the living room. Oma is waiting with such a hopeful expression that I don't want to disappoint her.

"Well? What do you think attached itself to that carving?" she asks.

"Fragility," I say, and Oma smiles and tells me again that I'm as bright as the stars.

She takes the bird and turns it over in her hands. "Sam carved this at a time in his life when he was emotionally frail. Vulnerable. And he carved that emotion right into the wood. That's probably why people who feel they must always be in charge and strong—even the ones who love birds—would rather just look at this figurine than hold it and be reminded of their own fragility.

"Sky Dreamer told me that when you're a sensate, you have to clear your space from negativity from time to time, because you absorb the emotions of others easily and can become overwhelmed. Here, I'll show you how." Then she demonstrates how to clear your space by lifting your arms above your head and whooshing them down to your sides, though I've seen her do it a thousand times already. Her left arm hits a plastic cup off the counter and it goes bouncing across the floor. Oma leans down to pick it up, then notices the dust bunnies under the fridge and goes for the scrub bucket. While I sit and pretend to study, I'm thinking about how the sadness, fear, and depression that attached themselves to Mom's words way back then are probably responsible for the emotions that make her swallow her Paxil and hide out in the clump of trees at the edge of the yard now.

I'm restless, so while Oma pulls the refrigerator out so she can clean under it, I wander off.

There's nowhere to go, really, since it's begun to rain outside. I peek in the study, but Milo doesn't look up from his books. Feynman is asleep at his feet. So I wander off and end up outside Grandpa Sam's room. I look in at him and I don't like him, remembering that he broke things and said mean words to Oma and Uncle Clay and gave their toboggan away.

He's lying in his bed, awake from his nap and staring at the ceiling. I think of how it would be if that's all I had to do all day—lie and stare at the ceiling, or at flashing TV stations with my broken mind—and then I can't see that mean dad and husband anymore. Only an old grandpa lying on his bed, sick and alone, waiting to die.

"You're awake," I say, stating the obvious—something that drives me nuts when other people do it but knowing that, in this case, the obvious may not be so obvious, so it's probably not a stupid comment after all. I slip into his room and stand by the bed.

I don't know if anyone's home inside that stare, but I feel like talking, and I decide that even if Grandpa Sam doesn't register what I'm saying, what difference does it make? Milo doesn't seem to register much of what I say either.

"You know what, Grandpa Sam? Upstairs there is a stack of notebooks Mom wrote in when she was a girl. My mom's your daughter, Tess, in case you've forgotten."

He turns his head to look at me when I sit on the edge of his bed, but I don't know if it's just his brain stem telling him to turn toward the source of noise or a conscious decision to look at me. I decide it doesn't matter.

"She writes about you being her dad and Oma being her mom. About the things that happened, and what she was thinking about at the time. She wrote about you making toboggans."

"I make toboggans," Grandpa Sam says.

"Did you make one for Mom and Uncle Clay?" I ask.

His watery eyes look away, but I don't know if that means he's thinking or not, because he doesn't rotate his eyeballs upward, like he's trying to search his mind for the memory. "Yeah," he says.

"Mom wrote about you making them one for Christmas, but you ended up giving it to Ralphy Bickett. They got a store-bought sled instead. They wanted the one you made for them, though," I say.

Grandpa Sam doesn't comment.

I want to ask him why he kicked the ornament box, but I don't want him to feel bad. "I never went sledding before, did you?" I ask.

"I was sick," he says.

"You mean you were going to go sledding once, but you got sick and couldn't go?"

"No. Then I had to go to work."

"Maybe this winter you and I can go sledding, huh?

There's a sled in the basement. Would you like that? I'd help you get on it."

Grandpa Sam lifts his head and strains. His stiff hands grab a handful of bedsheet and he tugs.

"You want to get up, Grandpa?"

"Yeah," he says.

I've seen Oma get him up, so I pull back his quilt and I take him by the ankles and swing his feet as far off the bed as they'll go. Then I grab his arms and yank until I get him in a sitting position. We both need a rest after that, so I use the opportunity to ask him the question I want answered the most.

"Grandpa? Did you know my dad? Howard Smith?"

Grandpa Sam actually looks like he's thinking for a minute, then he says, "Junice lives in the Howards' house now." He looks down at his bare feet, which have thick, flaky toenails—toenails that were so long yesterday that, as Oma was clipping them and Mom happened to walk through the living room and glance down, she said, "Crissakes, give him a tree branch and he could perch."

Grandpa Sam studies the floor. "What are you looking for?" I ask.

"Where's my slippers?"

I get on my knees and look under the bed, and I see them. They're brown suede, the toes scuffed. I pull them out and slip them over Grandpa Sam's feet, which are bony and feel cool like doll skin.

Wrinkled and dull-eyed as Grandpa Sam is, and with his hair sparse and white and standing on end, he suddenly looks as cute as a homely baby, and I reach out and give him a hug.

"I like you, Grandpa Sam. Do you like me too?" I ask

this as if the person I'm talking to isn't the same person Mom wrote about when she was a girl.

"Yeah," he says, but he doesn't smile like I do, so I'm not sure if he means it.

I reach out and pat his hair down, but it springs right back up. "Grandpa Sam, can you tell me anything about my dad, Howard Smith? Did you know him? Did he live here in Timber Falls?"

"You didn't have a dad," Grandpa Sam says.

Scientifically, of course, Grandpa Sam has to be wrong. But as he said himself, his brain is broken. I sigh, realizing I'm not about to get any answers about my father from him either.

"Lucy? Is Grandpa awake?" Oma shouts.

"Yes," I yell back.

"Okay. Tell him I'll be there in a minute."

Grandpa Sam is trying to rise from the bed. Or so it seems, since he's bending forward. I try to show him how to rock to gain momentum, but he doesn't mimic me, so I wrap my arms around his chest and clutch my hands together at his back, and with his help I manage to get him standing. I put the walker in front of him and take his hands, wrapping them over the metal bar, and I walk him out.

"You got him up?" Oma says when she sees us, a mop in her hand. "Oh, Lucy, he's too heavy for you!"

"We did it together, didn't we, Grandpa Sam?"

Oma helps Grandpa get into his lift chair, then hurries off to scoot the refrigerator back in place.

I watch Grandpa Sam as he gazes out the window, where a red squirrel is hanging upside down on the feeder's pole, gobbling bird seed. Grandpa tries to lean over far enough to reach the window with his knuckles. "Goddamn red squirrels," he says slowly as he gazes out the window. "Mean sons of bitches. They bite the balls off the gray ones."

I purse my lips to keep my giggle inside.

He turns back to me, and I realize that since we got here, I've not seen one expression on Grandpa Sam but this one. The sad one. As if his face were molded out of wax by a starving artist too poor to buy Paxil, and he is helpless to change it. I tap the pointed collar of his flannel shirt in place. "Grandpa Sam, did you like my mom? You know, when she was a girl like me?"

His eyelids slowly scrape down over his watery eyes. He opens his mouth like he's going to answer my question, but he doesn't say anything except to swear again at the squirrel at his feeder. I rap on the window and the squirrel scurries off. Two fat-bellied blue jays come to take his place. "Look, blue jays," I tell Grandpa. He opens his eyes and stares out the window. "Pigs," he says. "They chase away the good birds."

Once he dozes off, I go into the kitchen, where Oma now has the top of the range propped open like a car hood. She's clanking on the burners to free them of black crud. "Oma, what was Grandpa Sam like when he was young?"

"Well, it depends on when you're talking about."

"Like, when he was a kid."

"I didn't know Sam then, and he didn't talk about his childhood much. His mom died when he was ten. I know that much. And people say she was a sweet little thing. I knew his dad because he was still alive when we married. He was very hard on Sam."

"Was he glad Grandpa Sam married you?"

"That man wasn't glad about anything. Not that it would have mattered one way or another to me. I was head over heels in love with your grandpa. How could I not be? He was the most handsome man I'd ever seen. And so smart he was like a walking encyclopedia. He was obsessed with learning, as if knowledge was his water and he was always thirsty. You and your brother take after him like that."

Oma and I don't hear the hum of Grandpa's lift chair, nor do we hear the click of the front door. What we hear instead is the horn of Oma's car bleating frantically. "Oh, Mom must want help carrying stuff in," I say. Oma apparently feels the gust of cool air entering the kitchen at the same time I do, because she rocks back on one foot and peers into the living room, the grungy dishcloth dangling from her hand. "Is that the front—" Before she can get the rest of the words out, we hear a deafening crack and the echo it makes as it reverberates against the trees, followed by Mom's shrill scream.

"Oh, my God, was that a shotgun?"

Oma and I race to the front door, which is hanging open.

Grandpa Sam is at the bottom of the steps, one foot bare, a rifle lifted only high enough to tuck it against his side. The rifle is haphazardly lined up with Oma's parked car, its door open. I scream then too, because even though I can hear Mom, I'm suddenly afraid that she's lying on the front seat in a bloody mess.

But then I see her crouched alongside the car, a book bag dangling from one hand and a shopping bag clutched in her other. She lets go of the bags and makes a beeline for the maple tree between the house and the car. The tree is too narrow to hide all of her, though, and maybe that's why she screams and screams.

"Give me that gun, Sam! Sam!" Oma grabs the rifle and yanks it from his hand. She's shaking hard. "It's okay, Tess. It's okay! I've got the gun!"

Mom slips out and stands alongside the tree, hugging it as if she might fall down if she lets go. "I saw him with the gun and beeped for you. Why didn't you come?"

"What on earth did you think you were doing?" Oma shouts at Grandpa. Mom stumbles to Oma, and Oma wraps her arm around her, a hand nervously thumping Mom's back. "My God," Oma says again.

"He waited for me like a sniper!"

Grandpa Sam blinks at us with dull eyes, then looks to the tree Mom just vacated. "Goddamn red squirrels," he says.

IT TAKES Oma a solid week to get the house "in order." She pares down the clutter and boxes up mounds of knick-knacks, pans with peeling nonstick finishes, and the afghans she says Grandpa's third wife must have made compulsively. Then she scrubs the whole place with baking soda, vinegar, and salt, until the entire house smells like a pickle. When she's finished scrubbing, she feng shui arranges the house, moving the kitchen table from the center of the floor over toward the living-room doorway, so close to the cupboards that I can't see how a full-grown adult or even a kid—or chi, for that matter—is going to be able to squeeze around it to roam freely through the house.

Mom knocks over a green vase with artificial flowers in colors that don't quite match as she sits at the table working on Missy Jenkins's tale and surfing the Net with the DSL hookup she finally got (but only after she called to harp at Connie Olinger at least twice). She cusses as she scoops it up. "If you were cleaning out junk, why in the hell did you leave these ugly fake flowers everywhere? Whoever came up with the idea of making flowers out of feathers should have been shot. And what's up with all the mirrors?"

"She's using the flowers to create chi, as a remedy against shars—negative energy," I say. "And mirrors reflect shars."

"I wish I had my crystals here," Oma says to herself.

Mom tilts her head to the side and glances into a small mirror tacked up under the cupboard. "This one looks like a fun-house mirror," she says, "which is somehow wryly appropriate."

Oma leans over Mom to check the mirror and gasps, since mirrors that are distorted have a negative effect on chi—then she asks Mom to move her chair so she can take it down. "Damn it, Ma, I need to find a way to get some work done here, since here seems to be where I'm stuck for now. You understand?" Mom gestures toward the living room, where the TV channels are going spastic again, and Oma squeezes between the counter and table to get into the living room to grab the remote.

"What in the hell is the table doing over here, anyway? Never mind," Mom says. She sighs. "Between being back here and not having a damn thing to my name right now ... God, I'm ready to slit my wrists, even if I have to use a dull butter knife to do it."

"Tess, the way you talk!" Oma shouts from the living room.

I think even Mom believes she might bring some bad karma on herself for saying such a thing, because she apologizes quickly for her mood, blames it on the circumstances, suggests maybe she needs her antidepressant dosage upped, then tells me to get back to my reading. I put my head down before I roll my eyes.

In spite of what Mom says—that it's the stress of being homeless and back in this "dump" that is making her so edgy—I know it's about more than those things. "You're only crabby because you haven't talked to Peter in weeks," I tell her.

"Fourteen days, six hours, thirty-two minutes, and twenty-six seconds," Milo says, as he comes into the room and glides to the fridge to pour himself a glass of orange juice.

"Stay out of my business, you two."

I did a paper on the effects of love once, so I know that Mom's in chemical withdrawal. She's restless and not sleeping well, judging from the bags under her eyes. Eyes, I might add, that obviously cry in the night, because they're red and puffy when she wakes. And the other night, when she plugged the charger into her cell phone and the little red light wouldn't go on, she got so upset that she yanked it out of the wall and whipped it against the counter. If the charger wasn't broken before the crash, it certainly was afterward.

Oh, how I loved it when Mom was in the throes of new love! When her brain was shooting dopamine, estrogen, oxytocin, and testosterone into her body like an oil field, tempering her worrying and critical thinking system. During those first couple of months, even when I brought the mail in, she didn't flinch and go into distress mode. I knew, though, even back then, that we'd be in trouble when her brain calmed down and she and Peter had to rely on the bonding chemical, oxytocin, to keep them together. Oxytocin. It's also the "trust" chemical. The one Mom seems incapable of producing when it comes to men, just as some bodies are incapable of producing insulin.

Sure enough, a few months into the relationship, Mom started getting fearful that it wouldn't last—like she thinks all good things can't—and I saw her getting jealous and suspicious every time Peter was late. About that time, I noticed that Peter was spending the night less often too, because I stopped finding him on the couch in the morning, the pillow not even dented from his head, the blanket still folded neatly on the opposite end, and him stretching and giving a fake yawn so that Milo and I would believe (and Milo probably did) that he'd slept on the couch all night, rather than in Mom's bed.

I wrote a second paper then, explaining how after those first five months or so, those outrageous hormones settle down, but a twenty-minute hug or cuddling session is all it takes for a good dose of the trust hormone to be released by the brain all over again.

I pointed out, too, how males need to be touched four times more than females, thinking maybe she'd make those small gestures—a hand on Peter's shoulder, a tap to his belly, or a brush across his back as she passed him to go into the bathroom or kitchen—like she used to do when her brain was going nuts. I was sure she'd get the hint and be grateful for the information and use it. So sure was I that on the night I gave her that second paper, I tagged after Milo when he went into our room to grab a library book and I asked him what he was reading. He turned it around so I could see the cover, some nonsense about quantum superposition and multiple universes. The poor kid got so excited I thought he'd have an asthma attack when I asked him a question just so he'd stay out of the front room and give Mom and Peter enough time for an effective hug. "So," I asked. "If there's more than one universe, how do you know we're both in the same one?"

I flopped down on my bed and endured a forty-five-minute lecture on the topic, thinking that Mom, deficient in the trust hormone as she is, probably needed a little extra time. At first I tried to feign interest, but then I remembered it was Milo and he wouldn't notice the difference. I let my mind drift aimlessly, studying his nostrils and wondering if mine were shaped like two puny peanut shells too and what that shape might mean in Chinese face reading.

Apparently, I suffered through Milo's lecture for naught, though, because after I thanked him for enlightening me, I headed into the front room and found Peter standing by the door. "A good-night hug?" he asked me. As I hugged him, I peeked under his arm at Mom, who was staring down at her laptop screen.

"Why are you leaving so early?"

"I have an early meeting tomorrow, kiddo."

Mom didn't even look up when she said, "Bye, Peter."

Even Mom's farewell to him upset me, because Oma says that people should say, "See you later," or something like that when they part from people they love, knowing they'll see them again (even if it's in the afterlife). Otherwise it can be like a bad omen.

I look back down at my almost-finished book report on the book that *did* turn out to be depressing enough that it made *me* want to swallow Paxil and slit my wrists with a butter knife. I jot a note at the bottom of my page, asking

Mom to please let me pick out my own books from now on because I'm sick of reading sad stories about girls with dead or dying parents.

When I finish, I scoot the report over to Mom, who takes it and stuffs it into the folder sitting beside her laptop. I see Oma out of the corner of my eye, suspiciously watching Mom. She goes off to her room, and when she comes back, she's got a conch shell filled with dried sage. Mom's head is down, but I know it's not going to stay that way long. Oma strikes a match and touches it to the clump of herbs. She gently blows into the shell to get the sage burning, then she starts fanning the thin ribbons of smoke into the air, right over Mom's head. Mom bats at it and cusses, which only makes Oma fan more smoke at her. "You need to be smudged, dear, like it or not. It will help rid you of negativity."

Mom cusses and coughs dramatically.

Oma squeezes between the table and counter, heading into the other room. She fans smoke over Grandpa Sam, who's blankly staring at the TV, then she heads toward the study. "Hey, where you going with that?" Mom shouts. "Oh, she's not taking that in . . ." Mom leaps from her chair. "Not in there, for God's sakes!"

When I get to the study, Mom is chasing Oma around the room, hopping behind and reaching around her like the boys who play basketball at the dangerous park do when they're trying to steal the ball. Oma manages to smudge the long shelf that is filled with books, fossils, arrowheads, and minerals before Mom yanks the shell out of her hand. Milo, working at the desk, barely even notices that he is no longer alone.

"What are you trying to do? Give him an asthma attack

that sends him to the hospital? Geez, Mother, he's doing better now. Leave it that way, will you?"

"Nonsense," Oma says as she follows Mom back into the kitchen. I tag after them both while Milo gripes behind us that we left his door open and he can hear the TV.

"Sage is healing, Tess. Sacred. It won't hurt him, it will help him. Tess, what are you doing? Tess, don't! Dried sage is expensive!"

Mom has the shell in the sink and she's dousing the smoldering sage with water. "Lucy, will you sit down and work already?"

As Oma tries to squeeze the water out of her soggy clump of sage, Mom leans her rear against the counter and rubs the sides of her head. That's when Grandpa Sam shuffles into the kitchen, his jogging pants sagging so that you can see a patch of gray pubic hair between the elastic waistband and his T-shirt. "Oh, for God's sakes. I'm in an asylum!"

That's when the phone rings.

"Lucy, can you get that while I help your grandpa to his chair?" Oma says this as she tugs up his britches and turns him around. "You have to use your walker, Sam, remember?"

I pick up the phone while Mom reaches for her purse strap, strung over the back of the chair by her laptop. "I have to get the hell out of here for a little while," she says.

"Lucy, is that you?"

"Peter!" I shout into the phone. "I was just thinking about you! Only a half an hour ago, at the most!"

Mom's hand freezes, her purse swaying from it like a hypnotist's pendulum.

"Lucy, I'm so relieved that I found you. I've been trying

to locate you guys since the fire. It's been a nightmare try-ing to get information, but I finally found someone in your grandmother's building who knew where she was. I figured you were all together. I've been worried sick. Are you all okay?" Peter is practically shrieking.

"We're fine. We were here in Timber Falls when it hap-pened. But everything is gone. Our books, our computers, everything! Did people die, Peter? Any kids or old people? And did they find out if it was arson? I haven't heard any updates, because Mom says I don't need to know." The minute I say this, I know I've just screwed my chances for learning a thing. And sure enough, he changes the subject abruptly, saying the one thing he knows will distract me. "I miss you, kiddo." He says this as sweetly as Scotty Hamilton ever could.

"I miss you too, Peter," I say. "I wish you were here, so you could ask me a question." Peter says he wishes that too, and Mom motions for me to give her the phone. He suggests that we improvise with another game, by him giving me a quote and me telling him who said it.

Mom tosses her purse on the table and puts her hand in my face, her fingers snapping. "Just wait! Peter is going to give me a quote!"

Mom's hand is as quick as a pickpocket's, so I crouch down and clamp the phone tighter to my ear, wrapping my arm up over my head like a seat belt. "Go ahead, Peter," I say.

He pauses for a bit while he thinks, then he says, "A friend who is far away is sometimes much nearer than one who is at hand. Is not the mountain far more awe-inspiring and more clearly visible to one passing through the valley than to those who inhabit the mountain?"

"I know that one! I know it!" I shout while hopping in

place. "Kahlil Gibran said that!" Then I stop hopping, because I know why he chose this particular quote.

I want to talk to Peter longer, but Mom's fingers are biting into my shoulder like talons. She snatches the phone from me, then jabs her index finger toward my school books. "Hello?" she says, as though she's answering a telemarketer's call.

"Who's on the phone?" Oma asks as she passes through the kitchen with a rolled Depends diaper that smells so acidic that my eyes begin to water.

"Peter," I say, and Oma's face brightens. She pauses and Mom waves her away, so she hurries the soiled diaper outside to the garbage can—removing shar from Mom's space, no doubt, because it's not like she doesn't have enough negativity to deal with already. I open my book and pretend I'm reading, even though I'm sure Mom knows I'm not.

"I'm sorry, Peter. I didn't think of it," she says. She pauses while Peter talks and I strain to make out his tinny words.

"Frankly, no," Mom says. "I actually *didn't* think you'd be worried." Once Milo was watching a special on PBS about Stephen Hawking—one of his favorites—at Oma's. Hawking has a muscular disease and uses one of those devices that pick up the vibrations of the vocal cords so he can speak. Even though the device made him sound oddly mechanical when he spoke, his voice still had more life in it than Mom's voice has at this moment. I think of how alarmed Peter must have been and wish that Mom would use the same tone she used with Mitzy yesterday, to make him feel better.

"No, I couldn't. My cell phone was dead. My charger quit," Mom says, as though her cell was dead this whole time and she had no land line to use. "I ordered a new one and just set it up five minutes ago."

All of a sudden, I hear a loud thump in Grandpa Sam's room. I whiz past Mom and rush to his door. "Mom... Oma... Grandpa Sam fell!"

"I have to go. We have a situation here," Mom says, and she hangs up. Oma comes running from the bathroom, her hands red and wet from the scrubbing she was giving them.

"Oh, my!" Oma says when she sees Grandpa sprawled out on the floor, his head butted up against the box spring.

Oma gets down on her knees and asks Grandpa if he's all right. He's panting and looks stunned, and he doesn't answer. "Give me a hand, Tess."

Mom helps Oma lift Grandpa, and they get him up onto his bed. For a split second there is pity in Mom's eyes. That is, until Grandpa Sam gets tetchy. "I want to watch TV," he says. "I want to get up." His mouth doesn't close all the way when he talks lying down, so his enunciation is poor, but we all understand him.

Oma takes his quilt and covers him. "In just a minute, Sam. Let's make sure you're okay first."

"Where's my keys? Where'd you put my goddamn keys?" he asks, as if he's already forgotten that he was getting out of bed to watch TV. His face is purpled from the effort of raising his voice, but still he manages to muster up enough energy to grab Oma's wrist. He clutches it so hard that the skin whitens around his fingers.

The disdain in his normally complacent face first appears to scare Mom, then it infuriates her. She slaps at his hand until he lets go of Oma. "You don't have a job anymore!" she shouts. "Which is a good thing, considering you're in diapers! Diapers this woman is good enough to change, I might add, even though she doesn't owe you one goddamn thing and never did. So don't you go disrespecting her by raising your voice to her or laying a hand on her. You hear me? Or I'll see to it that your pissy ass gets flung into a nursing home."

Shock blasts Oma's eyes and mouth open. "Tess!" she says. "He's not well. He doesn't know what he's doing."

Mom is breathing so hard that I instinctively count the probable steps to Milo's inhaler, just in case she needs it. "Oh, yeah? Did he not know what he was doing back then either?" Mom bolts from the room and out the door.

I help Oma get Grandpa Sam up and walk in front of him while Oma follows us into the living room. She hurries to get him his pills, saying, "I hope your mom's all right," as she goes.

I watch Mom from the bay window. She heads to the clump of trees I've seen her at before, and she stands for a moment, bent forward, her hands braced against her thighs like a long-distance runner who just made it across the finish line.

chapter

TEN

I'M SITTING on the ground, my arms wrapped around my knees. Oma told me that in the old days, in the Sioux tribe, after a baby was born, the mother would place the baby on the ground and tell her that she was lying on the lap of her mother. I think of this every time I come out here and sit down, only I tell myself that I'm sitting on the lap of my father.

I'm looking at the trees, and wondering when they'll shed in mounds, and hoping we're still here when that happens so I can rake them into a heap and cover myself with them like a blanket. And I'm thinking of how I wish that

I had been here in the summertime, so I could have spread a sleeping bag on my daddy's lap and slept under the stars.

"I'm fine!" I hear Mom shout, then the slamming of the front door and the sound of an engine starting. I move to my hands and knees and creep far enough forward so I can see around the side of the house. Mom is backing out of the drive. She reaches the end and jerks the car to a stop, then backs out so sharply that the rear tires of Roger's Mustang almost hit the culvert. I look up at the sky and wish an eagle would come. Then I'd run inside and beg Oma for some tobacco.

I take a deep breath, like Oma takes, and I lie down on my back, the ground pleasantly cool under me, and watch the clouds tumble by. I love the sky here, clear and sharp and filled with bright stars after dark. Last night I watched them out the window, instead of diving into Mom's notebooks as I had planned, and each one sparkled like glitter, every single speck brilliant.

The screen door opens and Feynman leaps off the porch, Milo behind him. Feynman races to me and slobbers on my face, then runs off to water a tree. Milo comes to me, and, surprisingly, sits down at my side.

"Oma says Peter called." I feel sorry for Milo when I realize that he didn't get to talk to him, because Milo likes Peter as much as I do.

"You would have gotten to talk to him, Milo, if Grandpa Sam hadn't fallen. I only got to because I'm the one who answered the phone. I would have handed it to you next."

Feynman brings Milo a stick, and Milo takes it but doesn't throw it. Instead, he picks at the bark.

"Do you like it here?" I ask him. He shrugs.

"I do." We sit quietly for a moment, and with no book

before him and a bit of sadness in his eyes, it's easy to think of us sharing the same womb.

"Milo, can you keep a secret?" I say in a rush. "I mean *really* keep a secret? Like, if the CIA had you in a torture chamber and was trying to beat the secret out of you, you still wouldn't tell?"

"That's an irrelevant question," he says. "Why would the CIA have an interest in anything you have to tell me?"

I punch him in the arm and he flinches. "Stop being so literal! I'm serious, Milo. I have something I've got to tell somebody, and, unfortunately, you're my only option."

I take a deep breath before spitting it out in a rush. "I'm reading Mom's old journals that are upstairs in her closet. They're full of things that happened back when she was a kid."

Milo's face screws up. "Did Mom say you could read them?"

I roll my eyes and groan. "Of course not, you idiot. If she did, I'd be discussing this with her, not you. Anyway, one Christmas, Grandpa Sam made them a toboggan, but—"

"Well, you shouldn't read them, then."

"Milo! Aren't you even a little curious about their lives back then? About learning why Mom hates Grandpa Sam so much and why Oma divorced him?"

"Not especially," he says, and I gasp in exasperation. "Milo, think of it like the big bang...It's the beginning of us. Our origin. That from which all of our family life force comes."

I can tell that Milo isn't getting it. "You're so frustrating," I say. "I might as well be telling Feynman." I'm forced to rethink that comment, however, because Feynman is watching me with acute interest, his eyes bright, his tongue lapping out of the side of his mouth.

Just then Oma leans out of the doorway and is about to say something but turns her head away. She glances back, lifts one finger to signal "wait," then disappears. I use the opportunity to grab Milo by the sleeve. "Listen. You tattle on me, and you're going to be sorry."

"Who am I going to tattle to? The FBI? The CIA? The Timber Falls sheriff's department?"

Even though I'm angry, I am rather impressed that Milo has made two funnies in such a short amount of time. I don't tell him that, though. Instead, I tell him, "If you even think of tattling, I'll tattle on you."

"For what?" he says, getting up and tossing the stick at last.

I stand up so I can have the advantage of towering over Milo, because I know that just as the alpha wolf will roost at a higher elevation than the rest of the pack to reinforce his position, I'll have an advantage over Milo by standing taller. "I know you were behind the health department coming to test our building. I saw the sites you were visiting online and the articles you were reading. And I saw you snooping at the pipes under the sink too and chipping at the paint on the windowsills when you thought no one was watching. You e-mailed them as though you were a concerned adult tenant, didn't you?"

Milo, who never gets rattled (except when he's having an asthma attack or can't study), suddenly grows pale. "I... I didn't mean for anything bad to happen. I couldn't breathe there."

I'm suddenly sorry I said it. "You didn't start the fire. I'm just saying... Well, just don't tattle, or I will."

Suddenly Oma bursts out the door, a box of old junk in her arms. "I was just about to bring this stuff to the shed when I thought of something. Oh, this will be such fun for you kids," she says. She zips across the lawn, half hopping, half jogging. "Come! Come!"

She leads us to the shed and shoves against the door with her shoulder. "I don't know why I didn't think of this before now."

The door is jammed, so we help her ram against it. It opens with a creak and a scrape.

A haze of moldy dust forms in the sunlight let in when we finally get the door open, and Oma tells Milo to wait outside so his asthma doesn't start acting up.

The workbench that runs against one wall is coated with dust, as are the tools hanging from Peg-Board above it and all along a second wall. The shed is cramped with things I imagine got stacked there over the years since Grandpa Sam last used it for making his wood projects. Things like a roll of chicken wire, a lawn mower, a rain barrel, a few crocks, and everyday items much too dull to have Oma so excited.

"Move, Feynman," Oma says as she shimmies behind an old dresser. "Oh, they're still here! Give me a hand moving this stuff, Lucy," she says.

"Bikes!" I shout when Oma backs one up far enough for me to see its skinny back tire and red wheel cover.

Oma and I work swiftly to make a path through the junk to steer the bikes out. Milo looks confused about all our enthusiasm. "We don't even know how to ride bikes," he says, and Oma says it's easy and that we'll learn. Milo doesn't look so sure.

We push the bikes to the backyard, then Oma hurries back to the shed to get some spray, because the chains are corroded with rust. The bikes are old-fashioned 10-speeds, with handlebars that are curved down like rams' horns. One bike, the red one, is a girls' bike, and the blue one is a boys'. The difference between them is something that's always perplexed me: why they would design a boys' bike with a bar for them to get wracked on and girls' bikes with none, even though girls don't really have anything to wrack. I ponder this as Milo and I stand across the yard so we won't breathe the fumes from the WD-40 Oma is spraying on the chains, her cheeks bulging as she holds her breath. I'm guessing that the barless bike for girls was created by some dad in the old days when girls always wore dresses, so that when his little princess swung her leg over the back tire to get on, the neighborhood boys wouldn't see her bloomers, which is what Oma said they called those big underpants girls used to wear. I like the boys' bike best but know that to grab that one and make Milo ride the girls' bike could get him beat up if there are any boys within a five-mile radius of here—even if they aren't gangsters.

"Now what?" I ask, holding the handlebars of the red bike propped against me, once Oma gets the chains rotating smoothly.

"Why, you get on them," Oma says. "Here, I'll show you."

Oma takes the bike, swinging her Tina Turner leg through the no-bar space and hoisting her butt onto the triangle seat. She props her slipper on the pedal and pushes down, setting the bike in motion. She rides in slow circles. "Oh, my," she giggles as she wobbles over the grass, "I haven't ridden a bike in years. What fun!"

As she rides, Oma explains that she's wobbling because she's on the grass and riding in circles, so can't get up enough speed to glide smoothly. "That's the trick of learning to ride a bike," she says. "You have to get up enough speed to stop wobbling." As she rides, making bigger circles until she's encompassing the whole yard, Feynman runs alongside her, his ears flapping happily as he goes.

Back home, there was a man who rode his bike every day during the warmer seasons. I'd watch him whiz by under the window in his tight-fitting cycling shorts, his helmet one of those high-tech kinds with an aerodynamic point at the back that always reminded me of a pterodactyl's head. Every time I saw him, I'd think of how fun it would be to ride a bike. Actually, however, riding a bike for the first time is not so fun.

I can't find my balance, which shouldn't surprise me, since I have no balance to speak of in the first place. I can't pedal more than two rotations before I'm yelling, "Whoa!" and tipping over again. Oma hurries to me then, helping me up and holding the bike 'til I get back on. She keeps her grip on the back of the bike seat and one handlebar and jogs alongside me. "That's it, that's it," she says ... until she lets go and I crash again.

Milo, on the other hand, is a natural. His face is screwed up in concentration as he pedals, going slowly and wobbling but going all the same. "That's it, Milo!" Oma shouts now and then.

I'm rubbing my leg where the pedal scraped my skin when I fell, and Oma has my bike half lifted when she stops and says, "Did you hear that?"

I listen. "Hear what?"

"I thought I heard a car in the driveway. I guess not. It must have been the wind."

That's not the only trick the wind is up to either, I decide after my hundredth fall. I look over at Milo, who is no longer wobbling as his bike scoots around the entire yard, and I am convinced that it *has* to be the wind that's foiling my attempts to learn to ride a bike. And, of course, it's not like the wind would be a factor with Milo, since he's so thin that there would be little wind resistance even if the winds were at the speed of an F5 tornado.

I try riding until my frustration level is maxed, then Oma says maybe we should take a break and go inside. "Sam is probably ready to go lie down for his afternoon nap," she says, though I'm thinking that her ending our afternoon bike-riding lesson has more to do with the way Milo's puny chest is heaving. "Come on, Milo," Oma calls.

Milo looks elated as he slides off the blue bike and fiddles to pull the kickstand down with his hand. "They don't call it a *kick*stand for nothing there, genius." My jibe goes right over his pointy head, so Oma goes over to show him how to lower the metal rod by kicking it with the back of your heel.

"Can we go on the road later?" he asks. "I could go much faster on asphalt." I can tell by the gleam in his eye that Milo has finally found one activity besides studying that makes him happy, and I easily imagine him as a grown man: pterodactyl head and hairy, skinny legs pumping beneath black Nike tights.

"Maybe after you get more skilled. But you'll have to talk to your mother about that," Oma says.

Oma holds the door open for us and calls to Feynman, who is sniffing something at the fence. Milo claps and calls, but the dog doesn't come. Milo says that he needs a drink of water, so Oma tells him to go inside and she'll wait for Feynman. I'm crossing the yard to join her when she casually turns her head toward the driveway and her peaceful, balanced mood crashes. "Lucy! Go see if your grandfather's in his chair. Hurry! His truck is gone!

"Oh, don't tell me..." she says, and we split up, checking

each room, calling his name. "I was sure I had every set of keys he owned hidden."

My quadriceps tingle uncomfortably, and my ears buzz with fright at the thought of Grandpa Sam behind the wheel. "Call 911!" I shout.

OMA INCORRECTLY dials twice, so Milo takes the phone from her and punches in the three numbers. Oma is a stammering mess as she explains our precarious situation to the voice at the other end of the line. "How would I know where he might be headed? He's not in his right mind!" she says.

"To work!" I say. "His lunch box is gone. It was sitting right here on the counter with all the other things you were going to bring to the shed."

"Oh, oh," Oma says. "Excuse me, sir. I think I know where he might have gone." Oma gives him the name and address of the paper mill where Grandpa Sam used to work, then she repeats the model and make of his black truck and ends with, "Yes, please hurry. That man is going to hurt himself or someone else. He can hardly walk or think anymore."

After Oma hangs up, she hands me the phone. "Call your mother's cell, Lucy. I imagine she's with Mitzy."

I call Mom as Oma paces and wrings her hands. Mom answers, and I hear Mitzy's musical laugh in the background. "Hi, Ma. What is it?"

"It's me, Mom. Oma told me to call you and tell you that Grandpa Sam is gone."

I hear an intake of breath.

"What's wrong?" Mitzy asks Mom.

"He's dead," I hear Mom say. "I don't understand . . . He looked okay this morning. He fell, but he seemed okay." Mom is obviously crying now, but her voice is muffled, like she has the phone pressed against her shoulder, receiver side down.

"Mom! Mom!" I shout into the phone.

The muffled sound disappears, and Mitzy's voice asks, "Lillian?"

"No, it's me, Lucy."

"You tell your grandmother that we'll be right there."

"No, wait! Grandpa Sam's not *that* kind of gone. He's gone, as in missing-in-action. He took his truck and drove off. Oma called the police, and then she told me to call Mom."

"Ohhh!" The sound muffles again, but I can hear enough to know that Mitzy is explaining the situation to Mom. Her voice sounds like squirrel chatter. She comes back on the line again and says, "We'll be right there."

I hang up the phone and take Oma's hand, which is shaking hard. "It'll be okay, Oma. The police are looking for him, and Mom and Mitzy are coming to help too. We'll find him."

When the phone rings, Oma snatches it quickly. "Hello?" she asks, her eyes pools of anxiety. "Oh, hello, Jeana," she says, grimacing. "No, no. Nothing's wrong. I was just waiting for an important call . . . Yes . . . No—Jeana? Can I call you back? I really need to leave the line open for my call."

Oma hangs up and we go outside and cross the lawn, our hair and clothes flapping in the wind. The trees are in full glory now, the countryside smudged with color as far as the eye can see. Stray leaves are skipping across the ground.

We peer down the road on both sides, looking for any signs of a vehicle. The road to the east is sloped so that there's a blind spot at the dip between the two hills. We stand long enough to see that there's no car rising up out of the depression, then pace back into the yard.

While we wait, Oma rocks from foot to foot and walks to the edge of the road again. She looks both ways, then comes back to stand by Milo and me. She does this every few seconds.

"May I go ride my bike in the backyard?" Milo asks, and I call him stupid and tell him no, because Oma's too busy muttering a prayer to answer him.

"Why not?"

"Your mother's coming!" Oma calls when she checks the road again. I run to the edge of the yard to look. Sure enough, there is a splotch of red coming down the second hill, followed by the sea green of Mitzy's van.

Mom hurries out of the car to us, as does Mitzy. "Well, he's not between here and Mitzy's, anyway," she says.

"Oma told the police to check the mill. He took his lunch box," I tell them.

Everyone is talking at once, then Mom stops. "Is that the phone ringing?" We all shut up and listen, but with the wind so noisy, we can't tell. "Run and see, Lucy," Mom says, and I sprint fast. I'm not even halfway through the living room when the ringing stops.

"It stopped ringing when I got inside," I tell Mom when she comes in.

"Shit," she says.

It's quickly decided that Oma will wait by the phone, Milo with her, while Mitzy and Mom drive separately to search. I'm going with Mom, but only because I don't stop begging and she says there's no time to argue.

Mitzy makes a left turn down a road marked Venison Drive, where Grandpa Sam used to go after work some-times to fish in a little trout stream that runs across the road, and Mom and I are heading down a road called Benders Crossing. When we reach the end, Mom turns around in a parking lot outside of a bar called Pauly's and heads back in the direction we came from, taking a right to lead us away from the house. At the moment, Mom doesn't look like a daughter who doesn't love her father.

We ride over one gentle hill, then come to a stretch of short, steep ones. I gawk from side to side, looking for any sign of Grandpa Sam's black Ford.

We come to a fork in the dirt road, and Mom slows as she ponders which way to go. That's when her cell rings.

"What? What in the hell are you talking about, Ma?" Mom listens, mutters a few more questions, then hangs up and dials Mitzy.

"You're not going to believe this one," she says. "The cops caught up with Dad just across the Taylor County line. He's driving, and two squad cars are chasing him. He's going thirty to forty miles an hour, but he won't stop.

They've been following him for about twenty miles now. It's a low-speed chase." Mom pauses for a second, then says, "No, I'm not kidding!...Uh-huh. He's looped around and is heading back toward Timber Falls. I'm going to head downtown."

Once we get to town, we have no trouble spotting Grandpa Sam. He's in the truck that's leading two squad cars down Main Street—sirens roaring, lights blinking—as though he's a parade marshal. On the street, one little boy lets go of his mother's hand long enough to wave at Grandpa Sam, and an old guy gawks at Oma's vintage car.

"I can't believe this!" Mom keeps repeating as we follow Grandpa Sam up one street and down the other.

"Look," I shout. "The officer on the passenger side has a megaphone!"

We roll down our windows, and we can hear the officer, even with the wind thumping into the car. "Pull your vehicle slowly over to the side of the road. This is police orders, Mr. McGowan. Pull your vehicle over to the side of the road."

But Grandpa Sam doesn't. He keeps driving, right out of town, the cops following him. Mom and I, with Mitzy behind us, add our vehicles to the parade.

I lean my head out the window to get a better view now that we're on a flat straightaway, and the wind smears my hair away from my face. "He's turning!"

"He's turning into the parking lot at Joe's Pub. Where in the hell does he think he's going?" Mom says into her cell to Mitzy.

Grandpa Sam's truck follows the driveway in, then loops back out. Three cars in the opposite lane of the highway are pulled over on the gravel in response to the police sirens, and Grandpa Sam almost sideswipes one of them as he pulls back onto the road. "For crying out loud," Mom says, "how stupid are they not to have thought of blocking both entrances with their cars when he pulled in?"

"Oh, it doesn't mean they're stupid," I tell Mom. "Look at Milo. He's brilliant, yet he couldn't figure out how to let down a *kick*stand."

We spin around in the feed mill's drive too and follow Grandpa Sam back down Main Street, where more onlookers have gathered, gesturing and nodding. "Crissakes," Mom says to Mitzy. "We've got Mr. Magoo on the loose, and no one to stop him but Barney Fife and Mr. Bean."

As we follow Grandpa Sam and the police out of town again, I grimace along with Mom each time we see his truck veer over onto the gravel or into the left lane. "Where in the hell could he be going?" Mom huffs.

"Maybe he's headed home," I say.

But he's not.

We approach our house, where Milo is circling the yard on his bike.

That is, until he hears the sirens and stops, straddles the bike for a second, stares in our direction, then dismounts his bike to run into the house. We barely pass the driveway when Oma erupts onto the lawn, her hand capped above her eyes so that she looks like she's saluting.

About a quarter of a mile past our house, there are two squad cars, one parked on either side of the road, and sawhorses painted hunters' orange strung across both lanes. "Oh, shit!" Mom says, no doubt because there's no sign that Grandpa Sam intends to stop.

And he doesn't.

He merely drives into the gentle ditch alongside the roadblock, skirts past them, then creeps back onto the road.

The two squad cars tagging Grandpa Sam don't stop, so

we follow suit. Down in the ditch we go, and back up on the highway. I turn around to look at the officers standing beside the road as we pass the blockade and see one remove his hat and whack it against his thigh.

Down the hill we go again, and then up and down two more. And when Grandpa Sam reaches the top of the fourth hill, he swirls into the first drive on the right.

As Mom follows the officers into the driveway, I spot the name *Bickett* slapped on the mailbox across from it in gold stick-on letters. Nordine Bickett. The mother of the Tiny Tim, the lucky recipient of Mom and Uncle Clay's toboggan. Even in the notebook, there was a mysterious feel surrounding her name, and now, as we enter her property, that same feeling returns, only stronger.

"So this is where Nordine Bickett lives," I say.

"I can't believe he came here!" Mom says into her cell, then turns to me. "How do you know about Nordine Bickett?"

I cringe a bit, realizing, of course, that I just used a name I knew only from Mom's notebook.

"Oma mentioned her," I lie.

I get off the hook for one reason and one reason only: Grandpa Sam has just plowed into the Bicketts' garage.

We jump out of the car and head to Grandpa Sam's truck. The front end is embedded in the old wooden garage door, steam sizzling out from the hole and rolling up over the hood. One of the officers has the driver's side door open by the time we reach him, and Grandpa Sam is sitting behind the wheel, blood seeping from the egg forming over his right eyebrow.

The officers—one tall and chinless, and the other short and shaped like the SpongeBob SquarePants character on my sticker—move so we can get to Grandpa Sam. "Dad, are you okay?"

He doesn't answer Mom, but his dull eyes find me and he says my name.

I take his hand and squeeze it. "You're going to be okay, Grandpa Sam."

A screen door squeals then, and a little man with wild white hair yellowed like a smoker's fingers and thick, protruding eyebrows that sit like canopies over his eyes comes out of the house. His plaid shirt is only half tucked into his greasy work pants.

"Mr. Bickett," the chinless officer says. "We've had a little incident here, as you can see."

Moving like a young man, the little old man shoots across the yard and stops at the garage, staring in disbelief. He scoots to the truck and leans close to peer through the windshield. "Sam McGowan, is that you?" His face screws up with rage, creating a million more wrinkles, and his flubbery lips bunch up to hide his bare gums. He lifts his fist—walnut small, like Milo's—and shakes it before the glass. "Didn't I warn you that I'd blow your head off if I ever caught you on my property again? You son of a bitch, you!"

"Henry," the shorter officer says. "No need for that, now. Sam didn't know where he was going."

Henry Bickett runs around the back of the truck, slips between the bumper and the squad car, comes up between the officers, and shoves at their arms to weasel between them. The officers are quick, though, and they grab his elbows, yanking him back. "Hold it there, Mr. Bickett. No need for this," the taller officer says.

I glance at Mitzy, who has a grin on her face, and at Mom, who's staring in disbelief at the little man who is on his tiptoes, straining to get loose.

"Calm down there, Mr. Bickett. Calm down."

It seems no one but me notices the small woman standing near the garden. She comes toward us. Her hair is pure white and all one length, parted at the side and neatly curled under just below her ears. She has a velvet bow on one side of her head, level with her eyes. Her face is heart-shaped and girlish-looking, even though she's Grandma Moses old. While the officers are squabbling with Henry Bickett, the old woman meanders around the garage and comes out on our side. She comes straight to the truck and slips between me and Mom.

Up close, I can see that Nordine's lips are painted a summery pink and that there's a hint of blue eye shadow shimmering on her creased lids. She smells like lilac talcum powder. She reaches out and touches Grandpa Sam's arm with a small, veined hand and says, "Ohhh." Her deep-set hazel eyes glisten, though I don't know if it's tears making them wet or just that watery eyes look that old people get.

"Nordine, I'm warning you. You get away from that scoundrel right now!"

"Now, now, Henry," SpongeBob says. "Mr. McGowan has dementia and he doesn't even know where he is, much less who's talking to him. And your Nordine . . . well, seems to me they're in the same boat."

But the officer's wrong.

I can see it in Grandpa's eyes, and feel it in the way Nordine's body softens as she looks at him, that there's a flicker of recognition in them both. Grandpa Sam's memory, though, is erased in a slow blink, leaving me to wonder if I'd only imagined it.

Nordine takes a lace-edged handkerchief from the sleeve of her sweater and dabs at the blood seeping from

Grandpa Sam's eyebrow. The gesture makes me sad. Not only for them because they are old, but for Oma, because I now believe I know what was true back then: Once, Nordine Bickett was Grandpa Sam's girlfriend.

Henry Bickett really goes nuts when Nordine wipes Grandpa's brow, and the officers have to grab him again.

The cops won't let us take Grandpa Sam out of the truck. "That cut above his eye needs stitches," the chinless cop says, his head cocked sideways as he talks to Mom and Mitzy.

"I'll take him to the hospital," Mom says, but the officers insist on calling an ambulance. "You folks don't get much action around here, do you?" Mom says, and the tall officer's already pink cheeks flush to a deep red. He reaches through the opened window of the squad car and grabs his radio.

We have to wait for what seems forever before we hear the siren screaming down the highway and even longer before we see the ambulance coming down the Bicketts' driveway. Mom cringes at the sound, as if the volume of the siren pains her, even though she's not profoundly gifted.

While they tuck Grandpa Sam up into the ambulance, Nordine Bickett watches, wringing the blood-splotched hanky in her hands. She sees me looking at her and we share a glance that means something, but I'm not quite sure what, and then she wanders off, walking aimlessly across the yard.

Henry Bickett doesn't have to be restrained any longer, but he's still in an uproar about his smashed garage door. The officers assure him that Grandpa's insurance will pay for the damage, but he's not comforted. "It doesn't, and I'll take it out of his hide," he says.

* * *

A<small>N HOUR</small> and a half later, a nurse is pushing Grandpa Sam out to our car in a wheelchair. He has a bandage over his swollen forehead. "He has six stitches," she says, "but his concussion is a mild one. You'll want to keep an eye on him for a while, though. Any vomiting and you should call us."

Mom thanks her, and we slip back into the car. "You'd have thought they would have changed him, for crissakes," Mom grumbles, because the car already stinks and we're not even buckled in yet.

When we pull in the drive, Oma rushes out of the house. "Sam!" she says. "I was petrified when the ambulance went by. Thank God Tess called to say you were all right." She opens the car door and unbuckles him. Oma, I notice, does not look at Grandpa Sam with moist eyes like Nordine did. Instead, she looks like the mother of a toddler who has just fallen and thumped his head.

"So what did he hit? A road sign?" Oma asks. Mom and Mitzy share an unspoken moment, and I know they're contemplating whether or not to tell her that he ended up in Nordine Bickett's garage. After much hemming and hawing, Mom tells her. Oma smiles at Mom's worried look. "Oh, honey. Do you really think that after all this time I'd be upset over hearing that Sam went to Nordine's?" She rolls her eyes and shakes her head, but when she looks back at Grandpa Sam, she doesn't exactly look like a loving mother anymore either.

We get Grandpa Sam into the house and into his room so Oma can change him, then Mom helps Oma bring him to his lift chair. Once he's situated, Mom sits down on the arm of the couch and stares at him. Mitzy moves to Mom and places her hand on Mom's shoulder. Mom looks up at her and smiles weakly.

While Mom and Mitzy have tea and Oma cooks supper in the kitchen, I go in the living room and stand by Grandpa Sam. Oma has cleaned him up, and his hair has dried into one wispy curl.

"You went for a drive today, didn't you, Grandpa?" He looks up at me, and he looks confused, like he can't remember.

THAT NIGHT I wait for Mom to tell me to go to bed the usual three times before I make my way upstairs. Before getting in bed, though, I sit cross-legged on the floor in front of the closet and search through the stacks of notebooks for any mention of Nordine Bickett or my father—Mom may have known him while she was still a girl, just like Nordine knew Grandpa Sam. I'm so engrossed in finding their names that I don't hear Mom's footsteps on the stairs.

"What's your light still doing on at—" She stops. She looks at the notebook in my hand, then at the opened closet. "Lucy Marie McGowan, what do you think you're doing?"

She yanks the notebook out of my hand, then scoops up the pile of loose ones from my lap. "I can't believe you'd have the audacity to dig through my personal things like this, Lucy!" she says. "Haven't I taught you to be more respectful of other people's privacy than this?"

"Actually, no, you didn't. You read my letter to Scotty."

"That's different!" Mom says.

"It is not!"

"But I'm your mother!"

"What does that have to do with it?" I'm getting lippy, and I know it, but I can't help myself. "It's not my fault I have to go snooping around. I want to know about my family, and I want to know about my dad. You won't tell me anything, so what am I supposed to do?"

"I don't care what your reasons are, Lucy. That's no excuse for poking your nose into my personal journals. You're grounded off the bike for a week. You hear me? A week!"

"That's not fair!" I shout, so angry that I can feel my face burning. "The punishment doesn't even fit the crime. And it shouldn't be a crime, anyway. My dad could be a doctor, an ax murderer, or your cousin, for all I know. It's not fair!"

"Not another word, Lucy. Stop it right now."

But I'm too upset to stop. "You might hate your dad, but at least you know what kind of a person he is. I don't know one thing about mine, but I have a right to."

"I'm warning you, Lucy. Not another word or you'll get more than a week!"

As if the issue at hand—having the search for information interrupted—isn't bad enough, I suddenly think of how much better at riding a bike Milo already is than me and of how much better he'll get in another week's time, and I'm double-fuming. "I'll bet you even lied about his last name. Smith!" I huff. "The most common surname in this country. You were probably sucking on a Smith Brothers cough drop when you came up with that one!"

"You just earned yourself two weeks."

I know I look like an angry baby, sitting on the floor with legs and arms crossed. I can even feel my chin jutting out like Henry Bickett's. I don't want any more grounded time, though, so I make myself take a cleansing breath. It helps some, even though I took a shallow one so Mom doesn't accuse me of turning into a New Age "wacko" like Oma.

I can't totally stop myself, but my anger level is lower. "Maybe I shouldn't have snooped, but I just want to know where Milo and I come from. And that means knowing who our dad is, and who our grandparents used to be too, for that matter. I already know that Grandpa Sam was mean to you guys in the olden days, and that he had Nordine Bickett for his girlfriend, even though he was married to Oma. I just want to know the whole story of our beginnings."

Mom reaches into the closet, sets the notebooks she snatched from me on the pile, then lifts the whole stack. "Lucy, listen to me..."

She stares at me for a moment, as though she wants to say something. I wait. But then all she says is, "It's been a stressful day for all of us. Let it be enough for today, okay?"

She sets the heap of notebooks on the edge of the dresser, then she reaches down to help me up. She presses her cheek against the top of my head and holds me for a while, her breath warm against my scalp, and she sways with me like we're slow dancing. "I'm sorry," she says in a whisper.

She pulls away, gathers the notebooks in her arms, and says, "But you still have two weeks," as she goes out the door.

Later that night, still upset about Mom finding me reading the notebooks but with nobody to talk to about it, I slip down the stairs. Mom is at her laptop and doesn't look up, and Oma is on the phone talking to Aunt Jeana. "No. No. There was just a problem with my apartment back home and I was waiting for a call on that... Yes, of course. He's fine. Sleeping like a baby," she says.

I go to Grandpa Sam's room, but I don't go inside. He's

lying on his back, like he always is, a couple pillows under him because Oma says it will help him breathe better. He doesn't look like a cute ugly baby to me now. He looks like a scary man who would kick boxes and be a cheater—which is what the rust-colored-haired woman on the stoop called her husband when she ranted at him that he should be castrated, after finding out he had a girlfriend on the side.

I leave Grandpa's door open a crack because Oma likes it that way, give Oma a hug, and go to bed.

ON SATURDAY **Oma** spends the whole day in the kitchen, whipping up gourmet recipes she gets out of the cookbook written by her favorite chef. He's some German guy with spiky hair and wacky glasses who has a PBS cooking show. She is cooking fancy today because we're having dinner guests: Mitzy and Ray, and Marie and her husband, Al, who wasn't going to come at first (because he's in pain over a potential hernia—potential because, who knows? He won't see a doctor) but he's coming anyway, out of fear that he'll starve to death before Marie gets home with his doggie bag. Mom doesn't like to cook, but she breaks herself away from her laptop at intervals to wash dishes as Oma dirties

them, and I sit at the table doing schoolwork, while Milo—
Mr. Lucky—pedals his bike like a pro on the road.

Oma is sipping lemongrass tea as she cuts parchment
paper into heart-shaped pouches. "Oh, I'm making the most
wonderfully balanced meal," she tells me. "Sole en papil-
lote on sautéed baby spinach with tomato fettuccini. But
your mother couldn't find sole in town, so I'm using floun-
der. The book says to use only sole, but what is a chef in
Timber Falls to do? See? You butter the pouches and stuff
the fish and vegetables inside." She holds up a heart and
points to the empty inside.

Oma has her recipe book propped up and braced open
on the table. On the cover there are three pieces of shrimp
lying belly-side-up in a death pose, their backs crutched
against a wad of greens. Two chives, grass-green and thin,
are propped into the salad and stick up like antennae. I've
seen the inside of this cookbook before, so I know that all of
the dishes created by this chef, who studied in France, are
arranged like this. When I first saw the food stacked up on
the plates like Legos and Lincoln Logs, I thought of how
unique cultures are. How here in America, if a child plays
with his dinner, making tunnels in his mashed potatoes and
towers with his broccoli sprigs, his mother is apt to scold
him. But in France, if a child plays with his food, his
mother is likely to say, "Look, Jean Pierre, our Paul Henri is
a genius! A master chef in the making!"

Oma has sticky notes marking the recipes she's going to
use. I ask anyway, rather than bother to look to see what else
she's making.

Oma proudly recites the exotic names of the dishes
she'll serve. "We'll start with an amuse bouche to entice our
palates: lemon-mint sorbet with red peppercorns. Our soup
will be..." I tune out temporarily, because I don't know

what any of those dishes really are, then tune back in when her tone tells me she's winding down. "...And we'll conclude our meal with a delicious dessert, pumpkin pots de crème. A perfectly balanced meal," Oma repeats.

When she starts reciting which ingredients will refresh and invigorate our "pitta," and which will reduce our "excessive dosha," Mom looks up from her laptop, blinks at Oma, then turns to me. "What in the hell is she talking about?"

"Ayurveda," I say, enunciating the Hindi word as clearly as possible. "*Ayur*, which means *life*. *Veda*, which means *knowledge of*. It's a holistic healing system developed by the Brahmin sages in India, some three to five hundred years ago. It—"

Mom waves her hand. "Okay, you can stop right there. That's more than I care to know." She shakes her head in quick little jerks so it looks like it's vibrating. "Was it too much to hope that her *balanced meal* would mean selections from the four basic food groups?"

"Oh, no," Oma groans. "I forgot to put walnuts on my list. Oh, Tess, you'll have to run back to town. I need them for the dressing."

"Mother, I'm working."

"Please, honey. Please."

Mom grumbles, then gets her purse and leaves.

"Oh, dear," Oma says as she pivots this way and that, two bowls in her hands, and some odd kitchen gadget pinned against her waist with her elbow. "This kitchen never had enough work space. Honey, could you please take your books in the living room or upstairs? I need the table."

I close my books and stack them, and before I can get them gathered in my arms, Oma looks at Mom's laptop, also sitting on the table, and she says, "Maybe you should take your Mom's laptop up to her room too."

In the living room, Grandpa Sam is watching—or not watching—some western from about 1902, so I head upstairs. I go to the guest room first and set Mom's computer on the nightstand, then head to my room, where I toss my books and notebook on the rolltop desk and sit down.

I'm slouched over the desk, my head propped on my hand, my fingertips tapping against my temple. It's hard to concentrate on my work with the good smells wafting upstairs—and with Mom's laptop sitting in the next room.

My pencil has rolled to the edge of the desk and is lying there. I hate writing with a pen or a pencil. It feels foreign, and my cursive hand looks like that of a five-year-old. I miss typing. I miss the soft click of the keys and seeing each letter nudge the cursor out of the way.

I glance across the hall and into the empty room. Back home, our computers are lying like burned toast under a giant heap of rubble. We had our own desktops, HPs. Twins just like us. I miss my computer terribly. I miss my favorite sites, like the Jungian forum, where bright (and sometimes not so bright) nonscholars hash out Jung's theories and play out the archetypes. I miss MySpace, where millions of nobodies like me have Web sites right along with the somebodies, and I can read Brad Listi's attention deficit disorder blog, which keeps me abreast of the stranger cultural happenings, and make friends just by clicking *add me*.

I miss *PostSecret.com* too, where people anonymously send in artistically designed postcards, revealing their darkest secrets. Once there was a postcard picture of Epcot Center, with a cutout picture of two babies pasted at the bottom. Two strips of white paper with typed fonts said, *He went up the elevator, and I went out the door. It was the last time he saw his kids.* For two weeks I asked Mom if she was *sure* Milo and I had never been to Epcot Center, but finally gave up because I never saw even one smidgen of defensiveness in her body language any of the ten times I asked.

I get up then and get Mom's laptop, bringing it back into her old room and setting it on the desk. It's hibernating, so I don't have to boot it, which is good, since that would probably require a password.

It's my intention to open a Word document and type simply for the pleasure of feeling my fingers tap-dancing over the keyboard, but then my curiosity gets the best of me and I open her documents box.

There are several folders inside, including one that says, *Latest projects.* I click it open. Inside, there are chapters from Missy Jenkins's latest struggle with Satan, and a file with *Mexico* in the title, so it must be another travel article, and the third document in the folder—the one that grabs my attention—is simply titled *September 21.* Just last night!

I open the file and read:

The house is quiet, the kids asleep, and Ma is in her room reading. I told her I needed to get some writing done, so of course she thought I meant on my novel. And I do need to work on the damn thing. I've got one month to make deadline, and Missy is still waltzing into the church bake sale, loaves of sourdough bread stuffed in her bag, horny Chase Milford sniffing her instead of it. She's been in this pose so long that that bread has got to be moldy by now.

I've got my travel article to write too, but Linda's laid up with two ruptured disks, and the only photo she's sent in three weeks is one of her lying down, taken by her latest toy from the foot of her bed, the bottom of her boobs spread out and showing under a shirt she cropped herself. She's holding up a bottle of tequila, the thumb of her other hand pointed toward her head, like she's too damn drunk—or too retarded—to figure out she needs to point it toward the ceiling if she's making a thumbs-up while lying down. Hmm, maybe I could write about Timber Falls. Ma obviously thinks it's a great vacation spot. For activities, I could list squirrel hunting and participating in the annual low-speed chase. And for the dining section, I could cite tuna salad croissants, stuffed with kettle corn chips and peppered with succulent dead skin cells.

God, I'm sarcastic.

I'm restless tonight. Distracted. I can't seem to think of anything but Peter, who called last night for the first time since Dad fell on his ass. He was waiting for me to call him back, he said, then he told me that he must be slow on the uptake, because it took him a good twenty-four hours to admit that the crisis that made it necessary for me to hang up on him had to have passed and that I really had no intention of returning his call.

I wanted to spill my guts to him. To sob and wail and tell him how messed up I am here and how badly I miss him. I wanted to beg him to come and hold me. To listen to me rant and sob and assure me that the past is over and that it can no longer sink me (which, considering he only knows a handful of my past, is an absurd wish to begin with). Instead, I gave him the vague excuse of my being too busy to return his call and muttered a quick "sorry."

It was obvious that he didn't intend to talk to me long, and when I tried to keep him on longer—just so I could extract some comfort from the sound of his voice—by asking him about his work, what he was reading, and other banal things, he interrupted and told me that he wasn't in the mood for small talk and that I could call him if I wanted to "really" talk. I hung up and avoided Lucy's eyes for fear that she'd be able to tell from my expression that it was Peter at the other end of the line.

I spent the remainder of the day wandering restlessly in and out of the house, trying to avoid thinking of anything but how I was going to maneuver Missy Jenkins through the next chapter. I came up with nothing, so I spent an hour with Milo, listening to his theories that support the concept of time travel. At least I kept my sardonic humor to myself, not saying out loud what I was thinking: that if science truly wanted to study time travel, they could skip the high-tech machines and just send a person back to their childhood home.

Ma came out of her room for water a while ago. I minimized this screen and put my book up instead, leaning close to the monitor as though I was trying to think up my next line.

She filled her water glass, and the rock sunk at the bottom—put there so the "energy" from it could be ingested—bobbled against the glass. I could feel her studying me. And finally she asked me if Peter was responsible for my mood today. Her leomongrass tea must not be working, if she needed to ask.

I denied that my mood had anything to do with Peter, of course. I told her that I have more important things to think of than a guy who only serves as a reminder of why I vowed never to marry and to use a sperm bank if I decided I wanted kids. (At least I kept one of those promises to myself.)

God, I hate when people stare at me. It makes me want to scream. I looked up at her and snapped, "Do you mind? I have work here to do."

She didn't make a move to head back to her room, so I ignored her, hoping she'd go away. She didn't. Instead, she asked
me why I try to hide how I feel about Peter. And she asked me
what exactly it is that I'm afraid of.

I could feel my shoulders rise up and draw in—as if to
protect my head and heart at the same time—when I denied
being afraid of anything.

Wrong answer.

She pulled out a chair and sat down and asked me if I
knew what she thought of today. I told her she's the psychic,
not me, so, no, I didn't know. She let my bitchy tone roll off her
like a bad shar (or whatever in the hell it is that Lucy said she
calls bad juju), and I knew I was in for one of her long-
winded, heaped-with-New-Age-bullshit stories meant to
teach me a life lesson.

She asked me if I remembered the young woman, Sally
Rutherford, who lived in the Norton place on Venison Drive
the summer when I was about nine years old. The woman who
painted the watercolor hanging in her bedroom back home,
and did I know which painting she was talking about? I reminded her that she has only one painting hanging in her
bedroom.

Even though I'd just told her I knew which painting she
meant, she described it. Talking about the woman emerging
out of the water, the crown of her head barely breaking the
water's surface. She reminded me of the first time I'd seen it,
when I reached out and touched it as though I'd expected the
water to wet my finger.

I typed a nonsensical sentence just so I'd look busy, hoping
she'd keep her story short. She didn't. She yammered on and
on about Sally's big, listless eyes. How she was so timid that
the sound of her own voice seemed to spook her, but how she

painted bravely, trying imaginative new styles, not afraid of color. Then she told me that she always thinks of Sally's painting at times like this.

I switched my tone from bitchy to bored as I asked her what she meant by "times like this."

She blinked at me like the answer was obvious, then she clarified it with, "Times like this, when somebody is too afraid to break the surface and spring out of the sea of whatever is drowning them. It always makes me wonder: What if they dared come up all the way?"

I glanced up and Ma was staring upward, her eyes focused on nothing. Her face had that look again. The look that reminds me, on occasion, that underneath the persona of a wacky New Ager, some sort of wisdom lies there.

Ma scooted her water glass aside, deciding on tea instead, and did I want a cup of chamomile? I shook my head. I kept my head down while she poured water from the Brita into the teakettle. While she set it on the stove and ignited the burner, Ma told me that we both know where things went wrong for me. With her, she said. Then she nodded toward Dad's room and added, "And with him."

I pretended not to know what she was talking about, though I don't know why. My feigned ignorance only served as an invitation for her to explain.

She told me that it doesn't take an eleven-year-old genius to figure out why I'm afraid to trust my heart, and men in particular. She recaptured the key events of my childhood, then told me that she hopes that while I'm here I'll open my eyes and take a look at whatever has me gripped at the ankle, not allowing me to rise fully above the waterline.

She was speaking in riddles, but I didn't bother telling her so.

Ma caught the teakettle before it whistled, then poured us both a cup of tea, even though I'd just told her I didn't want any.

As she bobbed a tea bag into her cup and sat down, she talked about how Dad's getting worse and how Marie thinks she should call a county nurse to come look at him. I couldn't stand listening to her talk about him, her voice so soft with concern. I partially closed the lid of my laptop and told her how it bugs the shit out of me that she's here—that any of us are here, but especially her—and that I hoped it didn't mean that she still loved him.

Ma smiled as she reminded me that there are many kinds of love and that while, yes, once she did love him, desperately even, he destroyed that love, and now the only kind of love she feels for him is the kind of love you feel for a sibling. She ended her clarification by saying, "You'd take care of Clay under the same circumstances, wouldn't you?"

The mention of Clay distracted her—thank God—and she suggested I call and give him an update on Dad, reminding me that he's two hours behind us so he'd still be up.

"You call him," I said, my snotty tone intact. Ma reminded me that Clay doesn't take her calls, and I told her that maybe then she needs to come up out of the water and deal with that situation.

I felt guilty the minute I said it and saw her brows wrinkled with remorse. Ma has tried with Clay. Many times over. So have I, for that matter. But every time I've managed to get a hold of him and dared to bring up the topic of Ma, he cuts me off quickly and tells me to give it a rest. I got pissed the last time he said this and asked him point-blank why he couldn't give it a rest. And what exactly did he blame her for, anyway? For being afraid of him? We were all afraid of Dad.

Clay reminded me that we were only kids. Ma wasn't, and he claimed that she could have walked away like he did.

His remark pissed me off all the more and I went off on him, reminding him that she had two kids to take care of and that she didn't have a penny to her name. No car. No experience being on her own, since she'd lived with her parents until the day she married Dad. But none of that meant jack shit to Clay. The phone call ended with me telling him to shove his self-righteousness up his ass.

Ever since that conversation, his calls have gone from once a month to three times a year: Christmas, Thanksgiving, and Easter. And he keeps those calls short. Polite. Like you would if you were calling an old aunt out of obligation.

Ma sat down at the table and took another sip of tea. She told me that the time would come for her to talk to Clay, but for now he's not ready.

I asked her if Sky Walker told her this, and she told me to stop it. That I know her name is Sky Dreamer. She took a deep, soft breath, and her face turned wistful as she informed me that she's thinking of changing her name.

I hoped to hell she was kidding. She wasn't. She was perfectly serious as she told me that Lillian is a nice enough name but that it represents the old her. She reminded me that Marie had her name changed for the third time right before we left. I reminded her that Marie's Indian, for God's sakes—and she's not—that it's part of Marie's culture. I groaned out loud, then looked back at my computer screen. I could feel her thinking up new names even as we sat there.

"I'm not staying here until he dies, you know," I said abruptly. "Maybe you love the guy enough to stay and tuck him in for his dirt nap, but I don't."

Ma gasped at my comment, then asked when I got so sarcastic and bitter, anyway. What could I say?

She sat quietly for a minute—okay, maybe a fraction of a

minute—then she brought up her promise to Dad again. How it never went away, even after his meanness chipped away at her love until there was nothing left. After all Dad put her through, I said, she should be absolved from that promise.

She blinked at me. "Absolved by whom?" she asked. Again, I had no answer.

Suddenly Ma looked almost small. Almost vulnerable. She shook her head slightly and gave me one of those bittersweet smiles. Then she told me how, from the time she was a girl, she wondered what her purpose in life was. She always knew that it wasn't something on a large scale—even though she admitted that when she was young, she wanted to do something great. "Youth always dreams of greatness," she added, reminding me of my own youthful dream of becoming a world-class novelist.

She went on to point out that she has no special talents. How she loves music, but can't play it. How she gets goose pimples over beautiful artwork but can't create it. But she's comfortable with that at her age, she said, because she looks at success a little differently than she used to. Then she started talking about how when she'd finally gotten herself together, she promised the "Creator" that she would keep her word and decided that if she accomplished only keeping her word for the rest of her life, that would be enough.

That's a noble ambition, and I told her so. But I added that I didn't see the point in this case. And then she brought up something that pained me. How she'd promised everyone— Marie and me and herself—that she'd stick with her commitment to put an end to the madness going on in this house, but she didn't do it. Not then, anyway. And that although she tries to live with no shame, no blame, and no guilt, she falters at *times and wonders if things might have turned out differently if she'd stuck to her promise the first time.*

I felt my whole insides stiffen when she said this. "It wasn't your fault!" I protested. "You weren't the cause of what happened!"

"Wasn't I?" she said. Ma wasn't so sure about that, and she wasn't about to test it out. "And whether you see my aim as worthy for a life's goal or not isn't the point. To me, it's every-thing."

I wanted to wrap my arms around her at that moment, but I didn't. Instead, I asked her if she knew what I was having the most difficulty accomplishing.

She made a smart-ass guess that it was "trying to come up out of the water," and, I swear, there was a little taunting curl to her lips!

"No!" I snapped, even though I had planned to reveal something akin to that. I told her that it was trying to get my work done when someone was chewing my ear off. I adjusted the screen of my laptop and stared at it fiercely.

Ma rose then, warming her tea with more water from the kettle and leaning her backside against the counter. She made a comment about how fear is a peculiar thing, following that gem up by reminding me of how Clay always accused Dad of being a phony and a coward. She surprised me by agreeing with Clay and talking about how Dad split himself into two halves and sent one half out into the world for others and left one half here at home for us. How in both places there was fear. Dad didn't go to college—even though he loved learning as much as Milo and Lucy do—because he was afraid he wasn't smart enough to rise to the top there. How he held on to his money with a gripped fist and would take a swing at her when she dared try to snatch some of it for bread or milk, *because he was afraid he'd run out. And she brought up how Dad had a string of mistresses and loved at least one of them but couldn't be with her because he was afraid that if she saw him at his worst, she'd stop loving him. "Everything that man did, he did while standing chin-deep in fear," Ma said, then she added, "I understand fear, of course. I lived in it too. We all have fears, Tess. But, well, at some point we need to face them."*

When I didn't respond, Ma said she'd leave me to my work. She set her cup in the sink and kissed me good night, then went to her room.

Ma's right. I am afraid. I'm afraid of a lot of things. I'm afraid that if I allow my love for Peter to take me back to him, he'll change, and he'll find my underbelly and rip it to shreds in the end.

I'm afraid to really look at Dad, for fear that I'll see too much of myself in him and that I'll break through the thin covering of indifference that sits over the hole in my life where a father should have been and fall into a pit of grief when he dies.

I'm afraid to look at Lucy when she asks about her father, for fear that in a weak moment I'll blurt out the truth.

I'm glad my old files from my time with Howard are gone, along with that old word processor itself, because if I had them, I'm afraid I would read them and go back to that time I never want to relive.

I'm just afraid.

I feel like I just walked into a stranger's room and saw them naked. I minimize the screen.

Downstairs, the back door shuts, and I hear Mom's voice. She's grumbling about something or other. I kick off my shoes, and in stocking feet—half crouching, half creeping—I rush Mom's laptop to her room and set it on the nightstand next to her bed. I hurry back into my room, slip my shoes back on, and head downstairs.

"I had Lucy bring it upstairs," I hear Oma say when I reach the landing of the stairs.

"It's on your nightstand," I add, then quickly lean over Oma's shoulder and ask her how the dinner preparations are coming.

"Fine, honey," Oma says. "We're going to eat like kings tonight."

I pride myself on the acting job I'm doing. Mom had that worried look on her face when I entered the kitchen—the memory of catching me rummaging through her notebooks still fresh in her mind, no doubt—but I played it cool by looking casual, even if I didn't feel that way inside.

I manage to give Mom a bit of eye contact and keep my voice at its normal pitch when I casually ask what time Mitzy is coming. Mom is buying it, apparently, because her shoulders relax when she says, "Around seven." Well, as much as her shoulders are capable of relaxing, anyway.

Mom's face might look exactly the same, yet after reading her private thoughts, I know that there is a lot more underneath that dry skin and emotionally void face than meets the eye. For a long time now I've prided myself on my skilled intuition, my ability to read body language and verbal tones, but suddenly I question whether I'm any good at any of it at all, because I always assumed that Mom—with her attachment disorder and abandonment issues and all—didn't feel very much past her love for Milo and me and Oma. Now I know that she feels everything. Intensely.

I watch Mom as she heads up the stairs, and I think that

maybe I should brush up on my math skills and just become an accountant or something.

As the day progresses, the aroma of Oma's cooking swells from the stove to fill the kitchen, and by the time Feynman begins to bark, alerting us that someone is here, the whole house is bathed in smells so enticing that we're salivating like Pavlov's dog.

The first thing I think of when I see Marie is Oma's fertility goddess earrings. Her skin is clay-red, and she's molded solid like the earth, with heavy breasts and wide hips and thighs. Her face is full, and her salt-and-pepper hair is pulled back and twisted into a fat knot at the base of her neck. She has a wide, square, attractive face, and she's wearing a long denim skirt and a white roomy blouse. Long earrings made of tiny red and yellow beads wobble and bend against a neck that is filled with rings like a tree trunk. Mom didn't specify which kind of Indian Marie is, but I see for myself—feather, not dot—and she doesn't seem old, even though I know she's around Oma's age.

"I can't believe this!" Marie says as she twirls Oma around so she can look at her from every angle. "Look at her, Tess. Just look at her. Can you believe it? My God, I can't even tell it's the same woman who left here. You look terrific, Lillian."

Oma giggles. "Oh, I don't look so great right now," she says. She lifts her arm and wobbles the skin that hangs from her upper arms. "I've not been to Curves or Nia for almost three weeks now, and it's showing. Look at my stomach. I'm starting to look like I'm pregnant."

Marie pats her own pooch of a belly. "Hey," she says. "If

someone looks at us and thinks we're still young enough to get pregnant, we should take that as a compliment!"

"Come here, you," Marie says. She wraps Oma in her arms and they hug with such gusto that their faces change color.

"Oh, I've missed you, dear friend," Oma says as they hug.

Of course Oma tells Marie that she looks good too, and Marie says, "It's my new bra, I'm telling you. Look at this thing. Can you believe it?" She lifts up her blouse and shows us her tight-fitting bra, which is icy peach, filmy, and looks like the wrap they put over Easter baskets. Her boobs crest above her bra cups like muffin tops. "So don't worry about TV trays if you don't have enough room at the table for all of us, Lillian. I'll just slide my chin off my shelf, and we can set a few plates here."

Oma laughs 'til she's teary-eyed, then she throws her arms around Marie once more for a quick squeeze. "Still the same Marie," she says.

"Say hello to Sam, Marie," Oma says as she swabs her drippy eyes, and Marie turns and sees Grandpa Sam sitting in his chair. Her dark-chocolate eyes grow wide and her clay cheeks rosy.

Grandpa Sam is looking right at her, same as he was when she lifted her blouse, his face impassive. "Well," Marie says, "either his strokes have done that much damage to him, or the years have done that much damage to *me*!" The women roar again.

Then Marie opens her arms to Mom. "Oh, sweetie," she says. She hugs Mom long and hard too. When she's done, she cups Mom's face in her hands, smiles at her with glittery eyes, then kisses both of her cheeks. "I love you like a daughter, you know." Mom grins.

"Where's Al?" Oma asks.

"Probably still trying to get out of the car. Stubborn old mule, he wouldn't let me help him." Marie spots me and her eyes get teary all over again. She glances at Mom with pride, like she did something wonderful by creating me, then she opens her arms and invites me to step into them. She pins me in a big hug that feels good—well, except to my ear, which must be folded over, because it hurts. "Last time I saw you, you were still wearing your umbilical cord," she says. "Oh, Tess, she's just precious. Just precious."

The back door scrapes against the floor as it opens, and even with my ear crushed against Marie's boobs, which are bobbing against me like buoys, I can hear the taps of Feynman's toenails, which are getting so long that *he* could perch.

"Milo, come meet your auntie Marie," Oma says when Milo comes in, pink-cheeked and sweaty from his bike ride. "This is our Milo, Lucy's twin," she says proudly. Luckily for Milo, he's still wearing the pterodactyl helmet Mom insists he wear when riding on the road, so his head is protected from Marie's crushing hug, while I'm still rubbing my ear to get rid of the stinging.

"I didn't know you were my aunt," Milo says, and I'm amazed that he can breathe enough to say it, with his asthma and having his face smothered as it is.

"I'm your auntie of the heart," Marie says.

"Hot apple cider?" Mom asks when Marie finally lets go of Milo. Marie says yes and Mom hurries off to the kitchen to get her some, leaving Oma and Marie to hug and giggle some more. I follow Mom into the kitchen, but dumb Milo, he just stands there, too polite to ask if he can be excused even though he's fidgeting because he wants to be.

In seconds, I hear Mitzy's voice as she comes in the door.

She fusses over Milo, then Feynman, and I hurry into the living room to get my share of fussing. Mitzy's hug is different from Marie's—it feels more like a burst of sunshine, while Marie's felt like the splashing waves of an ocean.

"Where's Ray?" Mom asks.

"Outside talking to Al," Mitzy says. "The poor guys are probably afraid to come inside."

Oma invites them into the kitchen, even though they'll be cramped, she says, but she's got to watch the pots on the stove. While Mom is waiting for Marie to squeeze her way around the kitchen table, Milo goes to her and pleads to be excused. She nods—probably because she fears Milo will end up armless, considering that his puny arm is stretched like a rubber band as he tries to keep Feynman from jumping up on our guests—and he tugs the dog back to their cave.

I like being in the kitchen with Mom and Oma and Marie and Mitzy. They are all talking at once as they uncover pans to stir and sniff and sample, and their laughter is as fragrant as the steam that rises up from beneath the lids. They talk in hurried bits, commenting on the simmering food and past events. Light, simple, happy times, but the occasional glances between Oma and Marie say that there are deeper memories they want to share too.

There's a sharp rap of knuckles against the front door before it opens, and then Al and Ray step inside. Al is the same height as Marie, white, round in his belly and cheeks, and has bulgy blue eyes. His ears are triangle-shaped, and the tips point out at a ten o'clock and a two o'clock angle—which, I decide, is probably from being crushed against Marie's boobs for thirty-nine years. I only know a little about Al. He trucks logs from the woods to the paper mills, and he (probably) has a hernia.

Oma hugs Al as she laughs, and he pats her back as she hugs him. He does the same with Mom. While they hug, Ray just watches with a nervous smile. Mitzy goes to him and slips under his arm—maybe so he doesn't feel left out in the hug department.

Mitzy doesn't need to worry about Ray not getting his share of welcome hugs, though, because Oma sees to it that he gets his, even though she doesn't know him from Adam, as she herself would say.

Ray has hair the color of Peter's, but it's buzzed to a fraction of an inch. He's rather nice-looking—though not nearly as handsome as Peter—even though he's as skinny as a tapeworm.

Mitzy puts her arm around Ray again as she tells Oma who Ray's relatives are, dropping names in the hopes of finding someone in his family that Oma knows. I study Ray as his head swivels from side to side, trying to keep up with Mitzy, Oma, and Al, as they volley names. When they finally find a relative of Ray's that Oma and Al know, there's relief, although who knows why. Maybe it's just important to identify the tribe of a stranger. I tuck this thought into my head to chew on later.

"Here, here, have a seat," Oma says, when she notices Al's posture drooping. "Those hernias are painful, aren't they?" she says, as though she's had a few herself. "After dinner I'll give you a Reiki treatment." She says this as though Al has no choice in the matter, which he probably doesn't.

"You do Reiki?" Marie asks as she follows Oma back to the kitchen. "Oh, I'm curious about that. A friend of mine went to an alternative healing center over in Marrington and had Reiki. She saw a medicine man on the reservation too, and who knows which did the trick, but..."

Mom offers Mitzy and the men chairs and apple cider, then they talk about all those things grown-ups who don't know one another well talk about. When the frost will set in. The high price of gasoline. Boring things like that.

I watch them as they make their small talk. Ray is soft-spoken and friendly, but the way he keeps brushing the legs of his pants and shifting his feet says to me that he's a loner and would rather not be in a group of strangers. Al's face is tense, and he sits tilted to one side. He's making comments back to Ray, but I think he's really thinking about the pain in his groin and wondering what could happen if he lets his hernia—or whatever it is—go. And then there is Grandpa Sam, who is too out of it to worry about his health or, for that matter, about behaving in a socially acceptable manner, judging by the way he's picking at his nose.

Oma comes to take Grandpa Sam into the kitchen for his dinner before we eat. She's got him almost through the kitchen doorway when she stops and turns to me. "Lucy, would you mind feeding your grandpa, so I can orchestrate the finishing touches on our dinner?" She sees me cringe, and her face mixes with sympathy and pleading. "Please?"

Despite my stomach growling from hunger, nausea kicks in with the first spoonful of orangy-green mush Grandpa Sam rolls back out of his mouth. I scrape it off his chin like Oma does and quickly scoop it back in.

The light above the kitchen sink is working on Grandpa Sam's eyes like a beam from an optometrist's light, showing me just how lifeless they are. Before him, the women are buzzing like bees making honey for the hive, and his eyes don't even budge when one of them brushes past to move between the refrigerator, the sink, and the stove. In the living room, Al is talking about the Packers and the outrageous amount of money athletes make, and I feel sorry for Grandpa Sam, having to be propped at the table to be spoon-fed like a baby, when he should be in the living room with the other guys.

I take the edge of the dishcloth and wipe his chin and cheek, and I don't cringe. Instead, I wrap my free arm around him and give him a pat.

When he's finished, his bowl is still half full. I tell Oma I can get him to his room and she lets me, but Marie comes to help me lay him down. She adjusts his pillow as I cover him to his chin, which is a bit glossy because I didn't use water to wipe him clean. I'll remember to do that next time. When we have him tucked in, Marie puts her arm around my shoulder and says, "It's all a part of the cycle of life, honey."

I LOVE THE sounds as we sit crowded at the table and eat our luxurious meal: the chiming of the silver against the plates, the moans of pleasure with the first couple of bites of each new dish, the clips of conversation that I listen to carefully for any clue that will shed light on the missing parts of my family—namely, the men.

The longer and more we eat, the slower the gestures and sentences get, until at last everyone is leaned back in their chairs, sipping coffee, smiling contentedly, and muttering softly. "You outdid yourself, Lillian," Marie says, and everyone agrees.

"May I be excused?" Milo asks. Mitzy looks disappointed by his request. She had insisted that Milo sit next to her and had fussed over him through the whole meal, asking him if he wanted more of this or that, sliding his milk glass over so he wouldn't tip it, and various other motherly gestures that would be more appropriate if Milo were an infant. But Milo is fidgety. Probably because he can hear Feynman whining from the study, where he had to be put so he wouldn't beg for table scraps.

"Oh, sit with Auntie Mitzy a little longer," she begs. "Don't you want some more dessert?"

"No, thank you, I'm full. And Feynman needs to go outside to do his duty." This makes Mitzy laugh, and Milo look confused.

"I'll join you," Mitzy says. Mom gets up to follow them out, as does Oma, her pack of cigarettes in hand. Marie starts clearing the table, so I help her. We leave Al and Ray's coffee cups, though, because they're still sipping.

Al looks at Ray. He stifles a belch that puffs his already plump cheeks, then says, "Only thing missing from this good meal is the nap that should follow it." Ray laughs and agrees.

"Why don't you boys take your coffee into the living room so we can get this table cleaned off?" Marie says. Oma is just coming through the door, the stink of smoke still clinging to her, when Al rises and stops abruptly midway to groan. "You okay, Al?" Marie asks as he winces.

"I'm okay. I'm okay," Al says.

Oma tosses her cigarettes and lighter on the counter and hurries to Al. "Come on. I'm going to give you a treatment. I've got a brand-new table."

"I was just going to go out for a smoke," Al protests. But he doesn't win, of course.

Al shakes his head. "You women and your hocus pocus," he grumbles as Oma leads him into the living room by the hand. Oma starts unfolding her Reiki table. "I'm so glad I had this sent with speedy delivery. I knew I'd be needing it. This will help you. You can count on it."

"The only thing I can count on is that when the Creator decides it's my time, He'll cue someone to turn down the sod."

Marie shakes her head, then she starts scrubbing the last pot. I figure maybe this is my opportunity to fish for information from her, but I know I must be clever in how I ask, because Marie's sharp.

"Are you Native American?"

"I am," she says.

"Oh," I say. "Then how come you don't live on a reservation?" Marie leans over and scrapes at some crust at the bottom of a pan with her fingernail.

"I did," she says. "But when I married Al, I moved off it. It's still my reservation, though, and they are still my people. I go back home to see the family and for ceremonies."

"Oh!" I say, suddenly remembering that Marie has an Indian name too. "I learned...Oma told me...that you have an Indian name."

"I do," she says, her fingernail still working. "*An Wantin Nibi Quae.* It means *Calming Waters Woman.*"

"That's a pretty name," I tell her. "Mom should have used that for my middle name, when she named me after you. Well, not that Marie isn't nice too," I add, just so she won't feel bad, even though I've never cared for my middle name.

Marie laughs. She hands me the pan she's finally gotten clean and rinsed, and I balance it on top of the mountain of pots and platters in the dish drainer. "On the reservation, does everyone speak in a different language?"

Marie squeezes the dishcloth until it's hardly dripping, then starts wiping off the counter. "Sadly, no. There are young people on that reservation who can't speak even one word in our native tongue."

"Do you speak it often?"

"Mostly with the older people when I go home, though the traditional songs help me stay connected to it too. I like speaking in my own tongue. Like going home, it helps me remember who I am."

Bingo!

I let my smile wilt for effect. "I don't know my people," I say. "Just Oma, and Mom, and Milo. And now Grandpa Sam and Aunt Jeana. You've known my family longer than I have."

Marie gives me a smile that looks bittersweet. "Yes, I imagine that's true. Your grandma was just newly married when we befriended each other. I was there when your uncle Clay and your mom were born, and I even helped welcome you and Milo into the world."

"Then you've probably met my dad too?" I say, more bluntly than I intended to.

Marie is swirling her dishcloth in circles on the counter, and her hand pauses for a moment while she considers this. Then she clears her throat. She looks at me, and although her eyes have pity in them, the firmness of her mouth makes it clear that she won't be saying a word about what she knows.

Marie turns her attention to the mound of dishes dripping in the drainer and says, "Maybe you could dry for me, sweetie. Where are the dish towels?" I point to the drawer on the other side of her, and she pulls one out. She sniffs it, mutters, "Mmm," then holds it under my nose. "I love the smell of things dried on a clothesline, don't you?" she says. "They absorb the warmth of the sun and the scent of the breeze. And just sniffing the scent when we unfold the clothes can makes us feel sunny and happy inside." I sniff, but at the moment—knowing that I can cross Marie off my list of possible informants—the smell doesn't do much to make me feel sunny inside.

By the time Mom, Mitzy, and Milo come inside, Oma has the living room lit with candles, Japanese music is playing, and poor Al is lying on the Reiki table like a sacrificial lamb set on an altar. Oma's hands are cupped together and hovering over his private parts like a loose-fitting jock. Mitzy giggles with embarrassment.

"Oh, God," Mom grumbles, peeking over Mitzy's shoulder into the living room, and Ray (who hurried back to the kitchen with his coffee when Oma got out the table) chuckles.

"Shush," Oma says, her eyes closed in a meditative pose. She moves her hands as though she's tugging long, imaginary clumps of rupture from him, tossing them away, then cups her hands over him again.

"Rupture remover extraordinaire," Mom says, and Mitzy giggles again.

"Do you girls mind?" Oma says. Al opens one eye for a second, so that it looks like he's winking. We're hardly back in the kitchen before we hear him snoring.

Mom and Mitzy and Ray visit while I dry dishes and put them away. Ray is attentive. I like the way he keeps his arm on the back of Mitzy's chair. When I grow up, I'm going to marry a man who does that.

"There, we're done!" Oma says from the doorway. "I

told Al to just lie and relax for a few minutes." Al's still snoring, so this makes everyone snicker. "I'm going to consult my intuitive, Sky Dreamer, to see if there's anything else I might do for him."

"You can save your phone call. I'll tell you," Mom says flatly. "You can convince him to see a doctor."

The kitchen is crowded with chairs butted up near the table sitting too close to the doorway, so Oma puts her hand on Mitzy's shoulder as she shimmies herself between Mitzy's chair and the counter to get to an empty seat. She stops, still wedged. "Ohhhhh!" Oma says. "Did you feel that? When I touched your shoulder?"

"Yes," Mitzy says, her voice slow, her eyes expanded.

"Mother," Mom warns, saying "Mo-ther" in two slow, deep syllables.

Oma ignores her. "I can feel him, Mitzy." Oma's words are soft, filled with awe.

"Who?" Marie asks.

"My baby...Dylan," Mitzy says, her eyes glistening.

Mitzy breathes in slowly, as though she's breathing in something magical. "I felt him the second Lillian touched me. Right here," she says in a whisper, tapping her right shoulder.

"His spirit is standing right behind her back," Oma says, her face filled with the same awe as Mitzy's but with concentration too.

I feel a little spooked, but more curious than anything. Ray stiffens, his hand moving up from the back of Mitzy's chair to wrap around her shoulder.

"He's showing me something," Oma says slowly. She scrunches her eyes, as though she's trying to peer closely to see what it is. There's not a sound in the house but for Al's snoring.

"It's a ball, I think? And it has something scribbled on it?" Oma says this more like a question than a statement.

Mitzy's hand moves up to rest on the top of her chest, and tears spill over her cheeks. Ray squirms in his chair and leans closer to Mitzy. He looks like he wants to scoop her up and run. Mitzy puts her hand on his arm, like a mom does when she is cueing her child to stay put and shush.

Oma cocks her head as though she's listening.

"He wants you to know that you don't need to feel bad that he never got it or to think that you did anything to bring on his early birth." Oma pauses again, cocking her head even more. "He slipped into that defective body knowing he'd not be staying, but he came anyway, because it was his chance to connect with you, even if only briefly. He wants you to know that time is irrelevant. And he watches over you as he always has, and always will, until you meet again."

Oma looks up then and lets out a big breath. She looks stunned. "He's gone. Just like that." She reaches for the back of a chair and Marie pulls it out so she can sit down. "My, I've never had anything like *that* happen before."

Mom hurries into the bathroom and comes out with a stack of Kleenex for Mitzy, who presses the wad to her eyes. Marie and Oma, and even Mom, gather around her and stroke her back, her arm, her hair.

Mitzy blows her nose, then clamps the damp tissue in her fist and drops her hand to her lap. Ray cups his hand over hers, and I decide that I want a man who will cup my hand too, even if there's a snotty Kleenex clutched in it.

"I can't believe you saw the football." Mitzy looks at Mom. "Did you tell her about it?"

I know Mom wants to say yes—to take the magic out of Oma's words—but she can't lie, so she shakes her head.

Mitzy tells the bare bones of the story about the football—the story I overheard in the restaurant but am now listening to (hopefully) as if I've never heard it before.

"You can forgive yourself for that now, dear. I saw your baby's spirit standing in a white light. Well, not literally, but as if I was seeing him in my mind yet behind you at the same time. Oh, I wish I could explain it. Like a super-imposed photograph, I suppose. But I *saw* him, Mitzy. I felt him. I felt him at peace."

"Well, *that* gave me the chills," Marie says finally, fill-ing the gap of silence. Mom opens her mouth to no doubt counter the experience, but then—perhaps so as not to rob her friend of a tiny bit of comfort—she closes it without ut-tering a word.

Al comes into the kitchen, where everyone is sitting quietly (but for Mitzy, who's sniffling), his footsteps groggy. He pats his big belly and belches again, causing a nervous twitter of giggles.

"Get Mitzy some water, will you, Lucy? And get Al a glass too," Oma says, then she asks Al how he's feeling.

"Full," he answers.

The second she hears the faucet run, Oma says, "Oh, I forgot to wash after Al's treatment." She jerks her hand away from her damp eyelids as though Al's rupture is conta-gious and might infect her eye. She gets up to wash at the kitchen sink.

Ray scoots closer to Mitzy and whispers something in her ear, and she nods. They stand up. There's a silence that sounds awkward, until Marie says, "Good food, good friends, a little hands-on healing, and a psychic experience—boy, Lillian, you sure do know how to throw a dinner party!" Everybody laughs.

* * *

OMA SENDS me for Milo, so he can be a part of the good-byes too, and after the hugs and thank-yous, Mom, Oma, Milo, and I stand outside and wave as the night wind blows the leaves and our company down the road. As we head toward the house, Mom says, "Mother? Messing with Al's rupture is one thing—I suppose—but please don't toy with Mitzy's grief. Please."

Oma takes short, bouncing steps to catch up with Mom, her long tunic billowing. "What is *that* supposed to mean?"

Mom stops. "You know what I'm talking about. The psychic reading—or whatever in the hell you'd call it—on Mitzy's dead baby. Ma, I know you're only trying to help, but don't go there with that magical shit. She doesn't need that."

"Magical shit? You think I'm making this up? Why, healing energy and angels are from God, not 'magical shit,' as you call it."

Mom goes up the steps and yanks the front door open. She stops. "Adding a religious element to it is supposed to make it more legitimate? Religion is not a science, and neither is your metaphysical crap."

"What about the *Christian* Scientists?" Milo asks—making me believe this kid really *is* developing a sense of humor.

"There's scientific proof that prayer works. Isn't there, Milo?" Oma says.

"Well, quantum physicists *are* studying many things once considered only paranormal parlor games," Milo says, his profoundly gifted seriousness safely back intact.

"And there are plenty of scientists who believe in God,"

I add. "Stephen Hawking himself said that when we know what caused the big bang, we'll be looking into the eyes of God. Isn't that right, Milo? And Einstein believed that religion, the arts, and science were all branches of the same tree. Tell her, Milo!" But Milo can't tell her, because he's darting behind the house to chase after Feynman.

"End of discussion," Mom says. "Just leave her be, Mother." Mom slams the door, leaving Oma and me standing in the yard.

chapter

THIRTEEN

TWO WEEKS pass, and in that time, according to Oma, Grandpa Sam suffers "ministrokes" and can no longer use his walker without help. He stops talking too, for the most part. Oma—or Persephone, as she insists Milo and I call her now, so she can "try it on" as her new name—arranges for hospice to come. They've got a whole team, and Mom says we'll take help from all of them, except the chaplain, thank you. Aunt Jeana, who has power of attorney for health care, says we'll take help from none of them (and doesn't offer a thank-you), and she arranges for the county nurse to come by instead. The county nurse, Barbara, sees to it that Grandpa Sam gets a wheelchair and a bed he won't fall out of. Oma orders him a chair he can sit on in the bathtub so she can bathe him more easily too. We all think it's the chair coming when I see the brown van and yell, "UPS is here, Persephone!"

Mom looks up from her laptop. "Will you stop calling her that!"

"She told me to! And what's wrong with the name, anyway? Persephone, the joyful queen of the underworld. *I* like it."

Oma stands at the back door and waits for the deliveryman to reach the house. "Hmmm," she says. "Two boxes of the same size? That doesn't look right. Must be something else. But I didn't order anything besides that chair. You order something, Tess?" Mom doesn't hear her.

"What's inside, Persephone?" I ask, as Oma stares at the invoice and I stare at the two good-size boxes.

"Why, they're from Best Buy and addressed to Milo and Lucy."

Mom hears that! "What?" she snaps. She grabs the invoice out of Oma's hand.

"Oh, my God," she says. "He sent the kids each a laptop!"

"Who sent them laptops?" Oma asks. I suddenly envision my dad having a rush of remorse for ignoring Milo and me since our birth and sending us these special gifts to show us he's sorry.

"Peter," Mom says flatly.

"Peter sent us laptops?" I shout, echoing Oma's question.

"Yes."

Now I know why people cry when they get good news.

I race to Milo's study, shove open the door, and shout inside, "He sent us laptops! Peter sent us laptops!"

Milo rips himself from his chair and chases me back into the kitchen. The minute he sees the boxes, he starts in with little asthmatic barklike coughs.

Mom calls Peter instantly. "What in the hell were you thinking, sending expensive laptops to these kids?"

While Mom is talking, I plead to talk with Peter. I bounce rapidly while I wait, and when I can't take it anymore, I snatch the phone right out of her hand. "Peter! Thank you! Thank you! Thank you!" I shout. "I've missed my computer sooooooo much! As much as I miss you!"

"Lucy, did you just tear my cell out of my hands? Give that back to me now!"

Then I start rambling, trying to fit in everything I can before Mom yanks the phone back.

"I learned to ride a bike, Peter. Milo learned right away, but I had to work at it. I kept falling down, so after I was done being grounded, which was yesterday—I won't go into that—I went right on the road because there's a hill, and I forced myself to go down it. It was sink or swim, but I made it to the bottom without falling, and now I can ride! Mom got us helmets and knee pads. Elbow pads too, and we can ride on the road now. It's so fun!" I'm speaking at such a fast clip that I can only hope Peter is catching it all.

Peter says something, but I can't hear him because Mom is shouting at me, Oma is trying to calm her, and Milo is whining and wheezing because he wants to thank Peter and open the boxes.

"You won't ride that bike for a month, Lucy Marie McGowan, if you don't give me that phone right now!"

But I want to tell Peter something, at least one of my secrets, and quietly enough that Mom can't hear. I cup my hand over the receiver and yell above the ruckus, "I have to pee! I'm going to take the phone with me so Peter can ask me my question, then I'll give it right back. Promise!" I dart into the bathroom and lock the door. Mom bangs on it. "Damn it, Lucy. Open this door this instant!"

"Oh, Tess, don't swear at her," Oma says, and then the two of them argue whether Mom was swearing *at* me or just swearing, period.

"Peter?" I say.

"Yes, Lucy?" and I smile, because I love the way Peter says my name. Like it's a part of a poem.

"If I were to tell you a secret, would you keep it a secret from Mom?"

"That depends," he says. "If it's a secret that poses any physical threat to you, I'd have to tell—even though it sounds to me like you're in enough trouble at the moment as it is."

"Well," I say, "it only possesses a physical threat to me *if* you tell."

I have no idea why I want to tell Peter something, but I do. I decide not to tell him that I read from Mom's childhood notebooks or that later today when Mom goes to help Mitzy wallpaper her kitchen, I'm going to get into her laptop again and read whatever I can find. Instead, I tell him the bottom line. "I'm finding out where Mom got her distrust of men from, and, well, just hang in there, Peter, even if she talks to you like you're a telemarketer. She'll resolve it. I really believe she will."

Mom pounds on the door so hard I can see it vibrate. "God damn it! Lucyyyyy!"

"Tess, please," Oma pleads again. To which Mom shouts, "I'm going to do more than swear at her in about three seconds if she doesn't open this door."

"Come on, Lucy. It's my turn. You got to talk to him last time!" Milo's little fist sounds like hail pinging against the door.

Peter seems to not know what to say. I flush the toilet to create the proper sound effects for Mom and call, "I'll be right out." I turn on the water faucet.

"Lucy?" Peter says, talking loudly because he realizes that I'm having a bit of trouble hearing him. "I've got an assignment for you."

"Yes?"

"I want you to do some research for me. Do you think you can do that?"

"Sure! Now that I have a laptop, I can research anything. I'm good at it too. It's all in what you type into the search engines. Sometimes Mom can't find diddly, so I help her find the more obscure facts for her travel articles. I'll help you, Peter. What do you want to know?"

"Not that kind of research, Lucy. Hands-on learning, okay? I want you to see if you can't add a few more children's activities to your bike riding. I really want you to do that and leave all this messy stuff to us grown-ups, okay?"

The doorknob jiggles, turns, and Mom barges in. She holds the inside of a Bic pen up for me to see. "I've got my tricks too," she says. She snatches the phone out of my hand before I can even say bye and motions me out of the bathroom. "And, Mother, don't you dare let these kids open those boxes." She slams the door behind her and the lock clicks.

Milo groans. "Geez," he says, then he goes to the table and looks longingly at the unopened gifts. "She wouldn't make us send them back, would she, Lucy?"

At last! At last Milo has learned to see the value of my genius. I tip my head back as though I'm assessing the situation with my acute psychological knowledge, then I say, "Nope. She'll let us keep them."

"I hope you're right." Milo has a hold of one box, and it

makes scraping noises as he rotates it so he can read the print on each side.

"Can you believe Peter sent these, Lucy?" he says. He looks toward the bathroom. "I hope she lets me thank him."

Grandpa Sam coughs in spasms, and Oma, who is hovering outside the bathroom door, her ear almost stuck to it, steps back and motions for me to check on Grandpa.

Grandpa Sam is in his wheelchair, propped in front of the window. Outside, a handful of chickadees peck seeds in the feeder. He's breathing okay now, so I call back, "He's okay, Persephone."

I'm about to leave him so I can get back to the action in the kitchen, but he actually turns his head and looks at me and says my name, like maybe this is one of those mornings where he's partly with it, so I feel bad just running off and leaving him all alone. I glance into the kitchen, where Oma is now at the sink, filling it with water, and Milo is sitting at the table, his face in his hands. It's obviously going to be a while before Mom comes out, so I sit down on the arm of the lift chair.

"Peter—that's Mom's boyfriend, or *was*, anyway, before she ruined it—he just sent Milo and me computers. I doubt if that means anything to you, but, well, it's a really big deal to us."

The bathroom door opens and the back door slams. Milo pops his head into the living room. "We still can't open them." He shrugs, then heads back to the table to stare at the boxes some more.

I lean forward and peer out the window. Just as I suspected, Mom is headed for the trees off to the side of the yard. "Mom goes there whenever she's upset or just wants to be alone to think," I explain to Grandpa Sam. "See? Right over there. She'll sit like that for a long time, her back against a tree. When she's really, really upset, she keeps her legs drawn up and her head down. She's only half upset now. I can tell because her legs are drawn—which means upset—but her wrists are propped on her knees, while her hands pull apart a leaf or something that she's picked up from the ground. That means that she's half upset and half thinking, which is a positive sign, because she just talked to Peter, the ex-boyfriend who sent us the laptops. I want him to be my new dad, if I can't find my birth dad. Or if I do and he turns out to be a creep."

Grandpa Sam is still looking where I pointed. Or not. "You know what I wish?" I tell him. "I wish your brain wasn't damaged and that you could think and speak and understand me. Then you could tell me about my dad. It's kind of like how someone has to get a divorce before they can marry someone else. I have to find him to see if he'll be my dad, or else how can I have another one take his place?"

A fly walks across Grandpa Sam's cheek, but he doesn't flinch. I brush it away, and it comes right back. "He's pesky," I say. "Just like me.

"Do you know why I want to find him? My dad, that is? Or at least find out about him?" I don't wait for a response, because what's the point?

"Because I want to know who the other part of me is. And I guess I want to know that I'm not a bastard. I mean that in the old-world sense too, so don't think I'm swearing. Not that there's any stigma attached to being illegitimate anymore, but to me, I guess there is. If they got married, then that means they loved each other once, and if my dad loved my mom, then he'll probably love me, because I'm a part of her.

"At first, when I realized that Mom has the same last name as you, I automatically thought I was a bastard. But

Mom could have taken her maiden name back after she divorced him. Well, if there was anybody to divorce in the first place. There wasn't, if you were right when you said I didn't have a dad, and if Mom's remark about using a sperm bank was an actual intention."

I look out the window and see a red squirrel scampering up the bird feeder pole. "Look at that," I say. I rap on the window to chase the squirrel away, even if he's already chased away the chickadees. Grandpa Sam doesn't react to the squirrels today, which leads me to believe that he *is* having ministrokes like Oma says he is. I put my arm around him. The squirrel is gone and the chickadees have returned. I like moments like this. Moments when it doesn't seem so important to me that Grandpa Sam wasn't the nicest guy back in the old days.

"It's kind of ironic, isn't it? Me wanting a dad so bad when I probably wouldn't even know what you do with a dad if I had one, not any more than you'd know what you do with a computer if you had one. And there Mom is, and she's got a dad but she doesn't even . . . well . . . anyway."

I think for a minute as I watch the squirrel return and pick up seeds to gnaw on. "I suppose having a dad would be like having a grandpa. I never knew what you do with a grandpa either, before I came here. Probably all I have to do with a dad is talk to him too." I rap on the window, and once more the squirrel scampers off and the chickadees return.

I sit quietly for a bit, watching sunflower seed shells ping from the beaks of the chickadees. "I'm going to miss you when you're gone, Grandpa Sam. Even if you aren't much of a conversationalist." I feel a pang when I say it, which tells me that when my laptop is up and connected to the Net, I'd better pause from my research on sperm banks

and do some reading up on dying. Maybe look for some articles by that Kübler-Ross lady, or that Robert Neimeyer guy
that Barbara told Oma about. Anything to help me prepare
for it when it happens.

I hear the back door scraping open and shut and Feynman
whining. I glance out the window and see Milo heading for
the grove of trees where Mom is still sitting. I watch him
talk to her, scratching his arm nervously. Mom doesn't look
up at Milo when she nods. He comes barreling toward the
house, moving almost as fast as he does when he's on his
bike, and shouts, "We can open them, Lucy! We can keep
them!" as he bursts through the front door.

I give Grandpa a quick peck on the cheek, then hurry
into the kitchen, stopping on my way in to grab Milo's inhaler off his paper-cluttered desk. I hand it to him. "Here,
Wheezer," I say, deciding that if Oma can have a new name,
then so can Milo. "You'd better have a snort." Milo sucks on
it quickly, one quick in-breath, rather than his usual two,
and he doesn't even try to hold the medication in as he waits
for Oma to open the boxes with a utility knife.

While Milo is ripping things out of the two boxes, Mom
comes in. She doesn't glance at the table. She just kicks a
piece of molded Styrofoam out of the way and grabs her
cell from the counter. She calls Mitzy, asking her if she's up
for a visitor. Mom makes her voice sound chippy, but it
doesn't fool me. Apparently it doesn't fool Mitzy either, because Mom's next words are, "No, I'm fine. I'll be there in
fifteen." She grabs her purse, tells Oma she's going out for a
while, and out the door she goes.

Milo picks one laptop out of its box and tears the plastic
from it. "Wow!" he says. I dig in the second box to find
mine. I leave it in its plastic membrane and pull out the

other items tucked around it. "What's this?" I ask Milo. He glances up. "A router box. Cool!" he says, sounding more like a normal kid and less like a profoundly gifted geek. "It's so we can tap into the Net without having to literally be plugged into the modem."

"And what's this?" I ask, pulling out a cardboard tube and tipping it upside down so that a little flat rectangular thing encased in clear molded plastic drops out.

"A memory stick," Milo says, scooping it off the table. "Wow, Peter went all out! Is there one for each of us?"

We rake through his box and find a second one.

"Oh, wow!" Milo says with a gasp.

"You'd better take it easy there a bit, Wheezer. You just had a hit and you can hardly breathe."

"*Wheezer?* Lucy, please don't call him that," Oma says to me, then, to Milo, "Take a couple nice cleansing breaths, honey."

I've never used a memory stick before, and though Milo hasn't either, he knows all about them because he's a frequent visitor to tekkie Web sites. He explains their function to me quickly.

"Now we don't have to worry about backing up our work. Two gigabytes—wow! That's enough to store everything we could possibly put on our computers in a year's time. If your hard drive crashes, you won't lose anything, because we can store every document we have on it for safekeeping. Everything can be downloaded to another computer. I wish we had these for our old files."

The memory sticks are small and dangle from a long black cord, so we can hook them around our necks like necklaces—though who would want to is beyond me.

Oma shakes her head and chuckles. "Uploads... gigglebites... it's all French to me."

Across from me, on the kitchen counter, Mom's laptop
sits, plugged into its charger. "So," I say slowly, suddenly interested in those memory sticks again. "You're telling me I
could upload all of my documents on this memory stick,
then plug it into your laptop, and my documents would
download right onto your computer? Is that what you're
saying? You know, if I wanted to, say, make a backup on
your computer just to play it extra safe?"

"Well, you could. You just plug it into the USB port, upload your files, then take the memory stick, plug it into my
computer, and download. But that won't be necessary. The
memory stick itself serves the purpose well enough."

"But I *could* if I wanted to, right?"

"Right," he says.

MILO HAS our computers up and running in no time,
and there it is, my browser, coming back to me like a long-
lost friend. I race to the sites I love the most to see what I've
missed, skimming them all. But even as I read the newest
posts on *PostSecret.com,* I'm thinking of one thing and one
thing only—using my memory stick to lift Mom's documents off her laptop so I can read them on my computer.

I have to wait until Oma's outside smoking and Milo's
back in his room with his laptop, but then I do it. I plug the
memory stick into Mom's computer, and in mere seconds
I've lifted a copy of every document in her Word. I feel a
wave of guilt but rationalize it by telling myself that God
Himself prompted Peter to buy us the memory sticks so
that Mom's memories—my beginnings—could be given
to me.

When I'm done, I unplug the stick and insert it into my
new laptop, already configured by Milo. And—*voila!*—

there it is: Missy Jenkins's adventures (which might amuse me the same way a mindless sitcom would, if I were allowed to watch them) and, most importantly, Mom's journal, with only dates for file names. I race up the stairs and into my room, shutting the door behind me and jamming a butter knife between the door and the door frame because there's no lock—and because, hey, *I* have my tricks too. I open Mom's journal.

I am holding my breath, suddenly feeling scared. Not so much of getting caught but more of learning something awful. I open an entry at random, trusting that what I need to know will come—just as Oma says it will—and up comes an entry written on September 24, just two days after Marie and Al and Mitzy and Ray came for dinner.

chapter

FOURTEEN

Earlier today, from the front yard, where I paced and ranted under my breath, I could see Ma and Lucy ambling back to the house, side by side, as if they were glued together. I had an explanation ready if Ma came racing across the grass to offer yet another technique meant to cleanse me, center me, and make me easier to live with. I'd tell her that I was trying to reach someone who could tell me where to apply for relocation benefits for displaced tenants. It was better than telling her the truth. That I felt desperate to talk to Peter. To tell him that I'm sorry and want to try again.

I'm coming undone, and I know it. Two weeks back in my childhood home, and I'm losing it. Lucy knows it too. I feel her

watching me at every turn, her photographic mind skimming through the pages of every psychology book she's ever read, checking off symptoms, no doubt, trying to figure out what kind of mental affliction has claimed her mother now. Her hypervigilance toward me is unnerving and makes me sorry that I ever supported her decision to delve into psychology.

I'm outside again. Sitting in the cluster of hard maples that were my refuge as a child, hoping I won't be seen, which is ludicrous since I'm sitting in the glow of my laptop screen, typing. The ground is cool under me, a tree solid against my back.

I try to tell myself that I'd have it together had I not come back home, but the truth is, I've not had it together for a long, long time. Ever since The Absent Savior *failed and unraveled my dream of becoming a critically acclaimed novelist. Ever since Peter came into my life and unraveled my determination to make it through life without falling prey to the traps of love again, turning me into a pathetic, sniveling woman who, before we came here, crept out at night three times in one week and took the bus to his neighborhood, where I paced below his windows, watching his blinds for the hourglass figure of a woman to appear and tell me he's moved on and found another subject for his love poetry. This is the only reason I agreed to drive Mother here, of course. To save myself from becoming a full-fledged stalker.*

The sky is darkening, the sunset a sickly mixture of muddy greenish-gray, like vomit. Inside, the living-room light flicks on, and I can see Dad, a brain-dead lump in a lift chair, his hair ridiculously swirled on his head. I think of how he always spritzed on Ma's Aqua Net hairspray when he went out in the evenings, and I want to spray what's left of his hair until the peak is as hard as coral. I want to make him sit in front of that monstrosity of a mirror so he can see what he's become.

Ma just went into the room to say something to him, Lucy at her side. Mother's hands are gesturing like a maestro's. One edge of Grandma's gold-framed mirror is visible, and I can't take my eyes off it. Nor can I steer my mind's eye away from the events that happened in that room years ago. The events that caused that mirror to be hung in such a ridiculous spot.

Clay was on the floor, his Matchbox cars spread out over the carpet. I was standing beside him, the doll I was holding by one arm dangling against my calf. Clay and I were four. Maybe five. It would have been a purposeless memory, really. One the conscious mind would never have cause to keep, if it were not for what happened next.

Clay was lining his cars up, making them ready for a race, and Dad was in his chair watching the six o'clock news. Ma was making spaghetti in the kitchen.

"Clay!" Dad snapped, his hard eyes squinted in irritation as he stared at the TV. Clay, who was busy vrmmmmmmmm-mmming his engines, didn't hear him.

"God damn it!" Dad shouted. "Quiet, I said!" I backed away from Clay, my eyes on Dad. His head looked as large and menacing as the horned bison on the farm Marie once took Mom and me and Clay to see.

There was a loud clatter of pans in the kitchen and Dad bolted from his chair, cranked his leg back, and thrust the steel toe of his work boot against Clay's thigh. Dad's German shepherd, Millie, leapt to her feet, snarling, as she did every time there was an outburst of rage. She snarled at Clay, not Dad.

Clay clutched his leg and let out a wail that brought Ma

into the room. I hated it when Clay cried. I hated the way his eyes teared up, flooding bright red as if they were bleeding, drool pooling at the corners of his mouth, his cheeks blotching. He looked ugly when he cried. So ugly that I wanted to kick him too.

"What happened?" Ma shouted as she burst into the living room.

"God damn it, keep this little son of a bitch quiet!" Dad shouted, turning up the TV until it smarted my ears, just like Clay's wailing.

"He . . . he ki-kicked me!"

I expected Ma to cower like she always did when Dad shouted, but she didn't. She stepped forward, her arms reaching back to move Clay and me closer to the archway separating the living room and kitchen. Her voice rose to the roar of an angered beast's as she told him that what he did to her was one thing but that she'd not allow him to lay a hand on her children.

Dad glared at her. There was a twitch under his right eye.

In one swoop, he crossed the room and wrapped his hand around Ma's neck, shoving her back against the wall. There were droplets of spit spewing from his mouth as he lowered his face to hers and shouted, "You want the kicks when your little sissy boy won't shut the fuck up while I'm trying to watch TV? That what you want?" His hand came up to clutch a fistful of hair at her widow's peak. He jerked her head forward, then slammed it back. There was a sickening cracking sound as the back of her head disappeared into the wall. Small chunks of plaster and its white dust skimmed the wall and dropped to the floor.

I hate that I remember this scene. And the one that followed.

That night, Ma winced with each thwack of the hammer she used to pound a nail into the wall, just inches above the hole her head made. As I tried to help her hoist the heavy mirror up to hide it, she told me that she had a headache that throbbed without mercy. "Maybe a drink will help numb it," she said after she dug through the medicine cabinet for Tylenol and found none.

The next morning before Dad left the house, he checked that mirror to make sure his thick, dark waves were behaving themselves. It was a ritual he continued from that day on, every single time he left the house to run to his whore.

That wasn't the only ritual that was birthed that day either. Every day, from then on, Mother opened her bottle of vodka. Through those years, Clay and I often joked about Mother's headache, saying that she had the longest concussion in the history of head injuries—seventeen years, which is how long her drunk lasted. We most often came home from school to find her dozing on the couch or at the table, her bottle of vodka (she bought it in the liquor department at the grocery store as if it were a staple like milk or bread) sitting beside her like an obedient dog.

Ma was too numb during those years to hear him call her an idiot, a worthless bitch, a drunken lush, and the mother of both a whining sissy and a daughter dumber than a turkey, just like her.

But I heard him. Even when I clamped my hands over my ears, his insults slithered through my fingers and crawled into my ear canals to burrow into my mind, becoming a part of me. They made me hate the half of me that was like her, and then, when I got enraged over having and hating those parts, that rage made me feel like him, and I hated that half of me too, until there was nothing left about me to like.

I just close the document when Oma calls to me from downstairs, asking if I'll give her a hand getting Grandpa Sam up from his nap. "Be right there!" I shout in a voice I hope sounds normal.

I feel shaky and like I might cry. I stand up and take a deep cleansing breath like Oma does, lifting my hands above my head, then whooshing them down to my sides. Then I call, "I'm coming!" because I'm starting to feel better. Better, but guilty.

"How come we're not putting him in his wheelchair?" I ask Oma as we lift Grandpa Sam into a sitting position on his bed.

"He needs to keep his muscle tone," she says, as she lifts Grandpa to his feet with a grunt, and I hurry to scoot his walker within his reach. Oma is sweet and wise and doesn't put bad things into her "temple," as she calls her body—well, except for the carcinogens in her cigarettes—and I can't imagine her being an alcoholic. The closest I ever came to knowing a lady drunk was the woman who lived in our building for a time. She was the only person I ever heard Oma talk about unkindly.

Her name was Rose Pottor, and she was a redhead. All seven of her kids had the same clown-red hair, only in varying degrees of color intensity, depending on their ages—the older they got, the duller it got.

Rose's oldest child was Lou Ellen. She was tall for fourteen, and her back was slumped from the burden of carrying woman-sized breasts and woman-sized worries. A few times I met Lou Ellen and her baby brother in the hall and tried to initiate a conversation with her. She never even gave me eye contact, though. She just kept walking, four steps behind little Petey, who toddled up and down the hall with his heavy diaper sagging between his horseshoe legs.

Sometimes at night, I'd sneak out of bed and sit by my window, watching the homeless strolling along with their bags of newspaper, rummaging through the trash cans along the streets. And if it was late enough, I'd see Rose Pottor staggering toward the stoop, a beer bottle swinging from her arm. Folks said that she traded her commodities— a can of beef here, a hunk of cheese there—for beer.

Every time Oma caught sight of Rose leaving the building or we met her Raggedy Ann and Andy children in the hall, Oma's face would pinch up tight and she'd make a rude remark. Once Oma even called her a stain on motherhood and said she deserved to lose her kids. I always gave Oma a second look when she said mean things about Rose Pottor, because my Oma never talked mean about anybody. And if anyone within her earshot did, she made them apologize, even if their remarks were made in fun.

Mom was gone for a couple days with Marcus (the guy who felt like string cheese) and Oma was babysitting us when social services came to haul the Pottor kids away. Oma and I went into the hallway when we heard the ruckus. "Who's that lady?" I asked Oma, as other tenants lumbered out of their apartments like sleeping bears to see what all the pounding was about. The woman wore bangle bracelets that jangled as she rapped on the door and pleaded with Lou Ellen to open up. A cop waited behind her.

There wasn't even a hint of distress in Oma's voice when she said, "She's a social worker. They've come to take the kids away because Rose is a bad mother."

The cop went to get the superintendent when Lou Ellen wouldn't open the door, even after he ordered her to.

It was an awful sight, the cop's beefy fingers sinking into Lou Ellen's freckled upper arms and pulling her out of the apartment. Lou Ellen didn't scream words, just wails, as they tugged her to the elevator, little Petey in the social worker's arms, the rest of the kids following like a trail of muddy footprints. Little Petey was sobbing so hard that his wails stopped coming, leaving his mouth a round, silent circle of terror. Oma watched the whole scene with me, and when I looked up at her—my whole insides shaking—I expected her to have tears in her eyes, like me, but her eyes were dry. "Will they find them a good home?" I asked Oma.

"Hopefully, three or four good homes. They won't be able to keep them together. There's too many of them. But even apart, they'll be better off than they were."

Oma's voice sounded so hard that if I hadn't been watching her mouth move, I would have sworn those words were said by someone other than my Oma.

"Keep his walker steady, will you, honey?" Oma says, using the sweet, gentle voice I need to hear right now. I do, and I keep one hand on Grandpa Sam's back too, as he takes shuffling baby steps toward the living room. "That's it. That's it," Oma says to him.

I man the controls on the lift chair so the seat rises, and Oma helps Grandpa Sam turn around so his butt can meet it. He teeters a bit, and I reach out quickly to grab his arm, careful not to touch his dangling hand.

"I'll bet Rose Pottor got hurt lots of times," I blurt out without meaning to.

"Where on earth did that come from?" Oma asks as she lowers Grandpa Sam's chair. The phone rings then, so I don't need to answer Oma. While she talks to Aunt Jeana, I stare down at Grandpa Sam. I decide that his left hand is the one that carved beautiful birds and made toboggans, and his right hand—which is equally lumpy and knotted with blue veins but boasts a nasty scar on the knuckle—is the one that put Oma's head through the wall. So I reach over him and pat his left hand before I leave the room.

While Oma reassures Aunt Jeana that things are going well here, I gently stroke the back of her head and remind myself that Oma was not a drunk like Rose Pottor. She made chili, and turkey, and gingerbread cookies, and she bought Mom and Uncle Clay a sled when they didn't get a toboggan.

chapter

FIFTEEN

I DON'T LOOK at Mom's documents the next day or the day after that. I decide I don't want to know any more about Oma and Grandpa Sam in the old days—I want to know only about my dad.

So I resume my Internet search. I'm busy Googling when Oma and Marie come in from outside, where they were planting some flower bulbs that will come up in the spring, even though we won't be here. I pause to make tea for them both while they scrub the dirt from their hands. Chamomile for Marie—who has a tension headache because Al still won't take his hernia to the doctor, even though he's complaining almost nonstop now—and green tea, a natural

energy booster, for Oma, who says she's pooped out from all the work she's done since we got here.

"I told Al I'd give him more Reiki. I wish he'd come by," Oma says.

"Oh, that stubborn old coot," Marie says. "I'm ready to give him another hernia, or worse, if he doesn't stop all his bellyaching and just go in."

It's what Marie calls Indian summer, so they take their teacups with them when they go outside so Oma can smoke. I know they'll be out there for a while, sitting on the two old chairs Oma dragged from the shed, and I settle in to do my homework, which, for some reason, I don't mind doing today.

An hour later, Marie comes in to get her purse because she has to leave. She gives me and Milo each one of her bear hugs, and I go back to my schoolwork.

I'm reading but can feel Oma staring at me. When I look up at her, she comes to the table and sits down beside me. "Lucy?" she says. "Peter called when you were riding bikes with Milo earlier."

"He did? Oh, I wish I had gotten to talk to him!" I expect Oma to acknowledge my disappointment with an empathetic smile, but instead, her smile looks only happy.

"He's going up to Bayfield for his cousin's wedding next weekend. His whole family is flying in, so he's taken some time off, and, if it's okay with your mom, he wants to stop here on Thursday."

I suddenly get so excited I can hardly sit still. "That's just three days away!"

"Peter's coming?" Milo asks as he enters the kitchen to bring his cookie plate to the sink.

"*If* your mother says it's okay," Oma repeats.

"Why wouldn't she say yes?" Milo says with a blink. I roll my eyes. He's *so* oblivious!

"I sent your mom to the pharmacy. She should be back in about twenty minutes—if she doesn't stop at Mitzy's. But please, children. Let me be the one to bring this up. She'll need to be eased into this delicately."

"Okay," I say. Then, while Oma sits down to read from her *Tibetan Book of the Dead,* I sit and think about Peter's visit. And of how, if he and Mom were still together, I'd be going to Bayfield too and meeting his niece who's read *Little Women* fifteen times and his dad who can still walk on his hands.

SHE'S HOME!" I shout.

"Already?" Oma glances out the window and flaps her hands at me to settle down. "Go back to your studying, Lucy. And please. Say nothing. Let me handle this."

I try. I try real hard to keep my mouth shut when Mom comes in, sets down the white bag of pills, and announces, "I stopped at Mitzy's, but I didn't stay more than a minute. She's not feeling well. She's got a stomach bug."

"She should try ginger root or charcoal tablets," Oma says as she lines the new pill bottles on the cupboard shelf.

"Wait, those are mine," Mom says, grabbing two of the bottles from Oma—Paxil and Ambien. She struggles with the cap on her antidepressant, then grabs a glass from the drainer and turns on the faucet.

Without missing a beat, and while reciting a few more herbal remedies that might help Mitzy, Oma grabs the glass from Mom, pours the water down the drain, then gets the Brita from the fridge.

"Mother! Will you stop doing that? I like the taste of well water."

Oma's been wearing a half grin since Mom got in the

door, and I know it's only a matter of time before Mom gets suspicious and asks why.

"Have you had lunch?" Oma asks. "I made a nice shrimp salad."

"Later," Mom says. "I've got to get off an e-mail to my agent and tell her what fabulous progress I'm making on my book. Good thing I'm a fiction writer."

Peter called," Oma *finally* says, after Mom hits *send* on her e-mail.

Mom stiffens but does not look up. "What did he want?" she asks, trying to sound casual.

I don't mean to blurt it out, but I can't hold it in any longer. "He's coming to visit us!"

"Lucy," Oma moans, as Mom stares at me, her jaw going slack.

"Well, that's not exactly what he said," Oma says. "He's going to a cousin's wedding up in Bayfield this weekend. He's taking a few days off, since much of his family is flying in for the wedding, and he said if you didn't mind, he'd love to stop in and see you and the children along the way."

"He thinks Timber Falls is along the way? The guy never did have a sense of direction," Mom says. She's composed herself—or so she thinks—but I see the slight tremble in her hands.

"He's calling you tonight."

"I don't know why," Mom says.

I feel anger crunching my jawbones. "You have to let him come, Mom," I cry out. "It's not fair if you don't. I miss him, and so does Milo. Even Persephone misses him."

"Will you stop calling her that!"

"She told me to!"

"Well, it's stupid, a grown woman making her grand-children call her a Greek goddess."

"Tell her that, not me. And stop changing the subject."

Oma, who is now standing at the stove behind Mom, puts her index finger up to her lips to shush me. But it does no good, because I can't stop. "I don't see anything strange about it," Oma says to distract me. "Unusual, maybe, but not strange."

But I won't be distracted.

"It's not fair! You brought Peter into our lives and did everything in your power to see that we liked him. Then when we came to love him, you decided you shouldn't, and you said good-bye. And because you said good-bye, we had to. That's not the way it should be."

"That's enough, Lucy. Now get back to your studies. You've been slacking ever since we got here."

"Just let him come, Mom. Even if you don't want to see him. You can go to Mitzy's or something. Just let Milo and me see him."

Oma scoots around the table and puts her hand on my head, like we do to Feynman when we don't want him jumping on people. "Well, you just think about it, honey," she says to Mom. And then to me, "Lucy, would you check on your grandpa?"

"Why? He's sleeping. You can tell by his snores."

"No, I'm sure I heard movement in there. Check to see that he's not slouched over in his chair, please."

"You don't need to bother trying to get her out of the room," Mom says, closing her laptop. "I'm going outside. Maybe I'll be able to get some work done out there. Obviously I'm not going to find any peace and quiet in here."

Mom gets up, grabs her laptop, and heads to the front

door. "Sure! Go hide in your trees like you always do!" I shout.

Mom doesn't acknowledge my words. She slams the front door behind her, and I thump my book shut and head to the back door, grabbing my own jacket off the hook alongside it.

"Where you going, Lucy? Don't pester your mother now. It will only make things worse."

"I'm going for a bike ride!" I shout, even though I don't mean to shout at Oma.

"But your mother said..." I don't wait for Oma to finish.

W HEN MOM sees me zipping down the driveway, she yells, "Where are you going? And where's your helmet?"

I ignore her too and keep pumping, the old bike rattling beneath me as I hit the bumps in the graveled drive.

I pedal hard, tears rolling across my temples as the wind blows them out of my eyes. *I hate her*, I repeat with each rotation of my pedals. *I hate her! I hate her! I hate her!*

I don't think, I just ride at the edge of the road until I'm winded, then I stop the bike, straddle it, and wait for my lungs to stop heaving. While I'm resting, I see a mailbox with gold stick-on letters that spell out the name *Bickett*. As soon as I catch my breath, I pedal to the mailbox and turn down the long drive that runs alongside it.

Anger sure does make a person brave—or stupid—I think, when my legs don't hesitate for even one millisecond after I see Henry Bickett's beat-up pickup sitting in the drive.

Nordine is in her garden, wearing a straw hat that looks

like it was confiscated from the head of Scarlett O'Hara. I let my bike clank to the ground and head over to her.

"Hi, Mrs. Bickett," I say. Her white hair isn't curled today, and it hangs around her head like pulled lamb's wool. She's not wearing makeup either, and her cheeks have round brown splotches on them. Somehow, though, she still manages to look pretty.

Nordine is holding a bucket with yellowed fronds spilling over the sides, and a large carrot dangles from her other hand like a headhunter's trophy. "Hello," she says. She seems confused about who I might be, but she's not staring at me in that same vacant way that she did on the day Grandpa Sam drove into her garage.

"Look at this. It must have frozen last night," Nordine says, looking down at a row of plants dripping with string beans that are scabby and shriveled. It's frozen many nights in the past two weeks, actually. "All these beans, ruined." She lifts the carrot in her hand, "These are still good, though," she says, as she uses her foot to part the fuzzy leaves that are only partially hiding a few pumpkins and squash.

I know from what I've read that those in the earlier stages of Alzheimer's can slip in and out of dementia, and even though Nordine can't remember me (which is understandable, considering the circumstances under which we first met), her comment about her garden tells me that—at least for the time being—she's standing in the house of coherency, so I know I'd better start knocking. And fast.

Nordine hands me the carrot she's holding. "You can have that one...uh...I'm sorry, I don't know your name."

"I'm Lucy McGowan," I say, looking at the cold, dirt-coated carrot and not quite knowing what to do with it. "Sam McGowan's granddaughter. We're in Timber Falls to take care of him because he's not doing so well. Sam used to be your boyfriend, didn't he?" I don't know what makes me speak so bluntly—maybe my lingering anger at Mom, or maybe my desperation to leap through this window of opportunity before it slams shut—but I can't seem to stop the bluntness any more than I could keep from blurting out the news about Peter's visit. "I know he used to love you," I say. "Maybe still does."

Nordine Bickett steps closer to me. "He does?"

My words work like the strokes of a spatula across cake icing, filling in the furrows on Nordine's face so that she looks younger. "Of course he does. He told me so himself."

Nordine smiles, but her eyes gather a few tears too.

I wonder if I'm making bad karma by lying, but then I remind myself that Oma says that intention plays some part in karma too. And if she's right, then I'm probably safe, because what's so bad about a kid trying to find her dad and giving somebody trapped in a mental fog a little sunshine?

"Sam was my sweetheart," Nordine says. She looks first to the north and then to the south. "I can't recall where the school was now. Isn't that silly? I grew up in this house and walked there every day as a child, but I seem to have forgotten."

Nordine plucks at the collar of her worn work shirt, her sparse eyebrows dipping in worry.

"It's okay. Lots of people are poor with directions. Mrs. Bickett, I'd like to know more about my grandpa Sam. I didn't know him at all until we came here, because we moved away from Timber Falls when my brother and I were babies. I know the two of you were close, so I am hoping you'll tell me some things about him, since you knew him for so many years."

Nordine gives me that oh-that's-nice look that people absentmindedly give someone when they're not really listening. "Would you like to go inside for a glass of lemonade?" she asks.

I tell her yes, and I offer to carry the carrot bucket to the house.

When we get to the door, it's hanging open and clanking sounds are coming from inside. Henry Bickett grumbles a few obscenities, and Nordine stops and turns to me. "Why don't you wait out here, dear, in the lawn chair. I'll bring out our lemonade." I slip the carrot she gave me into the bucket and hand it to her.

I wait at the bottom of the steps. "Who?" Henry asks, his voice twice the size of him. And then, "That kid out there, that's who! What in the hell does she want?"

There's more mumbling and grumbling before Nordine appears from the house carrying one glass of lemonade. She hands it to me.

"Thank you. Aren't you having any?" I ask.

She looks down at her hand, as though she expects another glass to be there.

"Should we get you some too?" I ask. She doesn't answer, though. She just starts strolling toward two lawn chairs sitting under a large maple, so I follow her.

I'm glad that Nordine is walking ahead of me when I take a sip of my lemonade, because I have to spit it out. Not only does it have no sugar in it, but it's gone rancid. I don't think Nordine sees me, but in case she does, I half shout, "Eww, a bug flew into my mouth."

Nordine sits quietly, her eyes occasionally darting toward the house, where, from time to time, Henry's head butts up against the screen door to gawk at us.

"He jumped Richard Marbles because he bullied his girl, Louise Treder, in the parking lot. Shoving her so hard

that her thigh banged into the bumper of his truck, and she
cried out," Nordine says.

"Henry did?" I ask.

"No," she says. "Sam did. He pinned Richard down to
the ground and told him that if he was going to get his nose
out of joint and shove around some tiny slip of a girl, he'd
gladly give him a hand. He punched Richard so hard that
his nose is still cocked to one side today." Nordine rests her
hand on her bony chest as she laughs.

"When did he do that?" I ask.

"Last Friday night, at the dance."

Of course I'm surprised, but not for the reasons Nordine
Bickett would think I am, if she were truly thinking. I'm
surprised because the same boy who defended a girl who
was being shoved later went on to become a man who shoved
his wife's skull through a wall.

Just as I open my mouth to ask her a question, Henry
Bickett comes out of the house, carrying a wrench the size
of his forearm.

He starts toward the garage, then stops and turns. "You
ain't got time to be sittin' around gabbin', woman," he says,
like it's the 1800s and he's in the hills. "The rest of those
carrots aren't going to get themselves out of the ground.
You gonna let them go to hell like you did the rest of the
garden? Huh? You'd best get at it while you still have the
wits to do it."

Henry Bickett spits a wad of tobacco on the grass, then
glares at me. I glare right back at him. "Who'd you say you
were?" he asks.

"Lucy," I say.

"Lucy who?"

"Just Lucy."

He stares at me. Hard. Then his eyes squint until they look shut. "You were with that bunch that came to get McGowan out of my garage, weren'tcha?" He jabs the wrench toward the garage, where plywood is still tacked over the door. "You can tell that son of a bitch that if that damn door isn't fixed by the end of the week, I'm comin' for him." Then he stomps off, his bowed legs and porcupine hair so comical that nobody in their right mind could be afraid of him, which explains why Nordine is.

"He's not a very nice man," I say to Nordine, after he disappears behind the garage, where a rusted tractor sits in a group of half-assembled junky cars. I look at her and ponder what in her past made her a woman who found herself attracted to such mean men.

"He's got his ways," Nordine says.

"My grandpa had his ways too," I say.

Nordine looks confused, but I'm not sure if it's confusion about what I just told her or the Alzheimer's coming back to cloud her brain.

"Sam and I are going to get married," she states, and my question is answered.

I sigh. "Um, you can't do that, Mrs. Bickett. You're already married. To Henry."

Nordine gets up without saying anything and walks to the house like a sleepwalker, leaving me sitting in the metal lawn chair, wondering if she's coming back.

I wait for what seems a good ten or fifteen minutes, and just as I'm about to get up and follow her inside, she comes out the door. She has a box that says *Sorel Boots* cradled in her arms and a photograph pinched between her knobby knuckles. "What do you have there?" I ask. "May I?" I set the glass of sour lemonade on the grass, making sure to tip it a bit first so some spills out, then I slip the picture from her fingers. It is black and white, worn at the scalloped edges, and creased down the center. In the photograph is my grandpa and Nordine, both of them young. Grandpa is good-looking, I suppose, his grin stretched across his face, his arm wrapped around Nordine, who stands as small as a child under his arm, her hair frizzed around her upturned, heart-shaped face.

"He's a handsome man," she says. That comment alone tells me that Nordine has no recollection of the broken garage door or the man in diapers who clunked into it.

I hand her back the picture, and she holds it with both hands, as though it is just as heavy in weight as it is in memory.

"Mrs. Bickett," I say bravely. "I know that you and my grandpa Sam were, well, close over the years. So that means you might know something about my mom, Tess, and my real father. Do you remember Sam talking about his daughter, Tess? Did he tell you anything about her after she came back from California?"

Her eyes glaze over. "Sam's in California?"

"No. His daughter went there. About fifteen years ago."

"I don't have a daughter," she says. "I have a boy." She's obviously struggling to recall his name.

I take the photo from her hands again and point to Grandpa Sam. "No. *Him. He* had—he has—a daughter. Her name is Tess. She left Timber Falls to go away to college. And she came back pregnant with me and my twin. Did my...did Sam...tell you anything about that? Did he tell you about the father of her babies?"

Nordine's face is blank in the shade of her hat's wide brim, her eyes shadowed by her disease.

I sigh, knowing that I've lost her. "What do you have in the shoe box?" I finally ask her.

She looks down at her lap as though she only now realizes that there's a box resting on her legs. "Oh, let's see, shall we?" she says.

When she makes no move to do it herself, I reach over to lift the lid from the box. Whatever is inside is wrapped in grayed tissue paper. The kind that is dotted with colored glitter. The glittery specks cling to my fingers when I peel the paper back.

"It's a marionette puppet!" I say.

I pull the puppet from the box and it clanks like wooden wind chimes. The puppet is a boy, his head large and full of wooden curls, his body thin and gangly and dressed in homemade pants and a button-up shirt. He is about a foot tall and carved from pale wood that is scarred with nicks and gouges from the point of a knife. His wooden head is lolled to his chest, and when I pick it up and see his big, sad eyes—a sharp contrast to his full, smiling lips—I say, "Ohhh," out loud.

"Did Sam carve this?" I already know the answer. Even though it's carved crudely, unlike his birds, I can feel the same thing in it that I felt from them, only there's more sadness seeped into this wood, along with a whole lot more anger. So much so that I'm convinced that even Milo could feel it if he held it.

"It's him," she says. "His name is Sammy." And then she makes her voice deeper, rougher, and she says, "Always a puppet. Always a puppet."

Nordine Bickett gets up again, the photo floating to the ground as she wanders to the center of the yard, her head tilted back. She moves in slow circles, her face searching. I get up, the puppet in my arm, and hurry to rescue the photograph from the grass. I hand it to her and she stares down at it as though she doesn't know what it is. "I know my school is around here," she says.

The clanking of Henry's hammer against metal stops, and I don't know what to do, because I don't want Nordine's husband coming and seeing the picture or the puppet. Nordine lets the picture slip from her hand again, then she wanders back inside, leaving me standing there when Henry Bickett appears from the side of the shed. I have a split second to react before he looks up, so I slide the photograph into my pocket as I'm turning away from him and I stuff the puppet up my windbreaker.

Henry glances at the empty lawn chairs, the shoe box alongside one and the glass tipped on its side alongside the other, then he looks at me suspiciously. He goes over and picks up the box, peering inside, rustling the tissue paper, then carries it back to me. "What's this?"

"A shoe box," I say. "Your wife brought it out."

"What was in it?" he asks.

"Nothing." I don't even feel bad lying to him, even if it means a little bit of bad karma later.

"She's tetched," he says, tossing the box back on the ground. "You get out of here now. No relative of Sam's is welcome here."

"I want to say good-bye to Mrs. Bickett first," I say.

"Never mind that. She wouldn't know you said good-bye anyhow. Now, beat it."

I pull the drawstring on my jacket and tie it tight to keep the puppet secure, then head to my bike. "And don't come back. You hear me?"

As I pedal home, I think about Alzheimer's disease and how god-awful it is and how I hope Oma doesn't get it. And I wonder if I shouldn't go into medical research and try to

find a cure, since it would be work dealing with the brain at
least.

When I reach our place, I want to ride right past it
because I'm still upset with Mom. But I can't. I have to pee,
and besides, Mom is still in the trees and she rises when she
sees me.

I pull into the yard, toss my bike down, then dart for the
house even though Mom's yelling my name. I race up the
stairs to the bathroom, but not before tucking the puppet
and the photograph under my pillow.

While I'm peeing, the door downstairs opens and shuts,
and I know Mom has come inside to yell at me. I just step
into the hall when I hear Oma say to her, "No, Tess. Leave
her be. She's at that age now where she's going to have some
outbursts. And this is really difficult for her. She was very
attached to Peter, and you know how much she longs for a
father figure in her life. Just let her be for now. Please?"

"Let her be? I should be grounding her for a month for
that little stunt." My mouth turns as sour as if Nordine's
lemonade is still in it. I stomp into my room and slam the
door. Then I open my laptop and click on one of Mom's
journal entries at random.

chapter

SIXTEEN

I hate this house the most late at night, when Ma and the kids are sleeping and I can't. I hate the sounds of Dad's labored breaths and the eerie echoes from the past. The sights, the sounds, the smells—all of it—are enough to make me want to bolt out of here. But there's nowhere to run but the trees, and it's raining.

I can't believe I'm back here. I thought I'd left it for good.

On what I was sure would be the last day I ever set foot in this house again, Mitzy drove me home so I could pack my things. It was raining then too.

"Are you sure you don't want me to stay and help you pack?" Mitzy asked, her face tight with guilt when I opened

the car door and the interior light clicked on. I reminded her that I was only packing one bag for now and tossing the few things I planned to take with me in boxes for when I knew where I was going. I assured her that her helping wouldn't get the job done any faster, since I'd have to keep pausing to tell her what I wanted packed and what I didn't. "Just for moral support?" she said.

The truth was, I did want Mitzy to stay for moral support, but how could I ask her to? She was one month away from getting married and starting tech school to become an X-ray technician. It was Brian's birthday, and she had two bags stuffed with ingredients for spaghetti and meatballs and the lopsided chocolate cake she'd baked earlier sitting on the backseat. She was so wired with the anticipation of cooking him their first dinner together in their new home that she couldn't keep her mind on much of anything else. So I told her to go. That I'd be fine. I reminded her that Marie was picking me up in two hours and that she'd come sooner if I needed her to.

"Are you sure they're keeping your dad overnight?" she yelled as we ran the empty boxes across the darkened yard, squealing because we were getting wet. Once we reached the shelter of the porch, I assured her that they were and told her to stop worrying. "Just go. I'll be fine. Have fun. Screw your brains out."

"God, you're awful!" she said, and I told her that apparently I am. Her face fell and she hugged me, telling me that I was the best.

As she drove away in her five-year-old Grand Am, I envied her. Not because I wanted the life she was etching out for herself (marriage, a dozen babies, meat loaf once a week), but because she had a place to be, and a plan.

It was strange walking into my house that night to gather my things. It was the house I'd grown up in. I knew every crack, every scuff, and every stain on the walls, and once I had even loved it. When I was very young, that is. Way back before I realized it was such a dump. Before Dad got mean, and Ma started drinking, and Clay walked out. Even after those things happened—even after I stopped loving it—it still felt like home. But not that night, as I stood in the doorway with my empty boxes and flicked on the kitchen light.

The chair was still lying helplessly on its side, and the table was cocked so that one corner was butted against the counter.

Without a thought, I picked a dirty plate off the table to carry it to the sink. I stopped in the middle of the room, then turned and set the plate back down where it was. Maybe it was time to stop trying to clean up the family's messes, like Marie said. I headed up the stairs, my boxes scraping against the stairwell walls.

My room was just as I'd left it one hour before my graduation ceremony: the torn plastic bag from my robe and cap on the floor, my bed scattered with skirts and dresses I had tried on, then discarded, as I searched for something pale enough not to show through my flimsy white gown.

I didn't know how to start packing any more than I knew how to start a new life. I'd slept in this room since I was born, and everything I had ever owned was in it, from my stuffed toys and books to my stacks of journals.

I packed in a rush, not bothering to sort the things I wanted to take once I had a place to bring them—my favorite pens, my clothes, a few books, candles, odds and ends. I left the journals behind, as if by doing so I could leave the memories behind, and I scooted the boxes alongside the wall. Then I

packed my duffel bag with the things I'd need immediately—
a couple of changes of clothes, my toiletries, the book I was
partway through reading—and I carried the bag downstairs
to leave at the back door. I went back for my word processor,
still in its box.

As I carried the heavy box down, I kept my shoulder
propped against the wall to keep my balance, my side brushing against the darkened smears on the paint where my fingers had trailed each time I went up or down the stairs. Stains
Ma tried to cover with fresh paint every couple of years, but
they always bled through, just like Clay's handprints that
were smudged above the door frame where he leapt to see how
high he could reach.

I waited at the back door for Marie, the porch light on,
watching the rain glint as it fell in dotted lines from the eaves.
When the wind kicked up, the rain bobbed the fronds of the
spindly fern Ma had set at the edge of the porch a few days
before and blew the drops through the mesh of the screen to
spatter on my face.

I closed the door and there they were, the half-inch hori-
zontal lines Ma etched in pen, an A or a T next to each of
them, along with the date. Lines Mom used to mark our
height from the time we could stand up, no matter how much
we protested once we'd grown past the age of caring about
"getting big." I reached out and touched the marks near the
height of my shoulders. About there, I decided, was when I
first moved out of this house; I just hadn't packed yet.

I stood looking at the closed door for a time—at the hinges,
the worn rim around the doorknob, at anything "safe"—as if
in doing so I could keep the ugly, random slidelike images
that had been pelting my brain for two days from connecting,
from speeding up, from turning into a horror movie that I
didn't want to see. But staring at the door didn't help.

It's strange, the way you can enter a house and feel down to your bones that something is terribly wrong, even before you see anything amiss.

The minute I stepped inside the house that morning after graduation—just two days before Mitzy brought me back to pack—I knew something was dangerously wrong. I felt it in my skin at the nape of my neck, which had gone as taut as my breath, and in the sudden buzzing in my ears.

I pitched my cap and gown on the kitchen counter, my gaze fixed on the table, sitting at such an odd angle. There was an empty space where the chair that normally sits at the end should have been. My sudden fear made me call out Ma's name, even though moments ago my intent was to make it to my room without being seen or heard, so I could pretend that I hadn't stayed out all night at Settler's Hill.

That's when I saw Ma sprawled on the floor on the other side of the table, her sleeveless nightgown twisted around her hips, one bruised leg draped over the other.

"Ma!" I stepped over her and knelt down, rolling her onto her back.

Her eyes were only partially open, one iris a sliver under its lid, the other swollen shut and purpled. There was a cut on her left cheek, just below the swollen eye, and clotted blood smeared to her ear. Purple-red fingerprints spotted her upper arm and rimmed the sides of her neck.

I dropped to my knees and slipped my hand under her head to turn it toward me. There was a lump under the fingertips of my left hand, just above her ear. I leaned over, putting my face close to hers to feel for breath. What I felt coming from her alcohol-drenched mouth was so faint that I wasn't sure I hadn't imagined it.

I screamed for Clay, even though I knew he wasn't there, and I yelled for Dad, even though when I got home seconds ago, I had sighed with relief when the empty driveway reaffirmed what my watch already told me: that Dad had left for work. I called for him, even though I knew it was he who had put her on the floor.

I slapped Ma's unbruised cheek with quick taps and called her name, begging her to wake up: a scene straight out of one of the soap operas Ma occupied herself with in the afternoons while she medicated herself with vodka.

Not knowing what to do for Ma, I called Marie—the same as Ma called Marie every time there was a crisis—my hands so clumsy that I could hardly dial. "Tess, is that you? Honey, take a breath. Slow down. Auntie Marie can't understand you," she said.

Marie reached the house quickly. "She's breathing, honey," she said, after she laid her head over Ma's chest, then pressed her fingertips to the side of Ma's neck. "She's going to be all right."

But I wasn't convinced.

Marie leaned back on her feet and tenderly picked up one limb and then the other, her fingers gently stroking Ma's bruised skin. Silent tears ran down her cheeks and she didn't bother to brush them away.

Marie wrapped her arm around my waist firmly as two white-coated EMT workers slid Ma onto the gurney. And when a police officer told me he'd have to ask me a few questions, she stepped in quickly, telling him that I was too upset and could answer his questions later.

"One question, then," the officer said. "Miss? Do you have any idea who did this to your mother?"

A new assault of fear slammed my body as I answered, "My father."

My legs started shaking, and Marie pulled out a chair so I could sit down. She gently pushed until the base of my neck was resting below my knees, and she told me to breathe deeply.

And I did. At least until the sirens began their screaming descent toward town.

Marie took me to her house after we left the hospital, saying I could pick up my things in a day or two and stay with her until I left for California in August. "I'm so glad you're getting out of here, honey," she told me. "You get yourself an education and a better life than your mother's."

Dad cried when the police plucked him from his station and escorted him through the mill. That's what people were bold enough to tell me later, anyway, their retarded eyes filled with pity—for him.

When Mom was released, Marie brought her home too and wasted no time giving her opinion of things. Ma insisted that Dad wouldn't have done it had she not had "a little too much" to drink.

Marie jumped all over Ma then, reminding her that Dad had been slamming her around for years and that the only difference this time was that he'd gotten caught. "You are a battered woman, Lillian, and that's all there is to it," Marie said, her voice as sharp and hard as an arrowhead. She stopped for a breath, then quickly added, "No, I take that back. That isn't all there is to it. You aren't only a battered woman. You're also a drunk."

Ma looked like she'd been punched all over again. I glanced at the door, thinking of bolting. Marie must have sensed this, because she pinned me to the couch with one glance before turning her attention back to Ma.

"You know what you and Sam need... well, besides a divorce?" she said. "You need to start taking responsibility for your actions. It's time you both stop blaming the other and

*start owning up to the truth about what you've allowed your-
self to become. I don't give a shit how many times you do
something that irritates that man, he has no right to physically and emotionally beat you as he does. And I don't care
how many times he knocks you to the floor, that's no excuse for
hiding yourself in a bottle."*

Marie pointed her finger at me then and told Ma that I
had suffered for years, living in that house with the two of
them, and that Clay had lost his home for the same reason.
She told Ma that even if she and Dad didn't have any concern
about what they were doing to each other and themselves,
they should at least be suffering some distress about what
they're doing to us.

Ma was sobbing, and I made a move to grab her a
Kleenex from the box on the end table, but Marie put her
hand up to stop me. "You aren't going to take care of your ma
in this house," she said, and I was forced to sit there and watch
Ma sob and dab her runny nose with the back of her hand.

For a time the room was silent but for Ma's crying. I
watched Marie from the corner of my eye. Long strands of
her hair had come loose from a rubber band and were hanging over a face that was more serious than I'd ever seen it, the
softness normally there replaced by something as solid and
immovable as a boulder.

Marie pulled a corner of an envelope from the pocket of
her sweater and fingered it. She told Ma that she knew a
woman who was a recovering alchoholic and she'd given her a
call. The woman would be glad to take Ma to tonight's AA
meeting, but she'd have to call the woman herself if she
wanted to go. Marie said she'd leave the woman's number on
the end table. She reached over and set it there.

I glanced at Ma, who sat on the other end of the couch, her
elbow crutched on the armrest, her face propped on a fist

*clutching the crumpled tissues she'd taken from the box her-
self. She looked up at Marie then, her eyes singed with fear.
"I…" and sobs claimed the rest of her words.*

*Marie's face softened, and she went to Ma, settling her
large frame down beside her. She wrapped her arm around
Ma and tipped Ma's head to her shoulder. She told Ma that
she loved her. That she'd kept her mouth shut in the past for
the most part but that things had just gone too far and needed
to stop. She stroked Ma's hair, a gesture that always made my
insides go soft.*

*"You can't do a damn thing to make Sam straighten up
and fly right, Lillian," Marie said. "But you can choose to
straighten up and fly right yourself. Now. Before he kills you,
or you kill yourself." She revealed that Ma's wounds from
Dad's beating this time were superficial and that it was her
blood alcohol level that had her knocked out cold—the first
I'd heard this. "One more drink," she said, "and I could have
been bitching at you in your casket, Lillian. And that scares
the hell out of me." Marie's voice broke and she rocked Ma as
she repeated, "Just scares the hell out of me."*

*I went to stay with Mitzy that night. Marie insisted, saying I
needed to just go and be the teenage girl I was and talk about
boys, and movies, and whatever else it was that eighteen-year-
old girls talk about. I didn't want to go, because I knew I'd be
keeping Mitzy from Brian and because I didn't want to leave
Ma, but Marie gave me no choice.*

*Marie called after Mitzy and I finished a pizza to tell me
that Ma left with her friend for the AA meeting. She told me
that we shouldn't bank on anything, but that we should pray.*

*I didn't pray, though. I'd talked to this so-called God the
night Dad put Ma's head through the wall years before,
pleading with Him to not allow Dad to ever lay a hand on her*

again. I prayed the way I'd seen the child pray in that paint-ing that hung in the basement of the Lutheran church where Ma dragged me on Sundays when I was little: with my knees on the floor, my elbows propped on the bed, the palms of my hands pressed together. Had there been a God, He would have stopped the beatings, I reasoned, because anyone with the goodness of a God would not have let someone like Ma be beaten.

It was a good thing that Marie and I didn't bank on anything, because Ma went back home the following week. Marie's face blotched with anger when Ma told her she was going, but she didn't try to talk her out of it. Instead, she told her flatly that if she wanted to subject herself to that hellhole some more, she could go right ahead but that I wasn't going back with her.

I could see from the way Marie stood—legs parted and stiff, fists on hips, chin lifted high—that she meant business. Ma knew it too, because she didn't tell me to pack as she gath-ered her things.

While she folded her nightgown—the same one that had twisted around her as they hoisted her onto the gurney—I begged her not to go home. "He'll do it all over again. You know he will," I said.

Ma pointed toward the flowers and card on the night-stand and told me how when Dad brought them by earlier he promised that he was going to do better. She reminded me of Dad's hard life and the hot head he'd inherited from his dad, then followed up with his lame promise that he'd keep it in check from now on. I looked at the roses sitting on the night-stand, still wrapped in plastic, the green plant food cartridges still fastened to their stems, and I wanted to shred them into a thousand pieces. "Did the bastard promise to stop screwing his whore too?" I snapped.

Ma spun around to face me head-on and reminded me that I was talking about my father. She rattled the clasp on her tattered suitcase and gave up in tearful defeat, blaming her shakiness on my upsetting her.

I probably shouldn't have said it, but I was so upset that I couldn't help but ask her if that was it or if it was the fact that she needed another drink that had her packing for home.

Marie must have heard our raised voices, because she came into the room and took me by the elbow to steer me out.

I pleaded with her to stop Ma, saying that we couldn't let her go back there. Marie's hold on my elbow tightened and she tipped her head so that it was resting on mine. "Honey, people will do what they're going to do. You can't save anyone from themselves."

I wish those words had sunk in.

I DELETE THAT journal entry, as if by erasing it on my computer I can delete it from my mind. I can't, though. I see every little happening even after the words are gone, plus the extras that my mind fills in. I see the lint from Oma's Kleenex as she cries, hovering like a cloud in front of her face. I hear the groan of the box spring as Oma pushes her suitcase closed, the click of the lock. I smell the roses, sickening sweet, and see the tiny air bubbles through the clear green plastic of the tubes at the bottom of each stem. I see these things, and my mind can't stop screaming, *Don't go back there, Oma. Please, don't!* as if it is all happening now, not over fifteen years ago.

I lie down on my pillow and feel the bulk of the puppet against the side of my face. I yank him out by the arm, and I'm about to throw him, but I know that he'd only make a loud clunk that would bring Oma running. And although I want her to come—so I can see with my own eyes that she didn't stay back in this house this whole time, that she did move out and get sober and happy—I stuff him under the pillow next to the one I use and push down, smothering him.

I don't know how long I doze, but when I wake up, I hear women talking in the kitchen: Mom, Oma, Mitzy, and Marie, and I can smell cake baking in the oven.

"Well, look who woke up," Oma says when I get downstairs. She opens her arms for a hug. As I'm hugging her as hard as Marie hugs, Mom slips her hand between Oma's big breasts and my forehead and asks me if I'm okay. "You never nap unless you're sick," she says.

"Oh, I hope she's not coming down with my bug," Mitzy says.

"I'm not sick," I say, as I stand in Oma's hug, not wanting to let go.

"It must be all the fresh air," Oma says.

The timer on the oven goes off, and I scoot aside so Oma can take the cake out. It's golden brown on top and has juice bubbling up from the edges. Pineapple upside-down cake. One of Oma's specialties.

The women start yakking, and Oma watches the clock so she can tip the cake onto the cookie sheet waiting alongside the pan at just the right moment. If she tips it over too soon, it will break. But if she waits too long, it won't come out at all.

"God, that smells good," Marie says. "But I'm not sure I should have any. I'm getting so damn fat." Of course, this prompts them all to talk about their weight and exchange dieting tips.

"Speaking of fat," Marie says, after they agree that watching carbs is the key to losing weight, "this morning I walked in the bedroom and found Al standing in front of my full-length mirror, his Fruit of the Looms wrapped around his thighs, his hands down here." Marie stands up and grabs her belly near her groin. "Good God, I didn't know what bulge he was grabbing there, and it sort of threw me, you know?" The women snicker. "Turns out he was trying to get a good look at that hernia of his, and Lord knows he couldn't do it by staring straight down." The women snicker all over again.

"He looked like he'd just been caught cross-dressing, when I walked in." Marie contorts her face to mock his fear. She lifts her hands, rolls her eyes, and sits back down. "He told me he thinks it's a tumor," she says. " 'Cancer of *what*?' I asked him. 'Cancer of the fat part?' "

Mitzy laughs so hard that she snorts.

Marie looks at Oma. "You remember what a hypochondriac his mother was? She'd stay up three days in a row to sew a damn quilt, practically around the clock, then think she had cancer because she was exhausted on the fourth day. Every damn ache or pain she had was cancer. Well, turns out my Al is a closet hypochondriac too. I should have known; that man has been making jokes about dying since I met him.

"He finally let me make him an appointment for Thursday. Good thing, or he'd be going there for more than a hernia, I'll tell you. What is it about men when they're sick or hurt? Damn big babies! I should have married Robert De Niro like I'd planned to." The women giggle.

"If only Ray *were* like that," Mitzy says. "I always want

to pamper him when he's sick, but he never lets me. His mom wasn't the warmest of mothers, so he thinks that when you're not feeling well, you should just wander off by yourself like a sick dog."

"Don't complain," Marie says. "I'd take that any day over a man whining like a teething baby over every little thing."

Oma successfully inverts the cake and taps it onto the cookie sheet with only one circle of pineapple sticking to the bottom of the pan. She returns it to the white circle shape it was pulled from, then sticks the maraschino cherry back in its center. "Oh, it doesn't pay to think of death like that. Remember, Tess, when I bought enough deodorant at one time to tide me over for the rest of my life?"

Mitzy laughs, and says, "What? Why?"

Mom laughs too. "Yes, I remember." She gets up to get dishes and forks and asks me to get the napkins. While she slips small plates from the cupboard, she tells them the story—one I haven't heard before. "So, Ma uses this special deodorant. All because some retired mortician in her apartment building told her that when he cut into the armpit of a woman, she had aluminum an inch thick in her underarms from her antiperspirant. Ma was suddenly convinced that that's what killed the woman—even if she was ninety-two years old—and she rushed off to the health-food store to find an alternative to the antiperspirant she'd used for years."

"They still bleed people under the armpits?" Marie asked. "I thought they drew blood from their veins now."

"I don't know," Oma says.

"Anywayyyy," Mom says, to draw Marie's attention back to her story, "so Ma comes back with this mineral stick—"

"Did I show you that, Marie?" Oma interrupts. "It's amazing. I've been using it now for about seven years. You just dip it under the faucet and put it on like you would any deodorant. You don't even notice you're wearing it—it feels like water when it goes on, no smell, no feel but the water—and the whole stick lasts for a year! Here, smell. I haven't used it since my shower yesterday morning."

"Mother, for crissakes!" Mom says as Oma lifts her arm and sticks her pit in Marie's face.

"That's incredible, Lillian," Marie says. "Simply incredible."

I laugh with the rest of them, the lightness of the conversation and their laughter melting the ugly pictures I had in my head just minutes ago—well, except for the image of the mortician cutting into the armpit of the dead lady.

"Which gets me to the point of this story—which I'm going to forget in about ten minutes if you two interrupt me again," Mom says with a laugh, her eyes crinkled at the corners, as if she wasn't upset earlier either.

"Ma was so in love with that damn mineral stick that she suddenly started worrying about what she'd do if they stopped selling it. And since it lasts for a year, she calculated how many she thought she'd need for the rest of her life—"

"Thirty-five," Oma interjects.

"She bought twenty-five sticks—that's all they had on hand—and she ordered ten more," Mom says. "She dropped one hundred and ninety-nine bucks that day!"

"Oh, my God," Mitzy says, leaning over sideways as she giggles, holding her belly.

"You didn't!" Marie says incredulously.

"I did!" Oma says.

"Wait, wait!" Mom says. "That's not the best part of the story. Two months later, I'm at her house and there they are, stuffed under the sink in her garbage can. All twenty-five of them!"

"Not all twenty-five. I kept five of them," Oma says.

"Why'd you throw them away?" Marie asks, and she's laughing heartily, just like Mitzy.

"Well," Oma explains, "it dawned on me that they were just like one of those Advent calendars that mark the days until Christmas, and I knew that every time I opened that cupboard to get a new one, I'd see them staring at me, counting down the years until my death."

Oma is standing at the stove, a spatula poised in the air. "It was a good lesson for me, though. And I decided right then and there that a person is best off not thinking of those things. We have as much time left here as we have, and we should spend it living, not fretting about dying. You tell that to Al, Marie. You tell him the story."

"Shit," Marie says, "I tell him that, and he'll start tally-ing up how many deodorant sticks he thinks *he'd* need, just to prove that his death is coming sooner than yours!"

The ladies are still laughing as Oma and I pass out the warm cake, then the laughter turns into soft "mmmm-mms."

"So," Mitzy finally asks. "Did Al's mother die of can-cer?"

Marie swallows her mouthful, takes a quick sip of water, then says, "Hell, no. A brain aneurysm. She was eighty-seven years old."

Oma makes me bring Milo a slice, along with a glass of milk I have to pour—as if he doesn't have the nose to smell it and the legs to come out and get it—and when I come back, they're all looking oddly at Mitzy, whose cake plate is pushed to the center of the table, half full. "I, I don't know..." Mitzy says, then she bolts up and darts into the bathroom, her hand clamped over her mouth. She doesn't even have time to shut the door before she starts heaving.

"She should be over that stomach virus by now," Marie says, confused, and then her eyes go wide. She looks at Oma, who is nodding knowingly.

"I told you," Oma says in a hush to Mom. "Didn't I?" The women exchange looks, Marie and Oma nod some more, and Mom winces.

When Mitzy comes out, her face is water-damp and her eyes red and puffy. "I swear I'm never going to get rid of this damn bug," she says. "Sorry, Lillian. It wasn't your cake. I promise." Mitzy stops, because everyone is staring at her.

"I know. But I don't think you're sick either," Oma says. Mitzy looks confused.

Oma goes to her and puts her hand around her shoulder, leading her to her chair. "Honey. You're pregnant. I should have known by your aura alone."

Mitzy shakes her head. "No. It's just a bug. A girl in the office had it, and hers hung on for a good week."

Mitzy looks at the women one at a time, looking for affirmation, I suppose, that it *could* be a virus. And when she doesn't get any, she bursts into tears.

I don't think it's polite to keep eating cake while someone is sobbing, yet I like upside-down cake best warm, and since no one is paying an ounce of attention to me, I keep eating. I'm still listening, though.

"How long have you been throwing up?" Marie asks her.

"I . . . I don't know. Not long. Two, three days."

"Longer than that, Mitzy," Mom says.

"But not every day, and not usually in the mornings."

"You on the pill?" Marie asks.

"I can't take it, but we're careful. Really careful."

"Oh, honey," Oma says, hugging her. "Don't cry. It's a blessing."

Mitzy starts shaking her head. "But we're so careful. And I was never regular, anyway."

I press the back of my fork against the remaining crumbs and slip the fork upside down into my mouth. Mom moves to Mitzy, stroking her hair as she does me or Milo after we throw up. "It *could* be a bug," Mitzy says. "Couldn't it?"

"Yeah, the *love* bug," Marie says, and she grins at her own joke. Mitzy isn't amused. "Oh, God," she says. "I can't go through another loss like that again. I can't. I asked Doctor Peel to tie my tubes after Dylan, but he wouldn't. He said I was too young and that I might marry and welcome a pregnancy again. I asked him to do it, damn it."

And then they're all talking at once, and somewhere in that buzz of conversation it's decided that Mitzy needs a pregnancy test. Marie and Oma decide they'll run to town and get one, and I can keep my ear out for Grandpa Sam.

The house gets apparently quieter after Oma and Marie leave, and it's apparently only then that Mom realizes I've been listening this whole time. She asks me to go upstairs.

"I'm supposed to be listening for Grandpa," I say, so she tells me I can go into the living room and watch TV. PBS, of course.

PBS has a dumb sewing show on, so I only pretend I'm watching it as I keep my ears on the conversation in the kitchen.

"Oh, Tess. It can't be, can it?"

Mom tells Mitzy she'll know soon enough.

"Oh, God," Mitzy says. "I'm scared to death. Look at my hands."

"You want me to call Ray?"

Mitzy must shake her head, because Mom says, "Okay," and she doesn't call.

When Oma and Marie get back with the kit, the noise level skyrockets again, and I slip back into the kitchen to cut another piece of cake and get the lowdown on what's happening.

Oma tears the box open and hands a small vial to Mitzy, then nudges her toward the bathroom. Mitzy shuts the door, and Oma and Marie are pressed up against it, chattering at Mitzy that everything will be okay. Mom props her hands on her hips and wrinkles her brow at Oma and Marie. "Hey, you two. How's she supposed to pee with you hovering like that? Come sit down, for God's sakes."

While Mitzy is peeing, Oma looks for the kitchen timer. "Remember when a rabbit had to die to find out if a woman was pregnant, Marie? How cruel was that! Think of how many of them died."

"Rabbits?" Mom asks.

"It's how doctors used to determine if a woman was pregnant in our mothers' day," Oma says. "From the late twenties to the early sixties. They injected the woman's urine into a rabbit."

"People used to say, 'The rabbit died,' to tell someone that they were pregnant," Marie added.

"Yes," Oma says. "But the fact was, the rabbit died whether you were pregnant or not, because they cut the poor little creatures open to examine their ovaries to see if they had enlarged, then just left them for dead. Just think of how many of them died in those years between——"

"Ma, don't start counting again—remember the deodorant sticks," Mom says, and Marie and Oma laugh. Mom scolds them again, but in a whisper. "Please. She's really upset."

When Mitzy steps out of the bathroom, *she* looks like a scared rabbit about to have her ovaries split open. "I can't even look," she says when Oma sets the timer.

Mom goes to her and gives her a hug. "Let's go outside for a bit, Mitz," she says.

"Poor thing," Marie says quietly. "She's so scared of going through the heartache of losing another baby," and Oma nods.

"Yes, yes." Then Oma looks at me. "Honey, usually waiting to see if you're pregnant is a happy, happy event. But poor Mitzy, she lost a pregnancy, and then she had a baby that was born too early, and she's scared at the thought of losing another one."

"Was my mom happy when she found out she was pregnant with Milo and me?" I ask, and Oma says, "I'd imagine she was," like she doesn't really know.

When the timer goes off, Mom and Mitzy come inside. "You look," Mitzy says to Mom.

Oma and Marie are on Mom's heels as she hurries to the bathroom, and they bump into her when she reaches the door and stops abruptly. "Do you two mind? Geez!"

When Mom comes out of the bathroom, her face is the reversal of Sammy the wooden puppet's, in that her mouth is not smiling, but her eyes are.

Mitzy puts both hands over her mouth—as if there's double-danger lurking—and she breaks into fresh tears, and Oma and Marie swarm her as though she's just won the Miss America crown.

Mitzy asks Mom to drive her home, and she'll have Ray drop her off in the morning to pick up her car. As Mom gets her purse, Oma and Marie smother Mitzy with more hugs and reassurances that everything will be okay.

Oma stands at the kitchen sink, peering out the window as Mom and Mitzy leave. "Such scared young women," she says.

"We had our share of fears at that age too, remember?" Marie says.

"We did. But I guess after a while you just learn how to roll with the punches."

Marie pats Oma's arm and says, "Or we get better at learning how to avoid the punches in the first place."

WHEN MILO and I were little, we were both afraid of storms, Milo more so than me. The second we heard the low rumble of thunder, we'd freeze, and by the time lightning was flashing and the wind was rattling our windows, I'd be hovering close to Mom, while Milo stood next to her, his arms wrapped around her thigh, his face buried as he screamed. And even when we got to be about seven or eight—long after he was too old to clutch Mom's thigh— on those hot, humid days when Milo saw thunderheads forming above our building, he'd hurry for his inhaler. And by the time the storm broke and unleashed its winds, he'd have his inhaler almost down his throat. I was still scared of

storms by that age too, but no matter how scared I was, when Milo started shaking and wheezing, I'd calm right down. That seems to be the way it is with people. Probably it's a survival instinct; let's face it, somebody in the tribe has to keep a level head, because if the whole tribe panics, they'll all be toast when danger threatens.

I guess that's what happened to Mom when she saw how scared Mitzy was to be pregnant. When she got back from Mitzy's, the phone rang and it was Peter, asking Mom if he could stop in on his way to Bayfield. Mom didn't look nearly as frightened as she was when Oma first told her about Peter's request, and she told him he could come.

ON WEDNESDAY, Mom comes downstairs while Milo and I are eating our breakfast and announces that she's off to the salon to get her hair trimmed. Oma, who's paging through her gourmet cookbook, grins, and Mom snaps at her. "It's needed cutting for a month now, so wipe that grin off your face."

"Did I say anything?" Oma says, a smile still tickling her lips. She sets aside her cookbook and wheels Grandpa Sam into the kitchen. "Tess, I wish you'd have a good breakfast too," she says, frowning as Mom washes her Paxil down with a gulp of tap water, then starts filling her travel mug with coffee. Mom ignores her, until Oma asks how Mitzy's doing.

"I don't know. I called her last night, late, but she and Ray were still talking. I told her I'd see her this morning since she was going to call in sick today—she was so drained—so we'll see."

"Poor dear," Oma says. "I pray she'll be able to see this in a different light soon."

THANK YOU FOR ALL THINGS   255

"Me too," Mom says. She plants kisses on Milo and me, then says, "Be good, and get your work started right after you eat."

"Hey, why you telling me?" Milo says.

"I'll get my work done," I say to Mom as she hurries out the door.

"I don't see why she says that," Milo repeats. "I always have my work done ahead of time."

I roll my eyes. I'm not explaining it to him again.

I swallow my last bite of wheat toast, and as I watch Grandpa Sam waiting to be fed, I think about how hard it is to see things in a different light. For the moment, all I see when I look at Grandpa Sam is an overgrown toddler who can't fend for himself. Ever since I started reading Mom's journals, my image of him has been switching from the infantlike grandpa who I want to hug to the mean dad who kicks and shouts bad things and makes me want to hide.

In an old psychology textbook I had before the fire, on page 397, there was an optical illusion that promised to deliver two different images, depending on how you looked at it. One was the profile of a beautiful young woman, and the other, an old, ugly, crook-nosed crone. I saw the young woman first, but I had to try for what seemed forever before I saw the old crone. Then there she was. Sharing the same scarf, feather, and fur as the beauty, but the young woman's cheek and chin had become the crone's big nose, and the young woman's necklace had morphed into her face. I remember how once I saw the old woman, I had to struggle to find the lovely lady again. Back and forth it went, the figure changing shape right before my eyes, until I got frustrated and slammed the book shut.

Now I know what that book was trying to illustrate. How our minds interpret what we're seeing, and how once it has an image ingrained and a new image is introduced, it will struggle hard between the two images until it decides which image is the *real* one. It's what my mind does with Grandpa Sam, until I'm no longer sure who I'm looking at. And I know that for Mitzy right now, all she can see when she thinks of having a baby is dead little Dylan. And then there's Mom, who is trying to see love in a different light, but her mind can't switch over from some painful image of her past.

I look up and see that Oma is struggling to tie the dish towel that will serve as a bib around Grandpa Sam's neck. And because Grandpa Sam is that sweet grandpa that I love at the moment, I say to Oma, "I'll do that."

"That's okay. I have it now," she says, as she pats his bib in place.

"No, I meant I'll feed him."

Milo's fork stops midair. "I thought that grosses you out?"

"You're so dumb!" I snap, and Oma tells us to be nice. She hands me Grandpa Sam's spoon and gets his dish of yellow mush and gives it to me, but not before touching a spoon of it to her lip to test the temperature. "He's not swallowing very well," she says quietly. "I've asked the county nurse to come check on him tomorrow."

And Grandpa Sam *isn't* swallowing very well. In fact, twenty minutes after Milo and Feynman go out the door for their seven-mile jaunt, I swear I'm still scooping the same spoonful into his mouth. Finally he starts sputtering and coughing, and Oma gets fretful and takes the bowl away. She carries over a can of protein drink and pours a little into a plastic cup meant for babies—the kind with a lid and an upraised spout with tiny holes lined on it so the drinker can't get too much at one time and choke. She gives him as many sips as he'll take, then wipes rivulets of thin milky liquid off his chin. "Time for your nap," she says to him, in a voice much too cheerful to come from a battered woman.

Oma and I get him onto his bed, his weight making squeaking noises as it slides across the plastic mattress liner. I wait outside his room 'til she changes him, then step inside as she goes to scour her hands.

Grandpa Sam is getting littler by the day. I tuck his blanket up over his sunken belly and lift his arms out of the blanket. I set his good hand, his left (the one I'm now convinced carved the nice things), over his right hand (which I'm sure is the hand he hit with), and I pat them.

"Lucy, did you see that? He smiled at you!"

I turn and see Oma standing in the doorway.

"He did?"

"He certainly did!" Oma comes inside and stands next to me. "When you were patting his hand."

"Oma? Do you think there's a part of Grandpa Sam that knows when we do nice things for him?"

"Of course. That's why he smiled at you. He knows you were helping him get comfortable. And I'm sure he hears us too. Besides, even if his brain was totally gone—which it isn't—his spirit is registering everything, and it's communicating with you, right here." Oma taps me right over my heart, brushing one of the tiny new buds my chest is sporting these days. It hurts a little when she pats me. "And if you listen, you'll hear what he's trying to tell you."

After Oma leaves the room, I tell Grandpa Sam about visiting Nordine Bickett, and about the photograph and the puppet. He turns his head as I tell him these things. "Would you like to see them?" I ask, and his dry lips open and close, and although no words come out of them, I know he's said yes.

I run up to my room, put both items into one of Mom's old backpacks that I've claimed for my own, and go downstairs. Oma is busy cleaning the house for Peter's visit, so I slip into Grandpa Sam's room and close the door behind me. I take out the photograph and show it to him. I don't know if it's his poor health or his failing vision that makes his eyes water as he looks at the picture jiggling before him, but the sight of his tears makes my eyes water too.

"You loved her, didn't you, Grandpa Sam?" He doesn't answer, but I feel in my heart that the answer is yes, and that makes me sad. Sad for him, and for Nordine. But most of all, it makes me sad for Oma, because she's the one he was supposed to love.

I slip the photograph into a pocket on the backpack flap, then take out the puppet. "You gave this to Nordine," I say softly. "I think you gave it to her so that she'd have a part of you with her when you couldn't be."

I move the wooden X in my hands and try to make the puppet wave at Grandpa, but making him move as though he's real isn't as easy as one would think, and the puppet spasms as though he has cerebral palsy.

"Nordine told me this is you, but I would have known it even if she hadn't told me. And then she said, 'Always a puppet. Always a puppet.' I think she was reciting something you'd said to her when you gave it to her. Milo would call that pure speculation, and I guess it is, but it feels right in here," I say, tapping my chest.

"I'm people-smart, if you haven't noticed, and I think I know enough about you to guess that it was your dad who made you feel like a puppet. Was he bossy and mean to you?"

He turns away and closes his eyes, and I know he's no longer hearing me with his mind—and maybe not even with his spirit—so I gently put the puppet back in the bag and I just sit there for a minute, looking at him. With the shade drawn and the light in the room dim, his deep wrinkles aren't as pronounced, and it's easy to imagine him a young man again. A man young enough to love more women than a rock star and strong enough to cock the noses of nasty men and crash the heads of sweet, gentle wives.

He's moved his hands to rest on his belly. His right hand is over the left now, and I stand up. "Have a good nap," I tell him, then I switch his hands, left one up, and I kiss his cheek. I go into the kitchen and sit at my laptop. I have work to do. Not search for a topic for my oral report, as Mom keeps harping at me to do because she *is* going to find a place for us to give them yet, but to see if I can find all the sperm banks in California.

I HAVE JUST hit the jackpot when Milo comes into the kitchen, his pterodactyl helmet in his hands, his face flushed from his ride.

"Milo, come see. Hurry, before Oma gets inside. I've found our father! Well, not him per se, but I've found the place where . . ." I stumble over how to explain the links that brought me here, so instead I stop myself and give him the bottom line: "We are the products of artificial insemination. But not sperm donated by some derelict who just needed a couple bucks for a beer. Our donor was a Nobel Prize winner!"

"That's absurd," Milo says as he gets himself a glass of water.

"It is not! I read in one of Mom's notebooks that when it came time for her to have children, she was going to skip the relationship angle and go to a sperm bank. She wrote it twice. Once when she was a kid, and another time when she was grown.

"Now, we know that Mom went to school at UCSD and came back pregnant with us. San Diego is close to Escondido, home of the Repository for Germinal Choice, and—"

"So what?" Milo says after he drains his glass. "She was close to Cathedral Bible College too, but I bet she didn't go there either." Milo fills Feynman's dish with water and is whispering to the dog while I'm speaking.

"Will you shut up and listen?" I hiss. "I didn't jump to this conclusion based on that information alone, dummy. I came to it only after gathering enough data to support it. It all makes sense now. Why Mom and Oma never talk about Mom's years in California. Why she has no real name to give us. *Smith*—the most common surname in this country. Give me a break." I roll my eyes. "It all makes sense now, Milo. Why else would Mom and Oma have made the topic of our father off-limits? I mean, who would want to tell their children that their father was a tadpole in a petri dish?"

Milo is standing next to Feynman, watching him crunch his dog food, as if that is somehow more intriguing than the story of our beginnings. "Milo, listen, will you? Don't you see? This also explains why Grandpa Sam said we have no father *and* why we are geniuses, even though Mom and Oma—and probably Grandpa Sam in his day—are of only slightly above-average intelligence. Mom hates relationships, Milo. Something like this would appeal to her in the first place. Mix that with the family message she got from Grandpa Sam—that being stupid deserves a punch—and of course she'd resort to such a thing!"

Milo turns to me, his head protruding so far from his

skinny shoulders that he looks like a chicken ready to peck my eyes out. "I can't believe you'd believe such nonsense, Lucy. That's not gathering data. That's grasping at straws, grabbing one, then wrapping it in circumstantial evidence to reinforce it so it won't bend." I'm rather impressed with Milo's use of metaphor, but I don't say so.

"There's more." I grab my laptop and swirl it around to face us. I maximize an article from the toolbar. "Look at this. The sperm bank was started by an optometrist, Robert Klark Graham, who sold a patent for a hundred million dollars and used that money to fund the clinic himself—"

"What invention?" Milo asks, showing a spark of curiosity. I press the right lens of Milo's glasses with my thumb and twist it, adding my fingerprint to his collage of smudges. "These, Wheezer. The shatterproof plastic lens."

"Wow! A hundred million?" Milo leans over and starts reading to himself, his pale lips moving silently as he does.

"Yeah, well, before he becomes your hero, you should know that he was a eugenicist. He believed that the human race was slipping backward because stupid people were having the most kids and that the only salvation for this world was the birth of more intelligent human beings. I think this shows that he wasn't all that brilliant after all. A true genius would have realized that the problem isn't that we aren't smart enough but that we aren't kind enough. Anyway, in an effort to populate the world with more intelligent beings, he opened a sperm bank of Nobel Prize winners in 1980, in Escondido, California—only eighteen miles from where Mom went to school."

Milo is no longer paying attention to a word I'm saying but is reading the article for himself. He squints when he looks up at me and pushes his glasses farther up his nose with his middle finger—he doesn't mean it to insult me, of course, because I doubt that Milo even knows the meaning of that gesture. "William Shockley," he says, reciting the name of the one verified donor. "He received his Nobel Prize in physics in '56 for inventing a transistor. He was the father of the electronics era!"

Milo's eyes sparkle at the possibility that a prizewinning physicist could have fathered him. "There were nineteen donors by 1983," I add.

By the time Milo finishes the article, his eyes have lost their luster, and I realize that they sparkled only for the information itself, not because of our possible link to it.

"Nice wish, but I don't think it's a valid assumption, Lucy. It says that the clinic produced only 218 children, and of them, only one showed exceptional intelligence, with an IQ of 180. If we were a part of this, don't you think we'd be included in the statistics?"

"Knowing our mother, she probably ran off and broke contact with the optometrist, just like she does with every man in her life." But Milo's skepticism suddenly grates on my nerves. "Believe me or not, I don't care. I don't know why you'd doubt this, though. It seems obvious that this is our history."

"Two words to prove my point, Lucy: Scott Hamilton."

chapter

NINETEEN

I'M STILL on the road, five yards yet from the driveway, pedaling with all my might to catch up to Milo, when he cocks his head around as he coasts and shouts, "He's here! Peter's here!" My chest is already heaving, but I get a second wind when I see Peter's black Suzuki. It's the only vehicle in the drive, telling me that Mom is going to be caught off guard too, since he wasn't supposed to arrive for another two hours.

"Peter!" I shout when I get inside, racing toward him and hugging him with such force that he says, "Whoa!" as coffee from the mug he didn't have time to set down sloshes onto the table. He stands up, laughs, and puts his arms

under mine. He picks me up off the floor, twisting from side to side so my legs wave like pendulums until my foot bangs into the leg of the table. He sets me down and grabs Milo, giving him a bear hug too.

"Where's Mom?" I ask, suddenly scared that maybe they've already exchanged angry words and she's left—especially when I glance at Oma, whose face is morphing like grown-ups' faces do when they are talking about something serious and private but then have to shift gears quickly and look chipper because a kid enters the room.

"She was out shopping with Mitzy. I just got a hold of her and she'll be home soon."

"I learned to ride a bike, and now I ride seven miles per day," Milo tells Peter, pumping his hands up and down Feynman's neck.

"Wow, buddy. And it's showing too. You're bulking up."

Milo pulls back his shoulders to try and make his concave chest look a bit more convex.

I race into the living room to get the book I left on the end table while I sat with Grandpa Sam earlier and bring it to Peter. I don't need to tell him why. He opens it up at random, points down the page, and reads, *"Thinking is not only a cerebral process: but we also think with our emotions and our bodies—"*

"Page thirty-nine, third paragraph!"

Peter whoops, then turns to Milo. "May twenty-ninth, 1962?"

"Tuesday!"

Peter whoops again, then he reaches in his jacket pocket and hands us each one Hershey's Kiss. I am torn between saving mine and eating it, then decide that if I save it, it says that I don't trust I'll ever get another one from him again. So I unravel the foil wrapper and pop it into my mouth, sucking on the chocolate and saving the crunch of the almond inside for last.

When Mom comes through the door, though, our chatter and laughter stop, and it's suddenly as if the house itself is holding its breath.

Mom looks pretty in a subtly tiered turquoise skirt I've never seen before, flats the color of buttermilk, and a matching shirt. She rotates the turquoise bracelet on her wrist, then smooths the sides of her hair self-consciously (no doubt to flatten it, since Mitzy had moussed it and blown it dry until it was the size of a basketball), as she waits for Peter to move Feynman and rise. Her head is half dipped to the side so that she almost looks shy, and there's a nervous smile on her face as Peter stands up and shimmies between the table and counter to reach her. He puts his arms out and Mom walks into his hug.

Peter's hug for Mom is not a rambunctious bear hug, like he gave Milo and me, but one that is as intense and gentle as a deep sigh. Oma tilts her head and smiles—that is, until she sees the price tag dangling from Mom's armpit. Peter looks at Mom's lips when he whispers a hello to her, like he wants to kiss her, but he doesn't. Maybe because Milo and I are watching, or maybe because Mom has suddenly turned her head to harp at Oma, who's got her head bent right in Mom's armpit as she uses her teeth to free the price tag's plastic string.

It's only mid-afternoon, but Peter hasn't eaten lunch, so Oma bakes the lasagna she prepared earlier. Once we're seated, Milo and I chatter as Oma takes a pan from the oven and Mom slices French bread. Peter doesn't take his eyes off Milo and me as we babble on, but he occasionally reaches out and gives Mom's arm a quick stroke.

"Guess what I'm going to do, Peter?" Milo doesn't wait

for Peter to guess. "I'm going to work on beating the world record for reciting pi!"

Peter laughs. "A lofty goal, Milo," he says. "I'm sure you heard about the high school student who recited it to over eight thousand digits?"

"I did. I read it online. He recited it to 8,784! That's what gave me the idea to try it."

"Didn't a mathematician in Tokyo figure out pi to 1.24 trillion decimal places or something like that?" Peter asks.

"He did. In 2002, but he had the help of a super-computer. That's cheating. I wonder how far I could get on my own."

While we eat, Peter and Milo busy themselves talking about Milo's stupid quest. I don't participate. Partially because I hate math, but mostly because I'm busy watching Mom's and Peter's body language.

I know the gestures that show interest and even love, but unfortunately, from my vantage point at the table, I can't tell if their pupils are dilated when they steal glances at each other. I let my napkin fall to the floor and glance at their feet as I scoop it up. *Yes!* I shout inside when I see the telltale body language that I was hoping for. Peter's ankles are crossed, the sole of one shoe pointing toward Mom. Mom's legs are crossed too, one foot off the floor and pointed at Peter, her shoe dangling from her toes. I'm so happy to see that their feet are positioned like Cupid's arrows that I come up too quickly and whack my head on the table.

"You okay?" Mom asks, and I nod as I rub my head.

I ask Peter if his niece who's read *Little Women* fifteen times will be at the wedding. He says yes.

"Hey," Milo says. "If you don't have to be in Bayfield for the rehearsal dinner until Friday, you can spend the night tonight, can't you? You can borrow Lucy's bike and ride with me in the morning. We could race. It's really cold in the mornings, but there's extra stocking hats here if you don't have one with you. Gloves too."

I don't see Mom slip her shoe back on and stomp on Milo's foot, but I'm sure she does, because Milo groans an ouch and asks, "What did you do *that* for?"

Mom pretends she doesn't know what he's talking about and turns to look at Peter.

"I don't know. I..." Peter's eyes are on Mom as he speaks.

"You're welcome to stay if you'd like," Oma says. "We have a spare room downstairs." I hope she says this for Milo's and my sake, not for Mom's.

Peter thanks her and then says, "We'll see."

Mom is quiet through most of the meal, though she smiles a lot. She picks at her food, carving fork lines into the sauce on her square of lasagna and rearranging her steamed broccoli.

I alternate between watching her and Peter and thinking about all the great things we could do if he was my new dad. "Do you know how to ice skate?" I ask Peter, suddenly realizing that there's an awful lot I don't know about him.

Peter laughs. "A little."

"A little's enough," I tell him. "There's a sled in the basement," I add. "It used to be Mom's and Uncle Clay's. Grandpa Sam used to make toboggans, but there's none of them here. Do you like to sled? Not that we can do that now, but do you like to?"

"Who doesn't like to sled?" Peter says. "When I was a kid, my brothers and I went inner tubing down Bottle Rocket Hill every weekend in the winter." Peter takes his hand from Mom's arm and brings it to his face to show us a small bubbled scar a quarter of an inch into his hairline. "I got this as a reminder not to stop and abruptly hug a tree while whizzing down a hill," he says, and we laugh.

"So your father made toboggans?" Peter says to Mom, after we're mostly done laughing.

"He did," she says, stiffening her back against the chair.

"He carved too," Oma adds. She takes the cardinal off the windowsill and hands it to Peter, then gets up and goes into Milo's study. She brings back a number of small birds and a ferocious bear that's standing on a wooden block, paws arched and teeth bared.

"Wow, these are incredible," Peter says. "He certainly was gifted with his hands." Mom mutters something under her breath that I don't catch, but Peter apparently does, because he hands the carvings back to Oma and changes the subject, talking instead about a new class he'll be teaching next spring.

AFTER OUR meal, Oma heads outside to smoke and Mom takes her plate to the sink. We haven't had dessert yet, but that can wait until the table is cleared and our stomachs aren't so full, Oma says.

"Come see my study, Peter," Milo says, and Peter says he'd love to. I get up to follow, but Mom tells me to help her clean off the table. "How stereotypically sexist," I grumble. "I have to help clean the kitchen, but Milo, being a boy, doesn't. I get Peter next!" I call after Milo.

"So?" Oma asks as she comes back inside seconds later, smelling like an ashtray.

"So what?" Mom asks.

"Is Peter staying?"

Mom shrugs. "If he wants to, I suppose." Oma and I share subtle grins.

"I'll put clean sheets on the bed in the guest room," Mom says, "just in case." She talks slowly, deliberately, so I don't miss her point that Peter is going to sleep in the guest room rather than with her. It's her ongoing feeble attempt to keep the delicate moral fiber of her young, impressionable children from unraveling.

"You don't have to do that anymore, you know."

"Do what?"

"Pretend that Peter won't be sleeping in your bed. I read Freud, Mom, and you know how preoccupied he was with sex. Besides, I'm not a little kid anymore. I'll be getting my period soon. I've even been feeling a little crampy lately. I'm old enough to know that adults who aren't married have sex."

Mom stares at me with shock, and Oma nods. "She does have a point, honey," she says, and Mom tells her to stay out of her business, then adds, "You too, young lady."

I don't wait for Peter to come out of Milo's room when Oma has our chocolate silk pie on plates. I go to the study. "Dessert is served," I say, eager to interrupt them—that is, until I see Milo's animated expression as he dabs his pencil tip against a graph he's made. "You see," he begins, "if A represents…" I study Peter for a microsecond before he looks up at me. He seems genuinely interested as he studies Milo's paper, and I admire him for mustering up that interest for Milo's sake. As much as I want Peter all to myself, I know the importance of a father figure in a boy's life—so he doesn't grow up to wear women's lacy panties or something weird like that.

I go stand next to Peter while he's leaned over Milo's desk, but I don't interrupt. Peter gives my braid a soft tug, then drapes his arm across me as he listens to Milo drone on about God knows what. I study Peter's ear: firm and well shaped, and void of wax, even deep into the canal. I make a mental note to examine the ear canals of any potential boyfriend I might have in the future, then I study the stubble over his jaw and chin. The minuscule hairs jutting from his skin go in one direction in certain patches, then brush in another direction in other places, almost like crop circles drawn by a blind, microscopic-size alien. Peter feels me staring at him and turns to me and smiles.

I HAVE TO wait until almost forever before it's my turn to hog Peter: until dessert and coffee are finished, and Oma goes back outside to smoke, and Mom gets busy doing the dessert dishes and scrubbing the lasagna pan that was soaking.

"You want to meet Grandpa Sam?" I ask him.

"I'd like that," he says.

I take his hand and lead him to Grandpa Sam's room. Grandpa is lying flat on his back, and there's a drip bag stand next to him, the plastic bag filled with brown thick liquid that looks even more repulsive than the concoctions Oma used to whip up for him, if that's possible. The brown sludge moves down a tube that disappears around his torso, under his blanket. "That's how he eats now, because he can't swallow anymore," I explain. "He got the tube put in at the hospital yesterday. I didn't go with. Mom didn't either, but Oma did. They picked up Grandpa Sam in a medical van his nurse, Barbara, had sent over. Oma rode to the hospital with Barbara. Mom didn't want it done, but Aunt Jeana decides those things. I felt bad for not going to hold his hand while they did it, but Mom said it was surgery so I couldn't have gone inside anyway."

I sit down on the bed next to Grandpa Sam and place

my hand on his chest, right over his heart, and feel his breathing quiet the best it can. A calm comes over him. "Did you see that? I think he knows I'm here, even if he can't show it outwardly." Peter nods and smiles at me without showing his teeth.

"He sleeps most of the time now, but you can wake him up if you try hard enough. I still talk to him, even if he doesn't talk back anymore."

"I'm glad you do," Peter says.

"When we first came here, he could walk some and talk a bit. He could drive too—or so he thought." I start laughing and ask Peter if Mom told him about Grandpa Sam's getaway and parade down Main Street. He says no, so I tell him the story. Peter tips his head back and laughs and laughs.

When we get done laughing, I tell Peter, "I like having a grandpa, but I'm not going to have him much longer. Before Aunt Jeana dismissed hospice, their volunteer gave me this." I take a little white pamphlet, *The Dying Experience*, from the nightstand and hand it to Peter. "It explains what someone looks like and how they act as they're nearing death. They say in there just what Oma says: that Grandpa Sam has one foot in this world and one foot in the next. You know what else Oma said? That a lot of times, as people are dying, they talk to people on the other side. Ghosts. Well, Oma doesn't call them that, but that's what they are. Dead people like their parents, siblings, and friends, who come to help take their spirits to the other side. Mom says that's hogwash and that it's nothing more than their failing minds wandering."

"What do you think?" Peter asks.

"I think that I hope Oma's right and that someone nice comes for him."

We sit a few more minutes with Grandpa Sam, then I ask Peter if he'd like to see my room. He says yes, and we leave Grandpa Sam lying in the soft glow of the night-light and head upstairs.

"This was Mom's old room," I tell Peter as he walks the perimeter of the room. "I found her old notebooks in that closet right there. Notebooks she wrote as a kid. And I read them. That's how I found out that Grandpa Sam was mean when he was younger and that he had a girlfriend. That's also how I learned that Oma used to be a drunk."

Saying the words out loud makes them sound even worse than they sounded in my head.

Peter goes to my bed and sits down. He pats the mattress beside him, and I sit down too. He puts his arm around me.

"Lucy," he says. "People make mistakes. Sometimes very bad ones. But people change too. Sometimes."

"I don't want to think of Grandpa Sam as bad," I say, "but sometimes I do. And I can't touch the hand that I think he hit Oma with."

We sit quietly for a moment, then he says, "Did you do my assignment I asked you to do? On playing?"

"I did," I tell him, just because I don't want him to be disappointed in me.

"What did you play?" For the life of me, I can't think of one little fib to tell him, because I don't know of any games, except for riding bikes.

Peter pats my upper arm and removes his hand. He goes to the window, pulls back the filmy curtain, and looks out into the backyard. "Tell you what. There's a whole yard full of leaves that need raking. How about we all go outside and take care of them?"

"Really?" I ask with a laugh.

"Sure, why not? I've been sitting for hours, there's still enough daylight left, and I could use a good stretch. Come on."

"That's what I've been waiting to do! The leaves weren't falling all that much until yesterday's wind."

When we get downstairs, Peter calls to Milo and to Mom—but not Oma, because she's in Grandpa Sam's room, changing his diaper—then he leads us into the backyard like the Pied Piper himself.

Milo gets the rakes from the shed, but there are only two, so Mom and Peter use them and Milo and I kick leaves together with our feet before dragging them into one mound in the center of the yard. "Stop that, Feynman," Milo shouts when the dog keeps scattering our leaves.

The air is fresh and brisk as it teasingly tugs leaves from our arms. Peter pauses in his raking to take a breath that stretches the front of his sweater. "Just smell that fresh air, will you? Ahhhh."

For a time, nothing exists but the desire to make our pile higher, and wider. And when almost every fallen leaf in the yard is in our heap, Peter instructs us to form a circle around the pile. "On the count of three, everybody in," he says.

Mom shakes her head. "I'm in a skirt, Peter!"

"I won't peek," he says, and laughs. "But okay. Miss all the fun, then." He turns to Milo and me. "Okay, on the count of three.

"One. Two. Three!" And in we go. Feetfirst, but for me, who belly flops in.

"Everybody under!" Peter orders, and the leaves crunch and crackle as we burrow our way under.

"Everybody up for a leaf fight," Peter shouts, and up our heads come, crumbled yellow and red-orange leaves sticking to our hair. We grab handfuls and toss them at one another. Even Mom laughs, as she watches from the tree she's leaning against, one arm straight, the other crossed over her waist, holding it.

"Hey, Lucy," Milo shouts. "Let's stuff Peter like a scarecrow!"

"No, no! I'm ticklish!"

Peter giggles like a little boy as Milo stuffs handfuls of leaves down the front of his sweater, while I stuff them down his back and up his sleeves. Peter's laughing so hard that he keeps tipping over.

Soon Peter's sweater is fat and he's begging us to stop. He's laughing so hard that he's weak and can hardly get the words out. Then he stands up and holds out his bulky arms and makes his expression still, like a scarecrow. He leaps out of the heap and does a crazy little skipping dance, wobbling like a drunk. He goes to the tree where Mom stands and wraps one arm around her middle while the other holds her left hand, and he dances her to the mound of leaves, then pulls her right down into it with him. Mom screams and Milo and I crack up.

I fall back on the leaves and rock myself from side to side, holding my belly as I laugh. The sunset above is bright with hues of pink and violet, and I know that even when I get as old as Grandpa Sam, I'm going to vividly remember the look and the feel and the sounds of the four of us lying on this bed of leaves.

We are still laughing as we get up and brush the broken leaves from our hair and clothes. Mom holds out her skirt and fans it, and Peter lifts off his sweater and shakes it, then he pulls off his undershirt, even though it is cold, and brushes the crumbs of leaves from his red-patched skin. When we get mostly cleaned up, Peter wants to put the leaves in trash bags, but I inform him that Oma won't allow it, because she loves leaves on the lawn.

While the others go into the house, I follow Peter to the car so he can grab his bag and change out of his leaf-infested clothes. "I think I've found him," I tell Peter as he rummages through neatly folded shirts and sweaters.

"Found who?" he asks, as he slips a clean white undershirt on.

"Our father," I say. Peter looks up.

"He was one of the Nobel Prize donors at the sperm bank Mom went to when she lived in California."

Peter sets his suitcase on the ground and slams the hatch shut. He sits on the bumper and flops a clean sweater over his leg. He stares down at the gravel in the drive, not looking at me as I tell him the same things I told Milo. The story sounded like an absolute truth when I told it to Milo, but for some reason, when I tell Peter, the story sounds ridiculous even to my ears.

Peter's legs are spread, his hands resting on his thighs. "You know I can't tell you anything I might know about your father, Lucy. It's not my place to say anything, and, really, I know very little, anyway. But what I can tell you is this: You and Milo are *not* the products of a sperm bank. Can you trust me on this one?"

I have that sinking, hollow feeling in my middle again. The one that comes every time I think of Grandpa Sam dying, or of not finding my father, or of Peter not becoming my second father in the event my real dad doesn't want me. "Okay," I say. My head is down, and Peter puts two curled fingers under my chin and lifts it so that I have to look at him.

"Lucy, I've asked your mother repeatedly to please tell you children the story of your father. Lillian has begged her to too. Many times. But your mother has to feel that the time is right, and so far that hasn't happened. Try to be patient, okay?"

"I'm still a kid. How much patience do you think I have? Besides, I've waited all my life to know about him. Isn't that long enough?

"You want to know what, though? Sometimes I don't even know why I'm still looking. Because most times, I just want you to be my dad. And not only for selfish reasons that could bring me bad karma either. You'd make a perfect husband for Mom, you being patient and loving and all that. Okay, maybe she'd think you were more perfect if you were an atheist, but an agnostic should be good enough. And for me and Milo, you're perfect, no matter what your beliefs are."

Peter's smiling, but there's sadness in his smile too. "Ah, I'm not that perfect, Lucy. I drink straight out of milk cartons when no one's looking, and I'm fanatical about my books being in order but I leave dirty clothes on the floor. I'm grumpy when I don't get enough sleep, and I fart in the morning."

"That's okay," I say, "... well, except for the farting part."

Peter laughs and takes my hand as he leads me to the house.

"Lucy?" Oma's voice rings out from Grandpa Sam's room the second we get inside. "Could you please give me a hand?" Oma wants to distract me so that Peter and Mom can spend some time alone now, of course, and she doesn't need to ask twice. I want Mom and Peter to have that time. I want them to gaze into each other's eyes with dilated pupils and to feel a surge of warmth when their hands meet. I want Mom's trust hormone to kick into overdrive and then, before the night is done, Peter to reach into his breast pocket and pull out a poem that makes Mom want to be his forever.

As I skip off to Grandpa Sam's room, I leave Peter in the kitchen, where Mom has two cups of coffee waiting on the table. For the moment, I don't mind not knowing about my birth father.

I SIT CROSS-LEGGED on my bed in the quiet house, Sammy lying in the nest my legs make. I'm watching out the window. Staring at the patches of road between the night-blackened trees, waiting for the beams from Peter's SUV to light them.

"Don't wait up, honey," Oma told me before she turned in. "They'll no doubt stop to have a drink or go for a drive after leaving Mitzy's. You need your rest; you've had a long day." What she really meant, of course, was that Mom and Peter need their privacy. And while I know that's true—and I want them to have it—I just need to know that something magical and permanent has happened between them tonight.

I doze off while sitting upright and don't wake until I hear Feynman's three short barks. "They're back," I whisper to Sammy.

My legs are stiff when I unbend them. I hurry to the window and peer down into the drive.

The passenger door opens first, then slams shut with a *whomph*. I see a dark shadow hustling toward the house. The driver's side door opens next, and I hear the muffled call of Mom's name.

I'd left my door ajar so I could hear Mom and Peter pad up the stairs when they got home, and I hurry to it to listen. The back door scrapes across the floor, and then the bathroom door closes hard. I hear Peter's low whispers as he repeats Mom's name at the bottom of the stairs. My heart falls when the bathroom door opens and Mom's footsteps— a single pair—begin up the stairs. "Tess, please," I hear Peter plead quietly. "Don't do this. Let's finish this discussion."

The stairs stop creaking. "I've nothing more to say," Mom says. "Just leave it alone."

"Leave what alone? Us? Tess, you can't shut out the reality of what we have together any more than you can shut out the reality of your past. It works for a time, maybe, but it's still there, whether you're looking at it or not. It's all there."

"Are you saying that I'm *not* facing the reality of my past?" Mom says in what is supposed to be a whisper but isn't. "I'm living in this graveyard, Peter. I face it every single day I'm here."

"Honey, please. You'll wake your mother and the children. Come down. Let's go outside. It's a nice night for this time of year. Let's grab a blanket and sit on the back porch like lovers, and talk." Peter makes his voice boyish as he says the last part.

For a moment there's no response, which means Mom is caving. I don't waste any time. My room overlooks the porch, and with my window cracked and the night air in the country void of any sounds on calm nights but for the soft murmur of nature, it's likely I'll hear something.

I sit on the floor, my head just to the side of the windowsill, and wait for the downstairs door to open and close. Then I hear them, talking. I can't make out any words, only the low hum of Peter's voice. That is, until Mom gets upset, and her voice rises.

"I have a right to my privacy!" she says. "And she had no business telling you anything! What is it with this family, anyway? Can't anyone respect anyone else's privacy? Crissakes, I can see where Lucy gets it from.

"And besides, what my mother told you is probably not even the truth. We don't talk about what happened—I don't want to!—but I know her well enough to know that by this point she's filtered reality through a sieve of New Age beliefs in an effort to find the good in something that was only heinously tragic."

"I wouldn't know if she told me the truth," Peter says, and he sounds annoyed, "because you've never told me your version of what happened—only that he 'had problems' and that you left him. Why didn't you tell me the rest, Tess? Jesus, don't you see how it would have helped me understand you better? What good has it done to keep this a secret? From me, or from the children, for that matter? You give it more power by keeping it hidden."

I make two fists, lift them above my head, and silently give Peter a cheer.

"Upstairs you have a little girl who is so desperate to find her father that she's checking out sperm-bank donor information. She thinks that she and her brother were conceived through artificial insemination with sperm donated by a Nobel Prize winner. Did you know that?" I unclench my fists and drop them to my drawn knees. Peter can add another flaw to his list, right above farting. He's also got a big mouth!

"Look, I understand you not wanting to tell the kids. That's heavy shit. Of course you couldn't really tell them when they were very young, but you can't keep something like this a secret forever. Okay. Okay. I know it's not my place to judge how and when you tell them, but to not tell me? We've been together for over two years. We love each other. And you didn't see a reason to tell me what happened? Just that it ended badly? Crissakes, Tess, that's what you say when a relationship ends and both parties walk away with hard feelings. Not what you say when a relationship ends like yours did. Why in hell would you shut me out like this?"

Mom's voice is still raised. "Me shut *you* out? You're the one who walked out on me, Peter. Are you forgetting that?"

"I know. And I've told you how sorry I am for that. I was acting out of desperation, thinking that if you were forced to decide between making a commitment to me or losing me, you'd choose to let me into your life all the way. It was an adolescent stunt, I admit, and it backfired, but, damn it, I didn't know what else to do. We'd gotten to the point where something had to give." Peter's sigh sounds like a groan.

"Honey, don't pull away from me like this. Come here. Please. Open up to me. Talk to me."

"I don't know what to say." Mom's voice is husky with tears.

"Just talk to me. That's all. Tell me what happened."

"I don't know what you want from me, Peter. What?"

"The truth. About what happened—your side of the story—and what parts of it you still struggle with. I want you to tell me if you're working on it, and if you think we have any future at all. But if you can't do that at this point, then at least tell me that you love me, if you do. At least that. I've waited for two years, and you still haven't said those words. If you can't say them because it scares you to say them, but you feel them, then tell me that. And if you can't say them because you just don't feel them, then I want to know that too. So I can give up on asking you to marry me."

My mouth drops open. Peter asked Mom to marry him? Mom has never told him that she loves him? I want to leap up and lean out the window and scream at her, "Are you nuts? Tell him what you wrote in your journals about loving him, and say yes!" I don't, of course.

Their voices quiet and I get on my knees to put my ear closer to the breezy crack. I don't hear their words until Mom gets upset again. "Are you saying that I'm lying to myself about what happened?" She's all but shouting.

"Tess, please. That's not what I said at all."

It gets quiet again, but something in the air is so thick that it almost feels solid, and I sense that Mom is telling Peter the story that I long to hear.

I wait. And I wait. And occasionally I hear Mom cough on her tears, or a soft murmur from Peter, but no words. Long after the bones in my butt are sore from sitting against the wood floor, I hear Peter say, "Yes, difficult or not to say—and for them to hear—yes, I think you should tell them. Your mother thinks so too."

"Don't you condemn me for trying to protect my kids! You have no right to judge me on this one."

"Oh, geez, Tess. Where do you get that I'm condemning you for not telling them yet? Where? Did I say that?"

"Your tone said it," Mom snaps.

There is a pause and then Peter's voice, softer and slower this time. "Come sit back down here beside me, honey. Let me hold you."

I can hardly make out Peter's next words, but I think he's thanking Mom for telling him the story. Then he says, with conviction and in a voice loud enough for me to hear, "Just know that I will never, ever become like Howard."

"I'm tired, and my head is pounding. I just want to go to sleep," Mom says.

Peter laughs lightly and says something that I can't hear.

"Alone, Peter. I just want to be alone right now."

"Don't open yourself to me like that, then close up like a fist right afterward," Peter says, his voice firm.

"I'm going to bed. I'm exhausted."

"Tess. Please."

The screen door squeals, and I can hear Mom padding across the kitchen and up the stairs. I have tears in my eyes when she shuts the door to the guest room. She's ruined it with Peter again, and anger and disappointment tighten my jaw and clog my throat.

I hear Peter come in, and I listen for him to come upstairs and tap on Mom's door. Or at least for him to open the door to the spare room downstairs. I wait, but I don't hear anything at all. I picture him standing there, his hands on his hips, as he decides whether to come upstairs and try to talk to Mom again or to leave.

Peter decides to leave.

When I hear his engine start and see the glow of headlights outside my window, I fly down the stairs as though I have wings and race out the front door. Peter's Suzuki is already heading down the driveway, his headlights skimming the dewy lawn that is cold under my bare feet.

I run across the yard, waving my arms and screaming out his name, but I'm in his blindspot and he can't see me. I can hear drums thumping from a CD, and I know he can't hear me either. He pauses at the end of the driveway just long enough for me to catch up, and as his SUV starts to roll, I dart right in front of it and pound on the hood for him to stop.

Peter jams the SUV into park and gets out, the engine still going. "Lucy, my God. I could have hit you!"

"Peter," I cry. "Don't go! She didn't mean it. Whatever she said, she didn't mean it!"

Peter picks me up and carries me over to the gravel, my bare feet dangling. "You scared the shit out of me, kid," he says, and he sounds morning-grumpy when he says it too.

"Peter? Is Lucy out there?" Oma shouts from the front door. The fact that she's awake lets me know that she was eavesdropping on Mom and Peter too. Peter yells back that I am and that he'll bring me in in a minute. He slips me into the front seat with him and backs the SUV all the way into the driveway. He leaves the engine humming because it's chilly and I'm in my pajamas, but he shuts off the music and the lights. I can still see him, though, because the moon is harvest-moon bright and big.

"I hate her," I cry. "She chases you away over and over again. I hate her for that! You're the best thing that's happened to Milo and me. Her too, but she won't admit it. I just hate her! She's a weakling!"

Peter ruffles the top of my head. "Come here," he says, and he pulls me to him and rests my head against his wide, warm chest, filling my ears with the soft thumps of his heart. Hearing them makes my anger melt to something both bitter and sweet, because it sounds just like the way I imagine a dad's heartbeat would sound as he rocks his little girl.

Through the windshield, the moon runs like milk through my tears. I sniffle and cough, and Peter roots through the glove compartment until he finds a napkin from Subway, then lifts my chin and swabs at my face. He doesn't even seem to care if he gets tears or mucus on his hand— probably like a real dad—which makes me cry harder.

"I just wish Mom would stop this, Peter. She loves you. Trust me, I *know* this. I read it in her journals—the new ones she writes on her laptop. And I know why she's bitter about men. It's because Grandpa Sam was a mean husband, and she's afraid you'll get mean like him. But you'd never beat her up like Grandpa did Oma, and you'd never talk mean either. You brought her Tylenol when she was sick. You're not the mean one, she is. You'd never put her head through a wall, but she'd probably do that to you if she got mad enough."

"True, true," Peter says with a tired laugh. Then he leans his head back against the headrest and looks up at the moon.

"Did you ever hear the allegory about the gods' struggle to find a place to put man's personal power?"

I drop my cheek back to his chest. "Tell me," I say.

"Well," he says, "it is a story that I've seen attributed to the Native Americans but also to a couple other indigenous cultures. No matter where it comes from, though, it speaks a universal truth."

His tone changes then. It softens and becomes dramatically wistful as he starts the tale.

"Long ago, when man was first created, the gods gathered

together to try to figure out where they were going to put man's power—and I mean man, as in mankind," he adds. "Anyway, man was too new, too naive, they felt, to trust him to use his power wisely, so they decided it needed to be hidden. So they gathered together to try to figure out where to hide the power until mankind matured. One of the gods said, 'Let's hide it in the sky. They'll not find it there.' But another god said, 'No. One day they will build machines to take them into the sky, and they'll find it.' 'Deep in the earth, then,' another god suggested."

"Let me guess, let me guess!" I say. "They couldn't hide it there, because, of course, man would make drills to tap oil and find it there."

"Hey," Peter says with mock indignation. "Who's telling this story, anyway?"

"Sorry," I say, and settle back down against him.

"But you're right. That's exactly what the gods said. So another god said, 'Let's hide it in the ocean.' But, alas, another god in this fine circle of wise gods said, 'No. One day they'll build machines that can skim the tops of the sea and burrow down to the bottom.'

"So the gods were stumped. Where, where could they hide man's power so he'd not find it until he was equipped to handle it wisely? Having no more guesses, the gods decided to go to the one supreme god to ask his advice. The god listened, was quiet for a moment, then he said, 'Put the power inside man himself.'" Peter tapped his solar plexus area. "He'll never think to look for it there."

I look up at Peter, and he's smiling sadly. "I liked that story when I read it in one of Oma's books. It's good, isn't it?"

Peter laughs. "If you heard it already, why did you let me ramble on?"

"Because I never had a dad tell me a story before," I say.

Peter sounds choked up when he says, "Lucy, your mother's not really afraid of love, she's afraid of losing her power. Which means, of course, that she's never truly found it. But it's inside her, and sooner or later she'll find it. And when she does, she won't need to control her heart so much. There are good reasons why your mother's having trouble letting herself love me and telling you kids about your father, so don't be too hard on her, okay?"

I take the wadded napkin from the dash, because I know I'll need it again, and I tell him, "Peter, what if this is it? What if she cuts it off with you for good, and you can't even be my friend anymore, much less my dad?"

"I'll always be here for you, Lucy. No matter what." He squeezes my shoulder, then says I'd better go inside.

"Please try and talk to her one more time. Please?"

"Enough talking for one night, Lucy."

"But do you have to leave right now? Can't you come back inside?"

"No, I think it's best if I go. I'll go up to Bayfield for the wedding, spend time with my family, and give her space to think. Come on, I'll walk you to the house."

The moon stretches our shadows on the dark grass as we walk. A man and a girl, her hand in his. We look just like a father and daughter. From now on, I know, this very spot on the grass where our shadows fell will be my very own place-in-the-trees.

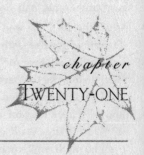

I N THE morning, Mitzy comes to pick Mom up on her way to her doctor's appointment. Oma hugs her when she comes in and pats her belly, asking her how she is.

"Queasy," Mitzy says, and Oma asks, "In your heart still, as well as your stomach?"

Mitzy gives a worried smile. "I guess you could say that. I called my doctor yesterday and he's going to give me something to help with my nausea so I can get back to work. Now if he could just give me something to ease my heart."

Oma hugs her, then yammers about using ginger root and charcoal instead of chemicals. Finally, she asks, "And Ray? How's he doing?"

"Mother," Mom snaps as she steps into the kitchen and hears Oma's last question. "Stop prying."

"He's happy," Mitzy says, then adds, "I'll just feel better after I pass the twenty-sixth week. You know?" Mitzy places her hand on her still-flat stomach. "This morning I felt almost crampy."

Oma looks at Mitzy, then at Mom, who is downing her Paxil with a glass of water, her puffy eyes closed as her neck ripples. "Painful memories can be hard to let go of," Oma says to Mitzy, though her eyes are still on Mom. "But we relive them every day of our lives—recreate them, even, at least in our minds—until we learn to let them go."

Oma turns to place a hand on Mitzy's belly. "This little one needs to feel wrapped in love and joy, honey. Not fear. What good will fear do, anyway? You have to think positively for positive things to happen."

"You know, Mother, I really hate that mind-set," Mom says. "What do you mean? That we cause bad things to happen because we have negative thoughts?"

Oma opens her mouth to say something, but Mom cuts her off. "Come on, Mitzy. Between last night and this morning, I've had enough sermons for a while."

Mitzy smiles at Oma, though her eyes are teary. "You're right, of course. What good will being afraid do me or this little one?"

Mom grabs her purse. She leans down to kiss the top of my head, but I duck. She hesitates and then pulls away.

Oma watches them out the kitchen window, then lifts her hands and draws her Reiki symbols in the air. "Everything will be okay, honey," she tells me after she turns around—as if her air-drawn symbols alone have just saved us all.

I sit down at the table, but I don't want the bowl of

oatmeal waiting for me, even though Oma has added raisins and crushed walnuts and drizzled it with honey.

"You told Peter something you won't tell me," I say flatly.

"Who told you that?"

"I know. That's all."

Oma sighs. "Lucy," she says, her head down, facing the sink. "It's a difficult time right now for the whole family. But I talked to Sky Dreamer last night, and she reminded me that boils become the most painful right before they burst."

She opens the cupboard, and she begins unloading the pill bottles—hiding her face so I can't study it. The pill bottles sound like baby rattles as she tosses them in the trash can.

"Why are you throwing Grandpa's pills away?"

"He can't take them anymore, Lucy. He can't swallow."

"But he needs his medication. How——" And I stop. "Ohhhhh, they're putting his medicine right in his drip bag now."

"No, honey," she says. "The medicine can't help him anymore." She closes the cupboard door and comes to the table. She sits down and puts her hand over mine. "Lucy? I'm so sorry that life hurts and is so confusing for you right now. If I could, I'd make every one of these things—your grandpa's impending death, your mom and Peter's breakup, your losing your home—reverse so that they never happened. I wish I could do that for you, but I can't."

Her words make tears pool in my eyes, and they're warm when they fall.

Oma squeezes my hand. "Oh, I just wish I knew what to say to you."

"You apparently didn't have any trouble knowing what to say to Peter," I say while sniffling.

Oma lets go of my hand and looks up. "Was that your grandpa?" she asks, even though there was no sound coming from his room. "I'd better go check on him."

I get up too and slam my chair against the table. "I'm going for a bike ride."

"Is Milo going?" Oma asks.

"No. He went when he woke up."

"I feel better when you ride with your brother."

"Why?" I ask. "If some danger arose, what would you expect *him* to do? Attack my assailant with an algorithm?"

"Lucy, you're being downright snippy now," she says. "But I forgive you because I know you're just upset." Then she tells me not to stay out long, to wear my helmet, and to not go far, since Mom has her cell phone so I can't take it with me.

I PEDAL WITH purpose, the wind flapping my loose hair, and I head straight for the main street of Timber Falls, where I'm convinced that the truth of my parentage, as well as other family secrets, can be pried out of *somebody's* mouth.

I reach town, and the streets are, I suppose, as busy as they can be for a town no bigger than a rabbit hutch. I get off my bike and push it down the sidewalk.

Now that I'm here, I don't even know where to start. The tea I drank at breakfast has moved into my bladder, and I have to pee. I look around for a store that might let a nonpaying customer use their restroom, then head for the restaurant where Mom and I met Mitzy.

I leave my bike propped next to the building and head

inside. There are two booths filled and one person sitting at the counter. Too few to slip off to the restroom in back without being noticed. "Can I help you?" the woman with dreadlocks who scratched skin cells into my sandwich asks. I give her eye contact and a smile meant to charm. "I'm waiting for my mom," I lie. "I'm a little early, so I'll just take a seat and wait. Well, after I use the restroom." Miss Dreads nods.

I hover above the toilet and try not to sprinkle pee on the seat, then wash my hands through both verses of "Happy Birthday" and turn the doorknob with my damp paper towel, just like Oma taught me to do to avoid diseases when using a public restroom. Then I step out.

"We'll take a booth, Lizzie," I hear, and see Miss Dreadlocks leading Mrs. Olinger and a fat guy with stubby red hair toward me. His belly hangs over his jeans, and his T-shirt is clinging to two man boobs the size of oranges. His toes point out when he walks.

Synchronicity, sweet synchronicity!

Mrs. Olinger recognizes me before I reach their booth. "Oh, hello there. Sam McGowan's granddaughter, right?" she says.

"Hello, Mrs. Olinger," I say. "Lucy."

"Remember I was telling you about them coming to town, Barry?" she says to the fat guy across from her, who is already mentally devouring the menu.

The fat guy, up close, has a ball face that is pocked with acne scars. He looks up and nods. Mrs. Olinger peers down at the menu. "I meet Barry here for lunch every Friday," she says. "We're having pizza. Deep dish, sausage, and extra cheese." She leans over and half whispers, "Barry's sweet on that new waitress with the funny hair. He likes her personality," she says. "I don't know about that hair, though."

"Geez, Ma!" Barry hisses. "Do you have to tell everybody my business?" He squirms in his seat, and the table edge cuts into his gut.

Mrs. Olinger asks what I'm doing in town, and I tell her that I'm waiting for my mother because we're going to have lunch too. I can tell by the tone of Mrs. Olinger's "Oh" that her opinion of Mom isn't favorable. And although I don't yet know how, I know I'll be using that to my advantage.

"Well, you're certainly welcome to sit with us while you wait," she says.

"Thank you. That would be nice." I slip into the booth alongside her, since she's scooted over to make room, and since Barry couldn't scoot over if he tried. Even from across the table, he smells like sweat and oil—the kind you fry chicken in, not the kind you pour into your car.

"How is your grandpa?" Mrs. Olinger asks me, her head tipping sideways toward me, like the bud of a wilting flower.

"He's not doing so well. He had to have a feeding tube put into his stomach because he can't swallow anymore, and he'll aspirate if he swallows wrong. He's getting a hoist today, because we can't get him in and out of bed anymore, and he's going to get bedsores if all he does is lie there."

"Oh, that's such a shame," she says, and Barry looks up. His small eyes are fringed with long, white, piggy lashes.

"Your grandpa was…is…a good guy. He sure did go to bat for me. When those assholes at the mill were giving me shit, he walked in and clocked two of those wise guys. Flattened 'em."

I can't know for sure yet, but I think Barry may be one of those compulsive liars.

Mrs. Olinger shifts in her seat and is about to say something, but then Miss Dreadlocks interrupts. "Well, what will it be to drink? Your usual, Barry?" she asks, flipping a sheet over on her notepad.

"Y-yeah," Barry stammers, and Mrs. Olinger sighs.

"Barry, what did Dr. Imm tell you about soda? Remember? He said if you're going to drink it, you're best having root beer, because it has less acid and is easier on your teeth." She looks at Miss Dreadlocks. "He'll have a root beer," she says. "Three please."

Miss Dreadlocks looks at me. "Hey, I remember you. You came in here with Mitzy and the woman who got all uptight because I had an itch." This seems to please Mrs. Olinger, who no doubt wants validation for her negative feelings toward Mom.

"This is Lucy," Mrs. Olinger tells her. "Sam McGowan's granddaughter. You haven't been in town long enough that you would have met him when he was well, but he was a wonderful man. Just wonderful."

"Nice," the waitress says. "You ready to order?"

"Yes. We'll have a deep dish. Large. Sausage and the fixings...well, except for the onions. They make Barry gassy. Oh, and extra cheese."

I try not to look at Barry, because I know he's humiliated enough at the moment, but it proves impossible since he's sitting right across from me and his face is turning the most interesting shade of maroon.

After Miss Dreads leaves, I swoop in. "Mom wasn't very nice to Lizzie when we came in here before, but she was under a lot of stress. You know, returning after all these years...after what happened."

"Ma, do you have to say stuff like that?" Barry interrupts. "You make me sound like some kind of farting freak of nature."

Mrs. Olinger acts as though Barry hasn't even spoken.

Her face softens. "Oh, of course. I didn't think of that, but, yes, your mother would be under a lot of stress right now. Why, I was just talking to Barry about the trouble your family had some years back, and——" It's as though she suddenly remembers she's talking to a kid, and a McGowan besides, and she stops.

I arch my back and sit up straight, hoping to make the most of my strawberry-size boobs and average height so I look mature enough to have a conversation about adult issues. "Mrs. Olinger, just so you know, I have an IQ of 144. And while that doesn't make me profoundly gifted, it does mean that I'm far enough above average to comprehend things better than most children my age."

Mrs. Olinger grins at Barry. "See? Didn't I tell you this girl was smart? Did you hear the big words she uses?"

"Well, I didn't say it to brag, Mrs. Olinger, because frankly, although I'm okay with my IQ, I don't think having good cognitive skills necessarily makes someone wise, or smart, for that matter. I was just telling you so you'd know that you don't need to talk to me like I'm a child. My mother and grandmother don't. In fact, they've told me the whole family story. Even that Nordine Bickett was Grandpa Sam's mistress."

"Oh, my," Mrs. Olinger says. She picks at the hem of hair at the nape of her neck. "Why, that *is* being open, isn't it? But then, Barry and I are very open with each other too, so I suppose..."

Barry's watching Lizzie and blushing, even though she's at the far end of the restaurant. "Yeah, and sometimes I'm sorry I ever tell you anything."

"I've heard folks say that your mother blamed Sam for what happened. I hope that's not true, dear. I mean——"

"Blamed him?" Barry huffs, turning his attention back

to our table. "Why in the hell would she blame *him* for what
happened? If that had been my daughter, I would have
done the same thing. No, I would have done worse! I would
have——"

But Barry doesn't get a chance to finish, because Lizzie
is coming to our table with our drinks, and the second he
sees her heading our way, his skin tone deepens and what
little neck he has disappears all the way into the collar of
his plaid shirt.

Lizzie sets down our root beers, made pale with ice
cubes packed to the rim, and starts yammering to Mrs.
Olinger, telling her that our pizza's in the oven and asking
her if she can get DSL out on her road *yet*, because she's
thinking of putting herself on an online dating site. "I
mean, really, I wish I could find a good guy here in town,
but I don't think that's going to happen."

"Oh, I think you'll get your wish soon." Mrs. Olinger
grins like she's Lizzie's secret Santa, which, I suppose, is less
humiliating for Barry than if she broke out into an im-
promptu infomercial for him.

"I doubt it. This town doesn't grow my kind of guys."
Lizzie shakes her head, and her dreadlocks crawl like taran-
tula legs. "I need a free spirit, like me. My friend hooked up
with a guy through one of those sites, and I could have
scratched her eyes out when I saw his picture. Long hair
down to here," she says, chopping at her elbow. "A muscle
shirt, cool tats from his neck all the way down to his wrists.
Mmmm, he was hot!"

"Tats?" Mrs. Olinger asks, and Barry mumbles, "Tattoos,
Ma. Geez, get modern."

"Oh, I don't..." Mrs. Olinger begins, but Lizzie stops
her.

"Tats are cool. I have them. Want to see my tramp

stamp?" She doesn't wait for a response before spinning around, tugging the back of her shirt up, and showing us a strip of waves with three dolphins leaping just above her low-rise jeans.

"Order's up!"

"Oh, there's your pizza. B-r-b," she says, using the computer lingo for *be right back*.

"Tramp stamp?" Mrs. Olinger says, as if the very sound of the words is digging in her throat like a fish bone. "Oh, she is definitely not the girl for you, Barry. Don't give her the time of day." She looks at me and rolls her eyes. "I guess I can count my lucky stars that she's not interested in him."

Barry straightens up. "She's just playing hard to get. I know she digs me. She as much as said so the last time I was in here." His ridiculous comment makes me think that maybe some people just can't tell the difference between a wink and somebody shutting their eyes to avoid looking at them.

I try to hide my frustration by concentrating on relaxing my facial muscles as I scramble to find some way to get the conversation back to my family.

I ask Barry for the time, and he glances down at his watch and tells me that it's 12:16. I sigh. "I wonder where Mom is," I say with just the right amount of dramatic flair.

"Barry can give you a lift home if she doesn't show up," she says. "I have to be back to work by one, or I would. He's a real good driver."

"I rode my bike here," I say. "But thank you anyway."

I take a sip of my root beer. "Maybe Mom's just having trouble tearing herself away from her dad's bedside. It's hard for her to see him like this. Like today. He was trying to tell me something about my dad, but he just couldn't get the words out. Mom burst into tears, she was so upset to see him struggling with something so important. I suppose he wanted to tell me what happened himself. He probably knows that ten different people are going to tell me ten different stories."

"Oh, how sad," Mrs. Olinger says, her face dripping with grief. And Barry says, "That's people for you. Such gossips."

"True," Mrs. Olinger says. "I know I sure heard my share of stories about that day. Why, the first story I heard was that your dad——"

"Here you go!" Lizzie says, as she swoops in and lowers the pizza to the center of the table, the grease at the edges of the pan still sizzling. She starts dishing a slice onto a plate, but Mrs. Olinger takes it from her. "I can do that," she says, wincing, as though she fears that Lizzie's thumbs might deposit an STD by touching the edge of crust, even though Barry is using his fingers and he inseminates cows for a living. Mrs. Olinger dishes up a slice for me and says, "Enjoy, honey."

The bell on the front door sounds, and Lizzie looks across the room. "Afternoon, Miss Tuttle. I'll be right with you," she calls. She gives Mrs. Olinger a grin and a wink, mumbles something about Miss Tuttle being her "fave," and off she goes.

"Speaking of *that* sort..." Mrs. Olinger says.

I'm sitting facing the back of the restaurant, so I have to turn and peer around the wooden bench to see her. There she is, the infamous Miss Maude Tuttle! She has big, shocking red hair in curls the size of juice cans hanging to her slumped shoulders, and her face is draped in sagging skin. She's wearing a black knit sweater flecked with silver glitter and ropes of silver necklaces and bracelets. Silver earrings hang long enough to show under the hem of her hair. She looks like an old movie star.

"Honey? Lucy?" Mrs. Olinger is tapping my shoulder. "Turn around, okay? Maude doesn't like to be stared at, and, well, she's just not the sort of woman that a young girl like yourself should pay attention to. She has a past."

"I'll bet she would have had a tramp stamp too, if they had put tats on the back, back in her day." Barry picks a string of cheese off his pizza, lifts it into the air, and lowers it onto his tongue.

"Boys!" Mrs. Olinger says, shaking her head.

"This seat okay, Miss Tuttle?" Lizzie asks, as she motions to a table toward the back of the room.

"I don't give a damn where I sit, as long as it's not a booth. I like to keep my eyes on my enemies."

Lizzie laughs, even though there's nothing in Maude Tuttle's voice to indicate that she's trying to be funny.

The second Maude Tuttle is seated, Lizzie starts reciting the specials to her. Maude cuts her off while she's giving the soup of the day and says, "Listen, sweetheart. I understand that you're relatively new, but after two weeks you should have figured it out. Since you haven't, I'll tell you. I come here every day for lunch, and every day I order a cup of coffee— black and strong—and a piece of pie. That's it. No sandwich. No soup. Just a piece of goddamn pie and coffee. Today I want lemon meringue. Now, cut the sales pitch and get me my order."

Lizzie is standing with her back to us, but it's obvious that she opened her mouth to say something, because Maude Tuttle snaps in a voice as big as her hair, "Just get my order, sweetheart. I don't small-talk."

As soon as Lizzie moves and the space between Maude's

table and our booth is open, and Maude sees Mrs. Olinger, Barry, and me staring at her, she lifts her middle finger and jabs it in the air.

Mrs. Olinger gasps and dips her head. "Oh, my, that she'd do something like that in front of children. That woman is crazy. Ignore her and eat, Lucy. Barry, you too."

"She's not crazy," Barry says. "She's just good and damn sick of folks in this town judging her. Good for her, I say. People here can be such assholes." Barry looks over at Maude Tuttle to give her a quick yep-we're-in-this-together thumbs-up, and she gives him the finger again.

I don't stare at Maude Tuttle, but I do glance at her from the corner of my eye now and then while she sips her coffee and Mrs. Olinger talks about the pizza, which she thinks is undercooked because the cheese in the middle is still stringy. Suddenly, I'm sorry I'm stuck at the table with the Olingers, because there's something about Maude Tuttle that tells me that if I play my cards right, I could learn everything I want to know from her.

"Uh-oh. The time," Connie Olinger says after she downs two slices of pizza. "I'd better get going. Barry, you take any leftovers home, okay? You can snack on them until dinner."

I pop the last bite of my pizza into my mouth and stand so Mrs. Olinger can get out. "Thank you for treating me to lunch," I say, and Mrs. Olinger smiles and says it was her and Barry's pleasure—that they'd treat Sam McGowan's granddaughter to lunch anytime. Maude Tuttle looks over at us, her eyes pausing to examine me. Mrs. Olinger notices and leans down to whisper, "You ignore that wretched woman, you hear me? In fact, maybe you should just go on home now, dear. It doesn't look like your mother's going to show up." I nod, but of course that's the last thing I intend to do.

I look at Barry, then down at the third of the pizza that's left, and I know he'll sit right here until every stray olive is plucked from the tray. I don't expect Barry to pay one iota of attention to me after his mother is gone, and he almost doesn't. Not until he sees me heading toward Maude Tuttle's table. I glance back when I hear the wooden seat groan, and, sure enough, Barry is leaning out of the booth to watch me.

I'm inches away from taking the seat facing Maude when the cowbell attached to the door clinks and jingles and I hear my name.

It's Mom and Mitzy. Mom has dark smudges under her eyes from lack of sleep, and she's pale. Mitzy doesn't look much better. "What on earth are you doing here?" Mom calls.

"Waiting for you," I say, loudly enough for Barry to hear me. I hurry to Mom and glance back toward Barry. I can see his squinty eyes peeking above the top of the booth, but when he sees me watching him, he dips his head down until all I can see is his orange orangutan hair.

Mom's confused, of course, and more than a little pissed, so I drop my voice. "I was out riding my bike and I had to pee, so I came here." I try hard to keep every ounce of snippiness out of my voice, but I'm not sure I'm doing such a good job, because Mom is giving me that look again. The one that says if I'm not careful, I may be ninety before I ride my bike again. I can't help it, though. I'm still furious at her for ruining things with Peter—again!

"Who said you could ride your bike to town?"

"Milo rides to town all the time. Do you yell at him for it?"

"Does Ma know this?"

"I don't know. But Milo does it, so why can't I?"

"I never said you kids could——"

"You hungry?" Mitzy cuts in.

I don't think it's a good idea to tell them I was freeloading off the Olingers, so I just say, "No. Not yet. I'll head home and have lunch there. Oma's making a chef salad."

Mom looks distressed. "We'll discuss this when I get home. All four of us. You have your helmet with you?" She digs in her purse as she talks, then she pulls out her cell phone. "If you have any problems, you call Oma or Mitzy's cell. Their numbers are in my contact list. You ride carefully, Lucy. Watch for cars, and if anyone stops, don't—"

"Geez, Mom, it's not like we're in Chicago anymore. I got here safely, didn't I?"

"I'll be home as soon as Mitzy and I finish lunch."

Mitzy gives me a kiss on the cheek, and I scoot to the door.

"Use your hand signals," Mom calls after me, and Mitzy tells her I'll be fine; I take note of the fact that Mitzy only fusses over Milo's safety, not mine. I don't take it personally, though. Milo is a boy, like Dylan.

I pedal my bike hard so I can get home in plenty of time before Mom does, for two reasons. One, so I can get some of the anger worked out of me and not get grounded again, and two, so I can lift some things off Mom's computer. I wasn't going to read any more, but I know that the more frazzled Mom is—and she is about as frazzled as I've ever seen her—the more likely it is that she's made some new entries in her digital journal.

chapter
TWENTY-TWO

WHEN I get home, Oma is on the floor, her back arched over her exercise ball, rolling back and forth and grunting, her face as red as the giant poppy on her workout shirt. "Oh, thank goodness you're here!" she says. "Give me a hand, will you? I never tried this position before and, oh, my, I can't get myself up, and Milo's in the shower. I was just going to spill over the sides, but a gal from my Pilates class tried that and cracked her tailbone."

I have to skirt around a big metal contraption so I can reach her. "That's your grandpa's hoist," Oma says. "It was just delivered. We'll have an easier time getting him in and out of bed now." I stand with both feet on either side of the

ball to keep it steady, then brace my arms tight as Oma holds my hands and pulls herself up to sitting.

"At least I didn't have to use Grandpa Sam's hoist to get you up," I say, and once Oma's on her feet, she laughs until her eyes get drippy.

"Speaking of your grandpa, I'd better check on him. Want to join me?" she asks.

"No. I've got things to do."

Oma pauses, wiping her eyes, though the humor is gone from her mouth. "Honey, you haven't been spending much time with your grandpa lately. I'll bet he misses your company."

"He's asleep most of the time now, anyway," I say.

"But his spirit knows you're there." She watches me closely for a moment.

"I'm fine, Persephone," I say, using her new name so I can stay on her good side. I know Mom is going to tell her I rode all the way to town.

Oma pauses. "Oh, you don't have to call me that anymore. I'm not sure it feels right. I'll just be Oma until the right name finds me."

The second she slips into Grandpa Sam's room, I hurry upstairs to get my memory stick. I don't run on the way back, though, because I don't want to make Oma suspicious by sounding like I'm in a rush.

I wait for Milo, since the shower's stopped. And after what seems like forever, he emerges from the bathroom, his hair sopping wet and dripping on his lenses, comb ruts separating the strands into tiny, uniform columns. "I did ten miles today. In record time too." Milo looks over at Feynman, who's sleeping so soundly that his tongue is lying out on the floor.

I wrinkle my nose. "You're such a bragger."

I say this to offend him, of course, so he'll get lost. "Geesh. I was just telling you," he says. He pats his thigh for Feynman to wake and follow, and Feynman does, though his head is low and his eyes are half shut.

The second Milo's door closes, I grab Mom's computer off the counter and plug the memory stick in. I'm just yanking it out when the county nurse's car pulls into the drive. "Oh, Barbara's going to show me how to use that hoist," Oma says as she hurries to get the door.

I don't want to learn how to do that, even though Oma wants me to so I can help her. Instead, I hurry upstairs and plug the memory stick into my computer and search for Mom's latest journal entry. It was written just last night!

He's gone. This time, I fear, for good.

I tried so hard to let what I was feeling on the inside come out, but it was like my body wouldn't cooperate. He pried until he got the story of Howard out of me. If only he had pried equally hard to get the words "I love you" out of me. I tried to wrench them out of myself, but the weight on my chest wouldn't let them rise. And because my body wouldn't cooperate, he's gone.

Everyone's asleep and I'm at the kitchen table now, trying not to listen to Dad in the next room. He's gone, for all intents and purposes. His mind has drifted off to wherever it is the mind goes before death comes. Now he only waits for his body to cooperate and release him. I can't look at him, and apparently Lucy can't anymore either. It's ironic that once again, Dad and I are alike. Both of us waiting to be set free.

I tried calling Clay again tonight. He never picked up. I guess this means I'm grouped with Ma now, because he doesn't take my calls either. Ma still leaves him messages. Sweet messages, telling him what's new with her, me, the kids, and now Dad. Occasionally he leaves her one back—dialing her around midnight, once he knows she's sound asleep, pretending it's the first chance he's had to call all day and stiffly making one or two comments before promising to catch her soon. Ma misses him, but unlike me, she has hopes that he'll let us in his life again.

I feel bad for Ma that Clay has shut her out of his life. She carries the school photos that Clay's wife, Judy, sends in her "Grandmother's brag book," photos of kids she's seen only once, even though Clay's oldest, his daughter, is almost as old as the twins—and she saves the thank-you notes they write her for the Christmas gifts and the few bucks she sends them on their birthdays. And what? Pretends that it's not Judy's hand that writes the notes from the boys, and that those nice granddaughterly words Brit writes weren't dictated to her by her mother? That can't make her feel all that special, can it?

I'm not as nice as Ma. The last time I bothered to call Clay and he actually picked up—just two weeks after we got here (picked up, I'm sure, only because he thought I was bringing him the "good news" that Dad was dead)—I confronted him. I told him that Ma doesn't deserve this. That she didn't do anything.

He told me I was right. She didn't do a goddamn thing.

I pretended I didn't get his point. I told him how she cried for him every day after he left, and I asked if he knew that. All he had to say about that was that she always cried when she was drunk.

I sighed and reminded him that she wasn't the same person anymore. Then it was his turn to sigh. "I'm just not one for visiting graveyards," he told me.

There was an awkward pause, and then I said, "Speaking of graveyards...are you coming home for Dad's funeral?"

He told me that he'd see what his schedule looked like. God, that burned me. I reminded him that I didn't want to do that freak show either, but I had to. I suggested that maybe he could come for Ma's sake, and mine, and I got snippy when I suggested that maybe his clients could wait a couple days to have their boobs perked and their asses lifted.

"That's not the kind of surgery I do anymore," he said flatly. "I do reconstructive surgery. Kids with deformities. Accident victims who got their faces rearranged. Those sorts of things."

I paused. I wanted to tell him that I was proud of him for making something out of himself. For having an honest career. Instead, I sniped that I would have known about his career shift if he ever bothered to talk to us. He said good-bye shortly after that, leaving me loathing myself for my knack for fucking it up with every male I ever had in my life, be it lover or brother, father or what have you.

It's hard to believe that Clay was only seventeen when he walked out of this house—this family—for the last time.

I never did know what started the argument. It could have been anything: Clay not dumping the garbage the way Dad wanted it dumped—the burnables in the burning barrel, the slop taken out to the trees behind the shed to rot or be eaten by wild animals, the cans tossed in the heap in the woods until the heap got high enough for Dad to bury. Or maybe it was just because Dad didn't like the look of Clay that day.

I was upstairs when I heard their voices rise, seemingly in unison. My ears perked instantly, my intestines cramping involuntarily.

I opened my bedroom door and stood frozen. Listening. Willing Ma to hurry home from Marie's, where she'd gone to have a new zipper put into a pair of Dad's work pants. Not that it would have mattered if she'd been home, of course. She'd only have done the same as me: stood frozen until things got totally out of control, then hovered at the edge of the scene, pleading with them to stop, her pleas not any more effective than mine in penetrating Dad's rage-reddened ears.

"You worthless little prick!" Dad bellowed "When I tell you to do something, why in the hell can't you do it right? You aren't worth the bucks it costs to keep you fed."

I heard the sound of breaking glass and Dad telling Clay he could clean that up too. Clay yelled back that he wasn't the one who threw it, his voice low and level. Challenging.

Dad's words weren't unusual, of course. I'd heard them all before. But what was different on this particular day was that his rage seemed to be starting at the same pitch it normally ended on.

Ma had warned us about this. How Dad was under a lot of stress. "Just try to do as you're told, and don't argue. We have to show him a little more patience right now. The bank turned down his loan application, saying that it's too risky to give him a loan that size and suggesting he find some investors, then come back. You know your father won't do that. I think it's finally sinking in to him that he's never going to have that sawmill and that he'll be working at the paper mill the rest of his life. He's losing his dream, kids."

I assured Ma we'd be good, but all Clay had to say was, "Fuck him and his sawmill."

Clay was even more defiant after Ma's warning. Not because he didn't believe that Dad was more volatile than ever, but maybe because he knew what was coming and he just wanted to get it over with. Nothing was worse than the calm before Dad's storms.

I hurried down to the kitchen and stood in the doorway. "Where's Ma?" I asked, as though I didn't know, and as if I didn't notice that they were standing with their chests a foot apart, jaws as tight as their fists.

Neither of them acknowledged that I'd spoken.

"Don't you get lippy with me, boy," Dad said. "I'll fuckin' deck you. Don't think I won't."

"Oh, I wouldn't be so stupid to think you wouldn't," Clay said.

Dad slowly, deliberately, moved in until his chest was butted up against Clay's, the pocket of his T-shirt level with the pocket on Clay's. "I don't know about that. You're pretty fucking stupid."

It hurt me, hearing Dad talk to Clay like that. When we were little, Dad let him walk on his boots, and sometimes he even got down on his hands and knees to be Clay's bucking bronco. Cuddled him once, when Clay was thrown into the coffee table and split his cheek open. And on weekends, Dad even took him fishing at Clement's Creek. I resented the special treatment Clay got back then, but I didn't have to hate him long, because it all stopped about the time Clay started school. In time, I had to wonder if maybe it didn't hurt Clay more than me, when things got so bad. After all, you can't miss what you never had. But Clay had it all once.

I silently begged Clay to do what he'd always done. Put as much distance between Dad and himself as he could, and do it as quickly as possible. But Clay—six inches taller in the last eight months, with arms bulky from using the weight room after school—didn't flee this time. Instead, Clay told him, "Go ahead. Deck me. And I'll fucking deck you back."

Clay swayed slightly, then thrust himself against Dad. Dad, not expecting any physical force from Clay, had to step back on one boot to keep his balance.

"Clay!" I shouted.

Shock stiffened Dad's face, but only for a moment; then the corner of his mouth curled up sardonically. "What? You put on five pounds and you think you can take your old man now? That it?" Dad moved so close that Clay had to tip his head back a notch to keep his gaze locked with Dad's. "You couldn't take down a goddamn pussy, you little punk."

Blotchy patches of red burned over Clay's cheeks. Not out of shame this time, but out of rage. "Oh," he said, mimicking Dad's mocking tone. "Is that what makes you such a big man? The fact that you've taken down a few pussies? Guess it's gotta be, since you aren't getting that big fancy mill that you were so sure was gonna make you a somebody." Clay shook his head and laughed. "You know what, old man? YOU'RE the fucking joke, not me. YOU'RE the fucking loser!"

In a split second, Dad grabbed the front of Clay's shirt, twisting it and yanking so that the armholes strained against Clay's underarms and exposed his belly. "You fucking little bastard. I should kill you!"

I was standing no more than a foot from the phone. I could dial Marie's, I thought in my panic. Marie would hear the trouble and come. She'd know what to do. She'd be here in—

But there was no time, of course. Already, Clay was in the process of doing the unthinkable, cranking back his arm. I shouted at him not to do it, but he did it anyway. His fist met Dad's jaw with a crack.

Dad's head jolted back, then cocked forward, his eyes bulging first with shock, then fury.

He let go of Clay's shirt, leaving the cotton twisted and

*bunched over Clay's heart like a crushed white rose. Then, in
a blur of movement, his fist rammed into Clay's face with double the force Clay had used. Vomit rose and soured my throat
while blood gushed from Clay's nose.*

*For a split second, I expected Dad to recoil at what he'd
done. Even though he'd slapped Clay around plenty in the
last couple of years, he had never outright punched him, the
way a man slugs another man. Even then, when it was only a
cuff, Dad apologized at some point, pleading with him (as he
did with Ma) to not push him so hard. "God damn it, boy,"
he'd always end up saying, "you know I'm a hothead like my
old man was. Don't make me act like him. For God's sakes, I
don't want to act like him."*

*But Dad didn't look sorry at all. And when he finally
found his words, it wasn't to apologize. "You gonna call me a
fucking loser now, boy? Huh? You had enough from this
'loser,' or do you want some more?"*

*Clay didn't bother trying to catch the blood that spilled
down over his mouth. "Go ahead. Beat me until you kill me.
You think I give a fuck?" Blood-tainted spittle showered from
Clay's mouth. "You'd do me a fucking favor by getting me out
of this hellhole."*

*Clay pulled his shoulders back, fists clenched, blood ooz-
ing down over the wadded white of his T-shirt. "Go on. Show
me what a big man you are. I dare you!"*

*"Oh, my God, oh, my God, oh, my God," I could hear Ma
say. But it wasn't Ma's voice saying those words. It was mine.*

*Dad looked confused. He stepped back and turned around,
as though he was going to walk away. But he didn't walk
away. Instead, he cocked his arm and bunched his fist. Then
he spun back and, in one movement, delivered his fist like a
cannonball into Clay's stomach.*

I don't know how many times he hit Clay. I closed my

eyes and clamped my hands over my ears, but I could still hear the thuds and the grunts that accompanied each blow. I cried out for Ma, for Marie, for anybody who could make Dad stop.

It took me a few moments to realize that my pleas and Clay's gasps were the only sounds left in the room. I opened my eyes and Dad was gone. Outside, I heard his truck start and saw a smear of black pass the window.

I hurried to Clay, who was bent over, one hand gripping the edge of the counter and the other clutching his ribs as he struggled to get to his feet.

I grabbed him to help him up, his skin damp and hot beneath his shirt. There was blood splattered on the linoleum and drops falling on the tops of my sandal straps, oozing between my toes. "Oh, God, Clay, you're bleeding all over the place."

Clay unfolded himself with a groan. His eyes were as red as the blood that drained from his nose.

"I'll call Ma!" I said.

Clay lifted the hem of his shirt and swabbed his face. "What the fuck good would that do?" he said between broken teeth.

I was babbling, and I couldn't stop. "I'll call Marie. She'll come and take you to the hospital. Al will come too, and——"

"Shut the fuck up," he said.

I stood silent, shaking, as he headed toward the door, groaning as he fished in his pocket for the keys to the beat-up Chevy he'd bought from Henry Bickett. Out the door he went, leaving me standing there in his blood.

Clay never came home again. Not once.

Mr. Walker called me into his office the first day Clay returned to school, asking if I knew what had happened to

Clay's face—which was badly swollen and bluish-purple, the bulges under his eyes tinged yellow. His nose was cocked and lumped.

There was no question in my mind about what to say. "He got into a fight with some boys from Larkston," I said. "They beat him up because one of them thought he was hitting on his girlfriend." It was the story Clay had told me to tell, when he grabbed my arm in the hallway while we changed classes, just seconds after my name was called over the loudspeaker, summoning me to the principal's office.

"You sure about that, Tess?" Walker said, scrutinizing me behind thick glasses.

"That's what he told me."

I packed his things in trash bags and moved them around the back of the shed, just like he asked me to do when he stopped me in the hall to ask how it went with Walker. He must have come for them in the middle of the night, because they were gone on the fifth morning.

If the school ever caught on that Clay wasn't living at home, they didn't question Ma or me. Clay's car was in the parking lot each morning when I got to school, and it was there when I boarded the bus each night.

Nobody seemed to know where Clay slept. Rumors circulated that he'd moved in with his girlfriend, Heather, and her family, but when Ma called there to check, Heather's father assured her that they hadn't seen Clay since "the incident," and it was better that way: Heather didn't need to be running around with "trash."

A couple weeks later, word trickled to Mitzy that one of the starters on the basketball team, Colin Blake, was convinced that Clay was living in his car. He'd caught Clay in the boys' bathroom at six o'clock in the morning when he came in for an early practice, and Clay had the sink stopped up with a sock and was washing his armpits with soap from the dispenser.

Clay got a job at the Piggly Wiggly after school, stocking shelves and bagging groceries. It must have afforded him enough money to make it, because every time I chased him down in the hall and tried to give him the small wad of bills Mom siphoned from the grocery fund, he shoved my hand away, saying he didn't want a thing from "those fuckers." I kept the money hidden in my room because I couldn't tell Ma that he refused her help.

"Ma didn't do anything. She wasn't even there," I told him. "And she's bawling her eyes out every day, worrying about you. At least give her a call so she can hear that you're all right."

But he never did.

Clay talked to me less and less in school in that last half of our senior year, until he wasn't speaking to me at all. Or anyone else, for that matter. He dropped Heather and his friends right after the big blowout, which was probably a good thing, since all they did was party—and his name appeared on the high honor roll that last semester. He didn't show up at graduation, even though he'd won scholarship money. And a week after graduation, somebody told Dad that they saw Clay boarding the Greyhound.

For the last hour or so—since I wrote the scene above—I've been sitting here, my body feeling too heavy to make it up the stairs to go to bed, even though sitting here means listening to Dad gasping for breaths. Breaths that sound like he was punched in the guts. It is a sickening sound, this sound of Ma's karma.

When I finish reading Mom's journal entry, I wrench the memory stick out of my laptop. I wrap it in a wad of Kleenex and throw it in the trash, promising myself that I'll never read it again. Even if that means never learning about my father.

WHEN I get downstairs on Saturday morning, Oma is in the kitchen, talking to someone on the phone. As I'm sitting down to pour milk into my already filled cereal bowl— not filled with something good like Cap'n Crunch or Lucky Charms but some whole-grain stuff that tastes like leaves, with dried strips of fruit that chew like shoelaces—I realize that she's talking about Grandpa Sam and that the voice at the other end is the county nurse, Barbara. She's been making increasingly frequent stops at our house over the last two weeks. I glance in the driveway and Roger's car is gone, which means Mom left before I woke up again.

"I did take it," Oma is saying. "It was one-oh-three last

night. This morning he feels clammy and downright cold. I don't know if he has a virus, or...Oh, uh-huh...Yes, I did that last night too. The top number was almost one-fifty, and this morning it's at about forty-five. His blood pressure's all over the place."

I wag my spoon in my bowl, clearing the flakes to the side until I form a little pool of milk, then scoop at it with my spoon. The little pool doesn't empty though, of course.

No longer hungry, I let my spoon rest against the side of the bowl and start paging through Oma's *Tibetan Book of the Dead*, which is sitting on the table.

"Okay. I'd appreciate that," Oma finally says, then hangs up.

Oma tugs the hem of her sky-blue tunic—as if it's not already in place—and forces a smile. "Good morning, honey," she says. She glances down at the page I'm reading and slips the book out from under my hand, as though she's merely straightening up, and then she suggests that maybe I'd like to join Milo on his bike ride.

I look up at her and see a worried half smile. She reaches down and puts her hand on my arm. "Your grandpa isn't doing so well this morning, so Barbara is going to stop by and take a look at him. She'll...Well, they know what signs to watch for."

So do I. From page five of the pamphlet from Ministry Home Care that the hospice volunteer gave us, underneath the heading: "One to Two Weeks Prior to Death." Second paragraph: *There are changes which show the physical body is losing its ability to maintain itself.*

"I think I'll go for a ride too," I say.

I pee, and Oma gives me Ma's cell phone, which Milo had forgotten to take with him. "You want to stop in and say good morning to your grandpa before you go riding?"

I shake my head. I don't tell her that when I see him, it's too hard to pretend that he's not dying.

Milo and Feynman always go west, where there are more-challenging hills, but I'm going east, toward town.

As I pedal, I try to think of what strategy I'll use to get Maude Tuttle to talk. I try to think of anything but Grandpa Sam, because I don't want to think of him anymore. I don't want to see him either. Yesterday afternoon, while I pretended to study, Oma and Barbara wheeled the hoist out of Grandpa's room. The contraption had him tethered around his waist and groin. His head lolled to the side, his arms hanging limply. He looked like Sammy, with no one manning the strings. As they made a wide circle around the couch, he lifted his head some, but I looked away. Mom says it's okay if I don't want to sit with him anymore, but it doesn't feel okay to me.

I find Maude Tuttle's house easily, and I'm only a little nervous when I rap on her door. Hard, in case she's half deaf, because she's old enough to need a hoist too.

It seems to take forever, but finally the curtain stretched tight over the long glass portion of her door slips to the side, and her wrinkled eye appears.

She opens the door about six inches, as far as the chain hook will allow. Not enough for me to slip through, but wide enough that I can see that she's not wearing any makeup. Her whole face looks like the wadded knot of Clay's T-shirt that Mom helped me vividly see with her words.

"I don't want any Girl Scout cookies, and, no, I'm not buying any chocolate bars so your band can go to Tim*fuck*tu to march in some ball game, so go away."

I put up my hand to keep the door from shutting. "No, no. That's not why I'm here."

She peers closer, her faded eye studying me. "I'm Lucy

McGowan," I tell her. "Sam McGowan's granddaughter. I saw you in Coffee Beans, remember?"

"What do you want?"

The plan I came up with just four blocks ago to woo her into talking suddenly seems lame, so I toss it out and just say it like it is—I'm convinced this is the best approach to take with someone like Maude Tuttle. "I want to ask you some things about my family, because when you're a kid, nobody tells you anything, even if it's stuff you have a right to know. I figure you might know something and that anybody bold enough to flip off Connie Olinger is probably bold enough to tell me."

Her wrinkly lids squint as she studies me.

"Please, Miss Tuttle. I'm trying to learn something about my father. You've been in this town forever, so you probably know my family's history. And no disrespect, but I figure that someone who once ran a house of ill repute is probably not going to worry much about telling the truth to a girl who's already getting cramps because she's old enough to get her period any day now."

Maude Tuttle opens the door and lets me in. The big deep-red hair she wore in the restaurant was obviously a wig, because all that's on the top of her head is a tuft of frail white hair that looks like a dandelion gone to seed, floating above pink turf. "Yeah, yeah," she says as she leads me across the living room. "I know I look like hell, but stop staring."

"I—I'm not staring," I lie.

"Of course you are," she says. "What did you say your name was again?"

"Lucy. Lucy McGowan. My grandfather is Sam McGowan. My grandmother's name is Lillian and my mother's name is Tess."

On the outside, Maude Tuttle is stark and bawdy, but her house is the exact opposite: soft-colored, refined, and classy. She shuffles her slippered feet to a rose flowered chair, where a white poodle with drip stains under his eyes is sleeping. She cracks her hands together, right next to the dog's head, and he leaps down. "Dog's half deaf," she says.

She sits down, not bothering to close her satin robe, even though her legs are naked, the skin puckered and hanging. She doesn't invite me to take a seat.

She watches me from the corner of her eye. "And just why should I tell you anything—*if* I knew something?"

I shrug. "No reason, I guess. But I'm hoping you will." I want to sound hard, like Maude herself, but there's nothing hard in me now. Not after reading what I read or seeing what I saw yesterday afternoon.

I take a deep breath, hoping I don't cry. "I've been looking for my father forever, but nobody will tell me anything. Everybody tries to protect me because I'm a kid. I didn't even know my grandpa Sam until we came here. And while I'm not thrilled with everything I've learned about him, at least now I know him. I want to know about my father too, and I figure you're the person to ask. It seems to me like you don't care much what you say to people."

"Sit down," Maude says, and I take a matching chair on the other side of the end table that holds her ashtray and coffee cup.

"I'd offer you something, but all I keep in the house is coffee and gin."

"That's okay. I didn't come here for refreshments."

Maude looks off in the distance, and I'm hoping she doesn't fade off like Nordine Bickett. "Did you know my family well? Or at least know of them?"

"I knew your grandpa well, once. I saw your grandma

around town now and then and heard bits of gossip about her. That's about it."

"Did you know that my grandpa Sam used to be mean? Or did you only know the nice part of him, like everybody else here in town?"

Maude laughs, her voice raspy. She reaches down and grabs a red box with the words *Swisher Sweets* on the front, and she pulls out a brown cigar, skinny like a cigarette, and lights it. Her mouth and cheeks fold into even deeper wrinkles as she draws on it until the tip turns orange. "Honey," she says, after she exhales, "you ever hear it said that a bartender and a hairdresser hear it all? Well, they might hear some things, but they don't hear shit compared to what someone like me hears."

She lifts her hand to make room for the old tabby cat that leaps onto her lap. She strokes her with long swipes and ruffles her hand after each caress to free the hair that's clinging to her fingers. "I always said that my bedroom heard more secrets than Father O'Reilly's confessional booth. Ha!" she says with a laugh, then adds, "Even after I got out of the business, some still came to me to purge themselves of their sins. I suppose they felt safe telling me their secrets, knowing I had no room to judge."

She looks from the cat to me. "Your grandpa told me himself about his temper. Cried like a baby each time he told me about his latest tantrum. Said he was going to stop. That he didn't want to become—he actually said 'become'— like his old man. Course, a couple months down the road, he'd be back again, crying the same old tune. That's people for you."

"His dad beat him too when he was young, didn't he?"

"Yep," Maude says, taking another pull from her cigar. "Sam got the shit beat out of him every day of his life, except for that year he was gone. Right up until the day his daddy died."

"Even when he was an adult?" I ask, baffled that any grown man would let his dad beat him.

"Not with his fists anymore," Maude says. "But there's more ways to beat someone than with your fist."

"True," I say.

"That old man of his was mean to the crotch. He went through three wives, you know. His old man beat the first two down until they probably welcomed that heart attack and cancer. Course, neither of them had a bit of backbone. That third time he met his match, though. The one he took after Sam was grown. A real junkyard dog, that one! Oh, he could still bad-mouth his son with the best of them, but when he got home to his woman, he was as docile as a starved kitten."

"You're kidding?"

"Nope. I don't kid, kid. It didn't surprise me, though. Those who get into doing the mean-dance, sometimes they like to lead, sometimes they like to follow." She clears her throat and crosses her legs. "Well, anyway, you didn't come here to learn what you already know, and you already know that your grandpa was a mean son of a bitch in his day, now, don'tcha?"

"Yes. I came here to learn anything you could tell me about my father."

"Your daddy," she says, lifting her chin as she takes another pull from her cigar, which is filling the room (and no doubt every fiber of my clothing) with smoke.

"I've been asking everybody I meet here if they ever met my father, Howard Smith. I pumped the Olingers for information, and I went to see Nordine Bickett, but her mind's too gone to tell me anything. She gave me a puppet my grandpa carved, though. Well, she sort of gave it to me. Anyway, did you know my father, Howard Smith, or anything about him?"

"Nordine Bickett!" Maude says with a surprisingly gentle laugh. "Ha! Now there's a gal for you—poor woman. That little thing came into this world with angel wings. Born to a preacher and a woman who buttoned her dresses up to her eyes. Nordine. Always did the right thing yet ended up in a spicy love affair that was so hot her undies almost melted.

"She might have been known for her goodness, and I might have been known as the devil's whore, but that sweetheart is the only woman in this town that ever gave me the time of day. Once, when—well, doesn't matter. All that matters is that she befriended me and defended me. Not that I needed defending, mind you. I took care of myself. But her trying just kind of warmed my heart, you know?

"She was the first and only friend I ever had, outside of my girls. Nordine didn't care if that weasel she was married to bitched at her for the company she kept. And if the president of the Lutheran Ladies Circle was at her table having coffee when I showed up, she'd just get out another cup and tell me to sit down. Course, I could have used one of the cups her uppity friends left on the table when they ran out the second I came through the door—acting as if they'd get the clap just by sharing the same table with me."

I don't know what "the clap" is, but I suspect it's one of those STDs that Mrs. Olinger fears Lizzie might give to Barry. And although I can't see what would be funny about having one, I laugh along with her, just to let her know that I'm on her side.

"I never forget someone who's good to me. Not ever. I

still slip over to see Nordine now and then, even though she doesn't know the difference between me and her chair at this point. I pretty her up—fix her hair a little, put some makeup on her. Some people just deserve some pretty in their lives, you know?"

The cell in my pocket pulsates against my hip, and I fidget, grateful that I at least had the sense to set it on vibrate.

"And my dad..." I say. "What about him? What kind of things did he deserve?"

One of Maude Tuttle's sparse eyebrows lifts. "Impatient little thing, aren't you?"

"Well, I'm not supposed to ride my bike all the way to town anymore, so I can't stay too long."

"Fair enough," Maude says. "And if your ma knew where you were, I suppose you'd be in deep shit. Ha! I admire scrappy little girls.

"I didn't know your dad," she says abruptly, as if she wants to get the act of disappointing me out of the way. "I know what happened, though," she adds quickly.

"I was years out of the business by then, but even before I was, I didn't give Sam McGowan anything but a glass of gin and tonic and an ear, once I became friends with Nordine. Hell, he only wanted me back then because I belonged to a Millard, anyway. Still, through the years, after I left the business, some of the old regulars came by—just for a drink and a purging of their sins. They'd tell me that no one mixes up a gin and tonic like me, but, hell, that's not why they came. They always left a nice tip on the coffee table afterward too—the high price they were willing to pay to be able to leave their sins behind when they went."

Maude Tuttle turns and looks me square in the face. "Be careful what you ask for," she says sharply.

"What do you mean?" I ask, sounding as dumb, I suppose, as someone who asks if Milo and I are identical twins.

"You ever go snooping around for information, then afterward felt sorry you found it?"

I think of all that I've learned from Ma's journals, and I nod my head.

"Yet you still want to know, don't you?"

"Yes," I say.

Maude rolls the tip of her cigar around the bottom of the ashtray and watches the ash peel off. "Funny how family secrets can't stay buried forever. Sooner or later, they come out. Sometimes it's because somebody like you goes snooping around. And sometimes they come out without anybody digging for them at all."

Maude's index finger busies itself outlining a pale flower on the arm of her chair. She looks out the window again.

"Mrs. Olivia Morgan and her husband, Russell. That's the couple who adopted me. They dressed me in finery and paraded me around town as their little darling. I had no reason to believe I wasn't either—and, oh, how sweet life might have been if *that* secret could have stayed buried forever. But it didn't, of course. I turned twelve, started sprouting a pair of perky tits, and Russell Morgan decided that I didn't look so much like a daughter anymore. That's when the truth came out. And it knocked me right on my ass."

"What truth?" I ask.

"That my mother was a hooker, and not a high-class one either. Who knows who my daddy was. Could have been any son of a bitch in a hundred-mile radius of that town. My mother gave me up right after I was born. Sold me for the price of a week's worth of tricks to Mr. Morgan, a man desperate to replace his wife's dead baby girl so she'd stop acting crazy and get on with her wifely duties, no doubt. He told Olivia that I was born to a young bride who died during childbirth and that the father, only a boy, wasn't equipped to raise a kid on his own. That's the story she knew, up until Russell decided to have his way with me. He turned the blame on me, telling Olivia where I came from and ranting on about how the apple doesn't fall far from the tree. I learned both stories then, right before they threw me out on my ass, to stand on the street in my nightie with nowhere to go."

Maude leans over and nuzzles her cat's head a bit, and the cat begins to vibrate like the cell phone in my pocket. "She had two other daughters by that time, so I guess I was just to tide her over until she could have her own."

She stubs out her half-smoked cigar and leaves it waiting at the edge of the ashtray. "Lots of times, through the years, I've wondered about that apple-not-falling-far-from-the-tree thing. I suppose if I'd ever been blessed—or cursed—with children, I would have found out for sure, but my guess is, had I had a daughter, she would have lain down for money too. And if I'd had a son, he would have fallen in love with a whore he could never marry no matter how much he cared. Who the hell knows. But what I do know for sure is that nothing could have hurt me more than being lied to for all those years. I would have been better off knowing that I was born to a whore from day one."

Miss Tuttle looks at me hard. "You know what I'm getting at here?"

I'm tempted to counter Miss Tuttle's conclusions with what I know about nurture versus nature, but I don't want to sidetrack her any more than she's already sidetracking herself.

I glance up at an old grandfather clock when it chimes. I've been gone far longer than I should have been for a bike ride already. "Yeah, I know what you're getting at. But, please, if you could get there a little faster I'd sure appreciate it, because I have to get home."

"Truth needs a proper introduction," she says. "And that *is* what I'm planning to tell you. The truth. As it was told to me by your grandfather himself. And I do believe he told me the truth too. He didn't have one reason to lie to me. Not one. He came to me that same night it happened, and he spilled his guts. Sat right in that chair you're sitting in now, all shook up and disheveled, his left leg sticking straight because it hurt to bend it, and he told me what he'd done.

"Course, by the time Sam showed up, I'd already heard the rumors of what happened. Word travels like brush fire here. I heard how Sam's daughter went out to California to go to school, met this guy, got herself knocked up, and came running home to hide when he got nasty. He came for her, though."

"Because he loved her and wanted her back. And her babies too?"

"Because the apple doesn't fall far from the tree, and your mom was your grandma's apple."

Loud rapping as sharp as gunshots sounds at the door, startling us both. "Lucy? You in there? Lucy!" Even through the thick old door, I can tell it's Mom calling to me.

"Shit," I say. Out loud.

"Raid!" Maude says with a chuckle. She lifts her cat and drops her to the floor, then rises and goes to the door, even though I'm pleading with her not to.

Maude pulls the door until the gold chain is taut, and Mom and Mitzy squeeze their heads together to peer inside. "Lucy?" Mom shouts. "Are you in there?"

Maude closes the door to create slack on the chain and she unhooks it. Without saying a word to Maude, Mom stomps through the room and yanks me by the arm. "What in the hell do you think you're doing here?" she says, and Maude Tuttle mimics her "*here,*" then tells her to...well... she basically tells her to go have sex with herself, only she says it the way a bawdy ex-hooker might say it.

I look back at Maude Tuttle, who's standing in the doorway as Mom tugs me down the front steps, hoping she sees the gratitude in my eyes and that she picks up on my silent promise to return.

Mitzy opens the trunk, and Mom, strong in her anger, hoists my bike into it before Mitzy can even get a grasp on the bike to help.

"I don't believe this! What in the hell's wrong with you? Do you go into just anybody's house? Is that what you do when you go for a bike ride?" Once I went into the apartment down the hall from ours with the guy who had the parrot, and Mom caught me and went nuts then too, but not quite this nuts.

Mom doesn't wait for an answer. She opens the back door and jabs her hand roughly against my back so I'll get in. "Oma says you took my cell phone; do you have it?" I retrieve the phone out of my pocket and hand it over the front seat. "We've been calling it for an hour and a half now. Why in the hell didn't you pick up?"

Mom calls Oma quickly to tell her she found me, and adds, "I'll tell you when we get home." She snaps the lid shut and pulls away from the curb.

"I don't know where your head is at these days, Lucy

Marie McGowan. Your grandfather's dying and the whole house is in chaos. Your grandmother is frantic because you were gone so long and Milo never saw you on the road, and what were you doing? Riding to town, as you were told not to, and getting cozy with Maude Tuttle, of all people. I wouldn't have believed it myself, if Ma hadn't called Mitzy's phone while we were picking up some things at the drugstore for Dad. Barry Olinger, that fat-ass busybody, was standing in line, eavesdropping, and told me he'd just seen you go into Maude Tuttle's house. I didn't believe it until we got to Maude's and saw your bike, half hidden behind her bushes. What in the hell were you doing *there*?"

I look out the window and watch as houses and trees blur by. "Just visiting," I say.

"Don't try jerking me around, Lucy. I know you better than that."

I spend the rest of the ride home sitting in silence while the trunk lid flaps, Mom rants, and Mitzy tries to distract her so she'll calm down. The wind that I didn't feel when I rode into town now feels icy, even through the thick car window, and even though the car's heater is humming full blast. And I don't know what to think. Not of what Maude had the chance to say or about the fact that Mom and Mitzy should show up just when Maude was going to tell me what happened when my dad came to get my mom. Oma says there are no coincidences.

Tiny snowflakes start to fall. I watch them and think of how soon winter will lie down over Timber Falls, and all the little creeks will freeze over. I lay my head back on the seat, and I close my eyes so I don't have to see Mom's angry eyes, shining cat-yellow in the rearview mirror, and I day-dream of ice skating, Scotty gliding toward me with his arms outstretched.

* * *

WHEN WE get back to the house, Marie's car is parked outside, alongside Mitzy's van.

Oma hurries to me and hugs me when I come through the door. "I was so worried about you, Lucy. Milo said he hadn't seen you on the road. Why didn't you answer the phone?" She squeezes me again, then says, "Well, at least you're safe."

"I found her at Maude Tuttle's house," Mom says.

"Maude Tuttle's?" Oma looks down at me. "What on earth were you doing there?"

I don't have to answer—either with the truth or a lie—because Marie comes out of Grandpa Sam's room and interrupts. "Lillian, I think it's time to call Jeana and Clay. Maybe you want to call the nurse to come look at him to get her opinion, but I think it's time."

Oma puts her hand over the top of her big chest. "I'll call her to make sure she's handy if we need her," she says. "But I trust your opinion, Marie. All those years working in the nursing home. You should know."

Marie pats Oma's back as she scoots around her and then squeezes around the table to get to the phone. She hands it to Oma, who calls Barbara.

Mom has her arms wrapped around her middle like a shield, though I'm not sure if that shield is meant to keep painful things out or in.

The minute Oma gets done talking to Barbara, Marie opens the cupboard door to find the numbers that are scratched on Grandpa Sam's old medicine schedule, and Mitzy gets out the canister of coffee. Marie calls Aunt Jeana, telling her everything she knows—which is plenty—about Grandpa Sam's faltering blood pressure, decrease in urination, spiked fever, increased restlessness, and all those other symptoms that the pamphlet—page seven, heading title: "One to Two Days to Hours Prior to Death"—says intensify. When Marie is done with the long list of symptoms, she calmly answers Aunt Jeana's questions and hangs up.

Marie dials Clay's number next, using her own cell phone for this call. She knows he won't pick up if he sees a call come in from Grandpa Sam's number. He answers promptly—probably because he thinks it's some frantic mother who just gave birth to a baby with a cleft palate, or no palate at all—and Marie tells him that his dad is dying and he is to come home right away. She doesn't give him time to counter her orders with excuses. "Your family needs you now, and you need them," she says, as if that's all there is to it. "We'll be expecting you, honey." She hangs up before he can respond.

Oma bites her bottom lip and looks close to tears. "Thank you for calling them, Marie. Jeana especially. I don't think I could have handled her right now." Oma fidgets. "I knew this time was coming, of course. But now that it's here, I have to say, I'm a little shook up."

While Mitzy pours steaming coffee into cups, I slip through the front door. I sit on the ground, on the lap of my father—right on the spot where Peter's shadow and mine fell—and I hate the day I'm in.

chapter

TWENTY-FOUR

O H, GOD," Mom says when Aunt Jeana's rental car rolls into the drive early the next morning. Mom looks over-tired, and I know why. Last night there was a blade of light showing under her bedroom door when I got up to pee. She was writing in her digital journal again, no doubt, trying to sort through the tangle of memories and feelings she has as Grandpa Sam's "time"—as Oma calls it—approaches.

Oma pats Mom's arm as she heads to the door so she can help Aunt Jeana bring in her clunky old suitcase and ratty dog bed.

Aunt Jeana looks stressed and nods her head in little jerks as she says hello to Marie—who has been camped out at our house almost nonstop for the last twenty-four hours, taking turns with Oma so that someone is always keeping vigil at Grandpa Sam's bedside—and to Mitzy, who has just arrived.

"Are you the county nurse?" Aunt Jeana asks Mitzy.

"No, Jeana. She's Tess's dear friend." Oma does her best to smile. "But the nurse was here yesterday, and she'll come again today if we need her."

"*If* we need her?"

"Past seeing that he's as comfortable as possible, there's really nothing more she can do for him, Jeana," Oma says. "Dying *is* as natural as childbirth."

"That may be true, Lillian, but we don't let a woman go through childbirth without medical help, stuffed in some back room by herself, now, do we?" She looks around the room.

"She'll bring him morphine, should he need it," Oma says, but Aunt Jeana ignores her.

"Who's sitting in with him right now?"

"I was with him," Oma says. "I just came out when I heard your car."

Aunt Jeana scopes the room, taking us all in. Her squinty eyes pause on Marie and Mitzy. "I don't know if it's a good thing to have the house filled with people who aren't family at a time like this," she says, and I wonder if she says it for Grandpa Sam's sake or because Chico is trembling in her arms, his bony head half buried in the sleeve of her jacket.

"I'm glad you could be here," Oma says, ignoring her comment. "Seeing as how Sam's the only sibling you have left, I can only imagine how hard this is for you, but I'm glad you came. Your brother needs you now."

Aunt Jeana bites her lip and nods.

"Hi, Aunt Jeana," I say, feeling a wave of pity for her. "I'm sorry about your brother."

She looks at me. "You're the one who was doing that odd thing on the ground, aren't you? What's your name again?"

"I'm Lucy," I say, suddenly sorry for saying anything to her.

Oma helps Aunt Jeana off with her coat—no easy feat, since Aunt Jeana won't put Chico down because she's afraid he'll get stepped on—and Mitzy and Mom quietly slip out the back door.

Aunt Jeana follows Oma and Marie into Grandpa Sam's room, and, amazingly enough, I hear Grandpa Sam's voice mingling with their soft murmurs. And what I hear him saying is my name.

I haven't gone into Grandpa Sam's room for a long time, but I go there now, weaving my way through Oma, Marie, and Aunt Jeana to get to his bed.

Grandpa Sam is sitting up against a wall of pillows—looking nothing like a limp puppet hanging from a hoist—and he's staring at Oma and talking more clearly than he has since we got here. "Where's Lucy?" he asks, his breaths a bit hard, but not too bad.

"I'm here, Grandpa! Right here!"

He turns to look me square in the face. "Lucy," he says, and I swear, the corners of his mouth actually turn up.

I can't help myself. I start laughing. I look at Oma and she's grinning too. It's a miracle! Maybe one brought on by Oma herself, with a prayer she probably offered up to an eagle who maybe happened to fly by while I was at Maude's. A prayer she forgot to tell me about.

My whole insides are soaring like an eagle too when I

sit down on the edge of Grandpa Sam's hospital bed and look into eyes that are looking back at me.

"She's your girl, isn't she, Sam?" Oma says, and Grandpa Sam nods and says, "She's my girl."

"Lucy and Sam got quite close in the six weeks we've been here," Oma tells Aunt Jeana. "She helped me feed him and get him around, and she spent lots of time with him."

The minute Oma says this, I feel bad. I lean over so it looks like I'm hugging him, but secretly I whisper into Grandpa Sam's ear, "I'm sorry I haven't been sitting with you. It scared me to see you so sick."

Grandpa Sam looks at me. "Don't be scared," he says slowly, his hand—his good left hand, the hand that carved pretty things—coming out and wrapping itself around my wrist, then bringing it up to his chest. I hear Oma sniffle.

"Clay's coming too," Marie says. "He called this morning. He's taking a red-eye tonight, and he'll be here in the morning."

"Clay," Grandpa Sam says, and Marie says, "You're waiting for him, aren't you, Sam?" Grandpa Sam nods and says, "Yeah."

I turn to Oma. "Imagine how surprised Uncle Clay is going to be to see Grandpa all better!"

The grown-ups exchange glances, except for Mom, who has slipped into the room, unnoticed, and is now watching her dad, her arms folded tight around her middle, her face tight.

Oma puts her hand on my shoulder and softly says, "Lucy, come with me for a minute, okay?"

"I want to stay by Grandpa Sam; he wants me by him. Don't you, Grandpa?"

"Come on, honey," Oma says. "Just for a minute. I'll bring her right back, Sam."

She takes my hand and leads me to the kitchen. Marie follows.

"Sit down, honey," Oma says, as she pulls a chair out for me. "You want some tea? Chamomile, maybe?"

"No," I say, feeling a little scared. "I just want to sit by Grandpa Sam now that he's better and can talk to me again."

Oma glances at Marie, then pulls out the chair at the head of the table and sits down right next to me. She takes my hand in both of hers, while Marie sits down and sets the pamphlet from Ministry Home Care down on the table. "Honey, did you read this?"

"Yes." My voice sounds snippy, like Mom's when she gets defensive.

"Well, here on page seven, it tells how a dying person may experience a surge of energy toward the end. Did you read that part?"

I blink fast. I read that whole thing. Not all at once, but in bits. If that part was there, I'd have remembered it.

Oma makes a soft smacking noise with her mouth, and her eyes get misty. She rubs the back of my hand. "You know what I was thinking of when I went into your grandpa's room and saw him perked up? I thought of your mom right after she was born."

Her tone has that dreamy quality people use when they read a story that begins with a "once upon a time" and ends with a moral, so I know I'm going to be sitting here for a while.

"Just minutes after she slipped into this world, before they'd even had time to wash the chalky white from her head, they put her in my arms, and oh, my, she was studying me *so* hard and cooing at me. The nurse walked in, and Tess even turned her head to see where the noise was coming from.

"Why, I could hardly believe my eyes. I didn't know much about newborn babies then, but I'd seen enough of them to know that they spend most of their time in a sleepy stupor. Yet there she was, as alert as a baby of six months.

"Clay was in an incubator because his lungs were giving him a bit of trouble, so I couldn't tell if he was as 'smart' as my baby girl, but I was sure he was, and I knew that would make your grandpa very happy.

" 'Look at her. Look at how alert she is!' I said to the nurse. 'It's amazing.'

"And the nurse just smiled. Then she explained to me what she'd seen many times before in that first hour or so after birth. How a baby will be alert, wise even. Seeming months older, before they slip into that newborn fog, where they'll stay for a few months."

I'm tapping the heels of my tennies against the linoleum. "Oma, can we talk about this later? I want to go back by Grandpa Sam now."

"In a minute, dear. Let me finish my story first." Oma rubs my forearm, then gives it a pat before continuing.

"Anyway, sure enough, forty-five minutes or so later, Tess's eyes began to glaze over, and the next time they brought her to me, they were as cloudy and dull as any other newborn's.

"The nurse told me it was nature's way, to make them hyperalert like that right after birth, so they can bond with their mommies and say hello to their new world. Life does seem to move in a circle, and death, well, like Sky Dreamer says, is nothing more than a rebirth. A leaving of this world to join the next. So it only makes sense that a person would become hyperalert again at the end of their life. So they can say good-bye to the ones they bonded with here. Now it's time for your grandpa to renew the bonds he has with those who are waiting for him on the other side. But he'll never forget you, just like you'll never forget him. You'll both have your memories, and the bond the two of you share will stretch like a rainbow from heaven to earth."

I can feel my eyes getting warm and wet. "But he looks all better," I say. "He even sounds all better."

Oma squeezes my hand. "I know," she says.

But she doesn't know. She doesn't know just how much I need Grandpa Sam to stay, because—as much as I don't want to admit it—I know now that I'm not going to find my real dad. I can feel that truth sitting deep inside me, in that hollow place that's filled with nothing but hurt. And I can't be sure that Mom will let Peter stay in my life either, to fill that space with something happy.

"Lucy?" Aunt Jeana calls from the other room. "Your grandpa's asking for you again."

"Sweetie," Marie says, and I look up at her. "At any time, if this gets to be too much for you, you leave the room, okay? Your grandpa will understand, and he won't be alone. We'll all be with him."

Oma takes my face in her hands and turns it toward her. "Don't be scared. Death is nothing more than another birth. We have our time with him to say our good-byes. Sad or not, let's send him off to the other side with love and joy, okay?" She stands up and holds out her hand so I'll take it. Then she leads me back into Grandpa Sam's room.

Grandpa is answering questions, and the room is filled with the kind of giggles that happen when tears are interrupted.

Someone asks where Milo is, and Mom says he's in the study.

"He should come spend this time with his grandpa," Oma says.

"I'll get him," I say, because suddenly I want Grandpa Sam to take memories of both of his grandchildren with him when he leaves.

I find Milo standing in front of his desk, chin up and shoulders back. He has Oma's round hairbrush held upside down and propped nearly against his chin.

"Hey, Lucy. Can you sit in as a judge? I'm going to do a practice run reciting pi. I've been experimenting with two methods. Remembering the digits in groups of ten by pretending they are the phone numbers of my favorite scientists, and converting the numbers into consonants and making words out of them. You'd think that the phone-number method would work best for me since I'm good with numbers, yet I seem to be equally good with the consonant-conversion method. To be honest, I actually find it more fun."

"I can't. We're supposed to—"

"Come on!" Milo whines. "All you have to do is follow along to make sure I don't screw up and watch the clock because I'm taking a ten-minute break every hour, just like they do in real competitions. I need to get used to the pause. Other than that, you just have to recite my position at the beginning of each hour."

"Milo, Grandpa Sam is dying. You're supposed to come and see him."

Milo blinks at me, his eyes round enough behind his spotty glasses to let me know my words scare him.

"Milo?" Mom is standing in the doorway, her arms still wrapped around her middle. "What are you doing?"

"I was getting ready to start my practice run reciting pi," he says. "I asked Lucy to pretend to be my judge, but she won't. She says I have to go by Grandpa...I don't want to."

"I'll do it," Mom says, flashing him a smile that looks carved from wax. She grabs a metal folding chair that is propped up against the wall and unfolds it. "Just tell me what I have to do."

Milo grins.

"But Oma says he should be with Grandpa Sam now, to send him off with love and joy," I say, interrupting Milo's instructions.

"It's okay, Lucy. You go sit with him."

I stand in the doorway for a second and watch as Mom sits with the stopwatch on her lap and Milo stands before his desk, reciting the first few digits of pi into the hairbrush handle. He emphasizes every other digit as though it's a period: "One, FOUR, one, FIVE, nine, TWO, six, FIVE, three, FIVE..."

I walk out of the room, not bothering to shut the door, because I know that, for both Mom and Milo, the door is already closed.

chapter

TWENTY-FIVE

ARIE IS in the kitchen pouring water into the teapot when I step out of the study.

"Milo is reciting pi," I say. "And Mom's sitting in as a judge. I don't know why they're doing that now." I'm scratching my earlobe, which is itching. Maybe because it's true that cells remember, and even looking at Marie's big chest and strong arms makes my ear remember being crushed. Or maybe, just maybe, my ear is itching because it *wants* to be crushed again.

Marie smiles a bit. "I don't even know what that means," she says, and I tell her that she probably doesn't want to know, because it's boring.

"You want to help me make tea?" she asks.

"I should go sit with Grandpa Sam. He wants me to."

"Sometimes a little break at times like this is good," she says.

I stand near the sink and reach up into the cupboard for the bin that has our tea. "Back at our house, we had a tea basket. I like baskets for tea better," I say.

Outside the window, I see Mitzy's legs as she sits on the edge of the porch, bobbing them. I contemplate telling her that Mom won't be back out for hours upon hours.

"Honey?" Marie is saying. Her hand comes down on my shoulder, and I turn and look up at her.

I expect her to say something, but instead, she wraps her arms around me and gives me a hug. Not the kind she gave me that first day—the kind that fit like a straitjacket—but one that fits more like a seat belt, making me feel securely held in place if there should be a crash.

"I know this is hard," she says, her voice a deep rumble in her chest. "You just remember that you only have to do the best you can do right now. That's what your mom and your brother are doing. The best they can do."

She loosens her grip on me and brushes away the clump of hair that is covering my eye. She smiles at me sadly. "It's going to be okay," she says.

"The cycle of life," I say, and she nods.

The teapot whistles, and Marie lets go of me so she can snatch it off the stove. She sets it on a cool burner, then takes down mismatched coffee cups and lines them on the table in case anyone else wants some. Mitzy comes into the kitchen then. "Oh, tea," she says, as though she's pleased. "I brought a loaf of pumpkin bread this morning. I'll slice it."

While Marie fills our cups, I help Mitzy with the pumpkin bread, lining the slices up on a plate like digits.

"Ray and I picked a wedding date," she tells Marie, who squeals and gives her the kind of hug that could squish an ear.

"I'm so happy for you, honey!"

"In six weeks. That's not a lot of time to plan a wedding, but Ray has ten days coming, and he has to take them before the end of the year or he'll lose them. He wants us to go to Hawaii for our honeymoon."

"Wonderful!" Marie says, then adds, "I can see you now..." She puts her hands out to the side as though she's waving and sways her wide hips back and forth to do the hula dance, singing "Ooo La La, Ooo La La," to a melody that *almost* sounds Hawaiian.

Mitzy and I laugh. A little too hard.

Marie stops her dance and eyes Mitzy carefully. "Honey, you okay with all of this now?"

"Mostly," she says. "But yesterday I didn't feel right: I had a backache and I panicked. I left work, without even talking to anybody, and I raced to my doctor's office and insisted they hurry me in. They asked if I had any spotting, but I didn't, so they told me to take a seat. I got hysterical and they took me in the back room to wait until the doctor finished up with a patient. Everything was fine, and I felt so stupid afterward."

"Aw, honey," Marie says, and she gathers Mitzy in her arms to squish her ear.

Mitzy grabs an empty cup and pours herself tea. "I hope Tess will stay awhile after this—or at least come back for the wedding. I want her to be my maid of honor and Lucy and Milo to be my miniature bride and groom."

I don't know exactly what a miniature bride is, or does, but I know it means I'll be in Mitzy's wedding, and that makes me happy. "Since I was married before, I'm not going to go overly fancy," Mitzy tells Marie. "I'm thinking of a nice fifties style, maybe a three-quarter-length dress. Puffed sleeves, a full skirt, a bow at the back. And pale pink for Tess, and a dress that matches mine in the same pink for Lucy." She turns to me. "I like pink, do you, Lucy?" I nod, even though it's not my favorite color.

"You'll carry a basket of rose petals to toss on the white carpet before I walk down with my dad."

"Oh, that will be sweet," Marie says.

I've never been to a wedding before, but I saw one on TV once. I'd slipped into Sonya-who-skipped-Barbies-down-the-steps' apartment one day and there was one on the soap opera her mother was watching. The camera shifted from the bride and groom to a bridesmaid who was trying to avoid the look of one of the groomsmen. But as someone with too much makeup sang, the bridesmaid looked up at him and, probably because she was caught up in the romantic moment, she gave him a look that was as good as saying, "Yes, I want to marry you too." Just the thought that this could happen at Mitzy's wedding makes me flood with happy feelings, and I know that if it happens between Mom and Peter, I'd get so happy, I'd probably toss every one of those rose petals straight up into the air as my way of saying, "Amen!"

"There you all are," Oma says, coming into the kitchen. She looks pale, wounded. She picks up her lighter, and I expect her to grab her cigarettes, but she doesn't. Instead, she grabs her conch shell and sage. "Lucy?" she says, pausing in the doorway. "Where's your mother and Milo?"

"In the study. Milo's practicing reciting pi, and Mom's helping him."

"What?" she says. "But Sam—"

Marie stops her. "We all handle death in different ways,

Lillian," she says. "You know that." And the way she says it stops Oma from addressing me, even though I know that she was about to ask me why I'm not in Grandpa Sam's room either.

"Of course," she says, and floats back into Grandpa Sam's room with her sage. Aunt Jeana is breathing enough negativity in that room to choke them all.

Mitzy slips right back into talking about her wedding plans—where they'll have their reception, who will supply the food, what kind of music they'll have.

"I suppose it's silly to go all out like this for a second wedding," Mitzy is saying, "but it's Ray's first marriage, and—"

"Oh, I think it's wonderful," Marie says. "I'm so glad, dear, that you set aside your fear and agreed to marry the man you love."

"Set aside my fears?" Mitzy gives a nervous twitter. "I'm scared shitless, but I *am* doing it, aren't I?"

"Yes, you are!"

I'm happy for Mitzy, but I wish it were Mom saying these things instead. If it were, maybe the thought of Grandpa Sam dying wouldn't hurt quite so badly.

All this wishing makes me think of Peter.

Once, a bird hit our window while Peter was over. I saw it happen and rushed across the room to peer down at the sidewalk, trying to see if he'd fallen or flown off.

When Peter saw that I was upset, he took me downstairs so I could check. The bird was lying near the stoop, his eyes open, but there was no life in them anymore. Two little boys from the second floor were bending over him, one of them poking him with a stick. Peter made him stop, then he picked up the bird.

There was no dirt to bury him in, but we walked down

one block and Peter stepped right over the tape sealing off a new tree that had just been planted to replace the diseased elms, and he dug a grave for the bird, patting a nice little mound over him. Then we walked back to our place, his hand holding mine. He never said a thing the whole time, but I felt better just having him there, knowing what to do.

Marie and Mitzy don't ask where I'm going when I open the back door and go outside.

The shade to Grandpa's room is open, the window reflecting the sun so I can't see inside, and I'm glad for this.

I feel bad, because Grandpa wants me with him, but I can't seem to make myself go back in there, now that I know he's still dying. Instead, I sit on the ground, right in my safe spot. A bird squawks and I look up, hoping it will be an eagle. It's not. It's a crow.

I settle back to lie in the lap of my father and look up at the clouds rolling by. When Milo and I were little and would get impatient waiting at the bus stop, Mom would have us look at the clouds and find pictures in them. I could never look too long, so Milo saw more pictures than me—usually stupid things, like a science-lab beaker or a telescope. If I looked too long, I'd get scared that maybe I'd fall right into that sky, as though it were the floor and the ground beneath me were the ceiling. I don't get scared as I look up into it now, though. Not with my father at my back. I tuck my hands under my head and stare above me.

I think Oma believes that heaven is in the sky, because she looks up there when she talks about spirits and the afterlife. Wherever it is—*if* it is—the only thing I know is that I don't want Grandpa Sam to leave here to go there.

I watch as the wind kneads the clouds into first one shape, then another. Then, suddenly, there he is. The image of Grandpa Sam himself forming in a cloud! It's the Grandpa Sam from Nordine's picture: big, and bulky.

One cumulus cloud makes up his head and torso, and poufs of wispy clouds drift together to give him arms. There's even a curled tail that forms his left hand. But on the other side, there's only sky where his right hand should be.

It's synchronicity. Pure, sweet synchronicity! Before Oma took *The Tibetan Book of the Dead* away, I'd read a section of it while sitting at the table. Page 191, third paragraph down. The section on averting death! It said that if you see an image of someone in the sky, and the image is missing a hand, you can keep them from dying by making a peace offering. Specifically, by creating a dough effigy.

It's like Oma always tells me—there are no coincidences! First I read a portion of Oma's book, even though she obviously didn't want me to and even though it seemed like a frivolous distraction at the time. Then I heard the squawk of a bird, coaxing me to look up, and *then* I saw Grandpa Sam's image in the sky, with the right hand missing. It's a sign! A sign that I should make Grandpa Sam a dough effigy to keep him alive.

I hurry into the house, to where the vase of fake flowers made of dyed feathers now sits beside the door, waiting to go to the shed, because Mom said she didn't care how many shars it removed, it was butt-ugly. The book said to use the feathers of a gull, but I know I'm not going to find one of those here, and besides, underneath the bright orange and red dye, these feathers *could* be from a gull.

As I'm contemplating how many flowers I'll need to pluck to give me seventy-eight feathers—one for every year of Grandpa Sam's life—Milo slips by me and into the bathroom. He's in a rush, of course, because he only has a ten-minute break, and I hear the toilet seat crack hard as he flips it up.

It's no coincidence that he is taking his break from reciting pi at this very moment either, I tell myself, and I go to the bathroom door, leaning close.

"Milo, how big is one cubit?" I yell through the door. One cubit is how big the book said the dough effigy should be, but I don't know anything about cubits, except that it is a biblical measurement.

"About eighteen inches," Milo calls back as the toilet flushes. He pops out of the bathroom without running water in the sink and scurries through the kitchen, yelling, "That's not an exact measurement, though," as he goes.

"You'd never know Sam was on his deathbed, looking at this family, now, would you?" Aunt Jeana says to Marie, as she walks into the kitchen. She goes to the fridge and pulls out the small package of raw hamburger she brought, struggling to open it without dropping Chico, who pokes his head out of Aunt Jeana's jacket only long enough to bark at me. "It's disrespectful."

I follow them to the counter and reach for the canister of whole-wheat flour. The instructions said to use seven grains when making the dough for the effigy, but is whole wheat a reasonable substitute? "How many grains are in whole-wheat flour?" I ask Marie, who is pouring Aunt Jeana a cup of fresh coffee. She says she doesn't know, and Aunt Jeana shakes her head.

I put the lid back on the canister and grab the bag of pancake/waffle mix, which is stamped with the label from Nature's Garden's health-food store on the front. Underneath the logo is written *7 whole grains of goodness*. No coincidences, I tell myself as I grab a mixing bowl and start pouring.

"What are you making there, young lady?" Aunt Jeana snaps. "Other than a mess."

"Something for my grandpa," I say, knowing Aunt Jeana wouldn't understand if I tried explaining it to her.

"He can't eat pancakes now!" Aunt Jeana snaps.

I take my bowl and dash out the door, grabbing the feather flowers—vase and all—on my way out.

I hurry out to the shed because, although the book didn't say the effigy needs to be made in the dying person's private sanctuary, I think it will give it more power if it is.

I mentally go over the instructions the book gave as I clear a spot on the worktable. I'm to create an effigy one cubit big out of dough made of seven grains. I'm to fashion it in the shape of a lion's open jaw, then poke one gull feather for every year of Grandpa Sam's life into it. Then I am to carry it down a main street to a royal manor at the north end of town. And I know just what manor house I'll bring it to too: the Millard mansion!

I run water from the spigot on the side of the house into an old tin dish, then carry the bowl back into the shed and get to work. I add only drops of water at a time, knowing that if I add too much, I'm going to make pancakes.

It's not easy making a lion's open jaw with no illustration to follow, but I do my best. And every time I get frustrated, I remind myself that I'm lucky that the hand that was missing in Grandpa's cloud image was his mean right hand and not his good left one. Had it been the other way around, I'd have had to find the fang of a black-striped tiger, which would have been impossible, of course, and the fang of a black dog, which would have been almost as impossible, since Feynman doesn't like his mouth messed with, and Grandpa's urine, which would have been particularly tricky, since I heard Oma say that he's not urinating anymore.

While the dough is still sticky, I start ripping feathers from the flowers and poking them into the lion's head. When I finish, my lion's jaw looks more like a lame science project of a mountain range made by some nongifted five-year-old, but, maybe like all gifts, it's the thought that counts.

I can't wait for the effigy to dry before I move it, so I dig in the burning barrel until I find a brown paper bag with damp coffee grounds stuck to it, and I tuck the effigy carefully inside. Then I get on my bike and pedal as fast as I can toward town, pretending that I don't know who's pulling into our drive when I get to the end, even though Mrs. Olinger is waving at me.

THE MILLARD mansion sits just down the street from Maude Tuttle's house. Even though I'd wanted to hear the rest of her story in the worst way, at the moment I can't think of anything but seeing to it that Grandpa lives, and I know I won't stop in to see her.

I park my bike three blocks from the Millard mansion, anyway, because the book said to walk down the main street with the effigy. I'm hoping three blocks is enough, because the late-October sky has clouded over, and all I'm wearing is my thin windbreaker. I flex my right hand, stiff from the cold and from holding the top of the paper bag folded over the handlebars so I wouldn't drop it.

I take the lion's jaw out of the bag, scooping up the feathers that fell to the bottom and poking them back into the dough. Then I hold it in the palms of my hands, away from my body—like I imagine an effigy should be carried—and for three blocks, I say prayers as Oma would: to the Creator, to my dead ancestors, to God, to Jesus, to

Buddha, to my guardian angels, to Mohammed, and to a couple of Catholic saints and Hindu gods whose names I happen to know. And I beg and plead for them all to use their power to help Grandpa live, because he's the closest thing to a father I'll probably ever have.

When I get to the Millard mansion, I don't know what to do with the effigy, so I say a final prayer and I set it down gently on the steps. I pause and I wait without knowing what I'm waiting for. Probably not for anything dramatic, like the gray clouds to part and some wise voice to call down to me, "You asked, now you shall receive" (because any god, I'm thinking, would probably use the word "shall"), but maybe something subtle, like a private inner feeling that makes me sigh with relief and cry happy tears. But I don't hear anything special at all. Just the whistle of the wind and the hum of cars on the street. And I don't feel anything but the cold wind nipping at my hands.

WHEN I get back home, there's a white car with a Hertz license plate sitting in the driveway. A tall man is standing beside it with his hands in his pockets, looking out over the yard, the wind ruffling the top of his neatly groomed hair.

"Excuse me," I say. "Are you my uncle Clay?" There's little ticking noises sparking under his hood, telling me he just got here.

He turns. He looks like Grandpa Sam used to look, yet his mouth and chin are shaped like Oma's. His nose and teeth are perfectly straight, which leads me to believe that he had them fixed after Grandpa Sam broke them. "If you're Lucy, I am," he says.

I don't know what the proper greeting for an uncle you've never met is, but what I want to do is hug him. Instead, I tell him that Mom and Oma are inside. He nods, smiles with his lips shut, and with his hands still in his pockets, he follows me to the house, then removes one so he can hold the door open and I can slip in first. I'm not thrilled to go inside, since I know it's likely I'm about to get a tongue-lashing for disappearing again.

I don't, though. Not when Oma looks above my head and sees who's standing behind me. "Clay!" she cries, her hand going to her chest. Oma doesn't wait for him to offer her his arms. She goes to him, kisses both of his cheeks, then hugs him, rocking him from side to side. "Oh, Clay... Clay." Marie and Mitzy watch them and get smiley and teary-eyed, then wrap one arm around each other, as if this makes them part of the hug.

"Your dad's waiting for you," Oma says. "He was faltering, but I told him you were on your way from the airport, and he rallied around."

"How long ago?" I ask.

"Huh?"

"How long ago did he rally around again?"

"I don't know. A half an hour ago? Forty-five minutes? I'm not sure."

I grin to myself. The effigy! It had to be! The pamphlet never said a thing about a dying person having *two* bursts of energy!

"Welcome home, Clay," Marie says, before she crushes him to her.

Clay asks where Mom is, and I glance at the clock. It's nineteen minutes to three, so I tell him that she'll be out in nine minutes. He looks confused, so I explain just the basics of what Mom and Milo are doing. "We all cope differently," Oma says to him, since he still looks confused.

Mitzy hugs Clay a bit too, then she offers him coffee. "You hungry? The Olingers brought by a casserole and a chocolate cake a bit ago," she says. "And there's pumpkin bread."

"I'm not hungry, thanks," he says. "But I'll take a coffee." His hands are back in his pockets.

"I thought I heard you," Aunt Jeana says as she hustles into the kitchen. Chico is barking like a lunatic, but she ignores him long enough to give Clay a one-armed hug.

"I'm glad you came, Clay," she says, her eyes red-rimmed. "The place looks good, doesn't it?"

Clay looks around the room and nods, even though I can tell that he's thinking it's a rat hole, just like Mom thinks it is.

"Do you want to see your father now?" Oma asks.

"I think I'll have that coffee first."

Mitzy pours him a cup, and Marie offers him her chair and says she'll go sit with Grandpa Sam while they all visit. Uncle Clay's eyebrows dip and one corner of his mouth cranks over toward his cheek when he looks at the table butted up against the cupboards.

"How's work?" Mitzy asks, and Clay pulls his hands out of his pockets and starts talking about his job, his voice sounding happy and sure. I watch him as he talks, hands gesturing the whole time. He looks like a very nice uncle. He reminds me of Mom. But then, I remind myself, he is her twin.

"We'll have to go make arrangements tomorrow," Aunt Jeana interrupts. "Most churches won't bury someone if they're not a member, but I'm a registered Methodist back home so I'm sure the Methodist church here will bury him. We can have the church ladies provide the luncheon afterward."

Her words make me angry. "Grandpa's not even dead," I blurt out. "And who knows. Maybe he's not even going to die."

Aunt Jeana's head snaps toward me. "This is an adult discussion," she says. Then she looks at Uncle Clay. "I hope you don't allow your children to be disrespectful like this."

"Oh, Jeana, don't," Oma says, hurrying to put her arm around me. "Lucy's a sensate, like me. This is difficult for her."

"A what?"

"Highly sensitive," Oma says.

Uncle Clay glances at the door like he wants to run right through it.

The plastic grandfather clock in the living room sounds, and right on schedule, ten minutes to the hour, Milo rushes out of the room, Mom following. "I'm about to start position 11,111 plus," he announces, as he races to the sink for water.

"Good heavens," Aunt Jeana says. "Does no one in this family have any respect for the dying?"

"He's not dying," I say between gritted teeth.

Mom stops when she sees Clay. Her chin quivers. Uncle Clay gets up and gives her a hug. "Sissy," he says.

To my surprise, Mom allows her tears to come as he hugs her, making me wonder if I will ever be separated from Milo by hundreds of miles and almost as many years someday, and, if so, if we'll hug when we see each other. I look at Milo, who is waiting impatiently for Oma (who dumped his tap water down the drain) to pour him a glass of Brita water, and I have my doubts.

The minute Feynman moseys out of the library, looking all droopy and sleepy, he sniffs the air and picks up the scent of another dog. He wakes up then and runs to Aunt Jeana, his front legs hopping off the floor. Chico goes nuts, like maybe he's afraid he's going to become hamburger himself.

"Get that mutt out of here!" Aunt Jeana snaps above Chico's whining. "What's he doing inside, anyway? He's not supposed to be in the house."

Milo hurries to grab Feynman's collar, and Aunt Jeana starts heading back to Grandpa Sam's room, speaking into Chico's papery triangle ear loud enough for us all to hear her say, "We'll go sit by Sam, where you'll be safe, since it seems that no one else in this family intends to go sit with him."

I watch Aunt Jeana's bony back as she leaves, and I feel bad again, because she's right. No one in the family—except for Oma—wants to sit with Grandpa Sam, and at the moment even she wants to sit with Uncle Clay instead. "I'll come too," I say.

Grandpa Sam is no longer propped up on pillows but lying flat on his back, a thin pillow tucked under his head. His feeding tube dangles from the metal pole, the end of the tubing capped and lying on the floor. Marie is standing at the side of his bed, holding up the covers and examining his naked skin. I don't want to be looking at him, but I look anyway. His body looks like those starving people in Ethiopia that I saw on Oma's TV. He has a washcloth sitting over his private parts, like it's been hung there from his protruding hip bones. His legs are skinny sticks like Milo's, and there's a bunched scar on his thigh. "He hasn't started mottling yet, anyway," she says as she drops his covers.

"My dad didn't start that until minutes before he died," Aunt Jeana says.

Marie sees me and leans down. "Sam? Jeana and Lucy are here now, so I'm going to step out for a bit and get some coffee." She talks loud so he can hear her above his noisy breaths. "How about a drink first, though?" She picks up one of the short plastic sticks with a small blue sponge at the top that the county nurse left us, dips it into the plastic cup of water on his nightstand, and places it against lips that are dry on the outside of his mouth but glossy closer to the inside. He opens up and roots for it like a baby roots for his milk bottle, and sucks on the sponge. "Be sure to offer him water now and then," she tells us.

"Of course," Aunt Jeana says. "I'd never deny him water. Or food, for that matter. I can't speak for the rest of them, though."

Marie doesn't completely shut the door when she goes out, but she closes it within an inch. I think that's so Grandpa Sam can have a little peace and quiet, because it's mighty noisy in the kitchen, with Clay's loud voice, Mitzy's wind-chime giggles, and Milo protesting, "But you said you'd be my judge!"

"You use the stopwatch, Milo, and I'll keep checking up on you," I hear Mom call after him. The back door opens and shuts, and I can hear Feynman barking from his chain.

"No one in this family ever had any respect for you, Sam," Aunt Jeana says to Grandpa. He slowly opens his eyes but he doesn't look at her. His face is slack, but when he sees me standing at the foot of his bed, I notice that his eyes still have a brightness about them.

I scoot between his bed and the wall and sit down beside him. "Oh, don't sit on his bed," Aunt Jeana says. "Get another folding chair." I pretend I don't hear her, and she loses interest when Chico starts fidgeting, his skinny front legs clawing her sweater.

"I need to take him out to do his business. Is that mutt tied?" she asks.

"I think so," I say without looking at her, because I don't like the way she calls Feynman a mutt or the way his dishes were empty when we got here, and I'm afraid I'll get snippy with her.

The minute she slips out of the room, I lean down and say to Grandpa Sam, "I made an effigy for you, and I carried it to town. So that you would live. Everyone thinks you're dying, but I don't think that. You're more tired now, but you're always sleepy in the afternoons, and you've had a lot of company. Aunt Jeana alone is enough to wear anybody out."

I swear he smiles a bit after I make that comment about Aunt Jeana.

Grandpa Sam lifts his left hand, and it trembles as it reaches out to me. I take it and rest it on the bed and lay my hand over his. He doesn't leave his hand there, though. He slips it out from underneath and places it over the top of mine. He gives it two soft pats. "It's okay, Lucy," he says in a dry-sounding whisper.

I want to ask him what he means . . . but I don't have to. I'm intuitive. Maybe even a little psychic, and I'm people-smart, besides. And I know what he's trying to tell me. Even though I don't want to know it. Tears fill up my eyes and trickle down my cheeks. "You're going to die anyway, aren't you?"

"Lucy," he whispers, in between breaths so jagged that the metal bars on the bed rattle.

"Yes?"

He closes his eyes, and he doesn't say any more, but he doesn't have to. My spirit already heard him, and what it heard him say was yes. That he's going to die.

"Honey?"

I look up as Oma enters the room, Uncle Clay and Mom behind her.

"He's going to die," I say to Oma, my eyes blinking rapidly. "I made him an effigy from the instructions in your *Book of the Dead*, but it didn't work. He told me he's going to die."

Mom hurries to me and she puts her arms around me. "Lucy, go be a judge for your brother, okay?"

I shake my head, determination that feels older than me suddenly sprouting. "No. I'm going to stay with Grandpa." His hand gives mine another squeeze. "Did you see that? He squeezed my hand. He wants me to stay by him."

"It's okay, Tess," Oma says. "She needs this time with him."

"Ma, she's just a kid. For crissakes, this is too much for her."

"No." I look at Mom, and at Uncle Clay, who is standing close to the doorway—where Mom would be standing too, if she hadn't felt compelled to come to me—and I say, "It's too much for you, and for Uncle Clay, and for Milo. But it's not too much for me."

Uncle Clay fidgets, brushing something from his jacket, and Mom's lips quiver. I turn back to Grandpa Sam. "I'm going to stay with you, Grandpa Sam. I'm going to stay right here."

Oma leans down then and says loudly—even though Barbara told us at least three times that hearing is the last function to go in a dying person—"Sam? Look who's here. It's your son, Clay."

Oma steps back and gently nudges Uncle Clay to the edge of Grandpa's bed. Uncle Clay looks down at Grandpa Sam like he's a stranger—which I guess in a sense he is. Uncle Clay hasn't seen Grandpa Sam in sixteen years, and he probably looks a lot different than when Clay was seventeen. He even looks a lot different than he did earlier today. Like fifty years have gone by in just an hour and twenty minutes.

Uncle Clay leans over stiffly and says, "Hi, Dad."

Grandpa Sam opens his eyes and peers up. He makes his mouth move, but nothing comes out.

"How ya doing, Dad?" Uncle Clay says, which I think is a pretty idiotic thing to say to someone who's dying. Especially from someone smart enough to become a surgeon.

"Here, you sit by his bed, Clay," Oma says, shoving the folding chair up against the back of his legs, but he moves away from it. "You want time alone with him, honey?" Oma asks.

Clay shakes his head quickly. "No. No, that's okay." He moves back to the doorway.

Mom goes to put her hand on Uncle Clay's, but he bolts out of the room. Mom follows.

Oma watches them leave, then says to Grandpa, "He must be going to the bathroom. He just got here."

I take a deep breath. "That's not true," I tell Grandpa Sam. "He just can't be in here because he's scared and feeling emotional right now and he doesn't want to cry—or get angry—in front of everyone."

"Lucy!" Oma whispers sharply.

"He likes to be told the truth," I tell her. "Like we all do. Don't you, Grandpa Sam?"

Oma picks at her fingernail, looks at the door, then leaves the room. Grandpa Sam and I aren't alone for long, though, because Marie slips inside as soon as Oma leaves. I think Oma asked her to, while she talks to Uncle Clay.

"Mind if I sit with you two for a while?" she asks, reaching over and brushing her hand over Grandpa's forehead.

"No." And I don't mind; having Marie near feels comforting.

Marie hums softly as she tugs the folded blanket from the foot of his bed and lays it over the sheet that's covering him. He opens his eyes and looks right past me, up at the corner of the room above my head, as though he can see something I can't. Then he closes his eyes, and his hand goes limp on mine.

Grandpa Sam's eyeballs bob under their lids. His mouth is almost closed, but his cheeks billow, and his tongue butts against his teeth as though he's speaking.

"Is he trying to talk?" I ask her.

"Not to us," she says. "He's talking to the spirits."

"What spirits?" I ask, glancing around the room.

"Oh, we can't see them. But he can. They're the spirits of his ancestors."

"Really?"

"Yes. Really. Can you feel how the room has an energy about it? How it suddenly got colder? The spirits always bring a cool wind with them." She goes back to smoothing his blankets and humming peacefully.

I do feel the coolness, but I was thinking it was only a draft coming from the window behind me.

Oma slips back into the room then. She takes one look at Grandpa Sam, who is still mumbling busily under his breath, his eyeballs bobbing, and she smiles. "Ohhh, they've come," she says.

"Lucy?" Mom is standing in the doorway, her hand on the frame. I look up and she curls her finger at me.

I go to her.

"Come on," she says. She guides me into the kitchen, where some of Connie Olinger's nuked casserole is steaming on a plate and Mitzy and Uncle Clay are sitting. "Sit down and have something to eat," she says.

Milo is at the table too, shoveling the hamburger-and-rice concoction into his mouth, grains of rice dropping back to his plate. He glances up at me with only his eyes. He looks tired and like he needs a shower.

"How's it going, Wheezer?" I ask.

"You keep calling me that, and I'm going to punch you," he says.

"They sound like we did," Uncle Clay says.

"They sound like us now," Mom says, and they both give short chuckles.

Uncle Clay makes a jittery, jagged-sounding sigh, then sips his coffee.

"You should have tea, instead," I say. "Chamomile."

Uncle Clay drains his cup and gets up to grab still more coffee, maneuvering his body between the table and the counter. "Crissakes," he says, "why in the hell is the table over here?"

"I think it's a feng shui thing," I say.

Uncle Clay shakes his head. "Ma should come live out on the West Coast. She'd fit right in with the other New Age nut balls there."

I shift in my seat. I want to like Uncle Clay, so I hope he doesn't ruin it by being mean.

I look at Milo, who is draining the last of his milk. "How long are you going to keep this up, anyway? Um, until after Grandpa Sam is dead?"

Milo springs to his feet. "Seventy-two seconds," he says, and bolts for the bathroom.

"Leave him be, Lucy," Mom warns.

"Why? I didn't want to be in there either. At least not yesterday." I glance from Mom to Uncle Clay. "But Grandpa Sam needs his family now."

"Mind your own business," Mom warns. Mitzy strokes the back of my hair, then pats my back.

SOMETHING STRANGE and unsettling is happening in the house. I can feel it. And I'm not just talking about the fact that there are ghosts in Grandpa Sam's room either. I'm talking about the tension that's building. It feels like everyone in the family is holding an emotional rubber band between their thumbs and stretching it back. Call me psychic, sensate, intuitive, or what have you, but I have a strong feeling that when Grandpa Sam lets go—if not before—everyone is going to let go too, and those rubber bands are going to start flying all over the place, and somebody is going to get stung.

chapter

TWENTY-SEVEN

I GET UP from my half-eaten food, and Mom stops me before I can even scoot my chair in. "Upstairs for a little rest," she says. "It's going to be a long night. Set your alarm, if you'd like, but I want you to sleep until at least five-thirty. We'll wake you if anything happens before then."

"I don't believe this. You're going to let Milo recite numbers around the clock, but you're not going to let me stay up to sit with Grandpa Sam on what is probably going to be his last day here?"

"Just close your eyes and rest a little," she says. "Now, march."

My back teeth are gritted so hard that I can almost hear

them cracking. "It's not fair! Just because you don't want to sit by Grandpa doesn't mean I shouldn't be allowed to!"

Uncle Clay gets that my-kids-wouldn't-talk-to-me-like-that look, and Mom gets all the more headstrong. "What you're doing is more stressful. Milo's relaxing himself. Now, go. One hour, at least."

I stomp up the stairs and flop down on my back, my ankles crossed. I'm good and mad at Mom now. So mad that I think when I grow up and she ticks me off, I'm going to pretend I don't have time to call her either.

Brave in my anger and determined to get Mom back one way or another, I go straight to the trash can, which I never emptied because there was nothing in it but for that wad of slightly-crunchy-from-dried-tears Kleenex, and I pull out my memory stick. I take it into Mom's room, plug it into her computer, and lift her latest entry. The one she wrote in the middle of the night—just like I thought. I upload it on my computer and start reading:

I can't believe Lucy went to Maude Tuttle's house! Maude Tuttle, of all people. She's an ex-hooker, for crissakes. And she probably knows every grain of dirt on every family in this town.

I wonder what Maude told her. It was something, you can bet, because Lucy's got that preoccupied, haunted look about her again. Damn it to hell, why can't people leave my past alone?

But I can't obsess about what Lucy might be obsessing about. Not tonight. I have my own shit to deal with. Dad's dying. And although I know I should feel something, I don't. Just the tension that comes from having to listen to someone gasp for air for hours on end. I wish he (or someone) would clear his goddamn throat!

I can almost see my karma veering into a curve now, ready to fling itself back to me. Not just for those words, but for the thoughts that go with them. I'm glad he's dying. It's awful to admit, but it's true. I'm glad because maybe it will put an end to this agony that has been with me for most of my life. I just want it over!

"And what is that 'it'?" God, I haven't seen that shrink in years, and yet her voice—high-pitched like a drill—still bores into me at times like this.

Even with Dad practicing for his final death rattle downstairs, the kids upset, Ma burning spices in everyone's faces, I think of him. I think of him, and I miss him.

He called me the minute I got back home, that first day we met, to ask me if I believed in love at first sight.

I smile as I read this. That's Peter for you—an ENFP on the Jung-Myers-Briggs personality test I took on his behalf when Mom's endorphins were still raging and I was sure he'd be my daddy. A *Champion Idealist,* the test showed. Extroverted, intuitive, feeling, and perceiving. Only three percent of the population is an ENFP. More proof that Mom is making a disastrous mistake if she lets him go, because the chance of finding someone else just like him isn't going to be all that easy—as I tried to tell her once. Just reading about him makes me miss him more.

It was explosive, right from the beginning. I saw him first in class: History of Ancient Philosophy 320. How could I not notice him? He was animated. Engaged. Brilliant.

I don't recall how it was we paired off in the hall after leaving class, but a half hour later we were in his beat-up loft apartment, where books on Socrates and Plato were strewn here and there, wedges of unopened envelopes thrust between pages he'd marked. How I noticed these ordinary things, with that wall staring at me, I have no idea.

"Your wall," I said, and laughed, as I fell into one of the two mismatched recliners facing it like theater seats.

He scooted stacks of books, a bong, and empty tuna and fruit cans out of the way with his sandaled foot, so he could better reach the black wall. Simple shapes and scribbles drawn with sidewalk chalk ran nearly the entire length of it. "What is it?" I said, still laughing. "Your cave drawings?"

He got so excited, so animated, when he told me that that's exactly what it was. "It's the wall from Plato's The Cave!" He asked if I knew what he was talking about, but he didn't wait for my answer. He grabbed a torn sheet from the black wall, not bothering to remove the tack first, and shoved it into my hand. "From Great Dialogues of Plato: Complete Texts of the Republic, Apology, Crito Phaido, Ion, and Meno, Volume 1, Page 316*," he said. He asked if I was familiar with Plato's* Allegory of the Cave.

I told him I'd taken Theory of Forms in my freshman year and that, if I remembered it correctly, Plato likened people unschooled in the theory of forms to prisoners chained in a cave who aren't able to turn their heads. All they can see is the wall of the cave, where images made by the puppeteers behind them are casting shadows on the wall. They think the images ARE the objects, even though they are only shadows cast by the objects. When I finished, I asked him how I did, my voice deep and flirty.

He became on fire then—obviously thrilled that I knew of The Cave, *and his excitement excited me, though not in the same way as him.*

Maybe his fire ignited my passion because I'd felt dead

inside for so long. I don't know. But as he rattled on, scribbling more images to illustrate the points he was making, I watched his ass under his jeans and the way his T-shirt stretched against his shoulder blades with each chalk stroke he made. I watched his mouth when he turned to look at me—full, slick, inviting—and waited for glimpses of his tongue, rather than listening to his words. I wanted to feel his tongue against mine. To feel it flicking across my nipples, then edging down to find the lips I hadn't yet allowed anyone to kiss.

And right in the middle of his animated lecture, I got up and went to him. I pushed him backward until he fell into the chair next to the one I'd just left, giggling like a porn star, for crissakes. The back of the chair was broken, and with a thump we fell back until we were almost vertical with the seat. I climbed on him, straddling his lap, and ran my fingers through the short bristles of his hair and opened my mouth to his to take in his words, his breath, his fervor.

I can feel my cheeks flush when I read this. And I know I should skip ahead, but then I tell myself that I *am* feeling crampy these days, which means I'll soon be a woman and I'll need to know these things. I promise myself that I'll stop and skim if she talks about Peter's penis, though (because I can't even think of him having one, much less read about it), then look for my place on the document.

But before I can find it, I stop.

Mom took Milo and me to Peter's apartment for a cook-out once, shortly after they met. While Peter grilled steaks on the balcony, I snooped at his books. I took one down from the bookcase to examine it, then set it on the end table when Mom came inside to announce that the food was done. Mom scooped it up quickly. "He's a neat freak about his books, if not about anything else," she said, and she slipped the book back in its original place. Peter's hair wasn't in a rubber band that day, and it hung down long enough to touch the arm seam of his shirt.

My heart begins to pump hard in my chest, because I realize that Mom isn't talking about Peter. She's talking about him.

My father.

Howard Smith.

We made love so many times that my crotch burned, but still I reached for him again, stroking, cooing, trying to spring him back to life because I wanted him to crawl up inside me until he became a part of me. I wanted to stay feeling alive forever.

Mitzy called me a "lucky shit" when I called her the next day and told her that the insides of my thighs were chafed. Brian was coming home from work so beat that she was lucky if she got a quickie.

In four months' time, though, Mitzy stopped calling me lucky.

"I don't know, Tess," she said one night as we talked on the phone, even though neither of us could afford long-distance calls so we'd promised to write letters only. "There's something not striking me right about him waiting outside your classroom like he did again yesterday. It seems he's been doing that a lot, claiming that he can't wait to talk to you until your last class is over." She asked me to please not get offended, but to her, it seemed like Howard considered his studies, his grades, more important than mine. "I hope he doesn't do that when finals roll around," she said.

I was defensive when I told her that he wasn't doing it often, but I didn't admit to her that he'd done it again that very day. Actually knocking on the door during my journalism class and lying to the professor, saying there was a family emergency, when the "emergency" was only that he still couldn't find a slant for his latest essay.

Mitzy drilled me to find out if I was giving up too much of my life for Howard. She brought up Lou and Lacy, and how she hadn't heard me mention them in ages. "Didn't the three of you used to hang out together at Starbucks and study almost every day?"

I told Mitzy that Howard was just intense, that's all. I didn't admit that Lou found Howard arrogant and Lacy suspected that he was bipolar and a tad on the homophobic side when it came to Lou. "He's just going through a rough time right now. He needs me," I explained, then added that I didn't have a hell of a lot of time to spare, with my schoolwork and my job, and how I preferred to spend what little time I had with Howard.

"I'm not sure that's good, honey," she said.

I felt my insides clench. Mitzy had had a father all of her life. Cozy and familiar as an old sofa, he asked her how her day went every night at dinner and never let her leave the house without pulling a couple bills from his wallet. And after she moved out, he brought over two chocolate éclairs every Saturday morning so they could have coffee and catch up while Brian was working some side job or other. What did she know about being a dried-up sponge that had just been dipped in water?

She asked me what Howard's rough time was about, and I struggled to put it into words for her. How could I make her understand the angst of a thinking man? Brian, nice guy that he was, didn't think beyond what Mitzy was making for dinner and who the Packers might trade. "Look, I'm happy. Just be happy for me, okay?"

And I was happy.

For a time.

Howard was horrified when I told him I was pregnant. He scraped his hands through his limp blond hair—grown down over his ears, even though he once couldn't stand the feel of hair on his collar—and he paced.

I assured him that everything would be okay, that we could get medical coverage through social services, and reminded him that we were only three months from graduation. I'd get a job so he could enroll in grad school, and we'd plan our schedules so one of us was home with the baby. I'd work on my novel in what spare time I could find, and when it sold, we'd have it made.

He looked at me as though I'd gone stupid. "Are you fucking nuts?" he said. "Is that what you think I'm upset about? How we're going to fare financially?"

He spread his hands to encompass our ratty apartment, with crates still turned on end for chairs from when his friends Leon and Ian visited the night before, while I was at work, to smoke weed and argue about life's meaning. "Look around, for fuck sake," he said, as he kicked over an empty ravioli can (about all he ate anymore, cold, and straight from the can) and sent it rolling across the floor, scattering cigarette butts as it went. "Do I look like someone who gives a shit about having material things? About making it?

"You want to bring a kid into this totally fucked-up world?" He started ranting then about the things I'd heard him rant about countless times. How democracy was dying, and fascism rising. How we were going to obliterate ourselves, and how mankind had gone blind to what was real. "Is this the world you want to bring a kid into?" he asked.

I don't know why I didn't see it until that moment. How his jeans bunched at the belt, and how his face had thinned. And how long had it been since he'd slept for more than twenty, thirty minutes in one stretch? Just the week before, a noise woke me and I opened one eye to see him working on the wall opposite "the cave." He had taken down the paintings his former girlfriend had done in acrylic on cardboard—ghouls in priests' robes, Uncle Sam in camouflage, the American flag with swastikas for stars and red stripes that ran like blood over the white—and he was opening a black paint can with the tip of the screwdriver. He was animated, as he often was, but this time his explosive energy looked like madness instead of passion.

I rose up on one elbow, and I asked him to stop. The apartment was too dark as it was, and the fumes from the paint were making vomit rise and sour the back of my throat.

He looked at me with haunted, sunken eyes and started bitching about my lack of understanding of forms. How I was a slave to my chair, an idiot played by puppeteers. Couldn't I see how dumb I'd become? How my pregnancy was making me want to nest and fall in rank and file with the rest of the mindless fools?

It was the word dumb, *more so than his crazy ramblings, that hurt. And after a lengthy argument that drained me, I grabbed my purse and my car keys and headed for the door.*

"Where are you going?" he asked, his face and body liquefying. He pressed himself between me and the door, closing it with a click. He reached for me.

I was crying when I told him not to touch me.

He lost it then and begged me to never forbid him to touch me again. He looked down at his paint-stained hands and said, "Don't say they're bad."

He looked like a stranger, and at that moment it dawned on me that he was. What did I know about him, beyond his beliefs on philosophy and government and that he was brilliant? Who was his family, and where did they live? How old was he when he stopped believing in Santa? Did he ever have a paper route?

He wrapped his arms around me, pinning my arms to my side. He nuzzled his face against my neck, and his cheeks were hot and damp. "Don't ever leave me, baby." Just that. "Don't ever leave me."

I sit here writing this today, and I wonder where in the hell my mind was back then. Even Mitzy saw the red flags. How had I missed them? And why, once I saw them, did I continue to ignore them until they were flapping so violently that I could feel their wind chilling my skin?

I woke up each morning convinced that my belly had grown overnight. My skin had stretched so taut by the time I was five months along that my belly button protruded through the cotton of Howard's T-shirts like a nipple.

I waited until I felt the life inside me jabbing my ribs before I went to the doctor on campus. I walked out of her office with my packet of sample multivitamins and stood at the desk waiting to schedule a follow-up appointment while the receptionist talked on the phone.

There was another student there, her belly still flat, her hand clasped with her lover's. They laughed as they made up potential, silly names for their baby, and just listening to them made me want to cry. Howard wouldn't be with me for the ultrasound the doctor had ordered. He wouldn't be there when we proved what the doctor already believed: that I was carrying twins, just as Ma had, even though their position made it difficult for her to pick up a second heartbeat. And maybe he wouldn't even be there for their delivery. He didn't acknowledge my ever-growing belly, even though we had to make love while lying on our sides by the time I was four months along.

I didn't tell Ma about my pregnancy. She had enough shit

on her plate, because, of course, within a month or so after she left Marie's and went back to Dad, things returned to their usual hell, and she crawled back into her bottle.

I didn't tell Mitzy either, because we'd stopped talking. I told her I didn't have time to write letters anymore, being neck-deep in schoolwork, and that I was already a month behind on my phone bill. I promised her I'd get in touch soon, though, but I ignored her letters. After a month of silence, she sent me a card from Hallmark with some corny verse on it about being best friends forever.

The first time Howard physically hurt me, I had just come home from the hospital after having my ultrasound. I was slipping the X-ray image into a frame that Mitzy had sent me for my nineteeth birthday, right over the top of the photo of the two of us taken on graduation night, both of us glassy-eyed drunk, our hair mussed, our arms wrapped around each other's shoulders as we giggled over something too stupid to laugh about had we been sober. I was only too glad to cover it up. It was nothing but a photo of two girls who were too ignorant to know that adult life was going to be a crock of shit.

When Howard came in, I shoved the picture in his hands before he even had time to set his books down. "Twins!" I announced. I pointed to the baby the doctor said was a boy and told him I was sure that the second baby I was pointing to was a girl, even though she was partially tucked behind the boy, making it impossible for the doctor to verify this. "Look, she's waving," I said. "See her perfect little hand? 'Hi, Mommy, hi, Daddy.'" I used a babyish voice as I said this, then sighed, content. "God, Howard," I said. "Just look at them. We created them. You and me." I heard my excitement, my awe, and it surprised me. I'd never been one of those girls like Mitzy, whose arms ached when she saw a baby.

Howard was standing before the cave wall—the original wall—which he'd painted over the week before, black, of course, without explanation, leaving the ranting demons on the other wall holding puppets with no shadows and crushed chalk smudged on the floor. He looked at me with vacant eyes. He smelled of weed, again. Even though I'd asked him not to buy any more because we needed every dime we could save for disposable diapers and other baby things. He took two stapled sheets of paper from his book and thrust them at me, as though I hadn't just showed him our babies' first photo.

I asked him what the papers were.

"Fry. That fucker," he said. I looked down at the essay Howard had worked on feverishly for the last week. So feverishly that he couldn't pull himself away long enough to work his few hours in the campus library. Professor Fry had scratched the words, Incomprehensible gibberish, and Doesn't answer the questions, in red ink, under the F he'd given him.

Even now I have to catch myself. I find myself thinking that maybe, just maybe, if I had set aside my hurt over his lack of interest in my pregnancy, my feelings of isolation and loneliness, and just listened to him, maybe things wouldn't have gotten so nuts. That's old thinking, of course, and I have to stop myself all over again. Blaming myself, as Mom always blamed herself.

That night I flew into a white-hot rage when he ignored the ultrasound to obsess about his grade. I called him selfish and said that I was sick and tired of handling everything myself as he went on his crazy tangents. I screamed that my studies were just as important as his and that our babies were even more important. I vowed that if I had to take care of them myself, I would, but that I'd not take care of some self-absorbed, weed-whacked boyfriend while I did it.

He didn't cringe and cry at my threat, as he had a few

weeks earlier. Instead, his eyes showed that he had dived into the same pool of rage I was treading in, and he grabbed my wrist and twisted my arm around my back until my fingertips reached my hair. "Don't you ever fucking threaten to leave me again. You hear?" he hissed, his breath hot against my ear. "And don't ever call me crazy." I screamed that he was hurting me and begged him to let go.

His chest was rising and falling with strangled breaths— the same huffing pants I'd heard come from my father year after year, each time he hurt my mother. He shoved me, and I stumbled.

I put my hand protectively over my stomach, not wanting my babies to hear his enraged breaths echoing through the water in my womb. He grabbed my hair in his fist then and twisted it until it threatened to come loose. "Don't you ever fucking threaten to leave me. I told you that before."

I was petrified. I wrapped my arms around my belly all the tighter, not just to keep out the sound this time but to shield every inch of it in case he cranked his fist back.

He walked me backward until I thumped up against a black wall. "I'm sorry. I'm sorry," I cried, hating myself for cowering. "Just don't hurt them. Please, don't hurt the babies."

He stopped. He grabbed me. He stroked my hair where my scalp was still stinging. "I'd never hurt you, Tess," he said, as though I'd cried out for mercy for myself, not for my unborn children. "You're all I've got, baby."

Like a fool, I melted with those words. He was all I had too.

"I just want you to be a part of this pregnancy," I told him later, as we lay together naked from the waist down, his leg resting over mine. He'd made love to me so violently, his

thrusts pushing into me so hard, I had grunted with each of them. I tried to be discreet, pretending I had an itch as I slipped my hand over my belly and felt between my legs to make sure the wet was from him, and not from my womb, and then strained to see if my fingers were red. When I saw no dark patch, I took his hand and placed it on my stomach—a place he'd not touched since he'd learned I was pregnant— where the twins were bumping against my skin. I asked him to feel them. To acknowledge that they were real.

He pulled his hand away quickly, moving it to my sore, engorged breasts. He tugged my shirt up and scraped the cups of my bra above them, and he sucked on my nipples as though the milk they were readying themselves to make was his only sustenance.

I should have known from watching my own dad that Howard's promise to never again touch me cruelly would be followed by more slaps and shoves and, eventually, punches used like exclamation marks to make their point. I should have known.

And then one night it happened. He hit me. In the stomach. And afterward, he screamed how he hated that I loved my babies more than I loved him. "There! Are you happy you had to know how I feel about them now? Are you?"

I called Lou for the first time in months, the second Howard left for class, and he showed up with Lacy twenty minutes later. And even though I still had a month left before finals, we pooled what money we had and Lou borrowed some more from his brother, and they put me on a plane and sent me home.

I cried all the way back to Wisconsin. I cried because I feared that the cramping in my stomach meant something was seriously wrong and that refusing to go to the campus doctor before I left was a horrible mistake. Every twinge I felt seemed to reinforce my fear that the tiny hand waving in the ultrasound picture I had in my purse was a premonition. And I cried too because I missed Howard so badly that my chest hurt.

I told myself, all the way back to Timber Falls, that I wouldn't be there long. That when Howard saw that my things were gone, he'd be sorry about what he'd done and re-alize that he wanted his children as much as he wanted me. Then he'd find me and make things right.

I don't know if I should pity or despise the desperate girl I was on that plane ride home, or the idiot I was eleven days later when I lit up inside because Howard pulled into the drive. Ready to take me with him at any cost.

I close the lid of my laptop, swab my wet cheeks, and roll onto my side. I just had to go snooping again, and now I'm sorry. Real sorry.

I squeeze my eyes tight and I try to see Scotty and me skating. I try to see Peter stuffed with leaves like a scare-crow. I try to see an orphaned sperm squiggling in a petri dish. But all I can see is a madman shoving my mom—and shoving me—as I tried to wave to him.

Downstairs, I can hear Marie struggling to be heard above Chico's barking. "No, it will be a while yet, I think."

I take my pillow and clamp it over my head, pressing it tight against my exposed ear. I lie like that for a time, and then, when I can't stand it anymore, I go downstairs, not even caring that my eyes still have to be the color of beets and Mitzy's sitting right there. I grab Mom's cell phone off the counter.

"What are you doing with that?" Mom asks. She sees my face then, and stops. "Lucy? You okay?"

I go out onto the porch. Outside, where every pretty leaf has been ripped from the trees and is lying damp and rotting on the ground, I find Peter's number in Mom's contact list and hit *send*.

"I don't know, but she's crying," I hear Mom say from behind the screen door.

Peter's answering machine picks up, and when the beep comes, I shout into it, "Peter! I need you. Please come. Now!"

Mom gasps and bursts onto the porch, the screen door making a loud crack behind her. "Give me that thing," she says. I push her away, and even though I don't have a jacket on and there are snow flurries falling, I race for my bike and get on it, pedaling as hard as I can. Why did she put those things on her laptop? She knows me. She knows I'd dig!

I don't realize that I shoved Mom's cell in the pocket of my jeans until it rings. My bike wobbles as I tug it out with cold, stiff fingers. I look at the window on the front, and it says *Peter*.

I almost topple over when my front tire hits the gravel at the side of the road. I right myself, though, and I flip open the phone with one hand. "Peter!" I shout. "I know! I know my dad punched my mom's belly. I know she ran back here to get away from him because he hit us. He was crazy, Peter. My dad was crazy." I am sobbing so hard, my breath heaving from the exertion of pedaling with all my might, that I can only hope Peter can understand me.

"Lucy? Honey? Where's your mom?"

"At the house."

"Where are you?"

"Riding my bike. I don't know. Just riding." My sobs sound tight now, because my lips are stiff from the cold, or maybe from fear.

"Honey, stop the bike for a minute. Okay?"

"Okay. Okay," I say.

"Lucy, take a couple deep breaths. It will help you feel better. Come on, breathe with me."

But I don't want to breathe. I only want him to come. But he insists, so I make my breaths match his.

"What happened, Lucy?" he asks, when my breaths stop being so jagged. "Did your mom tell you the story and you ran out? Is that what happened?"

"It doesn't matter. Just come, Peter. Okay? Is the wedding done, so you can come now?"

"Yes. It was yesterday. I'll come, Lucy. I'll leave this very minute. But first I want you to go back to the house, okay?"

I hear a car in the distance, and even though it's hidden behind the hill at my back, I just know it's Roger's red Mustang. I expect it to come toward me, but instead the rumble fades as the vehicle heads toward town.

"Come now, Peter, okay? How long will it take you?"

"About three and a half hours," he says. "Just go home by your mom and Oma, okay? I'll be there as quickly as I can."

"Okay."

I tuck the phone back into my pocket and look behind me. I've ridden so far that I can't see Grandpa Sam's house anymore. Up ahead, though, I can see Nordine Bickett's mailbox, even though it's almost dusk, and a billow of white smoke rising up from between the trees. I pedal toward it, thinking of nothing but getting inside her house so that my teeth will stop chattering. Then I'll call home and tell them where I am so they can come get me.

I pedal with shivering legs, ordering them to go faster, and wobble up the Bicketts' driveway. I don't even care that another car is in her drive, where Henry's truck normally sits. I only care about getting warm.

Nordine doesn't answer the door. Maude Tuttle does. She's wearing her big wig and holding a rat-tail comb. "Well, if it isn't Lucy McGowan," she says. Her smile fades when she sees that I'm shivering. "Where in the hell's your coat?" she asks as she tugs me inside.

The kitchen is warm, and the scent and warmth from wood burning in a stove wraps itself around me. Nordine is sitting at the table before an opened blue case, where old-fashioned rollers with bristles on wire spines are piled. On the top of Nordine's head is a row of curlers, the rest of her hair wet and clamped to the sides of her empty face.

"You're shaking like a leaf," Maude says. She pulls me to the table and sits me down opposite Nordine, then goes into a bedroom and comes back with a quilt to tuck around me. "What in the hell are you doing out without a coat on a day like today?" she asks.

"I know," I tell her. "I read Mom's diary, and I know that Mom fell in love with someone just like her dad. He beat her up too, and he was crazy. And he punched me even before I was born."

Maude Tuttle takes a chair beside me. She looks on the table and then the counter, like she's looking for something, then she says, "Oh, hell," and grabs the towel slung around Nordine's narrow shoulders and gives it a jerk. She wads a corner of it, then dabs my face, clutching my nose with fingers wrapped in terry cloth, and says, "Blow. You've got snot running."

Maude wads the towel and sets it down on the table. She

folds her arms over the top of it. "Reality can be harsh," she says. "Sorry about that, kid, but it's a fact of life."

"He was mean," I said.

"I know. I told you that."

"My dad was smart. Real smart. But it drove him crazy. No wonder Mom watches Milo like a hawk for any sign that says he's not staying happy. And no wonder she gets squirrelly when I think too much. She probably heard that apples don't fall too far from the tree too."

"You *do* think too much, Lucy McGowan," Maude says. "How about some hot cocoa? It'll warm you up. Nordine always has some Nestlé's around here." She looks over at Nordine, who is staring at us with a smile on her face, though I don't think she knows why she's smiling. "You have cocoa, Nordine?"

Nordine nods and gets up, but by the time she gets to the counter, she's obviously forgotten what she went for. Maude rolls her eyes and stands. "She doesn't know her ass from a hole in the ground anymore. Sit down, Nordine," Maude says, then roots around in the cupboards until she finds the cocoa can.

"She's probably better off that way," Maude says. She gets milk from the fridge and pours some in a saucepan, and I grab the towel and dab my eyes with the clean end.

There's a plunk on the stovetop and then the hiss of the flame. Maude sits down beside me again. "Now, folks like you and me, we don't have the luxury of being in a retarded fog. And as if it's not bad enough, knowing what we already know, we have to pick at old scabs too. The truth may hurt like a son of a bitch, but yet we gotta keep picking and picking until we draw blood."

I like the way Maude doesn't talk to me like I'm a kid,

telling me everything's okay when it's not or that things will be okay when maybe they won't.

I sniffle the last of my tears back up my nose. "I wanted to find a dad who was smiley like Scotty, and who maybe ice skated. I wanted to find someone nice, who hugs, like Peter," I say, not bothering to explain who either Scotty or Peter is, even though I've always hated it when other people do that. I can't help it, though. I'm too upset to want to explain. But it's okay. I know Maude won't look down on me for sounding like an idiot by not identifying them, her being an ex-hooker who can't look down on anybody and all.

"Course you did," Maude said. "Who in the hell wouldn't want a nice, smiley, huggy daddy who skates? But we get what we get, kiddo. That doesn't mean that's all we deserved, though."

I rub my hands together to get more feeling back into them. "Maude? Did my dad come to Timber Falls because he loved us and wanted us back?"

Maude looks at me, one eyebrow rising. "You just have to keep pickin', don't you?"

"I just need to know the truth."

She hesitates awhile, then she puts her hand over mine. The silver band from her gaudy, bigger-than-the-Hope-diamond ring is cool against my skin and gives me a quick chill.

"What happened when my dad came to Timber Falls to get my mom?" I ask, even though minutes ago I'd shut my laptop because I didn't want to know that very thing. "Did he come to hurt her?"

"Who's to say? But the important part is that, one way or another, Sam didn't let it come to that."

"You mean my grandpa Sam prevented him from taking

Mom and us back to California, so he couldn't hurt us anymore?" I ask, feeling a sudden wave of love for Grandpa
and a sudden wave of guilt for leaving him.

"You could say that." We hear soft sizzling sounds, and
Maude gets up to pour milk into three cups with powdered
chocolate at the bottom. She gives me a cup and a spoon,
then starts stirring the two in front of her, alternating a few
twirls in each cup. I don't stir, though. I wrap my hands
around the mug to warm them.

"Your dad told your mom that he couldn't live without
her—which those types always say, and probably believe—
and that he loved her, which is also what they say, even
though they don't know one shittin' thing about love, except
how to suck from it. But he wasn't in his right mind, Lucy."

"So Grandpa Sam kicked him out, didn't he? And probably threatened to hurt him if he ever even thought about
coming around Mom again. My grandpa was big and strong
then, so my dad was probably too scared to ever come
around again."

"You could say that. Now, drink your hot cocoa before it
gets cold," Maude says. "You too, Nordine."

"But the apple doesn't fall far from the tree. You said so
yourself. What if my brother goes crazy like our dad? Or I
do?"

"That's not going to happen."

"How do you know? You turned out to be a—well, like
your mom, didn't you? Even though you didn't know her
either?"

"For different reasons, not because it was stamped in
my blood. You're going to be okay, kid. You just are. And so
is your brother. You aren't living your dad's life, whatever
that was. Your mom's seeing to it that you don't."

I look at Maude hopefully, then take my spoon and stir the powder that is clinging to the edges of my cup. "I still don't understand why my mom hates my grandpa, if all he did was chase Howard away because he was crazy."

"Well, young women are pretty dreamy, kiddo. All that love-conquers-all bullshit. You'll see what I mean when you're a little older and fall hard. It happens to the brightest of us. I suppose she believed that in time he'd have gotten his head out of his ass and come around so they could live happily ever after."

I stare down at the white milky swirls in my cup. "But my grandma did leave Grandpa Sam, so I guess that means she eventually stopped being dreamy."

"Well, I'd guess, more than that, she looked at her daughter and realized she was living the same life she'd been taught to live by example."

"Sam?" Nordine asks, as if his name was just mentioned. She's cocking her half-rollered head from side to side, then gets up and turns around, as though maybe he's in the living room waiting for her.

Maude shakes her head. "That poor woman," she says. "Loved that man from the time she was a girl. She's got one foot in the grave, and still she doesn't realize that she was better off not having him, even if her daddy did marry her off to that piece of trash Henry. She never was overly bright, but she's always been a sweetie."

I watch Nordine as she shuffles back to the table. Maude goes behind her and sections another clump of damp hair to roll.

"Did my grandpa love her once? I mean, really love her, not just to . . . well, you know . . . but did he really care?"

"He did. And he beat himself up every day for not

marrying her when he should have, in spite of what her daddy said. But who's to say if things would have been any different with her. And if they hadn't...I don't know. This poor woman is as delicate as a rose, not strong like a weed, like you and me and your grandma."

"I'm glad my mom and dad loved each other once, but I wish they'd gotten married. Even if he was...well, you know..." I take a sip of my drink. "He's never tried to see my brother and me. Not once, that I know of. Maybe he's in a mental hospital. I don't know. But maybe I can look on the bright side and hope that, if Mom marries Peter, our real dad will let Peter adopt us, since he doesn't want us anyway."

Maude smiles sadly. "Drink up," she says, as she pokes a little pink pick into another roller on Nordine's head.

"I'm not feeling so well," I tell her. "My stomach hurts. I think I should call my mom now."

"You do that, kiddo. It would probably be best if you were gone by the time Henry gets back from town, anyway. You've had a hard enough day already."

Milo answers the phone, and I ask him to send Mom for me. He must be on one of his ten-minute breaks from reciting pi, because he's too rushed to ask me any questions, which is all right by me.

I hang up and take a sip of cocoa just so I'm not rude, and I watch Maude roll another piece of Nordine's white hair. I watch the stones from her heavy rings flopping and spinning as she works. I know what those hands did long ago. They touched men's private parts, then they folded the money they gave her afterward. They flipped off people in restaurants and petted animals with runny eyes. But at this very moment, they are rolling Nordine's hair gently, so they won't hurt her tender scalp. "You have pretty hands," I tell her, and she does, even if they are spotted and old and have done some not-so-pretty things.

Maude—probably because she's a sensate, a psychic, or just plain smart—says, "We're all a little of both, Lucy. Good and bad. Some of us, though, like your grandpa and me, we've just got bigger parts of each."

MY STOMACH hurts worse as I climb into the back-seat of Roger's car.

"What in the hell are you up to, Lucy?" Mom asks as I fasten my buckle and she glares at me in the rearview mirror. "First I find you at Maude Tuttle's, now Nordine Bickett's. You call Peter, like there's some sort of emergency going on that only he can handle...What in the hell's wrong with you? And whose car is that in the driveway, any-way?"

She looks over her shoulder at the driveway as she backs out. "Crissakes, as if this day isn't stressful enough..." She hits the brakes when she looks at me. "Are you okay?"

Mitzy looks in the backseat too. "Lucy?" she says. "What's wrong, honey?"

My abdomen makes a fist, and something damp squeezes out to sit between my underwear and my skin. "I think I just got my first moon time," I tell Mom.

"Moon time?" Mitzy asks.

"Her period. Your period, Lucy. It's called your period."

All the way home, Mom and Mitzy remind me that getting your period is a normal part of growing up.

Mom and Mitzy hustle me inside and straight to the bathroom, where Mom tugs down my jeans and looks at the splotch of blood glossing the crotch of my pink panties. Marie and Oma talk in excited whispers outside the door while Mom roots around in her bag, then pulls out a tampon. She holds it up, looks at it, then stuffs it back in her bag. "Mitzy? Can you grab a few sheets of paper towel?"

"You should have come to me," Mom says as Mitzy slips out of the bathroom door. "Not run off like that. I was scared too when I got my first period, but, Lucy, I prepared you for this. And what exactly did you think Peter could do for you?" Mitzy hands Mom some sheets of paper towel through the door, and Mom folds them into a cylinder-shaped pad. "Here. Wear this for now. Mitzy and I will run to town and get you some real pads."

Oma hugs me when I step out of the bathroom. "She even looks more grown up, doesn't she?" she says to Marie. Marie eyes me carefully and nods. I think, though, that Marie senses that it's more than the blood seeping onto sheets of paper towel decorated with teapots that has made me appear older.

"I want to go sit with Grandpa now," I say.

"Okay," Mom says. "We'll go to the Rexall and get you

some protection. We'll be right back." Mom grabs her purse and Mitzy and hurries out the door as though it's vital they go immediately, leaving me to suspect that she's wanting to run to town for *her* protection, not for mine.

As I pass Milo's door—he's been at it for eight hours now—he's resetting his timer. He sees me and calls out, "I'm just starting position 48,551 plus. I'm averaging six thousand digits per hour, right up there with the current record holders." He sets the timer down and starts again: "Three, SEVEN, two, FIVE, four—I really like that part!— EIGHT, two, FIVE…." The sounds of Grandpa Sam's rutted breaths and rattling bed bars are filling every corner of the house, and Milo's working hard to drown them out. I can tell by his eyes that he can hear them too and that he's struggling hard to see the numbers in his mind rather than his grandpa fighting to breathe. I feel sorry for him, so I say, "Good job. Catch you later."

In Grandpa Sam's room, Aunt Jeana is sitting on the folding chair, bouncing Chico as though he's a squalling infant. There's a horrid odor in the room, and I think it might be the smell of death that I read about in one of those Mom-or-Dad-is-dying novels Mom picks up at the library for me to read when it's book report time.

When Milo has an asthma attack, his eyes bulge and his whole body strains for the next breath, but that's not how Grandpa Sam looks. His face has gone to bones, his eyelids are hanging at half-mast, and he can't breathe, yet he looks peaceful. As if his mind, or maybe his soul, is resting comfortably, even though his body is not. I want Milo to come see, so he can stop picturing Grandpa Sam struggling to breathe like he does during an attack—only worse—but I know it's futile to ask him to.

A forty-watt bulb on Grandpa Sam's nightstand supplies

the only light in the room, but it's enough to cast a shadow on the wall. One that shakes with each breath, then freezes as his breath stops. When Grandpa Sam's breathing pauses again, Aunt Jeana rotates her wrist and peers over Chico's bobbing head to stare at her watch, stealing quick glances at Grandpa Sam's still body. When he inhales, she sighs. "Sixteen seconds this time," she says, before easing back against her chair again.

"My mother was buried in a brown casket," she tells me. "She hated brown, but that's what she got, because Sam said it was the cheapest and what did it matter, since she was dead and didn't know what color coffin she was being buried in, anyway. I won't bury Sam in something like that, though. Even if I have to dig into my savings. He'll have a nice black casket with white satin lining.

"You'd think Clay would offer to pitch in for this funeral," she adds. "He makes enough to pay for it with the change in his pocket. Everybody in this town loved Sam, and they'll all be there. He didn't have enough in his burial fund to go extravagant, and I have to watch my money, but he's my brother."

Grandpa Sam's leg moves, his heel scraping against the sheets, and Aunt Jeana stops. "Is he in pain?" she asks, just as Marie steps into the room.

"I don't think so," Marie says. "But the nurse is on standby—she's only two miles away. If he starts looking uncomfortable, we'll give her a call and she'll come and give him morphine."

Aunt Jeana's thin lips part, and her two wisps of eyebrows crouch down over her deeply sunken eyes. "What are you all waiting for? He's dying, for God's sakes!" Aunt Jeana's voice is so shrill when she raises it that I flinch, just like Chico.

"Well, she said it will compromise his breathing even more."

"I want to be alone with my grandpa now," I say, before Aunt Jeana can harp at Marie again.

"Excuse me?" she says.

"I said I want to be alone with my grandpa now. Please."

Aunt Jeana lifts her chin. "What kind of a world has this turned into, when you have kids telling their elders what to do?"

"A break would do you good," Marie tells her. "Come, let's go see if we can round up another cup of coffee. It might be a long night."

I want to talk to Grandpa, but aside from telling him that I know the story of my dad, I can't find anything else to say. So I just put my hand over his instead. And again, Grandpa Sam slides his hand out from under mine and rests it on top.

Grandpa Sam starts moving his legs again. Both of them. His eyes open wider, and he turns to me. His mouth starts moving, but no words come out. Just the gurgling, raspy breaths that rattle his hospital bed.

His hand leaves mine and begins groping the sheets. I glance at the door, then stand up and lean over his bed. "Grandpa Sam? Are you in pain? Do you need your medicine now?"

His mouth moves and his eyelids open wider. He looks right at me and strains again to say something.

"I'll get Oma," I tell him. "She'll call the nurse to come give you something so you don't hurt."

My upper body turns, and before my feet even have the chance to follow, Grandpa Sam bolts up so that he's almost sitting erect, and his hand clamps around my wrist. I gasp, because the suddenness scares me. "No," he says, in a voice more powerful than I've ever heard him use. "I'm okayyyy!" He falls back against his pillow, and after a couple more jagged breaths, he tries speaking again.

I can feel his frustration as he struggles to find the energy to get more words out. "What is it, Grandpa?"

And then, just like that, I *know* what he wants to say.

I lean closer. "Grandpa Sam?" I say in a rush. "You want to tell me that you love me, don't you? And you want me to let Mom and Clay, and even Oma, know that you love them too." He turns toward me, his eyes saying, "Yes!"

"And you want them all to know that you're sorry too, don't you? And that you understand why Mom and Uncle Clay can't be in here right now." Grandpa Sam's whole body sighs with relief against his pillow when I say the words he can't. His face looks peaceful again, even though his breathing has worsened.

Grandpa Sam—though his body is mummy-dry now— leaks one tear from the outer corner of his left eye, and it slips down across his bony temple. The sight of it makes my eyes tear too. "I'll tell them, Grandpa Sam," I say. "I promise I will."

And then he drifts off. Not to death, but to that place that feels halfway from here, and halfway to there.

Oma slips into the room quietly. "Ten one thousand, eleven one thousand," I count under my breath, as Oma pulls his hospital gown down to expose his chest. "Fifteen one thousand, sixteen one thousand." There's only one patch on his skin, about the size of a grown man's hand, that has any pink left in it anymore. The rest is blotched with black, and his hands and arms are cold. He's mottling, just as described in the pamphlet, page eight, seventh paragraph.

"This feels just like when you're waiting for a child to

be born," Oma says quietly. "Rebirth feels the same. I'm glad it feels like this."

I reach twenty one thousand before he starts another breath.

I look up at Oma, who is staring at Grandpa Sam with sadness. "He told me to tell you all something," I say to her. She looks at me. "I heard him say it, but not with my ears. I was—"

But I stop, because Oma stops listening. She leans over Grandpa Sam's bed, alert, because he's stopped breathing again, this time in mid-breath.

Oma grips my arm, and I know it's because she sees what I see. That last handprint-size patch of life leaving, gushing out in one swoosh. And although I don't actually see a vapor, I sense that it leaves through the top of his head.

He's dying! And in a rush of panic—because I'd forgotten to say it back—I shout, "I love you too, Grandpa Sam!"

In a whoosh, he takes another half breath, and he comes right back into his body. He turns his head and his eyes are scanning until they find their place, locked right with mine.

And then, in a split second, he's gone again.

This time, for good.

"Did you see that, Lucy? Did you see that?" Oma says, elated, even though she's crying. "He came right back into his body when you said those words. He came back, as if to gather that love right up to take with him to the other side."

"I've never seen anything like that before," Marie says. We turn and look at her, and she adds, "I heard his breathing and knew he was going, so I came back."

Oma leaves the bed and hurries to the window, cracking it open. "So his spirit can leave," she says. She folds her hands below her belly, her head down. Standing respectfully still, like a spectator on the street during a veterans' parade.

Only after she believes his spirit is gone does Oma come back to the bed and close the eyelids on the body Grandpa Sam just left. "I'll go tell them he's gone," Marie says.

They all come in Grandpa Sam's room once it's over. Mom, Uncle Clay, Aunt Jeana, Mitzy, and Marie. Only they don't come all the way in. They crowd at the door, except for Aunt Jeana, who comes to the bed and pats Grandpa Sam's hand as though she's saying, "There, there, it's all right." She's crying but without making a sound.

We stand for a few moments in silence, staring at the still mound on the sheets, and then Marie comes to stand at the foot of the bed. She starts singing a song that sounds like a prayer, in the language of her people. Her prayer song reaches down deep in me and strokes the sad part sitting there, and I can't do a thing but put my head on Grandpa Sam's still-warm but empty chest and sob.

PETER COMES just minutes after Grandpa Sam dies, and, as I knew he would, he knows what to do. He shakes hands with Uncle Clay, then holds Mom and opens his arms so I can fit into their hug too. "You okay?" he whispers to me as we hug, and I nod my head. Peter's presence itself works like an antianxiety pill on Mom. At least for a time.

Aunt Jeana is sitting at the table, the phone book open. "I need to call Hartwig's," she says, her finger making little zigzags down the short list of funeral homes. She pulls her hand away and brings it to the side of her tear-dampened face. "Oh, I can hardly think," she says.

"Would you like me to call them?" Peter asks, and Aunt

Jeana nods. He takes the phone book and finds the number quickly. The funeral home tells Peter that it will be a while, because they're out on another call. Aunt Jeana looks alarmed. "So we just let him lay? Oh, my Lord," she says. "It feels wrong. Just wrong."

Maybe Oma feels the same, because without saying a word she goes to the sink and fills a small basin of water, then she gets her soft essential-oils bag, the one with a moon and stars on it, and slips into the bathroom. She comes out with a couple of towels.

"What's she doing?" Mom asks no one in particular.

"Washing his body," Oma says as she shimmies as carefully as she can around the kitchen table, a few drops of water sloshing over Aunt Jeana's head.

Clay snorts, then he leans over to Mom and says quietly, "Jesus...who does she think he is—*Jesus*?" Aunt Jeana doesn't seem to hear him, but she hears Mom's nervous snicker, and she scowls. I give Mom and Clay a dirty look, because all I want right now is for us to get along like a nice family.

E VERYONE IS still huddled in the kitchen, Aunt Jeana on the phone, when Oma comes out with the basin of dirty water, the damp towels draped over her arm. Mom scuttles away from the sink, as if skin cells from a dead dad are even more repulsive than those from a dreadlocked waitress.

Aunt Jeana hangs up the phone and moves around the kitchen like a nervous bird, her hand pecking in the drawers. "Does Sam have a decent suit to wear?" she asks.

"I found one last week. I'll air it out on the line and wash the shirt," Oma says, then adds, "What are you looking for, Jeana?"

"Paper and a pencil. I've got to write Sam's obituary for the paper and find a church that will bury him. I just found out that the pastor of the Methodist church is in the hospital with pneumonia, and their lay pastor was called away for a death in his own family. I don't know what we're going to do now. I know that church would have buried him, because I'm a member. Any of you a member of a church?" she asks. When no one answers, she says, "Well, I'm not surprised. Now we've got a problem on our hands. Sam didn't go to church. No church is going to bury someone who has no connection to them."

"How very Christian of them," Mom says.

"We shouldn't have dismissed hospice," Oma says. "They would have helped us with these plans. With all of it."

"Nonsense," Aunt Jeana says. "We don't need outsiders in our business."

Aunt Jeana barks at me to get out the phone book. "The big one. The one that includes the surrounding towns," she says. "If need be, we'll take him over to Larksville or Trent."

"Or we can just have it at the funeral home," Mom says. "Why does it have to be held in a church, anyway?"

"Well, who will preside over the service?" Aunt Jeana snaps, her head cocking toward Mom.

"I don't know. The funeral director...one of us."

"He needs a proper ceremony!"

"My people on the reservation would do his ceremony," Marie volunteers, and Oma says, "Oh, that would be lovely."

Aunt Jeana goes ballistic then, which makes Chico go ballistic too. "Are you crazy? Drums, and all that chanting? It's heathen!"

Uncle Clay laughs. "Heathen would be fitting, actually," he says, and Mom grins.

Aunt Jeana's face bunches up and deepens almost to the color of Chico's collar. "Is that how it's going to be with you two? Both of you making snide remarks about your dead father?"

"Jeana," Oma says. "They're just releasing stress."

Jeana stands up, clutching a still-twitching Chico. "Why do you defend them? They're being rude and disrespectful. But then, you've always defended them, no matter how out of control they got. Is it any wonder that Sam was the way he was? Someone had to crack down on those two."

Uncle Clay stops laughing. "Don't you fucking defend the old man in front of me."

Aunt Jeana gasps. "Your language, young man!"

I sigh because, just as I predicted, it's happening.

Snap!

Snap!

Snap!

"Oh, please," Oma begs. "Let's not argue at a time like this. Everyone, please, just take a nice cleansing breath, and—"

"And just what?" Mom snaps. "Sit here and pretend he was a saint just because he's dead now? Isn't it bad enough that over the next three days we're going to have to listen to what a wonderful, kind, caring man he was? Can't we at least keep it honest among ourselves? He was a bastard. A bastard! And frankly, I don't give a shit who does his funeral or where he's buried." Mitzy fiddles with her coffee cup, and Peter bites his lip and stares at the table.

"Are you going to let your children talk about their dead father that way?" Aunt Jeana says, moving so close to Oma that Chico has to turn his head or face being crushed by Oma's boobs. He claws at Aunt Jeana's sweater, and she moves him up to her shoulder and pats his ridged backbone.

Oma is holding some sort of talisman, her fingers stroking it anxiously. "They have a right to feel how they feel, Jeana."

"I'd expect something like that out of you," Aunt Jeana says.

"Jeana?" Clay says, no doubt omitting the "Aunt" from her name on purpose. "You don't know a damn thing about what went on in this house. You came to visit once every few years and spent the whole time patting the ass of one of your little rats. When he called Ma a bitch, and worse, in front of you, you just turned away like you hadn't heard."

"I know what happened here, young man! Your dad practically broke his back trying to save money so he could buy that lumber mill he wanted so badly, to give his family a good life. And your mother, she spent every dime he saved so he never got his sawmill. That's what happened here! She used his money to buy you kids more things than you deserved, and she drank up the rest."

Uncle Clay snorts. "Yeah, right. He spent his money on his whores. That's where his money went. And he wasn't trying to give his family a good life. He was trying to be a somebody."

"I don't know what Sam did with other women, Clay, and frankly, I don't care. He had to find some warmth somewhere, I suppose, because he certainly wasn't going to get any at home."

"Oh, please!" Mom groans.

Aunt Jeana goes up to Mom. "Talk that way about him now, missy, but your father was good enough to come home to when you needed a place to hide from that lunatic you got yourself in trouble with, now, wasn't he?"

Mom looks horrified. "Go up to your room, Lucy," she says.

Jeana doesn't wait for me to leave—though I'm not going to, anyway.

"He took a bullet for you, young lady. A bullet! Now, if that isn't a father sacrificing himself for his family, I don't know what is!"

Peter and Mitzy move to stand alongside Mom. One on each side, like pillars.

"Go to your room, Lucy. Now!" Mom shouts. But I don't. I step back to stand under the living-room archway, where I can see and watch and hear, but where I'm not directly in Mom's line of vision. And I struggle to figure out if Aunt Jeana is speaking metaphorically about that bullet or if she means it literally.

"How many fathers would have done that, for a daughter who sent the cops after him, saying he'd beaten his wife when she'd only whacked her head from falling down in a drunken stupor? Not many, I can tell you. My father certainly wouldn't have! He would have let my lover shoot me."

She means a bullet in the literal sense! My stomach feels more than crampy right now, as I fill in the blanks of the story Maude Tuttle told me, and I know that my dad came to Timber Falls with a gun. And that means that he not only beat Mom, Milo, and me, but he wanted to kill us too. The realization of something that ugly makes my body go as cold as Grandpa's.

Snap!

"Most fathers would have thrown you out on your rump for getting yourself in that predicament in the first place, much less after you told such horrid lies." Aunt Jeana nudges herself so close to Mom that Mom must be smelling the hamburger on both her *and* Chico's breath. "My brother risked his life for you, missy, and you can't give him even an ounce of gratitude, to say nothing of respect?"

Mom looks at Oma, silently pleading with her to get me out of the room. Oma, intuitive or not, is fingering the talisman in her shaky hands and blinking hard. She seems oblivious to Mom's silent cue. "Let's not hash over those times. They're over with . . . We are family."

Oma might miss Mom's cue, but Marie doesn't. She comes to me and suggests she and I go outside for a little bit. I shake my head.

"Of course you're not going to show him any respect now," Aunt Jeana says to Mom. "You didn't then, why would you now? After he saved your life, you ran off, taking his grandchildren with you. But then, that's what I'd expect from the lot of you. That man lost his dream, and what did the three of you do in his time of need? You left him high and dry, without even looking back."

"Oh, wait a minute here," Marie says, moving away from me. "I was here through it all, Jeana. Not the night it happened, but almost every day before that. And I can assure you that the way Sam treated Lillian and these kids, most women would have been gone long before Lillian left."

Aunt Jeana looks at Marie like she's seeing her for the first time. "Who are you, anyway? You aren't family. What are you doing in this conversation?" She jabs her fingers at Marie, then at Mitzy and Peter. "This is a family discussion. I own this house, and I'm telling you all to leave."

"Honey?" Peter says to Mom.

"I just want someone to take Lucy out of this room. Please, just get her out of here."

"No!" I shout. "I'm not going anyplace. I have a right to be here. I'm family! And so is Marie, and Mitzy, and Peter. Why do any of us have to leave?"

"Lucy's right," Peter says. "Blood or not, Tess and Lillian and these kids mean something to us, Jeana, and we're going to be here for them if they want us to be."

My insides melt from Peter's words, and I don't care if he snores or farts or is a tattletale. I want him to be my daddy now more than ever.

"But we have private matters to discuss," Aunt Jeana snaps.

"What is there to discuss?" Mom asks.

"There are arrangements to be made," Aunt Jeana says. "And I don't care how much you three despise him—God rest his soul—but he is going to have a proper burial. If it were up to the lot of you, he'd be tossed in a ditch to rot like a deer, but he's my brother, and he's going to be buried in a church by a minister, in spite of what you heathens think."

"Okay, Jeana. That's enough," Oma says. In my whole life, I've never heard Oma use such a harsh tone. Not even when she talked about Rose Pottor. "You have insulted us enough for one day, and you'll stop right now. Clay is right. You *don't* know what went on in this house. No one does, except those of us who lived in it, and you'll not be judging us like this."

Inside, I say, *Ha!* just like Maude Tuttle does.

"I know enough to know that you were a drunk, and that this"—she wags her finger toward Mom—"this *thing* here, came home with a big belly, then brought her trash following right behind her and almost got my brother killed!" Aunt Jeana turns to face Mom. "Shame on you, missy. Shame on you!"

Mom's hands go up to her temples. "Lucy, go outside, damn it!"

Uncle Clay is pacing in tight circles, his hands shoved so far into the pockets of his Dockers that they're buried past his wrists. "Yeah, the big man. Took a bullet for his daughter out of pure love," he says.

"You weren't even here, Clay, so what do you know?" Aunt Jeana snaps. "You'd already run off to California to make your millions, so don't tell me what happened that night."

"And you were here?"

"I wasn't. But I heard what happened. That lunatic pulled a gun and told Tess that he wasn't leaving without her. Sam went to knock it out of the way—so his little girl and her babies wouldn't be killed—and he fired, catching Sam in the thigh. You going to deny *that*? Sam's got a scar on his thigh that says it happened. Go look, then tell me I don't know what happened here!"

"That's bullshit! He did not!" Mom screams. "He didn't put himself between me and Howard. He didn't!"

Everyone stops and stares at Mom. Including me. Oma hurries to Mom and tries wrapping her arms around her, but Mom shrugs her away and continues.

"Howard pointed the gun at me, yes. And he told me to get in the fucking car or he'd take us both out. And Dad, he turned to me..." Tears bubble up in Mom's eyes, and she licks her quivering lips as if they've turned to dust. "...and... and...and...he told me to get my trashy ass out of his house and to take my 'bastards' and my 'scum' with me."

Oma looks like someone slapped her. "No, Tess," she says, shaking her head, her fingers loose over her mouth. "Your father never said that."

Uncle Clay glares at Oma. "You sure about that, Ma? You were drunk as a skunk that night, weren't you? Hard telling what you missed."

"I would have remembered it if he'd said something like that, Clay."

"She would have remembered, drunk or not," Aunt Jeana says, backing up to stand alongside Oma as if they are suddenly serving in the same army.

Mom moves to the spot on the floor where the table can't sit, and where no one ever stands, and she looks down. "Right here! Howard was standing right here!" She suddenly starts shaking so hard that it scares me. It must scare Peter too, because he hurries to put his arm around her waist to steady her.

"Howard had the gun on me the whole time, and Dad didn't make a move. Not one goddamn move!"

"No, Tess," Oma says. "He stepped in the minute Howard pointed the gun at you." There is desperation in her voice, but I'm not sure if her desperation to get at the truth is for Mom's sake or for hers.

"He was right here!" Mom screams, as if she has forgotten that I'm listening. "Howard was standing right here, and Dad told him to take me and get out. Howard turned to face Dad when he spoke, the gun turning with him. *That's* when Dad charged him. Not when he had the gun on me. When Howard turned it on *him*. He knocked his arm and the gun went off, and the bullet grazed Dad's leg. Dad had the gun then, and he knocked Howard to the floor." Mom has her fingers splayed, and her arms chop to show us all the place at her feet. "It happened right here!"

Mitzy wraps her arm around Mom, above Peter's, and tears are streaming down her face. "Oh, Tessy," she cries.

Mom continues, her face old and young and haunted.

"And he could have stopped there. Dad could have stopped right there. He had Howard on the floor. Dad was twice the size of him, for God's sakes. And *he* had the gun." Mom looks down at her feet, her whole body shaking. "He had Howard down on his back. Right here! After he'd knocked him down with so many punches that I thought he'd kill him. I screamed at him to stop the whole time, just like I'd screamed at him to stop when he was beating Clay so badly. I begged him, told him Howard was sick and just needed help. And he stopped... I thought he'd stopped."

Mom is crying so hard that her stomach is convulsing, but still she gulps and pushes the words out as Peter holds her up.

"I screamed at Ma to call the police, so they could take Howard to the hospital so my babies would be safe. So he'd be safe too. But she didn't make a move to call, so I did. And while I was dialing, I looked back, and Dad was on his knees, bent over Howard. Dad's whole body was shaking. And then... and then..." Mom stops and gulps for breaths, then she says, "Then he put the pistol right between Howard's tormented eyes and he pulled the trigger! He pulled the fucking trigger!"

"Jesus Christ," Uncle Clay says.

Mom folds at her middle, and Peter catches her. He turns her to him and holds her close, his hand cupped over the back of her head as she sobs, his other hand on her waist, as if to still her insides.

Aunt Jeana looks dumbfounded, but only for a moment. Then she pulls herself up a little taller and she says, "It was self-defense. That's what the law decided," and she brushes past me, walking in a jagged line, as if she's as drunk as she says Oma was, and goes into Grandpa Sam's room.

"I didn't know..." Uncle Clay says after Aunt Jeana leaves the room, filling the silence that stands on the outskirts of Mom's sobs.

Mom pulls her face from Peter's jacket—as if she can feel Uncle Clay staring at her, even if she's not a sensate—and she glares at him.

"You didn't know because you didn't *want* to know. I needed to talk to you after it happened, Clay, but I didn't even know where you were. And after the twins were born two months early and I was so scared that they'd die, I tried to find you again, because I needed you then too. I was in such grief Ma had to take care of the kids until I could get my shit together after they were released from the hospital. Luckily, she didn't touch another drop of booze after that night, but, damn, we were struggling. We could have used your support then, but I still didn't know how to find you. You didn't want to know anything about what was going on here after you left, any more than Aunt Jeana wanted to know. And when I did find you, you wouldn't even take my calls, so I had to leave you messages. You sent me a basket of flowers and that was it. A fucking basket of flowers."

Uncle Clay's face crumbles.

"You blamed Ma for the years she was drunk and oblivious, but you chose to stay oblivious too once you left. You just didn't use booze to do it. And ever since you walked out, you've treated Ma, me, and even the kids as though we were as bad as Dad. And maybe in some ways we were, but Ma got sober, and she's been my strength and my help since then. And I've done the best I could with what I had to work with, just like her."

"Oh, honey," Oma says, and she goes to Mom, taking over for Peter and holding her up. After a moment, Uncle

Clay goes to them and he embraces them both. He doesn't say he's sorry, but his hug and his tears do.

Peter moves to put his arm around me. "You okay, Lucy?" he whispers, and I nod, even though I'm not sure I am. He draws me close, and I can hear his heartbeat through his sweater.

The room is quiet but for the soft sounds of sniffling and the scraping noise as Peter pulls out chairs so Mom and Oma and Uncle Clay can sit down.

Someone knocks at the back door, and Marie hurries to answer it. I glance up to see two men stepping inside with a gurney. While Mom and Oma and Uncle Clay sit with their heads tipped down, their hands still clasped, I turn and look into the living room and watch the men carry Grandpa Sam out the front door, a white sheet over his face. Peter helps with the doors and talks quietly with the men until they are gone.

Mitzy and Marie sit down on the couch without speaking, sharing tearful looks between them.

I turn and look back into the kitchen, and I say, "He wanted me to tell you all that he was sorry." Mom and Uncle Clay and Oma look up. "And Mom...Uncle Clay... he wanted you both to know that he understood why you couldn't be in the room as he was dying."

I don't bother saying *how* he told me, because only Oma, and probably Marie, would understand. Instead, I just tell them the important part. "He wanted you all to know that he loved you."

We just stay where we are then. Frozen, like we're in a play and the final scene is over, but there's no stagehand to drop the curtain. That's when Milo comes into the room, rushing so fast that I can feel the breeze he stirs, Feynman thumping behind him. He grabs a cup from the dish rack and jerks the refrigerator door open. "I'm on position—" he starts to say, then he stops, his pointy head turning until he's scanned the room. "What's the matter?" he says. "Did Grandpa die?"

chapter

THIRTY

I T IS my first funeral, and I'm wearing a scratchy new dress, which Mitzy ran to town to buy for me when she bought the simple navy dress Mom is wearing and the black slacks and dress shirt Milo has on.

We sit in the first pew of the church Aunt Jeana found—Me and Oma, Milo, Mom, Clay, Aunt Jeana, Peter, Marie and Al (who is walking good now after his hernia surgery), and Mitzy and Ray, because we are all family.

Mom said this church isn't a real church, because it doesn't belong to any denomination and because they sell vitamins and make their money on a pyramid scheme, then hide their profits behind the exemptions that should be saved for *real* churches—or for none at all. It doesn't look like a real church either, in spite of the big wooden cross that hangs on the wall before us. It's made out of the same planks that hold up the clotheslines out back of Grandpa Sam's house.

The minister is wearing a white robe with a sash slung around his shoulder. It has patches on it, just like the Girl Scout sash the little girl who gave me the leaf wore outside to play in on Tuesdays, after her meetings. He is wearing round metal glasses and has a scraggly salt-and-pepper beard. The frayed cuffs of his jeans and the tips of his dirty sneakers show when he takes a step to the left or to the right. He talks about Jesus dying and about how women prepared his body for death. Then he veers off to talk about how we must honor God by tending to our bodies too. Oma's head leans in a little farther when he starts in about the empty food we eat and how it's God's wish that we replace what our food doesn't give us so that we can show our gratitude for the gift of our flesh. I glance at Aunt Jeana to see if she notices that Grandpa Sam's ceremony is starting to sound like an infomercial, but she doesn't seem to.

I can hear Connie Olinger sniffling, and a few other ladies too, but no one in our row is crying.

W HEN WE first got here, we all stood together so that the guests could give us their condolences. All of us, that is, except Mom, who went outside to sit with Peter in his SUV. Uncle Clay was talking to the guy from First National about the vineyards in Napa Valley, and Oma was trying to comfort Connie Olinger, who sobbed as though it was Barry in that casket. Barry waited beside them, nervously glancing at the door. He was wearing a short-sleeve Hawaiian print shirt and had the sleeves rolled once, to show his new "tat"—a trout leaping from a stream.

Aunt Jeana was standing in a pool of old ladies who were ogling Chico as they talked about what a "good showing" it was, with every folding chair taken and folks standing in the back of the room and in the opened doorway. "Everybody loved Sam," they agreed.

I went to stand by Milo for a bit, but we didn't talk. He was off in his own little world, probably still reciting the digits of pi in his head. That's when she walked in the door: Maude Tuttle, in her big red wig, dressed to the hilt, as Oma would say. Nordine Bickett was on her arm, her hair and makeup as pretty as her lavender flowered dress.

The old women that Aunt Jeana stood with stopped and stared, as did a few of the old men standing in circles— though unlike the ladies, they wore sly grins on their faces instead of contempt. There was silence for a moment, then the soft buzz of gossip.

I went up to Maude and Nordine and said, "Thank you for coming," as I'd heard Oma say to many while we stood in some sort of receiving line.

"Hi, kid," Maude said.

"Maude, Nordine...how nice of you to come." I turned and Oma was beside me. She reached her hand out and squeezed both of theirs, and the buzzing in the room intensified.

"I thought she should come," Maude said, jerking her head toward Nordine. "I hope you don't mind, Lillian. Course, she could be at the Taj Mahal, for all she knows, but I still thought she should come."

Oma nodded. "Would you like to see Sam? The service will be starting soon."

"Crissakes," Maude said when she saw Grandpa Sam,

his face caked in thick orangey makeup, his thin hair shellacked into crusty waves. His hands were folded on his chest, the right hand on top. "Who in the hell did his makeup?" Maude said. "He looks like a goddamn pumpkin."

Maude shook her head, then she looked down at Nordine. "Do you know who that is, Nordine?"

Nordine stared down at Grandpa Sam, while we stared at her. Finally she said, "I don't know. But I know I loved him very much."

Others came up to see Grandpa Sam and talk to Oma, so I wandered off with Maude and Nordine. "Miss Tuttle," I said when we found a spot to stand that wasn't crowded—which wasn't difficult, considering that folks scattered like stirred houseflies wherever Maude Tuttle stepped. "At Nordine's house, when you said that my grandpa stopped my dad from hurting my mom, 'one way or another,' what exactly did you mean?"

"Still pickin'?" she asked.

"I know about the gun now. But my mom and my grandma remember it differently. Mom claims that Grandpa didn't step in to protect her but only attacked my dad when he pointed the gun at him. Oma says that's not true, that he stepped in the second Howard pointed the pistol at her."

"I don't know about that part. Your grandpa didn't say."

"Why did my grandpa go to you afterward? What did he need to confess?" I ask.

Maude pursed her lips and looked up. "He was sorry, kid. Cried like a baby when he admitted that he'd taken a life. He knew he had a choice. He told me himself that he had the kid down and he could have stopped right there.

"Maude here, she always tells it like it is. And I told him why he pulled the trigger—though I think at that point he knew why himself. I told him that he wasn't trying to kill that boy. He was trying to kill the beast inside himself. The same beast that was looking him square in the face at that moment."

"Okay," I said, and for whatever reason, I didn't cry. Instead, I took Maude's arm, and I led her and Nordine to two vacated chairs. After they were seated, I pulled the photograph of Nordine and Grandpa Sam from my pocket and discreetly handed it to Maude. "Give this to Mrs. Bickett later, will you?" Maude glanced at it, nodded, and slipped it into her purse, and I went to join my family because the minister was about to start.

THE CHURCH organist is the same woman who sold us the lemongrass tea and herbal remedies at the health-food store. Dressed in a skirt the color of new grass, she bangs at the organ keys like a toddler pounding on the tray of her high chair. We're supposed to be singing "Amazing Grace," but right in the middle of it, Aunt Jeana leans over Oma and asks me, "You have his eulogy?"

She's talking about the words she wrote last night about Grandpa Sam. She asked me to read them because she doesn't like talking in front of crowds and because, she said, I was the one person in the family who was good to her brother while he was dying. I open my sweaty palm and show her the damp folded sheet of lined school paper, and she nods.

"And now," the minister says, "the family would like to share some final words about Sam. Sam's granddaughter, uh"—he glances down at his notes—"Daisy," he says, "will read them."

"Lucy. My name's Lucy."

I go up to the wooden pulpit, walking with my legs close together—because even if Mom says the adhesive on the bottom of my teen-sized pad will keep it securely in place, it doesn't feel like it will—and I unfold Aunt Jeana's paper. I stare down at the long list of names and dates and sketchy details. In the room, I can hear the sound of impatience: a shuffling shoe, a baby fussing, someone's nervous throat-clearing, and the creaking of a couple folded chairs. And still, I just stand there.

"Lucy," Aunt Jeana hisses. "Read the paper."

And then Oma's whisper: "Honey, you want me to do it?"

I don't answer them. I just fold the paper back up and scoot the little square into the corner of the podium. I look out at the crowd and see a hundred eyes watching me, waiting.

"This is the first funeral I've ever been to," I begin. "And I guess this is the part where we put something personal into the ceremony, so that the whole thing doesn't sound like just another sermon—though I suspect it already doesn't. Anyway, I believe what we say now is supposed to recap the life of the deceased."

I look down at the square of paper. "I have something here to read about my grandpa, but...well...I'm not sure that a list of when he graduated, and married, and what he did for a living says too much about who he was. And since I came here to learn just that, I think what I'll do instead is to tell you what I learned. About him and...well...what I learned."

"What's she doing?" Aunt Jeana says in a voice not quite a whisper.

I clear my throat, then close my eyes and let the words come.

"Every one of you in this room, with the exception of my mom's boyfriend, Peter, and my twin brother, Milo—and no, we're not identical—knew my grandpa Sam longer than I did. He was the one you worked next to, the one who stopped people from making fun of you, and he was the one who made your kid's toboggan, or the one who talked to you in the lobby of the First National. And the Sam McGowan you knew was friendly, and nice, and good. Well, unless maybe you were the one whose house he went to when he needed to purge his sins."

"Purge his sins?" Aunt Jeana says, and Oma makes shushing sounds.

"Up until a couple of months ago, I didn't know my grandpa Sam at all. But I thought about him a lot. Just like I thought about my birth father—a person most of you probably knew of before me too, at least from the gossip.

"Grandpa Sam was sick by the time I met him. He'd had strokes that damaged his frontal lobe, and his strokes made him turn the TV channels compulsively, until someone took the remote away. He said himself that his brain was broken, so I know he understood. What he didn't know, though, was that he couldn't work anymore. Lots of times, he'd take his lunch pail and head out the door. And once, after he'd found his truck keys, he got away and drove through three counties, probably looking for the mill, and nothing stopped him, but for the Bicketts' garage door.

"But you probably know all of this stuff already. So I guess I should tell you some things about him you might not know.

"My Grandpa liked dogs, and women, and cinnamon. He used to live in a boxcar and had to go to work when he was still a boy because it was the Depression, and his family couldn't afford to feed him. His dad used to beat him, so my grandpa grew up to beat people too. Good people like my grandma, and my uncle Clay, and maybe not-so-good people too, like Richard Marbles—my apologies for saying that, Mr. Marbles, if you're here.

"My grandpa didn't beat up my mom, but then, if you know anything about psychology, you already know that if a kid sees somebody beating up your mom or your brother, then they might as well be beating you up too, because you feel every blow in your own body, anyway."

"What is she doing?" Aunt Jeana says, loud enough now that they can probably hear her a good five rows back. Again, Oma hushes her.

"I know a lot about a lot of things," I continue. "I'm people-smart, and I can remember where in a book I've read things, right down to what paragraph I've read them in. My whole family is smart—my twin brother, especially— and Grandpa Sam, I'm told, was smart before he got sick too. He had a room in his house filled with books, and artifacts, and things he liked to study. He had a dog he named Feynman, after Richard P. Feynman. And he didn't like noise when he was watching the news, or red squirrels, or blue jays, or to be called dumb. I think maybe he was the one in the family who taught my mom and my uncle that being smart is the most important thing in the world a person can be, and then this belief was passed down to my brother and me.

"Being smart didn't help me any, though, when I came here to Timber Falls and tried to learn who my grandpa was. I learned it, all right, but not the way I normally learn things. I learned that he had a gift for working with wood. That he carved birds and bent the ends of slabs of wood so that kids could slide down hills on nice toboggans— something he himself never had the chance to do. Or his kids either, for that matter. And I learned that he once put my grandma's head through a wall and broke my uncle Clay's nose." I hear a gasp, echoed by more.

"My grandpa didn't like celery or for people to drop in and see the family messes, and he certainly didn't like how mean he was. But the one thing he *did* like in this world was Nordine Bickett."

"This is an outrage!" Aunt Jeana says, rising to her feet. "Lucy! Stop this this instant!" She turns to Mom, to Oma. "Aren't you going to stop her?"

"I'm not trying to be disrespectful, Aunt Jeana," I say. "I'm only paying my tribute to Grandpa Sam. To who he was."

Aunt Jeana cradles Chico in her arm, bends over and snatches her purse from the foot of her chair, and stomps out. People watch her go, and a couple of them grin, but most just stare, their eyes wide and blinking, as if they'd expected to go to a funeral but stumbled into a circus instead.

"Anyway," I continue, "I learned a lot from my grandpa in the few months I knew him. I learned that what we see in others is only a small part of who they really are. And that good and bad often go hand in hand. And I learned that being hurt causes hurt. What else I learned is that even empty places where a father or a grandfather should be aren't really empty, because they're filled with things like longing and hurt and mistrust. And I learned that love doesn't mean a real lot if it's felt on the inside but can't be shown on the outside. I learned, too, that we can, and do, love people who aren't perfect, because I really did come to love my grandpa Sam. And he sure wasn't perfect.

"Just like I learned a lot from my grandpa's last weeks on earth, I think he learned some things during that time too. From what I can tell, he was the kind who always did things for other people, but maybe he didn't let people do things for him. And I know that being strong was something he thought was important, probably as important as being smart. So maybe, as we spooned cereal into his mouth and my Oma changed his diapers, maybe he learned that sometimes we have to let people do things for us too, and that it can be okay to be weak sometimes.

"And I know he learned to be sorry.

"So I guess that's about all I have to say about my grandpa Sam, except that I'll miss him, probably like you will. Thank you."

The room is silent but for the *clip-clop* sound of my shoes on the scuffed wooden floor. And when I reach my chair, Mom and Peter and Oma reach over to squeeze and pat me and to smile in spite of their tears. Milo isn't smiling, though. He looks mortified as he turns to Mom and says, "We're giving our oral reports here? Nobody told me!"

EVERYONE GOES outside to smoke or to stand in small groups to wait and soak up the sunshine, which has decided to warm the day so that one can almost believe spring is coming instead of winter. Soon we're going out to the cemetery so Grandpa Sam can be put to rest—because the frost hasn't set hard in the ground quite yet—then we're coming back here to the church to have the lunch the ladies in this makeshift church prepared out of Franken-free food, which pleases Oma, of course. Peter holds one of my hands, and Oma the other, as we start down the church steps.

We head toward the string of cars lined up along the street, the black hearse first in line, because Grandpa Sam is going to lead this parade too.

As Peter is opening the door to his SUV so we can slip inside, a rusty blue Ford pickup comes barreling around the corner. I recognize it immediately.

The truck stops with a screech and a thud, right in the middle of the road, and Henry Bickett, wild-haired and wild-eyed, steps out.

"Nordine? Nordine!" he shouts.

He gets out of his truck and runs up the line of cars, where people hang half in and half out, staring at him. "Nordine? Where are you?"

He spots Maude Tuttle and races toward her, darting around to where teeny Nordine is standing tucked under her arm, like a chick hiding under her mother's wing. "Damn it, Nordine," he shouts, loud enough that we can all hear him. "I knew I'd find you here! How many times I gotta tell you to stay away from that damn scoundrel?" He grabs Nordine by the coat sleeve and tugs her back to his beat-up Ford, raising his fist toward us and shouting as he goes. "And I want my goddamn garage door fixed, McGowans!"

chapter

THIRTY-ONE

W E'RE OUTSIDE, three days after Grandpa Sam's funeral, standing under flurries falling down over the ten inches of snow we got early yesterday. Peter is putting our overnight bags in the back of his Suzuki, Mom is slipping into the front seat, and Oma is positioning her *Angels, protect me on my journey* pewter clip on the visor above the driver's side.

We're going on a weekend trip up to Bayfield to meet Peter's family, including his niece who's read *Little Women* fifteen times and his dad, who can still walk on his hands. Peter wants to see his family one more time, and he wants us to meet them. He says the little break will do us good, because we've all been under a lot of stress.

As I watch Oma pat the angel clip after saying a prayer, I think of how she's probably wearing that pretty skirt—shorter than she normally wears—and navy tights that hug her Tina Turner legs because of Peter's dad. She sure asked a lot of questions about him after Peter invited us to go, and she didn't exactly sound sincere when she said it was a shame that his flight was canceled yesterday because of the storm. "Is he heading out today?" she asked at breakfast, after Peter got off the phone with his brother. "Clay's heading out any minute now, so I suppose all flights are good to go today."

She grinned when Peter said his father decided to stay an extra day or two in order to meet us. And later, while I helped her put the washed bedding back on the bed Grandpa Sam died in, she got all dreamy-eyed when she said, "What do you think of the name Aphrodite? I think it has a nice ring to it, don't you?" Aphrodite. The goddess of fertility, love, and beauty.

Aunt Jeana's keeping Feynman until we get back, and she promised he can stay inside, as long as he sleeps in the study. Milo's filled his dishes, plus three more, to the brim. I can tell he's worried by the way he's staring at the house, though, his eyebrows dipped down under his plastic frames.

After we meet Peter's family, we're coming back here to Timber Falls—Mom, Milo, Oma, and me—to help Aunt Jeana ready the house for an estate sale. Mom and Milo and I are also going to get measured for our clothes for Mitzy and Ray's wedding, which is just a few weeks away. Peter's coming to the wedding too, and even though Ray doesn't know him well, he's asked him to be one of the groomsmen, because he doesn't have any brothers or male cousins and only one really close friend.

Peter's going to Chicago first, though, because he has to get back to his classes. When we're done in Timber Falls, we're heading back too, in Roger's Mustang. Milo's first pi competition is in five weeks, and Mom thinks that she'll have found us an apartment by then. Her first royalty check from her Christian romance is on its way, which she says means we'll be able to rent a nicer place, maybe closer to a better park, so Milo and I can ride our bikes and, as Oma added, sit closer to the earth. We're going to stay at Peter's while Mom hunts for an apartment. I'd rather stay at Peter's forever, and Peter would rather we did too, but like Oma says, Mom, she needs time to warm up to an idea.

In the meantime, Mom's started a new book. I know because I peeked last night in the kitchen, right before I threw that memory stick in the trash for the last time. I don't think she's writing a Christian romance this time, though, because in the first chapter a lady and man are dancing in a club, and I think I saw the f-word on page two, fourth paragraph down. I couldn't read much of it, though, because Oma was moving around behind me, right over that place where no one ever stood, wafting sage smoke around so she could move the table back to the center of the room where it belongs.

While Mom is pleading with Oma to hurry before Peter freezes to death—even though it's not that cold today and the temperature's climbing as it did last night, so that the top of the snow has crusted over from today's sunshine—I'm standing and watching the tiny flakes from one lingering cloud swirl as they drop.

The day after the funeral, when Milo woke and saw

winter's first real snow falling so heavily that you couldn't tell where the sky left off and the horizon began, he looked out at his bike leaning against a tree and almost cried. Yesterday, he was still in mourning, and Oma told him that there's lots of fun things to do in the snow too. She bundled us up like snowmen and took us out to show us how to make snow angels.

Milo wasn't impressed when Oma threw him down to make one. He cried out when he dropped, as though the fall had pained him. He got up and looked down at his skinny imprint, which didn't look much different than the print Feynman had left alongside it, and went inside in a huff, saying making snow angels was for girls, and dumb. He cheered up some, though, when during dinner Peter told him that the gym on campus—where he'd gladly take him if Mom says it's okay—has stationary bikes with milometers and speed gauges on them, and he can keep in shape over the winter so that he's all the faster when spring comes.

"Lucy?" Peter says. "I don't see a bag here for you. Did you bring it out?"

"Oh," I say. "I must have left it inside."

"Is she going in to pee *again*?" Milo grumbles, because he wants us to stay on schedule. Mom tells him to leave me alone, because she knows that I'm only going in the bathroom to check (like I've done at least ten times already today) and see if I can take this stupid pad off *yet* because I don't want to sit for hours, teetering on something that feels as big as a couch pillow.

I hurry in through the back door, stomping my feet on the rug so Aunt Jeana, who's sitting at the table trying to get Chico to eat, doesn't harp at me. My new winter coat, bought on Mom's credit card, swishes as I move. "I forgot my bag," I say. I find my bag in the bathroom where I left it and pick it up, and Sammy, who's tucked in alongside my clothes, clunks against my leg.

Last night when we lay in bed—me and Oma, because I had to give up my bed so Peter had a place to pretend he'd slept, for Milo's sake, come morning—Oma said, "I can still feel him here, can't you?"

I knew who she meant, because I could feel him too.

"I think he's hovering," Oma said. "People do that sometimes, you know. Hang around after they die, if they've still got some unfinished business to take care of before they go, or because they don't know they're dead yet. Oh, dear, I hope Sam doesn't do that. Where would be his peace, then?"

I think of this as I watch the flurries outside the bathroom window. And then I open my bag and I take Sammy out.

"Where you going?" Aunt Jeana snips as I open the basement door.

I don't answer.

She stands at the top of the stairs after I go down. "Lucy? What are you doing down there?"

I don't explain as I head up, Mom and Uncle Clay's old sled clunking against the steps behind me.

Aunt Jeana follows me to the door. "Where are you taking that, young lady? That's going in the estate sale."

She's holding the door wide open after I go out, and Feynman scoots around her and bursts outside, hopping happily alongside me as I drag the sled to the car.

"We don't have room for that!" Mom says, when I get to the SUV.

"Lucy, my brother has lots of sleds at his house, and a good hill too. We can use his while we're there."

"It's not for Bayfield," I tell Peter. "Please put it in the back, though."

While Peter's opening the hatchback, and Mom's trying to pry information out of me, Milo steps out of the car and wraps his arms around Feynman, who starts whining the minute he sees Milo. "If Lucy can bring a dumb sled, then why can't I bring Feynman?"

Mom peers back and says to Peter, "Can we just get going already?" Then she yells at Milo to put Feynman back in the house, and to hurry it up too.

"Mom!" Milo whines. "Aunt Jeana went back inside without him. She's going to leave him outside to freeze, no matter what she says." Milo runs to the back of the SUV, where Peter has the sled shoved sideways alongside the wall. "See? There's plenty of room for him. And we could keep Feynman and your brother's dog separated—not that we'd need to. Feynman's strong from so much running. He could hold his own with your brother's pit bull."

Peter looks through the truck at Mom, and she rolls her eyes. "Whatever you think," she says, and Milo whoops when Peter grabs Feynman's collar and prompts him to jump up.

I slip in behind Peter, and as he pulls down the long driveway, I ask him to go west.

"West?" Mom says. "Lucy, you know we have to head back to town to get on the highway." Peter thinks Mom's on edge this morning because she's meeting his family for the first time, but I don't think that's it. She's on edge because of how dependent she's been on him for support over the last few days. It's her anxiety and attachment issues acting up, so I forgive her and ignore her impatience. Peter seems to forgive her for no other reason than that he loves her.

"I know. But it won't take long, Mom."

"What won't take long, dear?" Oma asks.

I ignore them both and stare into the rearview mirror,

where I see Peter's blue eyes (a lot like mine, and with no yellow shards to speak of) watching me. "I need to stop by Nordine Bickett's," I say to him, since he's the driver.

"Nordine Bickett's?" Mom says. She turns to Oma. "Why in the hell does she need to go over there? And where did that puppet come from?"

"I don't really know," Oma says. She studies me for a moment, then says to Peter, "It's about a mile west."

Everyone's talking at once, trying to find out what I've got up my sleeve when I step out in the Bicketts' driveway and ask Peter to get out the sled.

"What are you doing? Lucy, answer me!" But I can't answer Mom, because for the moment I feel just like I did when I first lay on the grass the day we came to Timber Falls, and all I want now, too, is quiet.

Peter sets the sled down on the snow and gets back behind the wheel. I stand outside, my door still open, and I say, "Aphrodite, can I use your lighter for a minute?"

"Aphrodite?" Mom says. "Oh, good God, don't tell me..." And Peter chuckles.

While Oma digs in her purse for her lighter, I hold Sammy sideways, one hand on the X, the other grasping his feet, and I pull until the strings are tight. When Oma finds it, she snaps her lighter to make a flame, then, without being told what I want her to do, she holds it under each string until Sammy breaks free.

"What on earth is she doing, Ma?"

I leave Oma to answer that question—or not—and I head across the snow, the old boots Oma found for me to wear breaking easily through the thin layer of ice sitting on top.

I walk right past Henry Bickett, who's come out to stand on the steps. "You! Get the hell off my property or I'll have you arrested for trespassing. You hear me? Goddamn no-good McGowans!" he shouts.

I ignore Henry and walk between the garden, where a few dried corn stalks are still standing, and the shed. I go past the tractor that's sitting broken in the snow, and I look for the line of trees that sit behind the Bicketts' house—the one that Mom wrote about in her notebook.

And there it is. A gap between the trees, with nothing on the other side but a snow-covered field shining in the distance. I drag the sled through the gap and look down at the expanse of hill. Then I place Sammy on the sled and wrap the dangling strings around one of the slats so he doesn't fall.

I stand still for just a minute—wondering if I should say a prayer or something. Not finding any words for one and not really feeling a need for one, I just bend over and give the sled a push. It makes soft scraping sounds as it glides down the hill, carrying Grandpa Sam down until he reaches the open field and slows to a stop to rest on the lap of his mother.

How soon before the house gets sold?" I ask as we hum down the freeway, looking to the people who pass us, no doubt, like any other family, with a mom and a dad, two kids, a grandma, and a dog in the hatch.

"It will probably take a while," Oma says. "And if it's not sold before we go back for Mitzy and Ray's wedding, we'll stay there for those few days."

"Or in a motel," Mom says.

"Do we get the money?" Milo asks, and I roll my eyes. "Geez, genius, think about it. If Mom had taken the house, don't you think *she'd* be selling the place, instead of Aunt Jeana?"

I sit quietly then, my head lolling against the window, and I think of everything that's happened and about everything that might happen still.

"I'm going to miss Marie and Mitzy," I say, and Mom and Oma say they'll miss them too but remind me that we'll be back soon for the wedding. "And don't forget," Mom says, "next summer we're coming back again for two weeks. Mitzy's baby will be born by then, and Uncle Clay and your aunt Judy and your cousins are coming for a week too. Your uncle is going to see if he can find a big house to rent so we can all stay together."

I think of these times to come, and it helps me feel not quite so sad. Especially when I think about all the good things that could happen in Chicago between now and then.

I look over at Oma, who is watching the road ahead of us, her head bobbing with the motion of the truck, a faint smile on her peach-colored lips. Oma feels me watching her, and she reaches out and takes my hand and squeezes it.

I open my book once the car gets quiet. A nice book I picked out myself on Amazon, about a girl my age who never had a dad but gets adopted by her mom's new husband. I fan the pages to find my spot and stop at the dry, flat green leaf that marks where I left off, even though I already know.

We ride a little longer, and I get sleepy. I close my book and lean my head against the glass. I'm about to shut my eyes when I see him.

"Oma, look! An eagle! Stop the car, Peter. Hurry!"

"What's the matter?" Peter asks, as he hits the brakes and pulls over to the shoulder of the road.

"Oh, Jesus," Mom groans, right along with Milo, who's sick to his stomach in spite of a spoonful of Dramamine.

I can't help laughing as Oma digs in her purse for a cigarette. "Synchronicity, sweet synchronicity!" I shout, and Oma laughs right along with me.

While Mom is explaining to Peter that it's one of Oma's "wacky, hocus pocus rituals," and Milo grumbles about how long this is going to take, Oma and I leap out of the car and race to the side of the road, our arms wrapped together like the entwined strings of two tea bags.

ACKNOWLEDGMENTS

I wish to express my deepest appreciation to the following individuals, each of whom contributed something of value to this project:

To my publisher, Nita Taublib, who continues to champion my work with enthusiasm.

To Kerri Buckley, my phenomenal editor, who more than anyone helped this book become the best it could be. Her foresight, attention to detail, and love for this story seeped into every page.

To my agent, Catherine Fowler, who handles me with patience and my career with wisdom.

To "dodinsky," whose insightful poem graces the opening page of this novel, and whose friendship now graces my life.

To art director Paolo Pepe, who repeatedly sees to it that I get fantastic covers, and to Lynn Andreozzi, who put this beautiful one together.

To Kathy Lord, the skilled copyeditor who surely worked her fingers to the bone plucking unnecessary commas from my manuscript.

To the many folks in the marketing and sales departments (and probably many other departments I'm unaware of). Although I don't know your names, I appreciate your efforts.

To the two experts in their fields who generously answered my questions regarding mathematics and physics: Dr. Michael Naylor, associate professor of mathematics, Western Washington University, and Dr. Paul McEuen, professor of physics, Cornell University, and up-and-coming thriller author.

To my friends and family, who continually support me in my life and in my life's work.

And last but not least, to you, the reader. Thank you from the bottom of my heart for buying my books, sharing them, and writing to tell me what they meant to you. It is because of you that I get to wake each morning to spend another day doing what I love to do most. I hope my stories continue to inspire you, entertain you, and help you remember the wonder you felt and the wisdom you held as a child.

ABOUT THE AUTHOR

SANDRA KRING lives in Wisconsin. Her debut
novel, *Carry Me Home*, was a Book Sense Nota-
ble pick and a 2005 Midwest Booksellers' Choice
Award nominee. *The Book of Bright Ideas* was
a 2006 Target Bookmarked™ selection and was
named to the New York Public Library's *Books
for the Teen Age* list in 2007. Visit her on the
web at www.sandrakring.com.